From a thousand m_____ ballroom. From somew_____ ___ conscience the under-used voice of her good sense wheezed a warning.

"I can make you feel . . . a thing or two," Jonathan suggested on a whisper. Casually. As though it were a summer day and they were two bored people looking for something to fill the time.

"I doubt it."

He smiled faintly, almost pityingly. And slowly freed her from her prison by bringing his hands up to cradle the back of her head. Big hands, sure hands. Her head tipped into them too easily.

He gazed down at her for a second, one brow arched: See how easy you are?

And then his lips crushed hers.

By Julie Anne Long

Julie Anne Long

It Happened One Midnight

AVON
An Imprint of HarperCollinsPublishers

This is a work of fiction. Names, characters, places, and incidents are products of the author's imagination or are used fictitiously and are not to be construed as real. Any resemblance to actual events, locales, organizations, or persons, living or dead, is entirely coincidental.

AVON BOOKS
An Imprint of HarperCollins*Publishers*
10 East 53rd Street
New York, New York 10022-5299

Copyright © 2013 by Julie Anne Long
ISBN 978-0-06-211807-3
www.avonromance.com

First Avon Books mass market printing: July 2013

Avon Trademark Reg. U.S. Pat. Off. and in Other Countries, Marca Registrada, Hecho en U.S.A.
HarperCollins® is a registered trademark of HarperCollins Publishers.

Printed in the U.S.A.

10 9 8 7 6 5 4 3 2 1

To every reader, reviewer, and blogger who ever spread the word about a book they loved—I appreciate you more than I can say.

Acknowledgments

MY HEARTFELT GRATITUDE TO the terrific people I'm blessed to work with: marvelous editor May Chen; the talented, hardworking staff at Avon; my lovely agent Steve Axelrod; to my sis Karen, who makes brainstorming fun; and to every reader, reviewer, and blogger who spreads the word about books they love.

It Happened
One Midnight

Chapter 1

THE MOON LAY ON its side like a discarded pickax, the stars' diamond smithereens strewn all around it. It was a rare clear London night thanks to a stiff broom of a breeze off the Thames, and everything Tommy had seen on her way to her destination—barrels full of old rain capped thinly in ice, a narrow black cat holding its tail aloft in the shape of a question mark, each bar on the low wrought iron fence she'd just slipped through—seemed etched into the night, distinct as puzzle pieces, shimmering with portent and beauty and danger.

Just the way she liked it, in other words.

Just like *her*, some of the ton's bloods might say.

And oh, how they loved to hear themselves *talk*. Granted, she'd done little to discourage it. She could find something to like in each of them, but there was a sameness to them, to their self-absorption and to their compliments—and to her ability to manage them. Not one of them saw anything more than what they wanted to see. Or what *she* wanted them to see.

Still, it wasn't as though she hadn't been enjoying herself.

She hadn't realized things had gone a *little* too far until the pearls arrived.

Pearls notwithstanding, the most valuable thing she owned was a short broad ribbon hung with a gold wide-armed cross. The most important words of her life were etched into it. She gripped it so tightly now she wouldn't be surprised to find the heat had seared them permanently into her palm.

It would only be fitting. Her body told the story of her life in scars.

She hovered in shadows in the terraced gardens, crouching slightly. She had a flawless view of French doors and enormous windows and a room lit only by a fire burning low. Not a typical row house, oh no; only a recreation of a French palais would suit the grandeur of its owner, who had built it decades ago.

Her heart launched into her throat when a man moved into the room.

Every cell in her body seemed to loan itself to *seeing*. She gulped glimpses as he passed through. Nose like the prow of a ship: conspicuous, arrogant, but right for his face, which was all sharply hewn edges and broad planes. An edifice of a face.

Tommy absently rested the back of her hand against the smooth curve of her own cheek.

He seemed hewn from eons of privilege. She could very nearly feel the weight of it from where she stood. It was in the way he entered the room, cutting through it with the purposeful confidence of a warship as he headed for the bookcase.

It was him. It was him. She *knew* it.

He turned a fraction toward the window, and that's when she saw that his ruthlessly cropped hair was gray. *More, more, more.* She wanted to know more. The color of his eyes, the shape of his hands, the sound of his voice. Impatience thrummed through her, drew her nerves tight as harp strings.

Which is why she nearly leaped out of her skin when she heard the faint "snick" of a struck flint right behind her.

The blood instantly vacated her head. She nearly fainted.

Still, she was no stranger to surprise. She whipped about so quickly her cloak slapped at her calves, and the knife in her sleeve slid down to prick her palm, but remained hidden. She gripped the shaft.

A sucked cheroot flared into life, and round the light of it a man came into focus.

His posture was unmistakable. She'd inadvertently memorized it this afternoon at her salon, because he'd spent much of his time simply leaning against the wall opposite her and watching her through hooded eyes. Smiling very faintly, as though he was in on a private joke. As though he *knew* her, although they'd only just met, and never spoke after that first introduction. Then there was the fact that he was the sort of man no woman with blood in her veins would ever forget once she'd seen him. His face, shadowed intriguingly now, rather embossed itself on one's memory. So few men actually caused a sharp intake of breath.

Judging from his reputation, he took full advantage of this.

None of this mattered to Tommy. He hadn't a

title, and he was a rake, and everyone knew she had rules about these things.

Ironically, however, he'd said the only thing that truly interested her all afternoon. She'd overheard it.

"Well, if it isn't the celebrated Miss Thomasina de Ballesteros. What could possibly bring *you* to—" He peered into the window. "—a crouching position outside the window of a powerful married duke?"

His voice was very quiet, very baritone, and intolerably amused.

"It's not what you think, Mr. Redmond," she managed with icy elegance. Or as much elegance as once could muster whilst whispering. "And one might ask the same of you."

Above their heads, framed in the square of light of his French doors, the man moved to kindle another lamp, and even more gaslight flared into the room. He was as illuminated as if he was a player on a stage now. How very helpful.

Now she just had to get rid of the sudden new audience member.

"I'm smoking a cheroot. I'm the last to depart a dinner party at this very residence, to which I was invited. It took place *inside* the house. I must say, however, that I'm unutterably touched that you care what I think."

"Oh, I don't," she hastened to disabuse. Distractedly, because the Duke of Greyfolk was choosing a book from a bookcase now. Which book? What does he *read*? "It's just that it's too difficult to keep lies in order, and I'm busy enough as it is. Now if you would just leave me to my business, there's a good lad, Mr. Redmond, and good night."

Jonathan Redmond exhaled smoke. Politely, away from her, toward the sky.

"You speak from experience. The lying," he said after a moment. They still spoke in hushes.

She cast a glance his way. She resented every second her eyes weren't staring through the window. Inside, the duke settled into a chair with a book, and seemed to take his time burrowing in, finding just the right position for his buttocks. A new chair? Or one that bore his imprint and he was just trying to wriggle into it properly?

How she wanted to know the title of the book.

"Naturally. Everyone lies. Even you, I'd warrant. Perhaps *especially* you, given your reputation, Mr. Redmond, and the company you keep. The reason I'm standing here is most assuredly not what you think, so you may save your innuendoes for the next fashionable salon you choose to grace with your presence."

He merely nodded along, as if everything she said followed a script. The rudeness was *very* unlike her, but one tended to revert to childhood defenses when cornered.

Above their heads the duke stood up, reached beneath him, and gave his trousers a tug; they had lodged between his buttock cheeks when he'd sat down. He resettled himself.

"You still haven't told me what your business here is, Miss de Ballesteros."

She turned toward him and straightened to her full height, which was unfortunately a foot or more

less than his. She counted to ten silently. She could
feel her temper crawling up an internal thermom-
eter. The temper was evidence of how accustomed
she'd become to men vying to do her bidding.

"Why are you tormenting me?" she asked,
almost lightly.

"Why are you holding a knife?" he asked, mimicking her tone.

Shock blurred her vision.

The ease had gone out of his posture. Suddenly
she knew he was a man poised to spring if he
needed to. And this was what he'd been leading up
to all along.

She cleared her throat. "Oh . . . this?"

"Yes," he said softly. "That."

She remained silent. She idly tested the tip of
the knife with her fingertip. Very sharp. Perfectly
deadly.

"Let me guess. It's not what I think."

Think, Tommy, think. "I'm carrying a knife," she
said slowly, "because . . . I don't own a pistol."

He nodded at this inanity thoughtfully. "Oh,
one should always carry a pistol. In fact, I'm carrying one now."

And so he was. There it was, gleaming in his
hand. *How had he done that?*

She stared at it.

"It's a very fine pistol," she commented politely,
thinking of ways to divest him of it or run, should
it prove necessary. A knee to the baubles? A blood-
curdling scream?

"It is. Thank you."

More silence. He wasn't precisely *aiming* the

thing at her, but he held it with the same casual ease with which he held the cheroot. She had no doubt he knew how to use it. She'd heard about how he allegedly, nonchalantly shot the hearts out of targets at Manton's with tedious predictability.

"Mr. Redmond, do you really think my intent is murderous? If it was, I assure you I would have done *you* or him in by now, rather than just taking in the sights."

He made an impatient sound. "You never would have gotten the chance to do me in, I assure you. Come. Do better."

She inhaled deeply.

"Very well. I carry a knife for protection if I'm out at night. I do know how to use it. And I'm here now because I learned he'd just returned to town, and I'd heard so much about him I simply wanted to see what he looked like. As you may have guessed, we hardly move in the same circles. I swear it on . . . my mother's memory."

It came out more piously than she intended.

Though it wasn't untrue.

"Your Spanish princess mother? Oh, *well*, then. I don't imagine swearing gets any more sacred than that."

She flinched. She ought to be angry—she *wanted* to be angry. She felt a faint sizzle somewhere on the periphery of her awareness.

Trouble was, she'd begun to find him interesting. And it was a rare enough sensation, when it came to men.

"I can't tell you why I wanted to see him, and I won't. But it's absolutely *true* that I simply wanted to get a look at the famous Duke of Greyfolk, and I knew he would be in this evening. I swear to you. Call it . . . curiosity. Will you leave it be now?"

Above their heads, the object of her curiosity scratched his great nose and turned a page.

God, *how* she wanted to know what he was reading. The light glinted from an enormous signet ring he was wearing.

"Why are *you* so concerned about the duke's welfare, Mr. Redmond? Pure heroics?"

He hesitated.

"I shouldn't like to see him murdered until I can persuade him to invest in one of my projects."

He'd startled a laugh from her. The self-deprecating humor surprised her. "You didn't succeed tonight?"

A thoughtful hesitation. A suck on the cheroot.

"Let's just say that I will."

She liked the quiet arrogance. No bluster, just a sort of calm certainty. It reminded her of her own.

"Shall we?" Jonathan said after a moment, gesturing with his pistol.

Simultaneously they tucked their weapons away.

"I'm amazed you recognized me in the dark," he said. "You must have eyes like a cat, Miss de Ballesteros."

"Difficult not to recognize someone who hardly took his eyes from me this afternoon."

Another interesting little silence ensued. She could have sworn her frankness had rendered him silent with admiration.

"I couldn't decide whether I found you attractive," he said finally.

Her jaw dropped. She coughed a shocked laugh.

"I know I'm supposed to," he added almost apologetically. And wholly wickedly. "Everyone else does. After all, you're quite the thing now, aren't you?"

She could practically *feel* him savoring her discomfiture.

All of a sudden she knew a wayward surge of delight at his pure effrontery.

"As you can see . . . I don't care what *you* think, either . . . Tommy."

Bastard was laughing softly now. But not in an unkind way. In a way that invited her to join him. To best him.

There ensued a fraught, invigorating little silence during which they retook each other's measure. During which they were deciding certain things, silently, about each other.

And then at last she leaned forward confidingly.

"Quite liberating, isn't it?" she whispered.

And after a moment, his wicked grin lit up the night.

She responded with one of her own.

It was as good as a handshake, that exchange. It was an agreement to like each other.

And later it was *that* she would remember about this particular midnight: the wicked flash of his grin in the dark, like a much more beautiful and dangerous twin of that moon.

She ought to have been warned.

Chapter 2

HOW DROLL.

Only the Duke of Greyfolk, Jonathan thought dryly, could all but ruin a perfectly good word like *droll*. He suspected he'd clench every muscle in his body reflexively, for the rest of his life, every time he heard it.

He'd strategically, with great finesse and subtlety, obtained an invitation to a dinner party held in honor of the powerful Duke of Greyfolk's return from a long tour of America. After dinner, over cigars and brandy, the talk had turned to manly things, and Jonathan had strategically, again with great finesses and subtlety, nudged the topic from racing horses to buying horses to investing in general, in a series of moves as planned and elegant as a chess game.

The duke had gazed at Jonathan speculatively, lingering expressionlessly but tellingly on that damned bruise beneath his eye. It was small but rapidly turning a disreputable purple, and looked like what it was.

It's not what it seems, Jonathan wanted to protest.

Well, more accurately, it wasn't *quite* what it seemed.

The duke had tipped back his head and exhaled straight up, obscuring his heavy handsome head in smoke. The devil would likely materialize in the room veiled in just that fashion, Jonathan thought.

"Printing . . . how droll, Mr. Redmond. I suppose every young man needs a . . . constructive . . . hobby." He returned his eyes to the bruise. One of his eyebrows gave a twitch upward.

It's not like I make a habit *out of pub brawls.*

"Mass production in *color.*" Jonathan was gripping his brandy snifter so hard he could feel his heart pulsing in his hand. He kept his voice steady; not too eager, not too emphatic. Surely *anyone* could understand the idea's potential. Particularly a man as allegedly savvy as the duke.

The duke gazed at him impassively for a second longer. And then he turned to the man next to him. "Now, that Lancaster Cotton Mill . . . The damned solicitor seems to have requirements for sale known only to him. He keeps requesting additional financial details before he'll approve a purchase. Ah, but of course he'll sell it to me eventually."

There were scattered chuckles. Because of *course* the duke always got what he wanted.

"Did you decide to buy the racehorse?" someone asked him.

"They're holding an impromptu race outside Holland Park in a few days. I'll decide then whether he's worth the money they're asking for him. They say he's the fastest seen in a decade."

Just like that, the subject had been changed and Jonathan was dismissed and forgotten, because it was the duke's prerogative to dismiss and forget anything he pleased.

He would, of course, try again at the horse race outside Holland Park in two days.

Jonathan was as interested in horses as the next man, and if *he'd* the capital to spend at the moment, he'd buy one, too.

But it spoke volumes about his father, Isaiah Redmond, that he'd considered the duke the easier of two titans to conquer, and so he'd begun there.

Because that's what he intended to do in Sussex: conquer.

Droll. Finding Thomasina de Ballesteros holding a *knife* outside the duke's window seemed a fitting conclusion to the night. For a moment he'd sympathized with what appeared to be murderous intent.

He smiled slowly. Imagine finding the woman who haunted the fantasies of bloods the ton over, the sole reason his friend Argosy had dragged him to the Countess Mirabeau's salon, crouched and tense as a feral cat outside the duke's tall windows. He didn't believe for a moment her presence there had been idle curiosity or pure impulse. She'd looked *just* a bit too comfortable in the shadows.

Even if he'd never seen her lurking outside of the Duke of Greyfolk's house at midnight, even if she'd never said *I carry a knife for protection if I'm out at night. I do know how to use it,* he would have *known* Tommy de Ballesteros was trouble.

It didn't prevent him from liking her.

She was officially the only woman of his entire acquaintance who had ever said such a thing, and she'd managed to sound sensible doing it. She didn't tolerate fools, which amused him. In fact, talking to her had been a bit like taking off tight boots at the end of a long day: she had felt peculiarly comfortable, peculiarly *spacious*, in the way other women simply weren't, by contrast.

And he liked her laugh. Quite a bit. He wouldn't mind making her do it again.

He handed his coat and hat to the footman and now stood in the doorway of the parlor of the Redmond House, surreptitiously watching his sister Violet, who was being looked after by their mother while her husband was on business in London. She was ensconced on the settee, clicking away with knitting needles, some scarflike object unfurling at the end of them. Her shiny dark head was bent in concentration, and in the cool pale light pouring in the window, she looked like a serene, exemplary representative of English womanhood. Someone could paint her just so and call it *The Sussex Madonna*.

And then the Redmonds could hang it in the parlor, and her family would gather round it and point and roar with laughter. For a more accurate name for such a painting would have been *Appearances are Deceiving*.

"What are you making?"

She whirled. "Jonathan!" Her face lit. "Don't stand there gawking. You look splendid, if a bit dusty. Tell me how I look."

"Radiant. But if you get any bigger we'll have to haul you about in a sedan chair. Or perhaps we can buy you a stylish cart and have it pulled about by a little white donkey."

She squawked in outrage and hurled a ball of blue wool at him.

Or she tried. Her arm snagged on her bulging stomach, and the wool ball instead dribbled impotently to the floor.

They both watched it roll to a listless stop at Jonathan's feet.

He handed it back to her, scrunched his eyes closed, leaned toward her, and sat obediently still so she could throw it at him again.

It bounced feebly off his chest.

They both watched it wobble to a stop a few feet from the window.

"Feel better now?" he asked her.

"No. But now will you fetch it for me?"

"Of course." He retrieved it and handed it back to her.

"Now will you fetch me some marzipan? And perhaps some raspberries?"

He turned an incredulous stare upon her. "Woman, you have me confused with your willing slave, the Earl of Ardmay. And where on earth would we find raspberries at this time of year? Oh God, you aren't going to cry, are you?"

She considered it. "Not this time," she decided thoughtfully. "But I think the baby needs raspberries."

"I hope you have a girl and that she's *exactly* like you." He delivered this like a curse, and flung himself into a chair next to her, slouched, and hoisted his booted feet up onto a little upholstered stool. He would get away with this as long as his mother didn't see it.

"So does Asher," Violet said dreamily.

"He'd wish differently if he'd grown up with you, and had to pull you out of wells by your elbows and the like." Violet had once threatened to throw herself into a well over an argument with a suitor, and had one leg over before she was pulled back by the elbows, and everyone in England seemed to know this. "I warrant that big mane of hair of his will be gray by the time your child is two years old. And he's an earl, after all. He'll want a boy."

"Honestly. The way all of you do go on about the *well*. I never made it all the *way* into the well, and I didn't intend to. And besides, Asher's done a good deal more for me than that." She smiled dreamily again. "The things that man can do . . ."

Jonathan clapped his hands over his ears. "No! Not one more word."

She laughed.

"But you do look very well and so radiant it borders on the cliché, Violet, even if you are huge."

In truth, she looked a little weary to Jonathan. The faint lavender crescents beneath her eyes worried him. He supposed it was difficult to sleep comfortably when one was carrying living cargo, and possibly the earl's heir. It hadn't been an easy pregnancy for Violet, but then Violet wasn't known for making *anything* easy.

"Thank you. Can you lean a bit that way, please? You smell of smoke and smoke still makes me a bit queasy, and I shouldn't like to cast my accounts here in the parlor. Were you out throwing darts at the Pig & Thistle? Do you think you can take me on a trip, Jonathan?"

He obligingly listed a bit in the opposite direction from her. "I smoked a cheroot late last night." He contemplated telling Violet about his encounter with Tommy, but decided to keep it a secret. "It must still be lingering on my coat. Did you say trip? In your condition? Are you mad? Unless it's to the foot of the garden, and then I'll go and fetch a donkey and cart for you. Easier to obtain the two of them than it would be to obtain raspberries."

"Oh, please, say you will! It's a short trip I have in mind, and Asher is in London at the king's behest. So very selfish of the king to call him away in my time of need. I should like to visit the Gypsy woman Leonora Heron and her daughter, that girl, Martha Her—oh, my goodness! You should see your face! You've gone so white! Are *you* going to cast your accounts?"

"I don't like that girl." That girl had once made a prediction that chilled him to his very marrow. "And you know why. Why *do* you want to see the Gypsy girl?"

"Because I want to ask her about the baby."

He laid a concerned hand on her arm and lowered his voice to a hush. "Are you worried it might not be human?"

She brushed off his hand. "I want to ask her about the baby, because she was right about . . ." She stopped. She bit her lip. Her eyes flared swiftly in alarm.

It was too late. Jonathan knew her, and he was faster. "Right about *what*, Violet?"

Violet kept her mouth clamped.

"Right. About. What?" he demanded.

"Things. I've heard she's right about certain things sometimes."

He made a disgusted sound. "Try again. As I recall during our visit there with Cynthia, she said something about you taking a trip over water, Mrs. Heron did. And then that looby of a daughter of hers, Martha, blurted the word 'Lavay.' And . . . well, let me see. At the ball, you were oh so excited to learn that 'Lavay' was the first mate of the Earl of Ardmay's ship. You were convinced it meant Lyon was a *pirate* named Le Chat, of all things. The earl was given a mandate by the king to hunt down this pirate. And then," he said slowly, "and then you went to a house party. For a fortnight. And shortly after you returned from said house party, the Earl of Ardmay appeared here, and voilà! You're married to him within weeks."

Violet listened to this. "That was the sequence of events, yes," she allowed cautiously.

Jonathan glared at her.

She donned an absorbed, beatific Madonna-esque expression, and ran a hand absently over her belly, a ploy to make him feel guilty.

She ought to have known better by now. Nothing of the sort ever worked on Jonathan.

"Did this 'house party' by any chance take place on a ship?" he asked sardonically.

Her mouth remained clamped shut.

"Mother of God, Violet." He was awed and disgusted and quite furious. "What happened? All I can say is I'm glad the Earl of Ardmay has the keeping of you now. You're bloody lucky something didn't happen to you. I'm so unutterably tired of *secrets* in this family. Give that ball of wool to me. *Now*."

Violet, like a true penitent, handed it to him with great trepidation, squeezed her eyes closed, and hunched her shoulders.

He wasn't going to pelt his pregnant sister. He hurled it instead across the room with impressive force.

Just in time to strike their mother squarely in her expensively-clad bosom.

It bounced from her and rolled across the carpet, unfurling a streamer of blue on its way, and coming to a stop obligingly near Violet's feet, like a loyal pet.

Jonathan and Violet froze, half aghast, half, truthfully, delighted.

Their mother was stunned motionless for a moment. And then she stirred. "What have I told you about throwing things in the house, Jonathan?" she asked evenly.

He pretended to mull this. "Never miss?"

She laughed. Fanchette Redmond was always indulgent of her youngest son's glibness. Probably because for a long while after his oldest brother Lyon disappeared, his mother hadn't laughed at all. And Jonathan had been the one to make her do it when she finally did.

"Your father would like to have a word with you, Jonathan. I wasn't certain whether you'd yet arrived, but he's in the library now if you'd like to go up."

"Ah," he said.

What a lot could be conveyed with one syllable.

His father was considerably less indulgent of Jonathan's glibness than his mother was.

"Thank you," he remembered to add.

"It's just a *word*, not a sentence, darling."

It took him a moment. "A prison joke, Mother! Oh, well done!" he congratulated her.

She glowed. His mother perhaps naturally assumed that Jonathan was in some sort of scrape. There would be plenty of time to explain later.

He stood and stretched, and when he did, a swift startled yearning flickered over his mother's face, and then it was gone. And he knew it was because she was noticing, as had so many others, just how much he'd come to look like Lyon.

Bloody Lyon.

He loved his brother. But he knew well that Lyon had been no saint, which was something other people seemed willing to forget, if they ever even knew it. And Lyon had disappeared without a word to anyone, allegedly because Olivia Eversea had broken his heart. Fulfilling, as all of England seemed to know, an ancient curse: that an Eversea was destined to fall in love with a Redmond once per generation, with disastrous consequences. The deep-rooted enmities between the Everseas and Redmonds had simmered beneath a veneer of civility this century (in another century, around 1066, rumor had it they'd cleaved each other's skulls with axes), but the disappearance of Lyon had scraped open wounds, and made even this civility dangerously more difficult.

Jonathan collected the wool ball and wordlessly handed it to his sister. He kissed his mother on the cheek in passing, and went up to persuade his father to invest in a son who had no intention of disappearing, let alone falling prey to a curse involving inappropriate *love*, of all things.

No, *he* intended to conquer, rather than be conquered.

The way Redmonds always conquered—with unsurpassable wealth.

Chapter 3

❧

IF HIS FATHER'S LIBRARY had been a symphony, it would have been written by Bach—tasteful, controlled, masculine, orderly. Browns and creams and rich dense fabrics—velvet, wool, crepe. The better to muffle the screams of Isaiah's victims, Jonathan thought, amused. Not that scream-muffling was strictly necessary. His father could paralyze a victim—a recalcitrant son, perhaps, or a poorly performing bailiff—with a well-chosen word and a beam from his greenglass glittery eyes. Much like a . . . native armed with a poison-tipped dart.

Jonathan had learned about natives and poison darts and the like from his brother Miles, a famous explorer who'd nearly been eaten by cannibals out in the South Seas. Jonathan had naturally been more interested in the stories of affectionate dark-skinned women who went about wearing nothing above their waists, but residual facts about other things clung to this titillating notion the way fluff clung to a dropped candied sweet. And Jonathan never forgot anything he learned.

One thing he'd learned was that Isaiah never missed his target.

But then, neither did Jonathan. One could ask everyone in Pennyroyal Green. He'd taken home four Pig & Thistle dart tournament trophies, and possessed several Sussex shooting trophies as well.

And no one knew that every dart that entered the board struck a metaphorical target.

Besides, he knew his father well enough now to anticipate and deflect the darts. Being the youngest had its advantages. You learned what not to do, what to do, and how to do precisely what you wanted. Much of it involved staying out of his father's proverbial sight, so he could stay out of his father's proverbial mind.

"Jonathan!" His name, at least, was imbued with warmth and pleasure.

"It's very good to see you, Father."

Isaiah didn't offer him brandy, which seemed portentous—was the conversation about to be quick and painful? Did he suppose Jonathan was already drunk?—but then everything was bound to seem portentous when his nerves could be played like lute strings, so taut were they.

"Have a seat, son." He gestured at the documents arrayed on his desk. "I was just reviewing correspondence from a frustratingly obtuse Mr. Romulus Bean, the owner of the Lancaster Cotton Mill. I've been trying to persuade him to sell the mill to me, but he continually requests additional financial detail. The number of servants I currently employ, their ages, their wages . . . "Rather arbitrary of the man, but so be it. I'm certain I'll have it in the end."

Ah, to be possessed of his father's unshakable certainty.

Jonathan casually decided to lay a piece of information at his father's feet, an offering to soften him for the conversation to come.

"The Duke of Greyfolk is interested in purchasing the Lancaster Mill, too."

Isaiah leaned back slowly in his chair and stared at Jonathan. "Is he?" he mused after a moment. "How did you come by this information?"

"Over dinner at his house."

A pause.

"You were invited," his father probed

"I was, indeed." Jonathan didn't see a need to expound on how he got the invitation.

His father absorbed this wordlessly, the wheels of his inscrutable mind no doubt turning. "Will you be at home for long, Jonathan?"

"Back to London in a day or so, as I've accepted some invitations in town. I primarily wanted to speak to you. And of course to see how Violet was getting on."

"Your sister's doing well." It sounded careful.

Jonathan suspected Violet had been gleefully using her pregnancy as an excuse to make everyone jump to do her bidding, his father included.

"She's radiant," Jonathan concurred. Which he had learned was the safest compliment one could pay a pregnant woman.

A little silence pillowed his father's next words.

"About your proposal to join the Mercury Club, Jonathan."

Ah. So it was to be quick, then.

"Yes, sir?"

"While I understand why you would want to join the club's ranks, as all members benefit greatly from involvement and from the income of others, I do not see what qualifications you would bring to an esteemed and highly successful investment group."

Jonathan's mind briefly blanked. Of all the responses he'd anticipated and prepared for, this one wasn't among them.

"There's . . . my surname, for a beginning." It was meant to be humorous.

For Isaiah had founded the club. And if Isaiah didn't precisely control this investment group, he powerfully influenced the activities of the club, as well as the membership.

His father didn't laugh.

Jonathan cleared his throat. "I've many ideas, sound ones, and I think you and the other investors will be very interested to hear them. And haven't you always said that ideas are capital?"

"Have you ideas, then," his father said, in way that implied he doubted it very much indeed. "I never dreamed you'd been listening to me."

It wasn't just that it was dismissive.

It was *shockingly* dismissive.

As though Jonathan at no point over the years could possibly have begun to think for himself.

He recovered smoothly enough. "I've become acquainted with a gentleman named Mr. Klaus Liebman, who has developed a process for printing mass quantities in color, and I do believe it would be an excellent investment."

His father took this in expressionlessly. "Print-

ing is a . . ." his father paused to search for a word.
". . . small . . . idea, Jonathan. And Liebman . . . isn't
he the Bavarian fellow you met at a gaming hell?"
His father delivered those last two words with
faint but unmistakable derision.

"*Outside* a gaming hell," Jonathan corrected.
Which likely amounted to nearly the same thing in
his father's eyes, but there *was* a distinction. He'd
saved Klaus Liebman from thugs, too, loaned him
a little money, and bought him a drink, which was
when Jonathan had heard all about his brilliant
idea. Klaus was depending on Jonathan to return
from Sussex with good news. "I realize it doesn't
sound as dramatic as a cotton mill, but the potential is immense."

"Of course, of course," his father indulged. "Is
that the same gaming hell outside of which you
were involved in a brawl? During which you allegedly shouted epithets in the street?"

That damned bruise. It was all he could do not to
touch it now. How did his father *know* about that?

"I intervened to help a man who was accosted
outside the Boar & Bear, which is a pub, not a gaming
hell. I simply happened to be in the vicinity. Three
men attacked him for his purse. With *knives*. I was
fortunate I lost only my handkerchief, not my life."

What he'd shouted, specifically, was "Get off
him, you fetid bastards!" It could have been worse.

"Of course," his father said, as if it was inconceivable that Jonathan would leap into the fray to
save a man, but for him to leap into a melee in the
street for the sheer primitive pleasure of it was apparently in keeping with his character.

So far, Jonathan thought dryly, there seemed to be very little benefit in playing Samaritan. Curse it for the reflex it was. Of course, he never would have been anywhere near the Boar & Bear if not for that salon Argosy had dragged him to.

"And it's come to my attention that you've been frequenting the home of a known courtesan who lives hear Hanover Square."

Speak of the devil.

"She's not a . . ."

Hell. With those three words he'd just betrayed he knew exactly who he meant.

He scarcely knew her, and still here she was, introduced as a topic of conversation by his *father*, of all people, and was clearly about to be used to illustrate his alleged failings of character. He knew she was trouble.

"I'm afraid 'frequenting' is a bit of an exaggeration, Father. I *attended* a salon frequented by the sons of many of your friends, as well as a number of authors and poets and artists and the like, and yes, a particular woman acts as hostess on behalf of Countess Mirabeau. The young woman in question is not a member of the aristocracy, and she doesn't live in the home, from what I understand. But if she's a courtesan I'm entirely unaware of it. I know very little about her at all."

His father winced when Jonathan got to the words "poets" and "artists," which he seemed to find more troubling than "courtesan." Jonathan felt rather the same way about poets and artists, truthfully. He was interested in tangible things, not abstract things. He preferred action, building an idea into fruition, rather than sucking the marrow from it, which is what this sort tended to do.

"What kind of young woman typically plays hostess to a gathering primarily comprised of men, Jonathan?"

"I'm uncertain, sir. Why don't you enlighten me?"

Silence.

Soooo . . . his father wasn't going to laugh at all today. That much was clear.

"Her mother was a Spanish princess, who fled to England after the war." That was the myth anyway.

"Of course. Their mothers are always Spanish princesses."

"And she's invited at the behest of the Countess Mirabeau, who is the *true* hostess of the salon."

"The Countess Mirabeau is one hundred and five years old, if she's a day. I think she may have behaved respectably for approximately three of those years, and she's been daft for fifty of them."

She *was* daft, but it was in a way that Jonathan rather enjoyed. The countess tended to forget the current decade, and one never knew whether she would appear in a toga, or medieval tunic, or a wig and bustle and patches, or in the first stare of fashion.

"She is seventy-seven, I'm given to understand. The weekly gathering was entirely her idea, and everyone present is there at her behest."

His father raised a dismissive hand. "Irrespective of the salon, there's the matter of Lady Winslow."

Jonathan went still. Truly and nastily surprised.

And the surprise heated into simmering anger.

He was a grown man. His dalliances were discreet ones; he wasn't reckless, nor had he brought shame upon his family. And Lady Philippa Winslow, a widow, was entirely free to do as she pleased, and what he did with Philippa was entirely his business.

And how would his father have heard about her? He must have eyes bloody everywhere.

"Were you a virgin when you married, Father? I doubt it, somehow."

Or at least that was what he longed to say. What he said instead was, "I'm afraid I'm uncertain what any of this has to do with my proposal to join the Mercury Club, sir."

"You've no experience with investing, Jonathan. Unless one counts stamina in the gaming hells, or the purchase of gifts for a certain kind of woman, or an investment in time in Five-Card Loo or dart tournaments. The men of the club would be polite to you and all that was gracious, but they would resent the presence of someone who not only hasn't the personal income or the depth of knowledge to truly contribute to the growth of wealth, but has demonstrated certain, shall we say, caprices of character. They would come to resent me for indulging your presence there."

Caprices of character? Since when had being young, good-looking, wealthy, and male constituted a caprice of character?

And he *excelled* at both darts and Five-Card Loo.

Instead, he tried, "I believe I've an aptitude for investing. After all, I am your son."

Flattery: a time-honored softener of the flinty-hearted. Delivered with a soupçon of charm.

Little did his father know he did, in fact, have an aptitude.

Quite an aptitude.

Not only an aptitude, but a hunger for it, a deep pleasure in it, a sense of it as an art. It was the same sort of hunger that must have driven his father, and his father's father, to amass the fortune Isaiah Redmond used to control his family—and a good portion of England, in many ways—today. A hunger that none of his other sons had heretofore shown. And it surprised even Jonathan.

"And in what way have you demonstrated this aptitude?" His father said this almost indulgently. Which made Jonathan want to scream, "I'm not twelve years old."

Which of course would make him *sound* twelve years old. The irony wasn't lost on him.

He dug the nails of his fingers into his palm for restraint. "I invested in a cargo of silks and doubled my investment."

"Ah. And what remains of your profit?"

Jonathan hesitated. "At the moment . . ."

In truth, the answer was "nothing." But not for the reasons his father assumed.

His father knew the answer without being told. And it was when Jonathan saw the cynical satisfaction on his father's face, he decided he'd be damned if he was going to beg. Or even explain further.

"If you're short of funds, Jonathan, and this is the reason you wish to participate in the Mercury

Club, you can have your portion and more the moment you marry appropriately. Not until then. Then again, I suppose you could always rely on the turn of a card for your future."

The word "marry" landed on his ears like the very first note of a funeral march. *Now* he was good and wary.

It occurred to him that his father might actually be leading to something unexpected.

"What does 'appropriately' mean?"

His father sighed. "Why am I not surprised that *you* should ask such a question?"

"Forgive me. Perhaps I should have asked: what does 'appropriately' mean to *you*, Father?"

Jonathan kept his voice level, his face as impassive as he was able.

But the question was barbed.

And his father was no fool. He could sniff out a rebellion the way a fox can sniff out a rodent in a thicket. He fixed Jonathan with a cold stare.

Jonathan was both too angry and too curious now to be cowed.

Because the question was valid. His older brother Miles had married the wildly inappropriate (as far as Isaiah Redmond was concerned) Cynthia Brightly, and showed no signs of being anything other than gloriously happy, in that very sure, very *immovable* way Miles had that made it seem like he'd done the most right thing in the world. And then Violet had married an earl of all things, quite unexpectedly, which would have made most parents ecstatic, except that the earl she'd married was Captain Asher Flint, the Earl of Ardmay—purportedly part Indian, nicknamed

"The Savage," of unknown parentage, American-raised no less, who'd earned an earldom from the king in part through application of a set of unsavory skills, violence among them.

When his father had craved a title his entire life.

It was funny, when one thought about it. When he was a small child, Jonathan coveted his father's black stallion more than anything in the world, and he used to try very hard at night to dream of riding it; instead, he wound up dreaming of riding mules, or sawhorses, or tree branches, if he dreamed of riding anything at all.

For his father, getting his children married to appropriate people must be rather like that. So close, and yet so far.

Still, no one could argue that the Earl of Ardmay wasn't the only man alive who could tame Violet and get her happily, if queasily and tyrannically, with child.

"Appropriately means a woman of whom I approve, born of a fine family, preferably with a title. Surely you could have surmised this much without asking."

He paused weightily.

It was, Jonathan realized even as it was happening, tantamount to the moment before the judge reads a verdict in court.

"I have in fact decided any additional funds you receive from me will be contingent upon you marrying appropriately inside the year."

Jonathan went very still. As though some disgusting and multilegged and poisonous creature, something his naturalist brother Miles might have discovered or known the name of, had settled on him, and would bite if he moved.

How is it I never saw this coming?

Then again, his father had a few more decades experience with darts, the metaphorical kind at least, than he did.

Men who are fatally struck usually take a moment to drop. He felt rather suspended in that moment.

"If club membership is what you want, and if you believe you have an 'aptitude,' as you say, for investment, I think the gentlemen of the Mercury Club would be more inclined to trust the judgment of a married man, Jonathan. After all, marriage demonstrates one's willingness to shoulder responsibility and manage a household, and requires a certain steadiness of character."

This was such *balderdash* that Jonathan had to bite down on his back teeth to keep his jaw from swinging wide. Drinking and gambling had practically been *invented* in order to help married men forget about their wives. Everyone knew that.

My father really does believe I'm stupid, he thought, in some surprise. Or at best, he thinks I'm a feckless child.

And for a moment he sat feeling strangely hollow, as if someone had just taken a spoon and scooped him out like a melon.

How little he knows of happiness, despite Miles. Despite Violet. Despite Lyon. He still thinks he can manufacture *happiness. His* own*, that was. From the lives of his children.* As far as Isaiah was concerned, there really was very little difference between control and happiness.

"The end of the year is . . . six months away."

"Excellent arithmetic, son," Isaiah said dryly. "Surely you can manage to reach an agreement with a young woman of good family and fortune. You've a certain amount to recommend you—your family name and money, breeding, your good looks. Dozens of lovely girls come eligible every day. We can cement an alliance with an excellent family. There's Lady Grace Worthington, for instance. And surely marrying a beautiful girl will be no hardship."

A certain *amount*?

I've a "certain *amount*" to recommend me?

And really, if this was happening to someone else, it might be terribly funny. But as Jonathan heard his alleged assets inventoried by his father, he felt himself nearly lift out of his body, and he observed the proceedings as if he floated overhead. He was a name and a face, was he? He was a youngest son, and a place would need to be found for him, as if he was a . . . superfluous vase. And this was all he had to offer the world?

Ah, but damn Lyon and Miles, both of whom had escaped Isaiah Redmond's iron grasp. Not without cost, of course. Lyon, the golden child, the heir, handsome, popular, charismatic, brilliant, the basket into which his father had put all of his proverbial eggs, had vanished entirely. Miles was still struggling to find enough funders for his next expedition, for his father had refused to assist him in light of his inappropriate marriage. And of course, he was still not precisely warmly received by his father, given that he'd married Cynthia Brightly, who was not received in their home.

He'd been unable to punish *them*, or not as thoroughly as he would have liked, so Isaiah clearly intended to leave nothing to chance where it came to Jonathan.

And this, he realized, was what this conversation was truly about.

"I feel obliged to point out that I haven't yet disappeared, Father. Surely that fact numbers among my virtues, too."

Isaiah lifted his head. He pinned him with a quelling stare.

Clearly he wasn't at *all* amused. The "yet" in particular did Jonathan no favors.

But, God, it had been tremendously satisfying to say it. Because if his father possessed any vulnerability at all, it had to do with Lyon. His Achilles' heel.

Jonathan met his father's gaze evenly.

Blink, you bastard, he willed him.

"I feel certain you'll do your duty, Jonathan."

He said it almost gently. But under the circumstances Jonathan thought he'd possibly never heard more contemptuous words.

He really thinks I will do precisely what he says, he thought.

Good God. He doesn't know me at *all*.

How crushing.

How illuminating.

How . . . potentially very useful.

"Brandy, son?"

And Jonathan thought with dark amusement that his father had anticipated he'd need a drink at *this* point in the conversation. Always the strategist, Isaiah Redmond.

"No, thank you, Father. I best be off to compile a list of potential brides. Six months passes quickly, you know."

He departed with an exaggerated wink. Winks— *just* the sort of thing his father loathed.

Chapter 4

TOMMY WAS IN JUST a *little* over her head.

This realization solidified the moment she found another message slipped under her door. To anyone else the message might have looked like a bit of detritus carried in from the street on someone's shoe. She knew better.

She hesitated. Then she plucked it up gingerly between her fingers, and carried it to her table. Nonchalantly she lit a lamp, allowed it to flare into life and set her room aglow, and then settled down at the table, her chin cradled in her hands, and stared down at it.

Postponing the moment when she would need to make a decision.

She didn't usually mind being just a bit in over her head. She generally flailed like a becalmed ship, irritable and purposeless and panicked, when things were simple. And if no challenge could be found, she had the dubious gift of creating one. She'd never known any other way, really. Resistance was the headwind into which she sailed.

Thud! Thud! Thud!

She gave a yelp. The entire building, made of kindling as it was, rocked, shuddered, and creaked. She lunged to keep her lamp from hopping off the table.

The thudding stopped.

She smiled. "Greetings, Rutherford!" she shouted at the ceiling.

"Greetings, Miss Tommy!" he boomed.

Rutherford lived in a suite of rooms above hers, and he was huge. When he moved about, the whole building trembled and squeaked and groaned as if it were a ship on the breast of a stormy sea. But he wasn't generally home. Sometimes he found work on the docks or on a ship or as a builder, and often he was away for weeks at a time, engaged in something far more interesting and dubious.

As he had been, for instance, when he'd last worked for her.

Dubious occupations, in fact, seemed to be one unifying characteristic of the people who lived in her building. It was where her mother had ultimately died, young, ill, and penniless, and it was where Tommy, when she'd found her way back to it, had cobbled together a motley family of sorts, for they had loved her mother. Her rooms were small and as snug as a shoe, filled with the few fine things her mother had left behind when she died, and she was surrounded by the sounds of life, which in this building were primarily thumping: Rutherford walking from one end of the room to another, Maggie's bed slamming against the wall as she entertained gentlemen callers, the four Beatty children thundering up and down the stairs. Things of that sort.

All in all she had little time to feel lonely. And yet when it was dark, and she'd doused her lamp and the thumping had ceased for the night, she sometimes felt she was on a raft alone at sea, and would awake in a panic, gripping the sides of her bed. Loneliness had a sound, and it was the absence of thumping.

Still avoiding the message, she laid out the medal gently on the table and touched her fingers to it for courage. Last night at the Duke of Greyfolk's wasn't really a failure of nerve yet, not really. It had been just a start, she told herself—because honestly, imagine *her* nerve failing! The sky would sooner fall. Jonathan Redmond had interrupted her, that was all.

She took a deep breath and leaned over the scrap of paper, hands clasped against her forehead.

It appeared to have been torn from an old book by someone who couldn't easily obtain foolscap or ink. In the narrow margin, in tiny painstaking letters, scratched with a burnt stick most likely, were the words:

She'll be waiting at the place we discussed, at the day we discussed, one of the clock.

She recognized the careful even script of Lord Feckwith's cook. She hadn't, of course, signed it. Signing it could mean her death. Not to mention Tommy's.

She closed her eyes and drew in a long breath. Released it, fluttering her lamp flame.

Would she do it again?

Could she do it again?

Because the last time had . . . well, it hadn't gone precisely as she'd hoped.

She absently rubbed at her arm. It didn't hurt anymore, and there would be a little scar soon— The Doctor, who was never known by anything other than The Doctor, and therefore was clearly as dubious as everyone else—did competent work. Still, it was one more mark her body bore.

It would be the only scar of which she'd ever be proud, however.

The irony was they'd likely been aiming for Rutherford, who was an infinitely larger and more conspicuous target. And what kind of shooting was *that*, if they'd missed him? Pretty sorry shooting, if you asked her.

Now Jonathan Redmond . . . in all likelihood, given what she knew about him, he wouldn't miss his target.

A little half smile found its way onto her face. The *cheek* of the man. She liked cheek. She liked a man who spoke to her as if she was a person, an equal, as if she were in on the joke. There was a freedom in not *wanting* anything from each other, which so seldom happened between men and women.

There was much to be wary of about him, too. For instance, those vast shoulders, and those cheekbones that called to mind battlements, so chiseled were they, all of which contrived to whip female heads around like compass needles. But she suspected it was something else . . . she would have called it a fine veneer of cynicism, a sort of detachment, as if he'd seen things that others had not, knew things that others did not . . . that lured females into dashing themselves on the allegedly rocky shoals of his heart.

Not *her*, of course.

She liked a little wariness. The rest of the men were so bloody predictable. And there was something about Jonathan Redmond that felt like the first breath of air drawn after you leave a crowded smoky room. She liked him. She supposed it wasn't more complicated than that.

"It's a gift you share with your mother, my dear," the Countess of Mirabeau told her. "Men like themselves better when they're around you, it's just that simple. And Carolina, rest your dear mother's soul, attracted a duke for a reason. Perhaps you'll do the same."

As it turned out, the genteelly poor countess—who repaid a good turn done her by Tommy's mother by taking in hand the fiercely clever, vivacious, half-feral scrap of a girl she'd been after her mother died, and done her best to polish her—had been right. Tommy had rapidly become the chief attraction at the countess's Wednesday salons near Hanover Square. And it wasn't as though Tommy didn't enjoy the salons and all the male attention. And it wasn't as though she'd never occasionally indulged her sensual curiosity and hot blood. But when she lost her virginity to a gorgeous boy who had promptly disappeared, Tommy's native pragmatism—surely she hadn't inherited *that* from her mother—put a stop to further indulgence. It was terrifyingly easy to be swept up in a current of desire. And she wasn't *about* to live the way her mother had lived, or suffer her mother's fate.

And yet the money from the occasional, modest,

serendipitous win at a hand of cards, and the shilling or two the countess occasionally pressed into her palm dwindled quickly. And though she was accustomed to challenge, the challenge to survive was ceaseless and wearing.

And then the gift of pearls had arrived. Another way in which she was in just a bit over her head. They could very well represent the answer to all of her troubles. They most definitely represented another decision she would have to make. And soon. It wasn't one she relished making.

She shied away from it for the moment.

Because thanks to something Jonathan Redmond had said, she'd just realized there *might* be another option.

She stared down at the little charcoal letters and reread them, and the bands of muscle in her stomach tightened, and an additional beat seemed to join the rhythm of her heart.

Ah, bloody hell. She was going to do it. There was no question that it was what she was born to do. That she couldn't live with herself if she didn't.

She was forced to admit, however, that for the first time since it had all started . . . she was a little afraid.

The problem was, she'd begun to *think* about it. And once you did that, you were sunk, she knew. Once when she was very little, she'd been able to walk the narrow stair rail in this very building, one tiny foot carefully placed in front of the other, arms outflung for balance like a circus performer. The very moment she'd begun to exult in her achievement, to really *think* about it, was the moment she toppled and cracked her chin. She still sported a tiny scar.

Not that she didn't *enjoy* the thrill that followed surviving peril. It was just that, as nearly everything in her life so far, she could easily imagine it eventually crescendoing into a disaster from which she barely escaped.

She lay down the scrap of paper and took up the medal.

"You commanded a whole battalion," she said to the medal. "Were likely shot at dozens if not hundreds of times. What if you could help me? I *know* you could help. Or would you think I was mad and ought to be locked away?"

She'd had numerous conversations with that medal over the years. Sometimes she'd harangued it, sometimes she'd simply told it about her day. Each time she imagined the medal was loving and regretful and sentimental, all of which she knew deep down was probably very unlikely. And yet, where was the harm in laying down the burden of her pragmatism for just one moment? It was an indulgence, one of her very, very few.

"Thanks for listening . . ." She breathed in. ". . . Papa."

No matter how many times she said the word, she never felt entitled to it.

THE GYPSIES, BEING Gypsies, had a tendency to roam, so they couldn't always be found camped on the outskirts of Pennyroyal Green, and were often as difficult to pin down as quicksilver, particularly when it came time for the Cambridge Horse Fair. But Jonathan had seen the smoke from the cook fire at a distance, and so after a great show of reluctance, he decided that Violet would get her wish before he returned to London. The following morning they packed her up like blown glass, and transported her in a well-sprung carriage, hauled by four horses driven with great delicacy, as though they were arthritic and lame.

It was a *long* trip. For Jonathan, anyway.

Leonora Heron emerged from her tent at the encampment when she heard the carriage wheels, wiping her hands on her apron, smiling a greeting, then curtsying.

Her aspiring tart of a daughter—if Gypsies could be said to be tarts—peeked out from behind her, and her round harvest moon-colored eyes widened. Her habitual pout transformed into a sultry one, and she twined a strand of curly black hair round one finger.

Jonathan studiously avoided her gaze.

"Dukker fer ye, brother?" she said anyway, offering to use the tarot to read his fortune.

"I'm simply an escort to my sister. So bat your eyelashes in another direction if you will, please."

"Jonathan!" Violet scolded.

"Martha!" Leonora Heron scolded. To no avail, in both cases.

"But it's why we came today, Mrs. Heron. If you would be so kind as to read the tea leaves for the countess?" he asked pointedly to Mrs. Heron.

"I would be pleased to do it." Mrs. Heron gestured for them to enter. Inside the tent they were assailed by the usual clean, pungent smell of herbs. Mrs. Heron clucked and found a chair that would safely accommodate Violet, and they all helped get her settled into it. Martha stood against the back of the tent, her arms crossed over her chest in such a way that her bosom was lifted nearly to her collarbone.

She brewed the tea for Violet, who drank a sip. And then Leonora swirled it about, tipped the rest gently onto a saucer, and finally peered into them, scrying with the leaves floating over the bottom.

"I see the leaves have formed the shape of a harp. This means harmony and happiness for you." Leonora looked up, smiling. "I am pleased to tell you this."

Violet had just begun to beam when, "She will break hearts!" Martha suddenly blurted, sounding startled. Her eyes were wide, as if someone else had borrowed her mouth without permission.

Violet swiveled to look at her. "She? Do you think I'm having a girl? Am I having a girl?"

Martha shrugged with one shoulder.

Violet's face suffused with pleasure, and it was wonderful to see. Jonathan enjoyed it. And then she predictably turned an "I told you so!" expression upon Jonathan.

"She will break hearts," Martha repeated, as if she were in a trance. She wasn't. She was simply enjoying the dramatic reception of her prediction. Meanwhile, she'd traced the outline of Jonathan's entire body with her big round eyes so thoroughly he could hardly fail to notice, and when he did, she touched a tongue coyly to her lips.

Jonathan was perilously close to scowling at her. He settled for a mere frown, and returned his attention to Violet.

"Well . . ." Violet took in this information. "That stands to reason, doesn't it? The breaking hearts bit? It's what Redmonds do."

"Well, it wasn't so much that you broke hearts, as enslaved and terrified them before you married. Isn't that true, Violet?"

"Shhh," she said, entirely unperturbed. "And is that all you see in the leaves, Mrs. Heron?"

Martha whirled on Jonathan then, who, much to his later chagrin, for Violet would go on to imitate it for the pleasure and hilarity of their brother Miles and her husband the earl, threw his arms defensively across his face. As if he could prevent her from peering into his soul that way.

"*You* . . . children everywhere." Martha sounded astounded. And then made a big swooping circle with her arms, in case the word "everywhere" didn't illustrate it horrifyingly enough.

Jonathan turned his head slowly and sent a sizzling "I told you so" look to his sister. "She's not helping in the least. Shall we depart?"

"Jonathan, wait." Violet wasn't satisfied. "Allow me to help. How *many* children, Martha?"

"Maybe ten. Maybe one hundred." The girl shrugged indifferently.

He rolled his eyes. "Can you even *count?*"

"Martha, how many is this?" Violet flashed ten fingers. "Will he have this many children? Or mayhap this many?" She flashed them again.

"I think more like this many." And Martha flashed her fingers a good dozen times.

"Stop it! Stop it at once!" Jonathan demanded, aghast.

And when Violet burst into laughter, Martha, feeling encouraged, continued to do it, delighted to be so amusing. Ten, twenty, thirty, forty, fifty, sixty . . .

Jonathan flung a shilling into the empty teacup, where it spun round a few times and then clinked resoundingly, and stormed from the tent, gulping draughts of air, Gypsy laughter ringing in his ears.

Then he remembered his sister couldn't rise without assistance, which rather ruined his exit, but he stormed back in, gently helped her up off the chair, and led her at a stately pace from the tent before he began to yell at her.

"Thank you!" she sang on her way out.

Jonathan leaned against the carriage and folded his arms across his body, and turned on her. "Why is my distress so *amusing* to you?"

"Jonathan . . . it's just . . . why *are* you so distressed? One day you will need to care about *something*. Why not children?"

He stared at her, genuinely struck dumb. He opened his mouth. A dry squeaking noise emerged.

And when he was finally able to form words, they were all hoarse.

"I need to . . . care? I need to *care?* Does *anyone* bloody know me? Do you really think I don't *care* about things, as you say?"

Violet winced. "I'm sorry. I'm sorry. Good heavens! I'm sorry! Hush! I didn't mean to give you apoplexy. Pregnancy has addled my brain."

He stopped and blew out a breath, yanked off his hat, pushed his fingers through his hair, and jammed it back on.

"You're going to miss having that as an excuse for every little thing," he said darkly, finally.

"I'll find another excuse," she replied placidly.

"And I'm sorry to bellow," he added stiffly, and then bent over and spoke to her stomach: "And my apologies to you, too. I'm allegedly the cheerful Redmond. Your Uncle Jonathan. Ask anyone."

"It's just . . . you can't go on like this forever, Jonathan. Gaming, balls, hunts, races, that disreputable salon you've been attending. Endless frivolity. Do you really find it satisfying?"

He turned a look on her that was rich with incredulity. "Why the bloody hell not? And yes, I find it 'satisfying!' I'm not doing any harm—"

"I suppose that depends on who you ask. Marianne Linley, for instance."

"—I'm still young. I like things the way they are. It's just that simple. And I don't see any great marital happiness going on around me. Do you think mother and father are happy? Lyon actually bloody disappeared over a love affair. I see a good deal of upheaval and battle and struggle all in the name of love. And Marianne Linley misinterpreted two conversations and two dances—on separate occasions, mind you—as some sort of passionate attachment. But primarily she saw me dancing with Lady Grace Worthington an equal number of times, and you know how all the young women think of Lady Grace. I assure you, there was *no attachment*, and I implied nothing."

"Perhaps you underestimate your powers of appeal."

Jonathan was taken aback. "Was that . . . actually a compliment?"

"I suspect I meant it as more of a warning."

"I'm really more interested in Lady Grace Worthington, if you must know."

"Isn't everybody this season? Aren't you supposed to be?"

Jonathan paused, and then half smiled. *I know I'm supposed to,* is what Jonathan had said to Tommy outside of the Duke's big windows—almost but not quite entirely out of deviltry—when he'd told her he hadn't decided whether he found her attractive. She'd been shocked, then genuinely amused. By God, he'd liked that. Whoever the devil she might be, she was comfortable in her skin, and it was one of his favorite qualities in any human

"Everyone is interested in Lady Grace with good cause. She's the girl against whom all the other girls compare themselves. She's turned each of them into competitors, even the meek ones."

There was *always* a girl like that. Every season.

Violet shrugged. "If you like that sort of thing."

That sort of thing being blue eyes, golden hair, and a face like a cameo.

He shot her a dry look.

"Why are you so full of shouting and swearing today, by the way?"

He hesitated. "I may as well tell you. Father has denied me my allowance."

A silence.

"Oh, no." Violet was appropriately shocked.

"It gets worse. I'm to marry within six months—or at least become engaged—or he'll cut off all funds forever. Marry *appropriately*, mind you."

"Oh, *no.*" Now she was horrified.

He basked for a moment in Violet's very real sympathy. Though it probably contained a shred of glee, for she did love a controversy.

"What prompted this, Jonathan?"

He considered telling her about the Mercury Club, and about Klaus Liebman and the color printing press, and maybe even Tommy de Ballesteros, but he strongly suspected her eyes would glaze, at least over all but the last.

And the last, in particular, for some reason, he wanted to keep all to himself.

"I suspect he's trying to forestall any ideas I might have about . . . marrying for love." He gave a humorless laugh. "One dalliance with a widow—which, I might add, strikes me as my business only—and he thinks I'm on the road to perdition."

There had been other dalliances with other widows, but he wasn't about to tally them for Violet.

"You know, you'd think father would learn. He's always forbidding things or making rulings, and everyone ends up doing precisely the opposite of his wishes, or at least not acquiescing to them."

"A lifetime, Violet. Marriage is supposed to be for a lifetime. You may be happy now. Miles may be happy now. And I'm happy now. And I intend to live a good long while. I don't need a wife, let alone ten children. I honestly fail to see how it will contribute to my happiness."

"Children seldom happen all at once, unless you're a barn cat."

Jonathan snorted.

"And you do understand that you were once a child?"

"Yes, but I had the good sense to grow up into the magnificent specimen of manhood I am today."

She rolled her eyes. "And you do understand that I will be having a child."

"I will endeavor to tolerate it."

She smiled, knowing she could substitute the words "dote upon" for "tolerate," and it would be closer to the truth. "How do you *know* you're happy, Jonathan? Before I married, I wasn't happy, Jonathan. I didn't even know it. I could scarcely put a finger on why. It only felt like . . ."

She stopped.

"Go on."

"Like I would go mad from the constraints of being me. And of forever being watched. Sorry, that includes *you* watching me! Jonathan, you should know that I'm happy now and never knew this kind of happiness was even possible. And, granted, a portion of that happiness has to do with imagining the expression on Father's face when Asher asked permission to marry me. But I am. And I think I fell in love with him the moment I saw him."

"My guess is you would have *needed* to marry him whether or not he was right for you."

Her silence was truly of the aghast variety. Complete with a dropped jaw.

"You do get away with saying the most outrageous things! Perhaps mama *has* indulged you too much."

They both noticed she didn't deny it, however. And maybe it was the mauve crescents beneath her eyes, but he refrained from prying further about how she had come to know the earl, and whether she'd learned anything about Lyon being a pirate, of all things. Because being a pirate seemed the antithesis of everything Olivia Eversea, that embracer of causes, would want in a man, though of course that could be the reason. And besides, if Violet had learned anything about Lyon, Jonathan doubted she'd be able to keep quiet about it. The temptation to gloat about being right would have proved her undoing.

So he said nothing.

"All I'm saying, Jonathan, is . . . you'll know the difference when you truly care."

He was genuinely regretful. "Forgive me, Violet. That *was* a bit beyond the pale, even for me. Maybe Father is right. Maybe I do need reigning in. I'm glad you're happy. I suppose I could experience a coup de foudre within Father's time frame. Because destiny is always just that accommodating."

"No, Father's wrong," she said irritably. "I shouldn't like you to change. I don't like change any more than you do. I like you as you are. And I wish you could stay here in Pennyroyal Green longer. Will you?"

It was alarming, this sudden display of sentimentality and need in Violet. But then she had pregnancy as an excuse.

"Of course you like me. How could you not like me? I wish I could stay, but I have to go admit a failure to a Bavarian. I'll return as soon as I can."

He kissed her on the cheek and to her surprise, was just able to get his arms around her in a hug. And *he* didn't even have pregnancy to blame for that.

Chapter 5

TOMMY HAD FOUND HIM quickly: the duke of course stood near the racetrack rail, cushioned from the rest of the cheerfully boisterous crowd by a few Weston-clad acolytes, who intermittently nodded solemnly or threw back their heads and laughed, apparently depending upon what His Grace uttered.

How Tommy *yearned* to know what he uttered.

There was to be one race only, an entirely impromptu event organized primarily to persuade the Duke of Greyfolk of the wisdom of buying one of the horses. The track was short, straight, informal; and even though it wasn't officially racing season, word of a fresh diversion, not to mention the opportunity to place wagers, ensured word of the event traveled swiftly, and a delighted and socially diverse (riffraff and aristocrats were represented in equal proportion) crowd had amassed. A costermonger had even wheeled a cart of apples into their midst, and was doing a brisk business.

Tommy had long ago mastered the art of near invisibility. She was small and quick and could weave through a crowd as unobtrusively as a breeze or a shadow. She'd dressed for the occasion, too, in last season's funnel-shaped face-hiding straw bonnet, and a respectable and forgettable brown dress and cloak, and she was confident not a soul would look twice at her. She clutched the scrap of red ribbon and medal in her fist, and was just about to sidle closer to the duke when the only person who could drag her eyes away from him appeared.

She smiled slowly. There was a shivery pleasure in simply watching Jonathan Redmond move. His height, his bearing, the sleek fit of his clothing—it was a bit like happening upon a handsome wild animal in its habitat. And it was also amusing to watch him do precisely what she'd just done: take up a station at the racetrack rail not more than ten feet away from the duke.

She suspected he would artfully, strategically maneuver his position until he was within speaking range of the duke, who could not fail to acknowledge him.

And *that* was a conversation she wanted to hear.

She slipped back through the crowd, and circled around the costermonger's cart, when suddenly she heard an outraged roar.

The barrel-shaped costermonger had seized a scrawny boy by the forearm and hoisted him, shaking him until the apple he'd stolen dropped from his fist.

And then the bastard went *on* shaking him. As if he could shake every thieving impulse from his scrawny body.

Tommy lunged toward them. But she stopped abruptly.

For someone else had gotten there first.

"Why don't you unhand him now?"

Jonathan's tone was pleasant, almost gentle, very, very controlled. Something about it made the tiny hairs stand up on the back of her neck. She wondered if the costermonger recognized the grave threat in it.

"'e's a wee thief, 'e is!" The costermonger gave another shake. The child squeaked and his eyes rolled back in his head.

"Yes, but he's dropped the apple, so you may as well stop shaking him. Now." Suddenly Jonathan's voice was velvety and sinister.

The dangling boy made a hapless gulping noise.

The costermonger thrust out his lower lip mutinously. And gave one more shake.

Before anyone could gasp, Jonathan's arm shot out, seized the man's wrist, and twisted it hard.

The man squawked in shock and pain and dropped the boy, who scrambled off through the crowd like a little spider.

Whereupon the outraged costermonger whirled on Jonathan and took a swing.

Tommy gasped as Jonathan leaped back. Not quickly enough; his head whipped back a little with a glancing blow.

He recovered his balance easily. The two men stared at each other, chests heaving.

Then Jonathan bent to retrieve the apple, and handed it to the costermonger silently. Quite speakingly.

Tommy was riveted. Jonathan Redmond had just risked bodily harm to rescue a street rat.

Fascinating, that.

And potentially useful.

Finally, Jonathan turned to walk away.

And stopped short when he realized the horse race had already been run and the duke and his entourage had departed, oblivious of the little drama that had just ensued.

"Bloody. Hell," he said feelingly.

Tommy casually extended her handkerchief. "You seem to be bleeding a little." She pointed to the corner of her mouth.

He took the proffered handkerchief, seemingly unsurprised to see her. "*When* will I learn it doesn't pay to be a Samaritan?" And then he went still and studied Tommy.

And his face suffused with suppressed hilarity.

"Well, look at you, Miss de Ballesteros. In all that . . ." He studied the bonnet that nearly engulfed her face, and the voluminous brown shawl, his expression growing increasingly amused, and then he decided upon the word, ". . . *brown*, one would almost believe you didn't want to anyone you know to recognize you."

Very dryly said.

She merely pointed meaningfully and insistently at the corner of her own mouth. "Valiant of you to intervene. And you're still bleeding, by the way."

He shrugged. "Or foolish. Choose your adjective. That costermonger was triple the boy's size." He dabbed the handkerchief at his mouth corner, pulled it away to inspect it.

"Ah, very good. Only a drop or two of blood. Just a tiny cut on the inside of my lip, no doubt.. And thank you for the loan of this, by the way. My sister generally keeps me supplied with embroidered handkerchiefs, but I recently gave mine away."

She liked the wry way he said "my sister." Affectionate, proprietary, long suffering. "To someone who was bleeding?"

He gave a short laugh. Too late she realized he was running his thumb absently over the corner of her handkerchief, where initials should have, or would have, been embroidered.

He didn't precisely *freeze*. He was far too careful for that.

But he did go appreciably still.

Because instead of Tommy's initials, his thumb had encountered pinprick holes where someone *else's* initials had been picked out.

When he finally lifted his gaze to hers, his face was carefully expressionless. But there was something a bit too speculative dawning in his eyes.

Bloody Hell.

She'd bought the handkerchief from a certain Mrs. Bandycross in St. Giles, years ago, in different times. Mrs. Bandycross did a brisk trade in stolen linen. A penny per handkerchief. Pickpockets brought them in, and Mrs. Bandycross picked out the stitching and resold them.

She was certain Jonathan suspected. And it told him a little more about her financial circumstances than she preferred *anyone* to know.

"Did you wager anything on the race?" she asked smoothly, quickly. But her heartbeat had quickened. Damn the man for being so bloody *observant.*

"I wagered I would be able to speak to the duke. And lost." He sounded a bit abstracted. He was still watching her thoughtfully. "Why were *you* spying on him?"

"I wasn't." She said it reflexively, and too late realized she sounded like a child.

He sighed. "You were. I saw you staring at him rather avidly from beneath that unflattering bonnet. I could *feel* you staring at him."

"You *couldn't*—"

"Oh, for heaven's sake. Give *up*, Miss de Ballesteros." "At least you're not holding a weapon this time."

It was impossible not to smile at him. The *cheek* of the man."That could be because you didn't creep up behind me, this time."

"No, it was rather the other way around this time, wasn't it? I simply turned, and there you were behind me at the costermonger's cart. Almost as if you knew exactly where I was. Just as I suspect I saw you because I expected to see you."

An ambiguous, interesting, charged little silence followed. It thrummed with the tacit understanding that they had each perhaps made an actual *effort* to find each other in the crowd. Had in fact been *quite* aware of each other in the throng.

Wordlessly, they took each other's measure, two confident, beautiful people, neither of them giving anything of their thoughts away to the other.

He wasn't a blinker, Jonathan Redmond. More's the pity.

A woman strolled by, glanced at Jonathan, and then swiveled her head so violently to gawk that she stumbled over her feet and nearly fell.

Jonathan didn't appear to notice. It probably happened to him every day. It was probably so commonplace in his world he assumed it happened to everybody.

"He's wealthy, the duke," Jonathan said casually into the short ensuing silence, at last looking away from her toward the track. The crowd was rapidly dispersing, straggling past them. "One of the wealthiest men on this *continent*. I imagine a man like that can afford anything he wants. Spectacular things. Say, the finest box at the opera. The very best horses and carriages. The very best . . . mistresses. Things of that sort." He slid a sly sideways look at her.

She rolled her eyes at his attempt to fish for information, to his clear amusement. "What do *you* want the duke to invest in, Mr. Redmond?"

"A business venture." he said shortly. He turned back to her. "Why? Do you have a great superfluous pile of money you wish to invest, too, Miss de Ballesteros?"

That *was* pointed. Wicked, wicked man. He was far too astute for his—and her—own good. Her incriminating sorry little bloodied handkerchief remained bunched in his fist. Still, there wasn't a shred of accusation in what he said.

"I'm interested in the art of making money." This much *was* true.

"Isn't that a coincidence," he drawled. "Something else we have in common. That, and our hobby of stalking the Duke of Greyfolk."

She laughed.

His face lit then, as if her laughter was a prize he'd won. But she could feel a restlessness setting in; her native caution was reviving, coiling in her like a spring. She *really* ought to put a halt to this

conversation. It was far too honest and dangerously comfortable.

She tensed to move.

And yet she couldn't seem to do it while Jonathan's face was still faintly lit. He suddenly glanced
toward her feet. "You just dropped something.
Something red?"

Her medal!

She lunged to snatch it up just as he bent to retrieve it.

And now her heart was pounding.

He stared at her again, a faint frown between his
eyes.

"Ho! *Redmond!*" A cheerful masculine voice rose
out of the dwindling crowd.

Jonathan pivoted reflexively toward it.

And Tommy, who was astute at seizing the perfect opportunity to appear and disappear, slipped
away as swiftly as that street urchin had snatched
an apple.

Chapter 6

THE NEXT MORNING JONATHAN tossed a coin to decide whether to first go to Klaus, break the news about his failure to gain capital, watch his sunny hopeful face fall, and withstand a shower of emotional German, or whether he ought to spend the afternoon saving Argosy from himself.

He knew no particular joy when Argosy won the toss.

For Argosy dipped freely into the seemingly endless vats of his father's wealth and was allegedly given leave to marry whomever he pleased; he wished he'd gone straight to Klaus. Then again, he would likely find little comfort anywhere in London, given the sword of Damocles currently dangling over his head.

And yet when Jonathan and Argosy entered a room together, women tended to flock to the two of them like migrating geese. Argosy was fair, chiseled, handsome in a way that only generations of beautiful people mating with generations of other beautiful people could produce—and was heir to a viscount. He'd perfected the art of ennui, such that women yearned to be the one who finally made him come alive with passion, and would go to considerably risky erotic lengths to do so, which Argosy never discouraged. *Given the company you keep,* Tommy had said outside the Duke of Greyfolk's house, and doubtless Argosy was precisely whom she'd meant.

And Tommy was the object of Argosy's current inappropriate obsession.

A year ago the Countess of Mirabeau had decided she was lonely, and instead of calling upon people or holding dinner parties, which is what most sane aristocrats would have done, she'd begun inviting people who amused her to wait upon her—a poet she'd admired, or a painter who amused her, a renowned thinker or two (although the true thinkers soon tired of milling about in the salon talking to poets), the daughter of a renowned former courtesan (that would be Tommy), and soon enough her events became fashionable. Which meant all the youngbloods investigated.

And when they met Tommy, they returned again and again. And brought better liquor with them, since the countess had a grand title but a modest and dwindling fortune.

And thus was born the weekly salon.

That was the other reason Jonathan wasn't eager to attend the salon today; Tommy might be intriguing enough, but he knew her for what she was: trouble.

Baritone voices and soft feminine laughter mingled. A poet who aspired to Byronic fame stood in one corner, gesticulating wildly, while another man, a novelist of some sort whose hair was much too long, as if he was far too busy thinking deep thoughts to ever cut it, listened and bobbed his head in agreement. A painter named Wyndham, rumored to have painted a portrait of Tommy, but whom Jonathan knew primarily produced remarkably colorful and prurient works of art for a brothel called The Velvet Glove, stood near them not troubling to look anything other than bored and incredulous, which made Jonathan like him.

And then there was Lord Prescott, a viscount who was reportedly nearly thirty years old. Older than everyone present, too thin for his frame, he leaned against a wall, alone, and still, but for his eyes. His eyes tracked Tommy about the room.

And thus far he was the only person she seemed to be studiously ignoring.

Interesting, that.

Prescott was a viscount. Wealthy. Unmarried. "A rather dry chap," Argosy had once described him, upon meeting him once socially. An indictment, indeed.

The Countess of Mirabeau was enthroned in another corner near the large marble fireplace, which, to Jonathan, seemed unnecessarily cherubbedecked. Their fat little cheeks and buttocks bulged from the corners and crawled all the way up the wall, in a great debauched arc. Today the countess was dressed in a toga, a wreath ringing her head, sandals on her feet.

"Greek today, are we, my lady?" he'd asked her.

"Carpe diem, Mr. Redmond. Carpe diem."

"I shall endeavor to carpe, thank you. It's good to see you looking so well."

"Likewise, young man. But aren't you over-dressed? Wouldn't you be more comfortable in a toga?"

"No doubt," he agreed. "Perhaps next time."

He was contemplating migrating over to chat with the countess now, because her benign mad-ness suited his mood, when Argosy said, "Come to Tattersall's with me tomorrow, Redmond. I could use your advice about a new mare."

Argosy was trying to distract him from his brood, which he was just settling into nicely.

"I would, apart from the fact that Tattersall's is less a pleasure than a torment now that I haven't a damn sou."

"Which inconveniences me as much as it does you. Your decision has suddenly deprived me of my most tolerable friend."

Jonathan snorted. "Your pain is poignant, truly."

"Why *did* you sink *all* of your profits into another shipping venture, Redmond?"

"Because the time was right and I think it'll yield twice my investment, if not more, and very soon. The cargo of silks was magnificent. And be-cause I fully anticipated having my allowance to draw upon in the interim. It was a miscalculation I shall not make again."

Argosy frowned faintly through all of this. "Firstly, how on earth do you know this sort of thing? Wouldn't it be nearly as profitable or pre-dictable to sink your profits into the tables at a gaming hell? Secondly, I'm not certain a *man* should go about describing silks as magnificent. Thirdly, your father is rich. You don't need to know how to *do* anything in particular, apart from perhaps riding and shooting and dancing, all of which you already do uncommonly well."

"Firstly, I think nearly anything that will make a profit is magnificent. Silks are magnificent. Gaslight is magnificent. Cotton manufacturing is magnificent. The new color printing press I'd like to finance? *Magnificent.* Secondly, I suspect any sort of knack I may possess, such as it is, I inherited from my father, rot his soul. But I've a taste for it now, and I'm bloody good at it and I like it. Thirdly, I'm not sure a man should go about complimenting another man's dancing skills, but it's kind of you to notice."

Argosy grinned. "I'll tell you what's magnificent. Or rather, who." He gestured subtly with his very fine chin to Thomasina de Ballesteros, who stood angled away from them, busily captivating a guest.

Jonathan raised his voice a little. "Trouble de Ballesteros? That very ordinary ginger-haired female?"

She didn't stop talking. But her mouth quirked at the corner, and her shoulder turned every-so-slightly toward them, like a weathervane.

He'd *known* she was listening.

Argosy swiveled on him. "Are you *mad?*" he said on an indignant hush. "Just look at her skin. Like amber and cream! And her hair is . . . oh God, don't say another word she's coming she's coming over here she's coming she's coming . . ."

She had indeed graciously extricated herself from her conversation and was now gliding toward them.

They bowed to her, and she curtsied with the

grace of a silk handkerchief fluttering to the ground. She was in white muslin today, her hair dressed in the Grecian style, and her neckline, as usual, could only be described as adventurous, for which every man in the room was grateful.

A far, far cry from yesterday's big bonnet and homely shawl.

"Mr. Redmond. If you brood any more darkly I may need to eject you, lest you blot out all the light in the room like an eclipse and people begin speaking of omens. Although some women consider brooding picturesque, and perhaps that is why you do it? Something to do, perhaps, with the maintenance of your mystique? Or is it perhaps related to that little bruise you're sporting?"

Jonathan listened to this with a faint smile. He let a strategic little silence go by. "Have you seen any dukes lately, Miss de Ballesteros?"

She smiled tolerantly, as if he'd said something whimsical.

Her eyes, however, flashed a warning.

His smile broadened to indicate how very little he cared about her warnings.

"Perhaps it's just that you haven't had enough to drink, Mr. Redmond?" she suggested. "It's early, but champagne is a bit like drinking sunshine. It ought to do you and the rest of us who must look upon you good."

Argosy intervened. "You must forgive my friend, Miss de Ballesteros, but he's been deprived of his allowance, you see, which would darken the mood of any man. I'm certain a moment or two of basking in your charm will set him right. Your presence could make any man forget his troubles."

Tommy wordlessly watched Argosy's mouth move.

When he was done, she said, "Oh . . . *you*," she finally said, and gifted him with a tap from her fan.

Jonathan stifled a laugh.

She made a three-quarter turn and pointed herself at him. "I thought I heard the word 'silks.'"

She sounded shockingly businesslike.

"Do you like silks? I'll buy a shipload of them for you," Argosy volunteered casually.

"Be a pet and do that," she encouraged him just as casually over her shoulder.

Jonathan coughed a laugh into his fist. "You heard 'silks,' Miss de Ballesteros, because I invested in a cargo of them."

"And . . . ? Surely that isn't how the story ends. Entertain me, Mr. Redmond. Make me laugh or weep."

"*And* I doubled my profits."

She sighed. "I do love a happy ending."

"I suspect it's just the middle of the story. I invested those profits in another cargo of silks."

"And now . . . ?" Tommy prompted, starry-eyed, like a child being told a favorite bedtime story.

"And now we wait."

"In other words, it could very well become a never-ending story. Like *Scheherazade* and *The Arabian Nights*."

"You catch on quickly. Investment is *just* that enchanting. A fairy tale come to life."

She laughed. And now the rest of the room shifted restlessly because her laugh was husky and genuine, and called to mind bells and Spring and mating and all sorts of things that stirred a man, and they all wanted to be the one to make her do it.

"The last time you were here, Mr. Redmond, I believe you mentioned something about a color printing press."

She had a fixed gaze, he noted. Quite a green one, when observed in close proximity, the iris traced in a circle of silver. Almond-shaped eyes, like a Gypsy or a Persian, beneath slanting little dark brows. A pixie or a sorceress's face, Argosy would have called it, but then, he would. Jonathan preferred his women blond and cool. "Unusual" invariably equated with "complicated," in his experience, and "complicated" was synonymous with "anathema."

Argosy would have *completely* missed the pragmatism and intelligence that shone in them.

The thing was, he hadn't mentioned the printing press to *her,* and this was fascinating. Apparently not only did she lurk outside the homes of powerful dukes, she selectively overheard bits of conversation, and not the sort he might have anticipated. For all he knew the sole purpose of these salons was for her to gather intelligence.

And yesterday she *had* asked why he needed the duke's money.

"A friend of mine, a German gentleman currently living in London, has developed the capability to print mass quantities in color—chromolithography, it's called. I believe its possibilities are legion. He's not the only lithographer hoping to print in color, but he's the only one I know of in London."

Argosy's head dropped back in a pantomimed snore. "And Redmond would invest in *that,* too, but I may have mentioned he hasn't any blunt to speak of at the moment." He'd momentarily forgotten to be languid in a surge of desperate and unworthy-of-him competition. "He invested it all in the silks. He has. No. Money. At all."

Jonathan turned his head slowly toward Argosy and pinned him with an incredulous black look.

Argosy looked back at him almost helplessly, an apology in his eyes, as if he couldn't help himself. She *was* that sort of woman. She didn't particularly try to do it, but Jonathan suspected it was really only a matter of time before men came to blows—or pistols—over her.

He, of course, wasn't going to be one of them, but he didn't particularly want Argosy to be one of them, either.

Tommy seemed to be all but deaf to Argosy. "Mr. Redmond, has your friend considered that he could likely make a fortune printing . . . shall we say . . . colorful playing cards featuring . . . explicit images?"

Jonathan went still.

He briefly closed his eyes as the suggestion spiraled into the depths of his mind like a guinea tossed into a wishing well.

It was *brilliant*.

Illegal. But brilliant.

"Or perhaps . . . depicting members of the current court? Or members of high society?" he mulled, half to himself. Ideas rippled out from ideas rippled out from ideas.

"Do you speak euphemistically when you say 'members,' or . . . ? Because either, I'm sure, would be popular."

It was an excellent double entendre and he rewarded it with the wicked grin it deserved, and she grinned back at him, and the air surrounding them was dangerously effervescent for a moment, until he remembered he had no money and he was supposed to be married by the end of the year.

"Tell me, Mr. Redmond." And here her fan drooped forward to touch his chest, in something perilously close to a caress. "Are you good at this sort of thing? Investing?"

"Yes," he said shortly.

He'd just noticed that Argosy's eyes were fixed on where her fan met his chest, and he was reddening in a way that boded no good.

"*I* like investing in ruby necklaces that match the flames in a certain temptress's hair," Argosy volunteered curtly. Forgetting to be languid, but not to be hyperbolic.

Tommy swiveled to Argosy again. "Do you? I think Rundell and Bridge may still be open for business at this time of the day, but you may need to hurry," she said briskly.

Jonathan couldn't help it. He laughed. It was only what Argosy deserved, given the allowance announcement. But then he took pity on him. It wasn't as though he particularly wanted Miss de Ballesteros's attention.

"Why don't you tell our hostess what *your* particular talents are, Argosy, before she becomes bored of us and drifts away to pollinate another conversation."

Tommy sent Jonathan a sharp, unreadable, narrow-eyed glance.

Then turned a brightly expectant gaze on Argosy.

"Of the ones I may *properly* discuss in a public

gathering," he began, and she nodded, acknowledging the hint of suggestiveness, like a school-
teacher with a clever pupil—"I'm a *very* fine dancer.
I handle the ribbons of my high flyer as if I were
Apollo bringing the sunrise to the world. I excel at
anticipating a woman's needs. I can carry on a conversation about *many* topics, if not investing, when
I'm not competing for your attention with a dozen
other men. When I compete, I fear I tend to speak
in hyperbole."

Argosy looked mollified when Tommy laughed.
She gestured with the empty champagne flute she
was holding. "Can you anticipate the need I have
now, Lord Argosy?"

"Your wish is my command." Argosy bowed
low and whimsically and immediately went in
search of champagne for her.

Not, however, without trailing a suspicious
warning look back at Jonathan.

"Meet me at midnight tonight in Covent Garden
outside the Half Moon Theater," she said immediately to Jonathan, on a hush.

"*What?* No."

"It's not what you think, Mr. Redmond."

He aimed a look skyward. "Dear God, tell me
you didn't just say that again. No. I've no interest
in the affairs of complicated, circumspect, ginger-
haired women. No."

"And you know very well I've no interest in the
affairs of currently penniless rakes."

Well.

"I ought to say 'ouch,'" he said gingerly.

"You would, but you don't care what I think any
more than I care what you think. Since we share

a particular interest, I do however think you'll be interested in a business proposition I'd like to share with you."

"And every grain of sense I possess tells me I'd be wise to pretend I never heard you say that."

"How many grains of sense *do* you possess?"

"Let me see . . . three grains, at last count. I used to have four, but I forfeited one when I agreed to accompany Argosy to this salon. Again."

"That's such a shame! Three grains is one fewer than you need to prevent you from a trip to the Half Moon Theater at midnight."

Jonathan laughed. He couldn't help it.

If the two of them laughed again the whole of the place would likely call him out, such was the delicate tension she'd built with her strategically allotted attention and strategically low-cut bodice. And here she was, of course, talking to the one person who genuinely didn't care whether she talked to him or not, much the way a cat could pick out the one person in a room who loathed cats.

"Come now, Mr. Redmond," she urged, her voice lowered. "What else are you going to do with your time? It's not like you'll head to the gaming tables, not if you've sense, and from what I understand you have three entire grains of the stuff. You've been deprived of your allowance, and correct me if I have it wrong, but your father isn't the sort to cheerfully pay your vowels should you play without funds. So meet me at midnight outside the Half Moon Theater. You'll hear something of interest. Oh—and bring your pistol."

And with that she pivoted and aimed the full radiant beam of her attention at Argosy, who'd returned, champagne in hand, with the air of a warrior bearing the head of his queen's enemy.

"Lord Argosy," she greeted him delightedly. "How impossible it is to resist a man who sees to my needs."

Just like that, she threw what amounted to a net woven of sunshine and jewels over Argosy. He basked, captivated, his envy of Jonathan forgotten, and in a few short minutes he was convinced he was her favorite, simply by the quality of her attention. She *was* charming, Jonathan observed. Effortlessly charming, it seemed. She *enjoyed* charming. That much was clear.

It was also all a show, that much was *also* clear—to Jonathan, at least. But it was a show he appreciated, as long as he could remain safely in the audience. He observed, amused and somewhat relieved to be completely ignored, while she allotted Argosy a few more champagne sips worth of flattery and warmth before drifting off to enchant another guest.

He wasn't about to meet that woman *anywhere* at midnight.

But he did like the way she moved, Jonathan thought absently, watching her walk away. It was the way champagne would move if it was a woman, all light and fluid elegance.

Chapter 7

H<small>E LEFT A HOPEFUL</small> Argosy behind at her salon before the sun dipped too low in the sky, with a vague promise to see him at White's this evening, but only if Argosy was buying. He walked as far as Bond Street, taking great punishing, cleansing draughts of clear cold air, where he paused.

He was held captive in front of a shop featuring Italian confections.

For there, right in the window, nestled in among a number of different pastries, was a pile of fruit molded from marzipan.

And lo and behold, among them was what appeared to be a cluster of raspberries.

He smiled. It was an omen, he was sure of it. Surely things would go his way, despite his father's threats.

He fished through his pockets, decided he'd sacrifice a few pence for the sake of his sister. Violet would laugh when she saw them. He chose several, and the shopkeeper wrapped them as tenderly as eggs. Jonathan tucked the little bundle into the inside pocket of his greatcoat, and turned to leave, a smile on his face.

And the smile froze, for there, with her hand on the door of the shop, dressed in sleek scarlet wool, stood the beautiful Lady Philippa Winslow.

Except at the moment her eyes and mouth were narrow slits. Which was unusual, since both were generally large and generous and . . . open.

Right now her mouth seemed to be trembling with the effort of holding back some sort of verbal earthquake.

"Philippa!" His voice thrummed with memories and enthusiasm. "What a pleasure it is to see—"

"You might have *told* me," she hissed. And before he could blink or duck—*SMACK!*—up flew her hand and cracked him on the cheek.

It sent him staggering a step backward.

"The bloody *hell* . . . ?"

But she'd whipped around and was already gone, boarding her carriage again, trailing a look of melodramatic heartbreak over her shoulder.

The shopkeeper, witnessing the entire thing, was shaking his head to and fro, and tsking.

"The women, they are lunatics, si?"

"Si," Jonathan agreed fervently. Hand against his cheek. Staring, narrow-eyed, after the rapidly disappearing carriage. An awful suspicion uncoiling in his mind.

"The amore, it is worth it, si?"

"This is where, kind sir, I fear our opinions diverge," he said darkly.

Baffled and furious, he walked the rest of the way home, allowing the air to cool his face while he rifled through his memories, his assignations, his every move since he'd last seen her two weeks ago, to ascertain what he might have done to deserve assault.

Women were mad capricious creatures; this was the only explanation he could arrive at.

So much for omens. He would tell Violet about it, and then tell her it was all her fault.

THE THEME OF the day appeared to be rude surprises; he arrived home to find his parents unexpectedly in residence at their London town house.

"Mother. Father. What a pleasure." He tried and failed to inflect that sentence. "I thought you intended to stay in Pennyroyal Green for a time."

He stood still for a cheek kiss from his mother; his father lowered a newspaper, nodded to him, and raised it up again.

"Violet insisted I would enjoy a bit of shopping in town and said she would be just fine for a day or so without me, so I decided to accompany him. Just for a day or so."

I'll *bet* she insisted, Jonathan thought, bleakly amused.

"And your father has a meeting with the Duke of Greyfolk."

Ah. The Duke of Greyfolk. Jonathan suppressed a dry smile. So his father *had* been listening to him.

He tried to peer through his father's newspaper to read his devious mind, but his father didn't so much as twitch.

How unsurprised Jonathan would be if the Duke of Greyfolk was suddenly invited to join the Mercury Club. For men like his father and the duke tended to get what they wanted in any way they

possibly could, and they both wanted that Lancaster Mill.

And so at eight o'clock he sat down with his parents to a full dinner of lamb chops and peas. He
listened to his mother tell his father about a relative
who suffered from a liver complaint. His father actually appeared to be interested. Then again, he'd
had years to perfect feigning interest in all manner
of things in order to get what he wanted.

The conversation was giving *Jonathan* a liver
complaint. He absently thought it would be an
excellent idea to marry, if only in order to bear
progeny and then torture them with conversations
about liver complaints.

He'd learned over the years that a little wine was
often the answer to life's general other complaints,
so he took a hearty gulp.

"Your father tells me you intend to wed before
the year is out, Jonathan."

Jonathan choked.

"Smaller sips, dear," his mother said, as if he was
nine years old.

He recovered with some aplomb and gently
set down his glass. "I didn't precisely say that,
Mother," he began carefully.

"Your father isn't in the habit of mishearing
things, Jonathan. I think it's a wonderfully mature
decision and I must say I approve." She smiled lov-
ingly at him, damn it all. She was so *happy*, and this
was so rare. "We'll fill a nursery with your babies
in no time. Surely you noticed the heaps of invitations awaiting in the entry. I put the word about the
moment we got in. How fortunate you are that so
many beautiful girls have come of age this season."

And this "putting it about," as his mother put it, very likely explained Philippa and the insult to his cheek. News of that sort would spread like cholera in London.

Jonathan took this in, nodding, and eyed his fork speculatively. He had two options, as he saw it: He could drive it into his own heart. Or he could hurl it straight into the tiny black heart of his father. Perhaps his aptitude for darts was all in preparation for this moment.

He met Isaiah's eyes. His father was smiling blandly and indulgently.

No, his heart is too small and shriveled of a target, even for a marksman like me, Jonathan decided blackly.

It *was* true, however, that beautiful girls did abound this season. But beautiful girls were like flowers; he was quite certain he enjoyed them so thoroughly because he wasn't the one responsible for watering and tending and keeping them alive and happy, and listening to them discuss liver complaints.

There were also going to be a few *other* beautiful girls, some of them the sort who would never be invited to the balls he attended, who could potentially hurl things at him, sob, or orate about how he had allegedly wronged them. He hadn't a permanent mistress. But a few had . . . auditioned . . . for the role, so to speak. Including Philippa.

God. London, his favorite place, was going to be a veritable gauntlet for the next several weeks.

The walls of the dining room suddenly seemed to be closing in on him.

He *wasn't* a heartbreaker. Or rather, he never

set *out* to do it. He could never understand how women did it so freely, offered hearts without telling a man they were doing it, and then accused a man of stomping on a gift he hadn't known he'd possessed. Didn't they know what a *dangerous* business love was? How reckless it was to fall in? Falling in love *alone* was proof of insanity.

His last few bites of lamb chop tasted of sawdust. He swallowed them, finished his wine, and pushed himself away from the table.

"Well, I'm off to fashion a noose," he said grimly, by way of excusing himself.

"Ha ha!" His mother laughed indulgently.

His father simply smiled generally. Very likely wasn't listening at all.

Three hours later Jonathan, instead of meeting Argosy at White's, found himself in front of the Half Moon Theater in Covent Garden.

For if he was a condemned man, quite truthfully, what had he to lose?

Chapter 8

Aɴᴅ ʏᴇᴛ ʜᴇ sᴛᴏᴏᴅ alone on the street except for a few surly drunks and the occasional rat strolling purposefully by, as if they were laborers off to work. The Half Moon Theater was dark; it had been boarded and shuttered, it appeared, some time ago. Across from him, a noisy pub disgorged and admitted staggering revelers at regular intervals; a listless prostitute asked him if he wanted a go at her. He politely declined.

The moon grew brighter, the night watch called out "Midnight," and still there was no sign of Thomasina de Ballesteros.

"This way."

Christ!

One moment she *wasn't* there, the next she was.

And she'd seen him flinch, because now she was laughing quietly at him.

"Count yourself fortunate I didn't shoot you."

"You'll need to be more alert, Mr. Redmond, if you're to be of use to me."

She was draped all over in a dark cloak again, but the husk of her voice was unmistakable. She seemed to have eyes like a cat, too, for Tommy immediately proceeded to swiftly lead him on a mazelike journey through alleys, narrow lanes, once through a park, up a staircase, across the top of one building to another, down a staircase, and he could have sworn they doubled back once to do it all again.

"Is this an elaborate ruse to disorient me in order to divest me of my purse? Because Argosy wasn't jesting when he said I'd been deprived of my allowance. And, really, is two pounds worth killing over? Because that's all I have on my person."

"I wouldn't dream of it. You'd just shoot me with your pistol."

"Oh, yes. That."

She turned left down a narrow street.

"You're awfully small to be traipsing about London by yourself at this time of night, Miss de Ballesteros."

"Are you about to get protective?"

"No."

"Possessive?" A warning edge in her voice.

"God, no. Merely making an observation."

"I have friends all over London who emerge to do business at . . . varying times of day. They'll recognize my screams and come to my rescue should I require it."

They trod along in silence for a few paces.

"You're trying to decide whether I'm jesting, aren't you, Mr. Redmond?"

"I unfortunately am quite certain that at least part of your statement was true."

"Clever as well as pretty!" she said dryly. "This way!"

She made a sharp right turn and then an almost immediate left. Who knew the great arterial streets of London were fed by so very many squalid little tributary alleys and side streets? She did, apparently, because on one street a drunk leaning against the wall called out, "Greetings, Tommy."

"Greetings, Jasper!"

This exchange was hardly reassuring.

"Is this really necessary?" he groused. "This circuitous route to your lair?"

"Patience. My mystique is everything, Mr. Redmond. And what makes you think it's circuitous? It may very well simply be the shortest route to my . . . lair." She liked the word, he could tell.

And she brought them to a stop in front of an unexceptional door in the side of a tall, narrow nondescript building, though most buildings could be described as nondescript in the dark. He suspected a shop occupied the bottom of it, but the windows were shuttered for the night. God only knew where they were, though he was fairly certain she'd strategically led him on an elaborate figure eight of sorts around Covent Garden for the last ten minutes, and they were likely probably only a few feet from where they began.

He listened hard; a drunken chorus swelled up and was abruptly cut off, as if a door had thrown wide on a pub and swung shut again. The song sounded like "The Ballad of Colin Eversea."

She produced a key, the door creaked open, she beckoned him through, and it slammed what sounded irrevocably shut behind them.

"Is this where I need my pistol?"

"Don't be silly," she said absently. A lit lamp was

hung on a hook immediately inside the door, obviously awaiting their arrival. She seized the lamp and scampered down a flight of narrow wooden stairs like a squirrel, and he followed, his hands on the walls for balance. Through a short, dark, narrow corridor.

Into a very small, beautifully appointed room, lit by a crackling fire.

He hovered in the doorway, amazed.

The room had glow and warmth, and contained the elegance of a snifter of cognac. A coral velvet tufted settee arched like a stroked cat against one wall; the rug was cream and brown and apricot and floral; the curtains, great heavy columns of coral velvet, were drawn shut. Furniture had obviously been selected with care—he recognized Chippendale and a French screen—and was tastefully and strategically gilded here and polished there. The fire set everything aglow. The back wall, somewhat unusually, was papered in black and white.

Jonathan's heart gave a lurch. The bloody wall had just . . . *moved*.

He'd begun to entertain the possibility that Philippa had truly done some damage to his brain with her blow when, to his relief and subsequent alarm, he realized it wasn't a wall.

It was a man. The sort of man one might easily mistake for a wall.

His head, which was just shy of the ceiling, was bald and glossy as porcelain, and embedded with four lines across the forehead, like a musical staff. His shoulders were nearly as broad as the settee, his girth suggested he might have *eaten* a settee, and he sported a shining gold piratical hoop in one ear.

He was dressed spotlessly in black and white, the uniform of a butler.

"Good evening, Rutherford."

"May I help you with your cloak, Miss Tommy? And your coat, sir?"

He bowed deeply to Jonathan. His voice must be what Poseidon's voice sounds like, Jonathan thought. It was fathoms deep, as if it had needed to travel miles through him in order to reach the surface. He was lost in admiration at what a *creature* this man was. He slowly turned around to allow Rutherford to delicately help him from his coat. And continued to peer over his shoulder at him.

Rutherford neatly laid both the cloak and the wrap over the back of the settee.

"Rutherford, if you would bring our guest . . ." She turned to Jonathan.

"Ale, if you have it."

"Two ales, please."

"Is Rutherford his real name?" Jonathan whispered when he'd departed for the next room. Jonathan was positively alive with curiosity over what might be in that room.

"No, but it amuses us to call him that. It was either that or Necksnapper, after what he allegedly does best. Though I confess I've never actually seen him do it."

Charming. "Why, because you covered your eyes when he did?"

"I'm sure it's just a myth," she soothed. "He's as mild as a blancmange."

"Yes. I'm certain his real name is Perceval."

She laughed.

"Is he in your employ?"

"No. He's a friend who lives . . . nearby . . . who doesn't mind helping me on occasion. He was a special friend of my mother."

"Your mother, the exiled Spanish princess."

The Spanish *would* explain her coloring, however.

"Yes," she said without a trace of irony. "Why don't you have a seat here?" She gestured at a plush damask chair pushed up against a tasteful, gleaming little card table.

"Is this where you live?" He craned his head, attempting to get a look down the hallway where Rutherford had disappeared. Did she bring men here often?

Did she take lovers? No one seemed to know for certain. That much had been true.

"Why don't you have a seat here?" she repeated pointedly, gesturing to the chair, enunciating each word very clearly.

"Perhaps I'll have a seat here," he suggested, which made her smile.

But first he pulled out her chair and motioned her into it. She slid into it as gracefully as a rose sliding into a bud vase.

Rutherford returned with two pints of ale on a tray and served them with alacrity.

"I'll just be in the next room, Miss Tommy," he said meaningfully as he bowed his way out.

"Cheers," Jonathan said, and hoisted his glass to her.

She did likewise to him.

They sipped.

And there was a moment of silence when they looked across at each other. It occurred to him that she was the jewel and the room was her setting, and that she had likely planned it that way. Her dress was a pale champagne color trimmed in satin, the sleeves long and fitted, and her smooth, pale gold shoulders and throat rose up out of it, giving the ever-so-slightest impression of nudity, and the effect was most definitely not without impact. Her stays pushed a pair of lovely small breasts up to the very border of her deep neckline, creating a tempting little crevasse a man could slip a digit into. She was dressed to persuade.

"Hold out your hand, Mr. Redmond." She said it with a little smile.

And so he did.

She produced a little velvet bag and tipped it over his palm.

Out poured an extraordinary rope of pearls.

A mile of them, it seemed; they went on and on, and ended by pooling, gleaming in his palm.

He stared at them, bemused.

He looked back up at her.

She was clearly awaiting *his* response.

"They're unarguably spectacular," he began, "but I prefer to be wooed more subtly. Perhaps we should begin with a ride in The Row?"

She gave a crooked smile.

He *knew*, however, why she'd poured them into his hand. They had that lovely near-fleshlike warmth of real pearls; they nestled in. Once you held them you were reluctant to relinquish them. They were . . .

Well, they were magnificent.

"These have . . . recently come into my possession," she began.

"They're real." He knew his jewels, thanks to his sister and one discriminating almost-mistress.

"Hence the flourish with which I presented them to you."

"Were they a gift?"

"Yes. 'Jewel thief' is not among my skills."

"Yet," they both added simultaneously, to their mutual amusement.

She paused.

He gestured with his handful of pearls. ". . . and?" he said, mimicking her conversation at the salon earlier in the day.

"And I should like to sell them. I need rather a lot of money quickly. But if I can double the proceeds from the money I earn from the pearls, or even triple it . . ."

Ah. He began to understand.

Jonathan slowly, slowly levered himself backward in his chair, a deceptively casual posture, and drummed his fingers deliberately on the table, measured as a death march, and perused her unblinkingly for a long silent moment. He didn't know it, but he had his father's stare when he was having a good hard think; there was a squirm-inducing, almost accusatory quality to it that would have innocent people confessing to crimes they hadn't committed, just to get a little relief from its intensity. Jonathan normally aimed it at the dartboard in the Pig & Thistle in Pennyroyal Green, which was why no one in Pennyroyal Green had yet bested him.

Tommy was clearly made of stern stuff.

Still, her bum eventually shifted in the chair beneath his gaze.

"Why do you need a lot of money right away? Are you trying to finance a revolution? Do you need to bribe an official? Do you need to ransom a lover? Are you in gambling debt up to your eyeballs, which admittedly are not very high up, given that you are small?"

"I appreciate the rich variety of your guesses, but 'no' to all of them. And I don't need it for illegal purposes."

He waited.

"Well, my purposes are not *strictly* illegal," she allowed somewhat weakly.

He sighed dolefully. As if this was only precisely what he'd expected.

"And these pearls . . . what did you do to earn them?"

Every man he knew wanted to be the chosen lover of Thomasina de Ballesteros. It was sport, it was de rigueur among the bloods of the ton, who were always looking for something novel to do, and were all too willing to behave like sheep to jockey for the position at those salons. And naturally White's Betting Books reflected all of this. It was just that no one seemed to know whether she already had a lover, or indeed, had *ever* had one. Speculation swirled, of course, and hopeful exaggeration about her skills abounded.

Jonathan would wager all of his future earnings that she wasn't an innocent. No woman could be this preternaturally confident if she was. And there was something in her eyes—a depth, a detachment, a *knowing*—that only came with experience.

What kind of lover was she? His thoughts floated in that direction briefly. Would she be submissive for the right price? Was she fiery, like her hair? Cool and arrogant, requiring a very specific kind of seduction? Was she the sort to throw things? Did she have rules?

She wasn't the sort he wanted, if this much guessing was required.

"I fail to see how that matters," she said finally. Diplomatically enough.

"Very well. If I were to attempt to sell them at Rundell and Bridge, for instance, would the proprietor immediately recognize them and know the original buyer?"

"Don't try to sell them at Rundell and Bridge," she said hurriedly.

In other words, the answer was "yes."

"Would there be consequences for you?"

"The consequences would be my affair, would they not? And I assure you, I can handle *any* consequence." She said this coolly.

He didn't doubt it. He fell silent, mulling.

"Answer one question for me, Mr. Redmond," she said hurriedly. "Regardless of the circumstances involved here, no matter what they may be . . . do you really believe you can double my money for me?"

He hesitated for only a heartbeat.

"I can triple your money," he said quietly. A trifle arrogantly, but then he was a Redmond, and arrogance was fuel for determination, which was fuel for accomplishment. "Legally. And quickly. Within a matter of weeks."

She gave a short nod. "Enough to buy the pearls again, should I wish it?"

"Yes."

"Very good. I should like in particular to invest in your friend's printing press."

Before he could bask in her approval, she added, "However, I have a provision before we enter into business together."

"As do I."

"In exchange for my investment, I may require your assistance with . . . a matter related to why I need the money. I shall need it tonight. And perhaps on other occasions."

Of course. Here it was. Trouble. He could hear it coming, like a herd of stampeding horses far, far off.

Chapter 9

"WHAT WOULD THIS ASSISTANCE entail?" he said, very, very dryly.

She pondered this. "Excellent reflexes. The ability to see in the dark. A pistol."

Tension gathered in his jaw. He powerfully disliked games.

"Don't overestimate my patience, Miss de Ballesteros."

"I'm not being evasive for the sheer pleasure of it," she protested. "It's best that you know as little as possible, for your own sake, Mr. Redmond. I know from experience that you see well in the dark. And possess a very fine pistol. And you are less conspicuous than Rutherford, and you also possess certain other qualities that he does not, which will likely prove very useful. In truth, what I need to do tonight shouldn't take very long or be very difficult at all," she concluded brightly.

He supposed she meant that to be encouraging.

He waited.

"Unlike last time,' she said, a little less confidently.

He waited some more.

"I might have been a bit . . . injured last time," she concurred weakly.

"Are you appealing to my sense of *chivalry* now? You must be desperate."

"I'm small. So very small and delicate. The world is a dangerous place for the likes of me."

He rolled his eyes. The eye roll took his gaze down to his palm again. The pearls lay draped there like a sated lover. Gleaming and warm and pulsating with . . . potential profit. He didn't know another soul who would be willing to hand over this kind of money to him so easily right now. It was *everything* he needed, precisely when he needed it.

"Before we discuss this any further, Tommy, allow me to tell you *my* provision. It's this: I shall require a broker's fee for the investment of your money."

She slowly straightened her spine. She was suddenly all haughty incredulity. "I'm *giving* you these very fine pearls to invest."

"I'm a businessman. Not a bloody clergyman. Or a sap. And I see what you're trying here now, *now* that you've made your eyes so very wide and limpid and *imploring*, but it won't work, so stop it before you sprain one. You would have brought these pearls, or the profits from their sale, to a professional broker if you didn't have a certain investment, shall we say, in keeping this transaction entirely sub rosa, away from anyone who might question your objectives or your income."

Her brows met in a perfect V of indignation at the bridge of her nose. And for a time she glared icily at him.

Jonathan drummed his fingers. Then he studied his fingernails. He made a show of looking at the clock (ormolu, French). He yawned.

Until suddenly the tension eased from her posture as surely as if she was melting, and her stare evolved into something cool and speculative.

And then at last a smile spread from one corner of her mouth to the other, slowly, a wholly pleased-with-him smile. She sat back much like he did.

"Very well, Mr. Redmond. A small percentage."

"Why do you trust me?" he said instantly.

She immediately began counting on her fingers as though she'd given this some meticulous thought. "Because you're not a fool, you've a bristly sort of energy that makes me think you have something to prove, you've a look about you that implies a sort of worldly detachment, and you need money, too. You don't care what I think of you, I don't care what you think of me, which means there is absolutely no excuse to be anything other than honest with each other. We are free to be friends."

There was a little silence. An impressed one on Jonathan's part, though he wasn't going to let on.

"Oh, and I've a hunch about you. My intuition is generally excellent."

No one had ever called him "bristly." Everyone thought he was the cheerful Redmond. He wasn't sure whether he liked it, the bristly bit. He wanted to think about whether it might be true. And what might have changed in his life to make this true, if so. And worldly detachment? When and how had that happened?

It's valuable, he thought, to occasionally see one's self through the eyes of new people. Not the ones who see you nearly every day, and therefore never *really* see you.

"Friends, are we?" he asked.

She shrugged with one shoulder. "Certainly. Why not?"

"Why not, indeed."

A little silence passed.

"I'm not precisely a rake, you know."

"Oh, do forgive me. What *precisely* does one call a man who enjoys an allegedly unbroken string of conquests?"

"The word 'conquest' implies a great degree of effort. Can I help it if they just . . . fall at my feet?" He tried and failed to suppress a smile that was, admittedly, rakish. "It wasn't always that way. And only a fool would refrain from the occasional partaking of such . . . serendipitous bounty."

"They fall at your feet? The way birds plummet from the sky in a proverbial biblical plague?"

He whistled, impressed. "Not even my sister has yet thought to call me a biblical plague."

"Except instead of birds, it's blond women."

He thought he might have detected the slightest, slightest whiff of judgment around the word "blond."

"Yes. I prefer blond women the way I prefer spring days to winter ones, and I prefer simple women to the complicated ones, and I prefer an untroubled life to a troubled one. And while these may not be virtues, they are most certainly not vices. Surely you have preferences when it comes to men?"

"Wealthy and titled." Very briskly said.

Well.

Oddly, it did sting just a bit.

He recovered. "You see? In a way, we are both creatures of simple tastes. I don't set out to break hearts. Some are handed to me before I'm aware of it, and I am on occasion perhaps less graceful or perceptive about that than I prefer to be. I haven't the dexterity of some, who can skillfully juggle a dozen or so hearts at once without ever dropping or committing to just one."

She went still, suddenly alertly suspicious.

"Oh, yes," he continued, "I imagine *quite* a mess would ensue if said juggler ever slipped up, or put a foot wrong, or added one too many hearts to the armload she was juggling. Or perhaps added the *wrong* heart. It could even get dangerous."

She narrowed her eyes at that.

The clock swung off a few seconds.

"And you call *me* a rake," he said softly.

The mutual stare continued another few seconds.

And finally she inhaled a length, then softly blew out a breath.

"Sometimes . . ." she began cautiously, "sometimes jugglers are conscripted into the . . . shall we say, circus . . . before they really know what it entails. And then it's too late, and they're too good at it, and they know full well they can never drop a heart, or, as you say, chaos could ensue."

They locked eyes.

He suspected this was more than any other man knew about Thomasina de Ballesteros at the moment. Oblique as it was.

He felt the temptation: *ask*. Ask more. It was

like peering down an intriguing corridor, all full of closed doors. What lay behind them? Delightful surprises? Or things of the sort you wished you hadn't seen, as when he'd opened a door at the Redmond house and surprised a footman pleasuring himself over what appeared to be a lady's fashion plate? But he wasn't going to ask any more questions, because he knew one question would simply lead to another and another and another, until the bloody woman had him enmeshed.

"You see? It's not your fault any more than it's mine."

They sat in a moment of righteous complicity. They shared the curse of the profoundly charming.

"Tell, me Tommy—may I call you Tommy? There are far too many syllables in the I'm sure not-at-all-fictional name of de Ballesteros. And Thomasina is also quite a mouthful."

He watched amusement and irritation flicker over her features. "I was named for my father. My surname is quite real. And you may call me Tommy if I may call you whatever I wish to call you."

"Done. Tell me—what do you plan to do with all of those hearts you're juggling, Tommy?"

"I'll marry one of them, Johnny."

"Not Johnny. Or even John. You'll just choose one, then, as if they're truffles in a box? Yet again, I suppose every rake must retire one day."

She remained silent.

"I hear *your* retirement is imminent," she said finally, with a sly little smile.

Oh, God. The whole of London knew.

"We shall see," he said inscrutably.

She smiled at that.

Jonathan let the silence stretch. The warmth of the room was lulling and quiet.

Quiet, that was, apart from what sounded like feet pattering about overhead. Little ones.

He cast his gaze upward. "Mice?" he wondered aloud. "Obese ones?"

"Mmm," she replied noncommittally, without looking up.

The overhead pattering headed in the opposite direction, followed by a thump.

She sipped nonchalantly at her ale.

"My hair isn't ginger, by the way," she said suddenly.

"Oh, I know. It's more of an oxblood."

"*Oxblood!*"

He laughed silently. "Very well. Oh, let's say, mahogany then. I called it ginger in order to irritate Argosy, who can only discuss you using rhapsodic metaphor, an affliction that comes over him when he wishes to impress a woman. He really is a good sort, and I hope you will be kind to him. And I said it to amuse you. It worked on both counts. You called me pretty."

He'd slid the last sentence into the conversation so swiftly and surreptitiously, she almost didn't notice.

And then she stiffened, as though she'd been caught in the act of stealing a sweet.

"And pretty men are legion in London, Mr. Redmond," she said loftily. "Useful ones, on the other hand, are scarcer than honest ones."

"Mmm," he replied. With a faint smile.

I wonder if she knows, he thought idly, how perfectly her skin matches those pearls. No wonder a man was tempted to give them to her. He must have chosen them for that very reason. And he knew a moment of pity for the man whose hopeful gift was about to be heartlessly turned into cash again.

She looked at the clock. "Speaking of useful, Mr. Redmond, it's time to earn your pearls! Follow me."

She leaped out of her chair and flung on her cloak before he could push back his chair or offer to assist her or do anything gentlemen are bred to do, the way sheepdogs are bred to herd sheep.

Chapter 10

She led them once again on a circuitous, labyrinthine route that somehow ended with the two of them standing on Drury Lane.

And all along the way, surreptitiously, as often as he could, Jonathan pinched off and pressed little bits of one of the pink marzipan raspberry clusters against walls of alleys and buildings. He'd found them wrapped in his coat pocket, and he'd decided he could sacrifice at least one of them. Not all of his marzipan markers would survive until the next day, or even stay put for the night. But he suspected enough of them would. He'd be looking for them tomorrow.

"This is where all of this"—she swept a hand up and down through the air in front of Jonathan—"becomes truly useful."

" 'This?' " he queried dryly.

"The boots by Hoby, the coat by Weston, the accent, the eau de I'm-oh-so-wealthy-and-scrupulously-bred that wafts from your very pores like gin from a St. Giles footpad. We'll need a hack," she said decisively. "I warrant one will stop for you straightaway."

She was right. It was a cold evening, but fortunately Jonathan's conspicuous height, bearing, clothing, and his obvious and surprising sobriety, rare in an aristocrat at this time of night in London, got them a hack within minutes.

"Grosvenor Square, please," she directed the hackney driver, who was clearly *not* sober. But drinking was a requirement of his job, if one didn't want to freeze to death.

"Of *course* Grosvenor Square," he muttered dryly, and cracked the ribbons.

In the carriage Tommy was quiet for such a good long while, and her nerves were so clearly growing tauter and tauter, that Jonathan wanted nothing more than to yell "Boo!" He suspected her head would touch the ceiling if he did.

"Boo," he said softly but with a great burst of feeling.

She hopped gratifyingly.

He smiled crookedly.

"You are a *child*," she said irritably.

Her big green eyes in the shadowy light of the hack glowed almost spectrally. They *might* have spooked a less stalwart or sober man. He refrained from sharing this with her.

"If I guess correctly, will you tell me what we're about?"

"You'll never guess," she said absently

"Do you intend to steal something?"

Silence.

He could almost hear her mental *bloody hell* at his instantly correct assumption.

"A warning: I'll know it if you lie to me, Tommy. I don't recommend it."

She turned to stare out the window at London as if she'd freshly arrived from a foreign land. Or was seeing it for the last time.

"I don't *consider* it stealing," she said finally, carefully.

Oh, splendid.

"So we *are* stealing something."

She hesitated. "We are . . . liberating something."

And quite surprisingly, here she turned to him and grinned, a pure rascally grin, a grin that had a reckless swashbuckling quality to it. A do-or-die sort of grin.

Oh. Bloody. Hell. He *was* in trouble.

And yet a part of him thought: *I will of course excel at stealing whatever it is we're stealing,* because he refused to fail. Perhaps his father was right after all to attempt to rein him in, since clearly the promise of pearls could lead him so easily astray. The new things he was learning about himself lately were flowing thick and fast.

He imagined saying from Newgate, "Well, if you didn't want to visit me here, you shouldn't have cut off my allowance, Father." It was one thing the Redmonds could hold over the Everseas—not one of them had yet been in prison.

"You'll want to wrap your boot heels in a handkerchief or your cravat, by the way," she added absently. "We shall need to be silent as cats."

Surprisingly, he did as he was told without question.

Grosvenor Square was quiet. All the aristocrats were tucked up in bed or the houses shut up for the winter. They witnessed no comings and no goings. That could, of course, change at any minute. And suddenly Tommy thumped the ceiling, signaling the driver to stop.

Jonathan craned his head out the window and realized things had just taken a turn for the worse.

For he knew precisely where they were.

"This is Lord Feckwith's town house."

"Yes," she said, sounding faintly surprised, as though he was stating the obvious. "Why don't you pay the driver to wait for us and impress upon him the need for utter silence. And ask him to douse or cover his lamps. We shouldn't be more than a minute or two. Any longer and . . ." She trailed off ominously.

Jonathan cocked his pistol, a sound that never failed to stir his blood, pushed open the carriage door, and swung down. He immediately swiveled and lifted Tommy to the ground before she could squeak a protest. She was remarkably easy to lift, not heavier than, say, a sturdy chair. She gave herself a little shake like a disgruntled cat and immediately darted toward the narrow passage that led to the mews.

After he had a brisk word with the driver, he followed her, his bandaged boot heels muffled on the stone, her slippers barely more than whisperlike scuffs. She ran like someone who was used to running silently. Like a wraith. Her cloak like something cut from shadow, billowing behind her.

They were eventually going to crash into things, he just knew it. No light reached them from the moon or through a lamplit window. The shrubberies in these gardens were usually treacherously low. If he tripped, he'd likely shoot himself or Tommy.

"*Tommy*," he hissed.

She halted so quickly he crashed into her, sending her staggering and windmilling forward another foot. He grabbed a fistful of her cloak before she could topple onto her face. Apparently she didn't precisely have the eyes of a cat, because she went no farther. Instead, the two of them pressed themselves against the wall of the house and waited. In short order, shapes came into focus in the darkness and became recognizable as a low round ring of shrubbery, the door leading to the kitchen, and what must have been a servant's privy, tucked more or less discreetly behind another mass of shrubbery.

The hush was palpable. It was as if a dark cloak had been thrown over the whole world. He began to breathe more slowly, and on one breath he took in the scent of something sweet. *Tommy uses French milled soap,* he knew then. He leaned forward for another surreptitious sniff, wondering—

BAM!

They both shot a few inches skyward out of their shoes when the privy door banged open, releasing an unholy stench and a burst of light.

The light bobbed and weaved; it was a lantern. They heard heavy shuffling footsteps, as if someone large was having difficulty lifting his feet. A lantern carried by a staggering, likely inebriated servant.

Unfortunately, the swaying light threw a wayward beam right into Jonathan's face.

Christ! Jonathan crammed his hat lower onto his

face, seized Tommy, and shoved her behind him.

The servant halted his shuffling steps and hoisted the lamp high, peering into the dark.

"That be Lord Feckwith?"

"Yes," Jonathan replied coldly, muffling his voice in his cravat.

The lamp continued to sway. Fortunately the man couldn't hold it steady.

"Wiv a doxy?" Interestingly, the servant sounded entirely unsurprised.

"Yes. Wiv a—with a—doxy. Off with you now."

He couldn't tell if Tommy had stiffened with indignation or hilarity.

"Very well, sir. I be sorry to trouble ye. It's just we'd beef for dinner, and seems the beef turned, ye see, and . . ."

As the consequences of the beef turning were really rather self-explanatory, he bowed, the lamp clinking and swinging on down with him, and turned and shuffled into the house.

They waited. Jonathan counted to ten after the door shut behind the servant. Tommy's breathing was alarmingly swift now. And then she crept forward, out from behind him.

He followed.

And when they were close enough to the privy to make their eyes water, she whispered: "Sally?"

Seconds later there was a rustle.

All the little hairs stood up on Jonathan's neck. A tiny figure crept out from behind the shrubbery near the privy. "Tommy?"

And Tommy lunged for whatever it was, snatched it up, turned tail, and ran back down the passage.

"The *devil*—"

Jonathan bolted after her. She couldn't move very quickly with her bundle, but fright often substituted for strength in extreme circumstances.

The carriage driver laconically opened the carriage door when he saw them tearing toward him. Tommy transferred her bundle to beneath her arm, Jonathan gave her arse a nudge up with a shoulder to get her all the way in, and then he locked his pistol, and with a "Back to where you found us, and a shilling more if you go like the devil," to the driver, he leaped aboard.

The carriage lurched forward, tumbling the passengers a little. They righted themselves apace.

Across from him, Tommy flung herself backward and heaved a sigh of relief. She gently settled the bundle down next to her on her seat, patted and soothed it.

Jonathan stared. "It's a *child*."

No one, no one, had ever sounded more aghast than Jonathan at that moment.

Tommy was unaffected. "For heaven's sake. You say that the way someone else might say, "It's the *pox!*"

Just then the little girl—for that's what it was—seemed to notice Jonathan.

And she screamed.

And screamed.

And screamed and screamed and screamed.

It was a scream of exceptional quality. A nerve-shattering, eardrum-shredding, blood-congealing scream that shaved years off his life, hurled him backward in his seat, and nearly made him wet himself. He found himself clawing at the walls of the carriage, as if that could help him escape it.

Tommy was in a flailing panic, too. She'd whipped off her cloak, and Jonathan harbored a brief irrational hope she might smother the thing with it.

Instead, she whisked it over the little girl's shoulders and started up a nonstop soothing one-sided conversation. "Sally, it's all right. It's all right. Hush now. Hush. *Hush*."

Oh, *enough*.

"CEASE THAT NOISE AT ONCE!" he bellowed.

Sally ceased with remarkable equanimity and stared at him, wide-eyed. Clearly impressed with the power of *his* lungs.

Oh, the bliss. The bliss of silence. How had he never appreciated it before? He vowed never again to take it for granted.

"The . . . fekking . . . *hell* . . ." he said faintly.

Tommy clearly couldn't yet speak.

He felt like he needed smelling salts.

The horrible sound lived on in the ringing of his ears. He put one finger in and twisted it, as if he could return his hearing to its former innocent state. He wished he was one of those young bloods who carried around a flask of whisky.

Tommy's voice still had a certain tremolo quality when she spoke.

"Sally, this is . . . er . . . Mr. Friend. He is a good man and I trust him and he's here because he wants to help you. He will *never* hurt you. There is no need to scream."

"Mr. Friend would very much like to hurt *you* right about now," Jonathan muttered blackly to Tommy, through clenched teeth.

Tommy ignored him.

Sally was looking at him with wide-eyed equanimity. She had the sort of eyes possessed by puppies and fawns. Glossy and enormous and liquid with innocence. *The better to disguise evil*, Jonathan thought darkly.

"Cook said I'd get the collywobbles if I talked to strange men. And that I ought to scream if I see one, sudden like."

Jonathan snarled, "What the bloody hell are collywob—*OW!*"

Tommy kicked him in the shin.

He glowered poisonously at her.

She hiked her eyebrows to her hairline.

He sucked in a long breath, a symbolic attempt to siphon patience from the air of what had clearly become a rolling madhouse. He exhaled to steady himself.

He had only himself to blame. He knew it. He possessed a sixth sense for this sort of thing because he wanted none of it, none of the nerve-taxing complications that women like Tommy represented. It was bleak satisfaction to know that he'd been right, oh so right.

"The cook is wise to tell you not to speak to strange men, Sally. Fortunately I had the collywobbles when I was very young, a long time ago, and recovered nicely, so you can't get them from me."

Tommy coughed a laugh.

"Oh." This satisfied Sally, apparently.

He stared across at the little girl from beneath beetled brows. She was certainly a little thing, very pale, her white cap askew. Dark curls bounced like springs from beneath it. She was a servant, clearly.

A scullery maid, mostly likely. And couldn't be more than seven years old. Possibly younger, given her size.

She stared back at him shyly, curious now. And then she smiled. He almost rolled his eyes. A little flirt, this one, as capricious as the big one against whom she snuggled. He refused to be charmed.

And that's when he saw the white bandage on her forehead, beneath her cap. There was a dark spot on it, not a small one.

And he suspected it was blood.

"What happened to your head, Sally?"

"Master William coshed me," she said softly. She was young enough to lisp. "And when 'e did, I fell and broke me crown."

"Master Willi . . ."

Master William was Lord Feckwith, the younger. Who was Jonathan's age.

And easily three times the size of Sally.

Could this be true?

Tommy's eyes were on Jonathan. She seemed to be holding her breath.

"Why?" he asked Sally finally. The word was a bit choked.

Though he suspected the answer was "because he could." Because big men who would hit a little female child . . . let alone hard enough to knock her down . . .

"Shhh, Sally, love, there's a good girl," Tommy interjected firmly. "All is well now. We don't need to talk about that now."

All was well?

All was *well*?

Jonathan aimed a look of such sizzling disbelief at her, their hackney driver must have felt it through the ceiling on his bum, and might have been grateful for the heat.

But Tommy refused to meet his gaze. She promptly either forgot or pretended to forget he was even there. She softly sang some nursery song to Sally, who leaned back against her, comfortable and utterly at home despite the bizarre circumstances, her eyelids lowering.

Tommy had likely shushed Sally here because the more Jonathan knew, the more enmeshed he became in . . . whatever this was.

His head was a writhing tangle of questions.

And he'd have his answers. Oh, he'd have them.

For now, he shrugged out of his coat and thrust it at Tommy.

She stared at it blankly. Then looked up at him, clearly preparing a look of defiance.

But the abruptness of his gesture and the black quality of his silence warned her not to refuse it.

She took it from him and settled it over her shoulders.

"Thank you," she whispered regally.

He snorted. Softly, so as not to wake the little beast.

"I've something for you, too," she whispered.

She shifted the child on her lap and then he watched in some fascination as she fished about for a time in her bodice.

She emerged with a flask and handed it over.

He did note it was still warm from being nestled against her breasts. For a moment thought was obliterated in favor of sensation and imagination. He was male, first and foremost, after all.

She's infinitely too much trouble, Redmond.

And then he silently raised it in a sardonic toast to her and bolted half.

A FEW MINUTES later she thumped the roof of the carriage, and Sally, who'd been sleeping, stirred against her.

"I can get down on my own, but will you hand her to me?" she said quietly. "Mr. Friend will help you, Sally, all right?" To Jonathan she whispered, "Right, Mr. Friend?"

What could he reply? He could hardly nudge the child out of the carriage with the toe of his boot as if she were a sack of flour.

He gave a short nod.

Sally sleepily stretched her arms up. Jonathan ducked awkwardly between them and she looped them around his neck, as if it was the most natural thing in the world, something she did all the time.

He hoisted her up. Ironically, she weighed about as much as a bag of flour.

A man his own size had coshed her in the head, but someone she trusted told her to trust *him*, and so she had. He knew a brief sudden sweep of vertigo, near terror, as if he were walking a wire strung between buildings. God, what a perilous thing it was to be a child. To go from screaming looby to unquestioning trusting innocent in the space of a single hackney ride. And this, he suspected, was perfectly typical child behavior.

"Thank you, Mr. Friend," she mumbled sleepily.

"You're welcome, Sally," he said stiffly.

She was either nuzzling into his shoulder or wiping her runny nose on his coat right now. He very much suspected the latter. Mad disgusting creatures.

Not *entirely* without charm. But only just.

"I'll have the pearls sent over to your town house tomorrow morning." Tommy whispered it.

It was tomorrow morning already, but neither of them pointed that out. A wan light was pushing through London's haze of coal smut, and drunks all over were stirring awake from the light, if not warmth, in Covent Garden.

"I'll need answers," he said in a tone that really was more of a threat.

"You don't want them, believe me."

She hadn't phrased it as such, but Jonathan heard it like an accusation.

And she was likely right. He'd been utterly right about *her*, that was certain. That she was likely a labyrinth of a woman, and God only knew her true past or predilections. He'd be better off snatching her pearls and forgetting the night had ever happened.

"I'll have them." Each word was a dire promise.

They stared a stalemate at each other.

"How on earth did I help matters tonight, by the way?" he whispered.

"It went better this time," Tommy said. "No one was shot."

Christ. "Were *you*—?"

Sally stirred and muttered something against Tommy's leg, which gave Tommy an excuse to look down.

Her head snapped up again immediately, and she was clearly distressed. "I'm sorry, Mr. Redmond, but she has a toy, a tiny doll . . . it's really her only possession, and I think we've left it inside the carriage. Could you have a look? On our seat? Can I trouble you to do that for us?"

This minor inconvenience she begged prettily about?

Jonathan hopped aboard the hack again, patting his fingers along the seat, feeling along the floor with the heel of his boot. He found nothing. "I'm afraid I don't see—"

Tommy gave the side of the carriage a hard thump with her fist, the driver cracked the ribbons, and when the team lurched forward, the door of the hack swung shut and Jonathan toppled backward onto the seat.

He *might* have imagined the laughter behind him, but he doubted it.

Chapter 11

THREE SHORT RAPS. A pause. Two short raps. Pause. Four short raps.

Tommy dashed for the entrance, slid the bolt, and The Doctor slipped in swiftly and followed her briskly down the stairs and through the dark corridor.

She didn't know The Doctor by any other name, which suggested his occupation was just as dubious as everyone else's in her building, though no one knew precisely where he lived. Rumor had it he did a brisk business as a resurrectionist. Judging from his pallor, his work *did* take place primarily at night. She unfortunately had no trouble picturing The Doctor selling corpses, but he seemed competent enough about patching up the living. Rutherford had found him for her—it was a case of knowing someone who knew someone who knew The Doctor. She was hardly in a position to critique his pedigree, particularly since he worked on account, and her resources were thin indeed.

"Thank you for coming. She's in here." She'd already told Sally that The Doctor, like Mr. Friend, had also had the collywobbles a long time ago, to ensure a peaceful examination, and Sally, who fortunately was fascinated by anything and anyone new, sat wide-eyed, silent, one finger in her mouth. She'd slept like a rock—or rather, like a child—the moment they'd arrived home the night before.

"Let's have a look at your sore head, shall we?"

The Doctor peeled the bandage from Sally's head with his long thin white fingers and took a peek beneath. "It ought to have been stitched," he said. His voice was arid and sandy and scarcely inflected. He turned to her with a little smile. He looked, Tommy thought guiltily, like a fish. His watery blue eyes were small and round, his mouth was moist and pink and fleshy. "A bit late for that now, unfortunately. She'll have a scar."

Sally held onto Tommy's hand and squeezed hard. "You are a very brave girl. You'll have a grand scar. Scars are dashing. I've quite a number of them."

"Does Mr. Friend have scars?"

"Doubtless many of them. All truly dashing people do." Most likely in his eardrums this morning, Tommy thought.

Sally had mentioned Mr. Friend a good half-dozen times this morning. Jonathan Redmond had made another conquest. She felt a bit guilty about sending the truly dashing man off so ignominiously last night, but she'd fulfilled her part of the bargain—she'd sent the pearls over this morning.

Tommy held Sally's hand while The Doctor cleaned Sally's wound, bound up her head neatly and efficiently, and examined her vision and reflexes for any lasting damage.

"Does it hurt anywhere else, sweets?" Tommy asked her gently.

"Here." She pointed to her shoulder. When she'd been struck, she'd knocked into the side of a wood stove. The Doctor had a look. "Just a bit bruised, and it will feel right again in a few days with a bit of rest."

"Thank you," Sally said sweetly. And glanced at Tommy, who winked approvingly at her good manners.

"You're welcome," The Doctor said flatly. "Now, Miss de Ballesteros, if you would be so kind as to escort me to the door?"

"I . . ." Tommy hesitated. She'd squared her account with The Doctor, who had been kind enough to wait for payment in the past. Something else must be on his mind. "Certainly. One moment." She pulled from a shelf an aging but carefully tended picture book—colorful letters of the alphabet, accompanied by vivid illustrations.

"Will you be a good girl and wait for me? I won't be long. Here is a picture book I loved when I was a girl."

Sally took it in both hands with something like awe and settled down at the table with it, opening it with an instinctive care that squeezed Tommy's heart.

"Shall we?" she said to The Doctor. They proceeded up the stairs and through the dimly lit corridor in an odd silence. When he stopped near the door rather than opening it, she was suddenly intensely uncomfortable with his closeness in such narrow confines. She took comfort in the proximity of the door, and put one hand on the doorknob, gave it a half turn.

He noticed.

And he smiled a little smile that made the back of her neck prickle uneasily.

"As you are aware, Miss de Ballesteros, we've enjoyed a certain arrangement for some time."

"Enjoyed" was certainly an interesting way to put it. Tommy brought a number of patients to him or he came here to see them, he stitched them up or reset bones or administered powders as necessary, and departed. And though he had worked on account more than once, she'd recently paid him what she owed.

"Are you abandoning us, Doctor? I would regret it. I was pleased to settle our account recently," she said lightly.

"Ah, yes. About that. I fear I must raise your fees, my dear, for I find my own expenses have risen over the past year. And given the clandestine nature of our arrangement, I believe my silence on the matter may warrant additional compensation."

She went still. Her smile remained fixed and friendly. All the while she thought, *That's a whole bloody lot of words to use when one would have sufficed: extortion.*

It occurred to her then that she'd never seen the man blink.

"Come now," she cajoled faintly, trying to charm. "I thought you agreed that you were handsomely compensated for your work."

"I had another type of compensation in mind."

He said it bluntly. Evenly. Without a moment's hesitation.

His meaning was unmistakable.

Take this powder twice a day. Change the dressings once a day.

Spread your legs for me.

The tone was just that dry and officious.

Hot little worms of revulsion crawled over her skin. Breathing was suddenly more difficult.

"I see that I've surprised you. But I think you'll agree that you and I undeniably share a special rapport. You have made clear your attraction for me."

She blinked. Surely she was *dreaming* this conversation?

"Doctor," she said gently, carefully, "if you have interpreted my politeness and appreciation as something more, I am truly sorry. It was meant only as good manners."

"Nevertheless. I think you'll find me a thorough and considerate lover, Miss de Ballesteros."

She couldn't decide which of those words horrified her the most.

She *did* shiver then.

"And surely you can find room in your social schedule to accommodate me. I shan't be unreasonable. Once a week should suffice, beginning tomorrow?"

He closed his case. Gave a tight polite professional smile.

"Surely . . . Doctor, you can't mean it?"

He was surprised. "I never jest."

That she believed.

"But your wife . . ." Was he married?

"Will never know, now, will she? And for a

woman like you, one more man should surely be no hardship."

She drew herself up to her full height, rather like a spitting cobra. Such a wave of fury rippled out from her that The Doctor at last blinked.

"I'm afraid I don't know what you mean by a 'woman like me,'" she said evenly. "And the fact that you would say such a thing is evidence that you don't know me at all, let alone well enough to assume we share a special rapport."

He just smiled ruefully, as if they both knew she was lying.

"The child will still be here tomorrow, as well, Doctor."

"Well, I'm not an animal, Miss de Ballesteros. The door of her room has a lock on it. I shan't be long. I expect it will go very quickly, as I've been imagining it for a good long while, and anticipation has rather a way of hastening the outcome of these things."

This statement rather opened up a window on horror. She froze, helpless not to imagine *him* imagining it.

"I'll return tomorrow to collect what I'm due, and as I suspect you're a sensible woman, I expect you'll be in. One way or another, Miss de Ballesteros, I'll have my prerogative. I think, upon reflection, you'll agree with me that bartering for services is a very fair arrangement, and rather relieves you of an unwanted financial burden."

"Yes. You're an absolute Samaritan, Doctor, looking out for my best interests."

"Good day."

He donned his hat and bowed, and when he

was gone, she bolted the door and threw her body against it.

Imagine that.

Yet another way in which she was in over her head.

ALONG WITH THE suddenly sinister heaps of invitations, which his mother gestured to with a smile and a pair of raised eyebrows, the next morning Jonathan found a package wrapped in brown paper and tied in string, addressed to himself, from a certain "Thomas B."

"The most astonishing looking man delivered this to our doorstep this morning, from what I understand," his mother told him. "The footman quite took a fright."

Rutherford, no doubt.

He hefted it in one hand. And he set his jaw.

He would be damned if that woman would get the better of him. He wanted to know just what he'd done last night.

"It's a lovely day to ride in the row," his mother said pointedly. "And I've heard from Lady Worthington that her daughter Grace seats a mare beautifully."

"It is a lovely day," he agreed. "I've made plans, however, and my day is full."

Of selling pearls, cheering up a German, and following a marzipan trail, specifically.

HE KNEW OF a small jeweler, Exley & Morrow, who would be ecstatic to get the pearls at Jonathan's price rather than a merchant's.

The transaction was smooth and pleased both

Jonathan and Mr. Exley, who asked no uncomfortable questions about their origins. Flush with a comfortable amount of money, and feeling like he could exhale again, Jonathan stopped by the solicitor's to pay the arrears rent on Klaus's print shop on Bond Street.

He'd met—or rather, found—Klaus a few months ago when he'd bumped into him outside of a gaming hell. Klaus had been sobbing quietly, though not in a drunken way, and Jonathan learned (it was slow going, given that Klaus delivered his story in an arbitrary blend of German and English) he'd lost nearly all his money at the tables, and then had been robbed of the rest of it by a gang of thugs when he'd departed.

Jonathan had led him into a pub, bought him a drink, and loaned him a few pounds. Revived by ale and kindness, Klaus had become his voluble cheerful self and the whole of his story poured out in very good English—how he'd emigrated from Bavaria to London but a few months ago, had developed a process for printing cheaply in color and in great volume, and had rented a shop on Bond Street, which, due to a rare error of good sense (his first and last foray into a gaming hell), he could no longer afford.

And Jonathan had just . . . *known* the moment he heard. Good ideas were like that. It was difficult to describe, but it was if some internal bell sounded when one dropped into his mind.

And made his way to Bond Street to unfurl his good news to Klaus a bit at a time.

He told Klaus about the pornography first. Just to delight him.

Klaus thought pornography was a *wonderful* idea, but Jonathan, a bit to his own surprise, was regretfully yet adamantly opposed.

"You want to be associated with quality products. You want something seen as exclusive or unique, something all the ladies will wish to purchase or own, something a gentleman can purchase *for* them. You want something that will be coveted, traded, and commissioned. And you want to charge a price that's *high*, but not too high. Liebman, are you ready?

Klaus leaned forward eagerly.

"We'll start with playing cards with the members of the court on them."

Klaus's eyes went wide. He stared for a moment, mouth dropped into a little "O." And then his arm shot out and he clapped Jonathan on the shoulder to steady himself against the sheer glory of the idea.

And then he clasped his hands together and rattled off something ecstatic in German. Jonathan's French and Spanish and Italian were more than adequate, but German still sounded to him like blocks of wood being scraped and slapped together.

"Klaus! German! *Klaus!* Speak English! Please!"

"Oh, I am sorry, mein freund. It's a wonderful idea. Everyone will want them." Klaus had been in London long enough to get a sense for what oiled the wheels of the place: gossip and status and vanity. "We'll need an artist."

Klaus was practical, Jonathan had learned. And he'd vowed never again to visit another gaming hell. An excellent quality in a business partner.

Jonathan thought for a minute. And then snapped his fingers. "I know just the person."

Finally something useful about Tommy de Ballesteros's salon! Wyndham, the artist who painted suggestive portraits for the brothel, The Velvet Glove, and who had allegedly painted Tommy's portrait. His work was certainly competent enough to create simple plates for the color press.

He'd just have to persuade him to work for a percentage of profits.

"And . . . perhaps we shall need models." This realization made Klaus's face light up again with glee. "Imagine, Redmond, I lost my shirt in a game of cards, and now cards will give my future back to me. And models."

Jonathan went motionless. It was his turn to stare in wonder at Klaus.

You could rely on the turn of a card for your future, his father had said.

And then a slow smile spread all over his face.

A smile that boded no good for his father.

"Klaus. Klaus, Klaus, Klaus. I am brilliant," he crowed softly. "We are brilliant. You shall have your models. And we'll be making an *additional* deck that will likely prove just as popular, if not more so. With a little help from Argosy and the Betting Books at White's, and that river that nourishes us all. Gossip."

Chapter 12

With a bit of sun pouring into the little rectangle of her window, and Sally giggling over her bread and cheese breakfast—surely a carefree child's giggle was the sound of sunlight itself—Tommy couldn't make herself believe that The Doctor had been serious. He'd actually *met* Rutherford, for one thing. Surely the proximity of such a behemoth was enough to give a man pause.

The more she thought about it, the more it became just another potential obstacle to overcome, and what had her life been but a series of obstacles not only overcome, but triumphed over?

She would clearly, simply need to find another doctor.

The question of what was to become of Sally was perhaps a more pressing one, however. The little girl swung her legs.

At three o'clock in the afternoon she left Sally in the care of Rutherford to see if she could bargain for some bread and cheese and maybe, just maybe, a bit of beef, confident Rutherford would send The Doctor packing should he arrive.

The THUD rocked the building. Sweet Mary, Mother of—only one thing was capable of making such a sound. She scrambled through the door, not pausing to bar it, and plunged inside, dashing down the corridor, up the stairs, and into her rooms.

At first glance, naught was amiss.

And then she saw The Doctor seated casually on the settee, a glass of brandy clutched in his hand.

Mounded on the floor like a great marine mammal, an arm flung over his chest, was Rutherford.

Her heart stopped. She dropped her bundles and staggered, then fell to her knees next to him. Her hands went up to her face.

She shot to her feet again, her words terrified gasps.

"Is he . . . did you . . . ?"

"No, no. I'm not in the business of killing. I'm in the business of *healing*."

"Oh. Silly me," she said bitterly. She could see it now: the rise and fall of Rutherford's rib cage. "Then what have you *done* to him? Where is Sally?"

"He's merely in the arms of Morpheus. And will be for a good long time. Certainly long enough for us to take our pleasure. We had a drink together, he and I—what man can refuse a bit of good brandy? I pretended to be quite reasonable and resigned and understanding, begged his forgiveness, asked if he would like to toast our parting. I slipped a powder into *his*. I used the weight of a horse to calculate how much I ought to give him. The *sound* he made when he went down. The child is simply napping, as children do—she seems to have slept

right through it. I looked in on her, and she seems
quite well. Shall we repair to your bedroom?"

He was loosening his cravat.

"Shall we . . . ?" she choked. "Are you out of your
mind?"

"Oh. Do you prefer to do it here, then?" He perused the room. "Perhaps I can take you on this
little table, and you needn't bother getting completely undressed. More efficient for the both of
us, and Rutherford is unlikely to be conscious
of anything for a good long while. Or there's the
settee, and you can climb on top of me. Perhaps
you know some new and interesting ways we can
both enjoy?"

He was actually *unbuttoning his trousers* now.

"Not if you were the last man on earth, Doctor."

She desperately, desperately, desperately did *not*
want to get a look at the man's worm.

He paused, a little wounded. "Oh, now, surely
that is an exaggeration. I'm not entirely repellant.
Be a good lass, sit back here, and lift your skirts.
It'll be over before you know it. I've an appointment in an hour or so, so I'll be off right after."

His arid uninflected voice made it all the more
hideous.

He was advancing on her now. She reflexively
backed away, but she encountered Rutherford,
tripped, and ricocheted off him to find herself flat
against the wall.

"Perfect. Excellent idea. Right here against the
wall will do."

A knee to the baubles. A stomp on his instep.
These were time-honored ways of deterring a man.

But quickly, briskly as he did everything, he'd

seized both of her wrists in one hand and pinned them against the wall.

She growled low, like an animal. *God* how she hated anything wrapped round her wrists.

She tried to get a knee up, but he'd anticipated that. He pinned her with his body. His soft belly pressed against her, and she could feel his cock beginning to swell. Her stomach heaved.

His hands were cold and peculiarly moist, and for some reason it was this more than anything that made her want to scream and scream. Confirmation that he was indeed part fish.

And with his free hand, he began awkwardly dragging her skirts up.

If she twisted her arms, he'd likely break her wrists.

Fine. Biting it was, then.

She felt her father's medal burning inside her bodice, and willed courage and protection from it. She twisted her head in preparation to sink her teeth into his hand.

Suddenly his eyes bulged. His mouth fell open. He dropped her hands in favor of scrabbling for his throat, and gagging hideously.

And then he abruptly levitated.

Before her horrified eyes, his dangling feet kicked and thrashed, and his body arced. Every bit as though he'd been speared on a fishhook.

When she finally was able to tear her eyes away from the macabre spectacle of his face, she looked farther up.

To discover that The Doctor was thrashing at the end of Jonathan Redmond's fist. Jonathan had gotten him by the collar.

The Doctor's eyes were bulging dangerously. He was purpling rapidly.

"You'd best drop him now," she said faintly.

Jonathan did.

The Doctor landed with a nasty thud on his knees. Gagging and wheezing, struggling for breath.

Jonathan toed him with his boot gingerly, speculatively, as if he were a fungus of unknown origin on a forest floor.

He looked at her then.

"Are you unharmed?" What a terrifying expression he was wearing.

". . . unharmed?" she said faintly. "Yes. Thank you. You've exquisite timing."

They both stared down at The Doctor then.

"I can't decide whether to kill you now," Jonathan mused to the creature on the floor. "Or hunt you on the street, for pleasure."

The Doctor's voice was a scornful, tortured rasp. "You'll . . . never . . . find me. And your sort doesn't commit murder. You would have done it now, if you were going to do it."

"My sort?" Jonathan was amused. "I'm afraid it's just that I haven't time in my schedule today to dispose of a body. Tommy, if you will hand The Doctor's bag to me?"

She did. Jonathan fished around inside and came out with a pair of scissors. He clacked them together, tested the point with his fingertip.

The Doctor struggled to rise, truly unnerved now. "Now, Your Lordship, or whoever you might be . . ."

Jonathan lifted his leg and casually pressed The

Doctor into a kneeling position again with his boot.

"Point to something in the room, Doctor. Some part of the décor. Aaaaanything at all. Do it."

The Doctor didn't ask questions. He looked about the room. And then he pointed with a trembling finger at a small framed portrait of Tommy, dressed in green and gazing boldly out at the room. It was hung over the settee with a narrow ribbon. Fifteen or so feet away.

Jonathan eyed it. Tommy had never seen anyone so still.

And then his wrist flicked and the scissors hurtled across the room.

The painting crashed to the floor.

The scissors remained embedded in the wall, vibrating. They'd severed the ribbon.

Tommy slowly turned to stare at him in awe.

"I'll replace the frame," Jonathan said absently.

The Doctor was gaping.

"It makes surreptitious murder so easy, as you can see, Doctor. When I throw it at you, the dart tip will be dipped in poison, and it will enter that vein throbbing right there in your slimy scrawny white neck. I never miss. Would you like another demonstration? Shall I give you a head start and then track you down with a dart?"

The Doctor had gone a peculiar pale shade of green. "That demonstration will suffice, thank you," he managed.

"Get up," Jonathan ordered.

The Doctor struggled first to his hands and knees, and then to his feet. He coughed wretchedly.

"Shall I break one of his cowardly bones for you, Tommy, before he leaves, so that he can't practice medicine? Choose a bone," he said, as if offering up a platter of sweetmeats.

The man was sweating now. "I'll go. I'll go. *Please* just . . . let me go. "

"Really? Begging already? I'm not certain I'll let you go yet. Usually I torture my victims until they wet themselves first. The ones who want to harm women, that is."

The Doctor was terrified now. He squeezed his eyes closed, and something that may have been prayers wheezed from him.

Jonathan sighed. "Stop it. First, you'll apologize to the lady."

"I apologize," he whispered hoarsely. "I, in fact, rue the day I ever saw you."

Tommy suspected this reflected Jonathan's sentiment, too.

"And you will never set foot near her again, or your death will not be pretty." Jonathan cocked his pistol. His hand whipped out and he seized him by the collar once more, and nudged him at gunpoint down the corridor and out again.

Tommy stood frozen, dumbstruck.

Jonathan returned, tucking his pistol into his coat. As if this sort of thing was something he did all the time.

He paused, staring at her as if seeing her for the first time. And he shook his head slowly to and fro. Lips compressed thoughtfully.

She spoke first. "How did you find . . ."

". . . your house? Marzipan raspberries," he said absently. He was still white-faced with fury.

She felt it wisest not to request him to expound.

"The door was unbarred, which struck me as wrong, and when I approached your door, I could hear your . . . exchange . . . with The Doctor through it." He swept a look over her, ascertaining she was unharmed. "Are you certain he didn't hurt you?"

"Yes. Thank you," she said faintly. "He was going to."

She saw his jaw set at that. He strolled over to the wall and plucked the scissors from it. He hefted them in his hand thoughtfully.

"I'm going to need an explanation. Now."

His voice brooked no argument.

She began to babble. "He's a doctor. I brought him in to see to Sally. He's always been professional, if mysterious . . . He really *is* a doctor," she concluded lamely. "He decided he preferred a different type of compensation."

"Clearly," Jonathan said flatly.

She bit her lip and aimed her glance at Sally's door. It was still closed.

"What the hell happened *last night?* Did we kidnap a child? And I'm warning you. I won't tolerate evasion."

The warning was unnecessary. She knew better than to be evasive in front of this particular version of Jonathan Redmond.

She took a deep breath, and prepared to say aloud something she'd never said aloud, in its entirety, to anyone on earth.

"She was a child sold from the workhouse into indentured servitude as a scullery maid. She was given a shilling to sign a paper that says Lord Feckwith essentially owns her until she's twenty-one. She made that decision when she was six years old, Jonathan. Could *you* make that decision at six years old? They're disposable, these children."

"So what you're telling me is that you stole Feckwith's servant?"

She shook her head violently. "Do you think she would have lived to be twenty-one? Lord Feckwith beat her. Violently. More than once. Once, because she dropped the coal hod and it rattled when he was trying to sleep, and another time because she was accidentally underfoot in a corridor. That's when he swung an arm at her and knocked her over. She should have had a stitch in her forehead. Her shoulder was—" She struggled with the next word. It emerged faint. "—dislocated."

His head went back a little, as if he'd suffered a blow. He took this in wordlessly. It was a moment before he spoke again.

"How do you know these things?" His voice was steady. But subdued.

"This I can't tell you."

"So other people besides you are involved."

She was silent.

"You've done this before."

A long, long silence.

Suddenly, without warning, he reached out and lightly seized her arm and turned it slightly.

The bullet wound. With his sharp eyes, he'd seen it, and known it for what it was. And the sleeves of her day dress were short enough to expose it.

He gazed at it for a long while. She didn't pull away.

His face was darkened, unreadable, pensive.

"Oh, God," he said softly to himself. "I *knew* you were trouble."

Gently, gently he released her arm.

Jonathan's gut tightened. He could almost span her arm with his hand. The skin was vulnerably silky. And someone had *shot* at her.

Then again, it seemed as though she had a gift for putting herself in harm's way.

"Who *else* is going to help them?" She was anguished. "It all started quite accidentally. With the cooperation of, yes, a few other people, I was able to help a little boy get away from where he was being ill-treated, and find him a new home away from London, a place where he'll learn a trade and be treated well."

He couldn't speak through the enormity of this. His hands went up to push through his hair.

"It's madness, Tommy." His voice was frayed. He was awed by just *how* mad and dangerous it truly was.

Mad and dangerous and . . .

. . . grand and *noble* and wildly unexpected.

Never would he have dreamed it about her. The slimly elegant Tommy de Ballesteros, she of the gossamer clothing and effervescent charm. She was a Robin Hood, of sorts. A bloody lioness.

And he thought for a moment of beautiful, brittle, distantly charming Olivia Eversea and her antislavery pamphlets and her earnestness. And suspected passion drove her. And he understood a bit how Lyon could be drawn to that sort of thing, would want to warm his hands over it.

"No. Hurting and using children is madness. The practices that somehow allow it are madness. The laws are inadequate and never enforced, and not a single bloody politician seems able to change this. I'm nobody, really, but if *I* can help, if only one child at a time . . . and there are so many, Jonathan. So *many*. Tell me—" She lowered her voice to a fierce hush, and jerked her chin. "—Would you hit her?"

Sally was standing in the doorway, rubbing her eyes. She'd slept through everything, and this was a blessing.

"Mr. Friend!"

She was wholly delighted to see someone she'd met only once before in her life.

Jonathan stared at her. She was so . . . *small*. So willing to trust. To believe the best of people, despite what she'd experienced. To find delight in something simple.

A cold fist clenched his heart. Hitting her for *any* reason was inconceivable. The notion of it was grotesque. Not only was she a child, but a servant. Someone who would *never* be able to defend herself.

"Good morning, Sally," he said politely. Somewhat abstractedly.

She smiled shyly at him. "Do you have any scars?" she asked.

He blinked. "Do I . . . ?"

"Will you show me?"

She had anarchic glossy black ringlets and enormous brown eyes. How in God's name did anyone say "no" to those eyes? They were horribly unfair.

And now Tommy was biting back a smile.

"Go on, Mr. Friend. I told her all the most dashing people have scars. She will have a particularly fine one on her forehead."

"Oh, I've scars. It's just that there are so many to choose from," Jonathan hedged.

"The bravest one," Sally requested.

"The bravest one . . ." He inhaled. "Very well." He shook off his coat, unfastened his cufflinks, rolled up his sleeve, and knelt down near her.

There, on his forearm, was that raw red slash. From the last time he'd intervened to save someone.

"It's not yet officially a scar, Sally. But it will be, and a grand one, too. A gentleman was accosted by a group of ruffians outside an" —he substituted the word "establishment" for "gaming hell"—"and I intervened to help him. I was slashed a wee bit by a knife but all the *good* people got away unscathed."

Implying that the "bad people" had been scathed indeed. From the floor, the deeply sleeping Rutherford gave a snort and turned.

"He's just sleeping," Jonathan said smoothly, and Sally accepted this with apparent equanimity.

"Ooooohhhh." She peered at his scar admiringly, not at all upset by the violent story. "Does it hurt?"

"Not so much, anymore. This bruise, you see, went along with it, and it's going away, too." He pointed to the fading spot below his eye. The one that had seemed to brand him as a ruffian in the eyes of the Duke of Greyfolk.

Tommy was watching the two of them, and when he glanced up he found a look of studied innocence on her face, a certain triumph underlying it. "So you intervened, did you, Mr. Redmond, when you saw a wrong being committed?"

"How could I not?"

"Do you make a habit of intervening? Didn't you rather intervene in my circumstance today?"

"It's not so much a habit as . . ." He trailed off.

He thought about Klaus Liebman. And the costermonger, and the child thief, and how Tommy had given him her sorry handkerchief. And the mysterious gentleman outside the gaming hell, whom Jonathan had rescued from knife-wielding ruffians, and who had staggered, dazed and frightened, away into the night, bleeding on Jonathan's handkerchief, muttering thanks.

And then, of course, today, when he'd been quite prepared to do murder for the woman standing in front of him.

"Not everyone intervenes, Mr. Redmond. *You* simply have no choice. It's your nature."

"I haven't a choice," he repeated faintly. With grim resignation.

She'd made her point, then.

It wasn't quite the same thing, but he wasn't about to argue it now. And she'd also neatly taken advantage of this quality in him by enlisting his assistance, which, in a perverse way he admired, and he almost smiled ruefully. The woman was deucedly shrewd.

He sighed. Christ. What she did was untenable and mad, and it unnerved him greatly. The lawlessness and peril of it. The grandeur and heroism of it.

It terrified him to his marrow.

And frankly, it thrilled him.

God save him from complicated women.

She quite simply couldn't go on doing it. She would be caught. It really was only a matter of time.

Every muscle in his body contracted in protest. No. No. He didn't want to be Tommy de Ballesteros's savior. He quite seriously doubted Lady Grace Worthington, for instance, would ever need to be saved from a mad doctor. He indulged in a moment of imagining her serene, predictable, exquisitely-bred blond beauty.

Well, he'd demanded details from Tommy. He supposed he only had himself to blame.

He sighed. "Have you any tea?"

Very few circumstances weren't improved by the addition of a little tea.

"It isn't very good tea," she warned.

"When your investment pays off, your tea will be excellent."

Her face brightened instantly. "Oh, so is your plan underway?"

"I sold the pearls at Exley & Morrow, I came from Klaus's a few minutes ago, and then paid a visit to Mr. Wyndham, who will prepare the images for the plates. We should have the plates made and the decks printed inside a month. I predict you'll have your investment returned, and then some, quite soon."

She beamed and gave the slightest little gleeful hop, and this pleased him absurdly, and not only because she seemed to share his joy in the making of money. Her face was luminous when she smiled genuinely. She had the sort of smile one felt smack in one's solar plexus.

"Tea it is!" she said, and swiveled toward where

cups were stacked on shelves and stretched up for one. And for a moment he lost himself in the quiet pleasure of watching her slim back, the quick deft movements of her white hands selecting saucers. Her grace was innate and subtle, as though she moved to silent music. By contrast, the colors of her—the rich hair, the exotic eyes, the black brows—were as vivid and surprising as her personality. And for a moment he indulged in simply baldly admiring her as if she were a woman he'd never before seen. He understood how she could have captivated the imaginations of so many men.

And yet none of them truly knew her.

He glanced at the snoring Rutherford on the floor, and considered wryly whether he envied all those young men their ignorance of the real Tommy de Ballesteros.

The one who had a bullet scar on one slim pale arm.

He felt every muscle in his body tense again, as if he was springing to defend her from something that had already happened. As if he could take the shot for her.

"Tell me, Tommy . . ." he said slowly. "Who gave you the pearls?"

He hadn't realized he was going to ask the question.

She froze. And pivoted reluctantly. Her green eyes studied him, gauging whether the well of his patience had begun to refill.

"A gentleman. And that's all I'll tell you."

Apparently she'd concluded it was safe to be circumspect again.

After a brief staring contest, he acquiesced with

a shrug and a quirk of the corner of his mouth. He supposed, in the end, it didn't matter; he told himself he didn't care. It wasn't as though he had a claim on her, or remotely wished to join the ranks of besotted sheep who wagered absurd things about her in White's Betting Books. And yet, if they were to be friends, he supposed it would be useful to anticipate from which direction trouble would next come. Because with Tommy, trouble was inevitable.

Besides, he had every confidence in the world that if he truly wanted to know, he'd eventually have the information out of her.

"Very well." His chin pointed to Sally. "What are you going to do with her?" he asked sotto voce. "It's hardly safe for her here, is it? For her *or* for you."

Something flashed in her eyes then; a shadow darted across her face. A wounded defensiveness about the rooms she could afford, about her ability, perhaps, to keep Sally safe.

She composed herself swiftly.

"I haven't a place for her yet. And usually I have a place . . . it's just the timing of it was unfortunate . . ."

"*Usually* you have a *place*?"

How many of these rescues had taken place? And then he recalled the little thumping sounds he'd heard above his head the night she'd shown him the pearls.

"Was there a child upstairs with Rutherford the first night I was here?"

Again, a stubborn silence.

In other words, yes, there was.

In other words, she made a *habit* of this sort of thing.

She read his expression, and again her voice was a fierce, persuasive, unapologetic hush. "Nobody cares about these children! When they disappear, it doesn't cause an uproar or histrionic articles in the broadsheets. They haven't families. They're *property*. When you use up kindling, why, don't you simply go and get more? That's how they're used by the workhouses and by wealthy men like Feckwith."

Her words were appalling. And true. He just hadn't thought about it in this light.

He glanced at Sally, who looked up and beamed at him. She'd lost interest in their incomprehensible adult conversation, and was paging slowly through what appeared to be a little picture book. She had a dimple, he saw, on the right, and what appeared to be a crumb on the left. Reflexively, he pulled a handkerchief from his pocket and dabbed at the crumb.

"Thank you, Mr. Friend." She beamed. And returned to the picture book.

Well. He was charmed motionless for an instant, despite himself. Polite child, for all that.

He looked back at Tommy and found her as frozen as a pointing retriever, an aura of amazement on her face.

He frowned faintly at her. "And the reason you need money more quickly . . . is to fund this enterprise?"

There ensued more stubborn hesitation, which he knew heralded more circumspection.

"Why does anyone need money? Perhaps I want more than this." She gestured to her rooms.

"So you *do* live here."

Her silence, followed after a moment by a non-committal one-shouldered shrug, rather confirmed it.

"Ah, Miss de Ballesteros. But I thought you were going to *marry* money."

"Oh, of course," she said smoothly. "Just like you."

He couldn't help it. He grinned at that.

She smiled back at him.

He shook his head and turned away from her and sighed at length.

Damn the woman. There was still no question that he *liked* her. He just wasn't certain his world needed to be as . . . interesting . . . as it had become since she'd entered it. Then again, Argosy was also his friend, and Argosy could, on occasion, be a trial, too.

As Tommy pulled down cups and saucers with homey little clinking sounds, he turned his attention to Sally again, who was still absorbed in the book, her legs swinging gaily.

He wondered if she could read, or if she was just looking at the pictures.

And from that thought . . . an idea dawned.

He was going to regret saying it. He would only embed himself deeper into Tommy's quixotic madness.

But in truth, there was no way he couldn't say it.

"Tommy . . . about Sally . . . I've an idea . . ."

Chapter 13

ARGOSY ENTERED WHITE'S WEARING a smug secret smile, and wove through the club purposefully, greeting his friends abstractedly, which of course captivated all of them.

His destination was clearly the Betting Books; such was the languid Argosy's charged purpose, all heads turned to follow his progress.

He scribbled something in it, then wiped his hands with satisfaction, and turned.

To find that five young men had leaped from their chairs and clustered around him to read it.

I wager Jonathan Redmond one hundred pounds that he will marry the Queen of Spades by the end of the year.

They all reared back at once.

"What the *devil* does that mean, Argosy?" It was Harry Linley, whose sister Marianne yearned after Jonathan.

"Well . . ." He made a great show of reluctance. "Very well. I'll tell you. Do you know how Redmond excels at Five-Card Loo?"

"Took me for seventeen pounds last month," one of them said sullenly.

Argosy nodded. "He's going to let the cards choose a bride for him."

A silence.

"He's going to do *what?*" This was a general exclamation as the word "bride" and "cards" seldom occupied the same sentence, or even their minds, simultaneously.

"Do you mean he intends to *win* a *bride* in a card game? I'm going to the wrong gaming hells, if brides are on offer."

"Is that an option?" one of them muttered. "I'd like to trade in the one I've got."

Argosy held up a hand for silence. "Very well. I'll tell you, but you mustn't tell a soul." This admonition was critical to ensure that the gossip would be spread immediately. "Klaus Liebman & Co. on Bond Street is having a special deck printed. In *color*, mind you. A magnificent new process of printing. And the suits—all of them—will be represented pictorially by the most beautiful women in town. Only Diamonds of the First Water, the most beautiful women of the finest pedigree, you see, will be allowed into the deck."

This prompted much discussion among the little crowd.

"Imagine, a card deck immortalizing this season's most beautiful women. Who wouldn't want that?"

"Who wouldn't want to lay Lady Grace Worthington down on a card table?"

This resulted in unworthy-of-them chortling.

"I'll raise you Lady Margaret Cuthbert."

"She raised me just the other day while we were waltzing."

Appalled and delighted hooting ensued.

"These are ladies, gentleman, so if you'll refrain from this sort of talk . . . until we're a bit drunker."

"Or Olivia Eversea."

A hush greeted this. There was no question that Olivia Eversea was beautiful by anyone's definition. It was just that it was difficult for anyone to imagine winning her, let alone playing her.

"Redmond told me he thought it would be brilliant to let the turn of a card determine his choice of bride. *I* think he'll draw the Queen of Spades. Whoever she may turn out to be. You're all welcome to wager otherwise. But please be discreet."

They all absorbed this in delighted shock.

"Redmond is *actually* planning to get leg-shackled?" Linley asked.

"He always did have a diabolical panache," one of them said enviously.

"Where will the girls be posing?" someone else wanted to know.

"An artist will sketch them on the premises of Klaus Liebman Printing on Bond Street. Remember, he has the finest, most modern of chromolithography printing. Liebman himself will have the final say over who is featured in the deck."

"But . . . how will he get the girls to go to him?"

Argosy made a show of looking at his watch. "From what I understand, a young woman need only provide evidence of an Almack's voucher if she'd like a chance to be featured. For we all know that is a sign of *true* pedigree. I believe he may have personally invited only one."

"*Who?*" they chorused. For surely she was the standard against whom all others were measured.

Argosy shrugged.

"Where can I get a deck?" Linley wanted to know. "Maybe I want to choose a bride from it, too."

"You can place your orders with Liebman himself now, from what I understand. *And* your bets. The decks should be completed and available from all the best merchants in a month. But demand ought to be fierce, so I would place my order now, if you wish to be among the first to see the results."

He stepped aside and gestured at the book.

And as the idea was irresistible, they queued to lay wagers.

Having more than adequately fulfilled his assignment, Argosy strolled out of White's whistling.

"THIS SORT OF thing," the formidable Miss Marietta Endicott said after a long silence, "one might expect of the Everseas, if you'll take my meaning, and also forgive me, Mr. Redmond."

"She's not my by-blow, Miss Endicott. I swear it."

Never in his life did he dream he'd have to say those words to Miss Marietta Endicott

The Redmond family name—and Miss Endicott's admiration for Jonathan's skill at darts, which she witnessed whenever she took a pint at the Pig & Thistle—were what got him an immediate audience with her in the middle of the school day. He'd watched the heads of young girls crane as he walked through the long hallway to Miss Endicott's office. Giggles and whispers and reprimands followed in his wake.

Tommy remained with Sally and the Redmond's driver across the bridge on the opposite side of the river, lest anyone notice and wonder why a carriage bearing the Redmond crest was there. Certainly no one in his family had any immediate business with the school.

Miss Endicott still looked unflatteringly dubious. "Do you know anything about this girl's family, her true age, her temperament, Mr. Redmond? Can she read and write?"

He reflected upon the carriage ride there, during which he'd learned that six year olds never stop moving. As if they've just discovered all of their limbs, and fingers and toes and tongue, and need to break them in, like a new pair of shoes. The conversation had gone something like this:

Don't kick, Sally."

She stopped kicking, and beamed at him, as if she'd been kicking specifically to get him to say things to her.

And then she inserted her finger in her nose.

"Don't put your finger in your nose," he ordered.

She pulled it out of her nose and wiped it on her dress.

"Don't wipe your . . ."

He wondered if all children required constant calibration. It was like learning to manage the ribbons of a high flyer drawn by unpredictable horses.

And then there was the "Baa, Baa, Black Sheep" incident. Sally had pleaded, and she'd looked so bloody hopeful . . . but he'd been adamant. In the end those incredibly unfair eyes were at last what did him in. It was like being held at gunpoint by a doe. Those eyes . . .

And he'd sung "Baa, Baa, Black Sheep." For two. Bloody. Hours.

He cleared his throat. "She is an orphan. I believe her to be about seven years old. She is a cheerful and even-tempered child, with unobjectionable manners. She likes picture books. She enjoys singing. She . . . has a dimple."

Miss Endicott's face was a picture as he described her.

And then a slow, amused, faintly wondering smile appeared on her face. Her steely blue miss-nothing schoolmistress eyes pinned him, and he was awfully tempted to squirm.

He felt himself flush. He swallowed. "She was retrieved from a . . . circumstance in which she was ill-treated."

"Ill-treated in what way?" Miss Endicott was relentlessly crisp.

He hesitated.

Miss Endicott raised a prompting brow.

"She was beaten, Miss Endicott," he said quietly.

Her features became utterly immobile. And then her head went back, and came down in a nod of comprehension. They engaged, for a time, in what appeared to be a staring contest. Miss Endicott's lips were pursed in thought.

She longed to ask questions, Jonathan could tell. But she was also shrewd enough to know that his family was instrumental in the continued survival of the academy.

"I shall have to meet her."

"You can meet her within the hour, if you like."

"That would be acceptable."

"I must, however, request that my involvement in her circumstance remain entirely secret."

"I am nothing if not discreet, Mr. Redmond."

Which made him wonder just how many other interesting secrets she knew. Then again, when one's academy is stocked with aristocratic pupils, utter discretion was critical.

"And I suppose we can find room for one more girl. But how do you propose to pay her room and board?"

"Doesn't my family provide a scholarship for the occasional girl from a, shall we say, more challenging background?"

"The scholarship is awarded at my behest, Mr. Redmond, and my judgment is expected to be impeccable. If your protégé—"

"I hope you do not intend to refer to her as such in the future, Miss Endicott, as it's critical that my involvement remain unknown. Even to my family." *Especially* to my family, was what he really meant, and Miss Endicott, the epitome of astute, grasped this.

Another short silence ensued. As did another short staring contest.

"Very well, Mr. Redmond. If the young lady in question should be found suitable, she will be admitted."

He had a suspicion, however, that Miss Endicott had already found her suitable.

Chapter 14

Aﬕer a lengthy chat with Miss Marietta Endicott—Sally wanted to know if Miss Endicott knew how to sing "Baa, Baa, Black Sheep," and to her astonished delight, the woman was familiar with the song—Sally became a pupil of Miss Marietta Endicott's Academy.

Sally gave both Tommy and then him a kiss on the cheek. And Tommy watched a faint flush paint his cheek.

Imagine. Jonathan Redmond, of all people, blushing over a kiss from a girl.

They watched her go off with Miss Endicott, skipping a little, delighted by the idea of having other young ladies for friends, as well as the promise of tea cakes.

She never once looked back at them.

"Out of sight, out of mind," Jonathan said ruefully.

"They're resilient, little ones," she said softly. "Be grateful for that, Mr. Friend."

But because she couldn't help it, she watched Sally until she disappeared entirely from view, as if she could make sure, very sure, she would at last be safe from harm. This was one child who would be warm, fed, safe, and one day, hopefully, cherish a family of her own. Just one child. But still.

She exhaled a breath she hadn't realized she was holding. In a sense, a breath she'd been holding for days. She felt both loss and triumph.

When she turned, she found Jonathan staring at her, an expression she couldn't decipher fleeing from his face. She might have called it rapt. Or surprised. Or thoughtful. Some fascinating hybrid of the three.

"Shall we?" he said simply. And swiveled on his heel. She followed, and they plunged out into the cool bright day. She inhaled with relish the rare clean scent of country air, as if she could store it in her lungs and savor it while she was in London.

"Save some air for the rest of us," Jonathan ordered mildly.

She laughed. "I've forgotten that I do love the country."

"So do I," he said simply. But there was a world of meaning in those words. Pennyroyal Green was his *home*, the place where his ancestors had lived and died for centuries. Eversea and Redmond bones probably fertilized the ground all over the countryside.

What must it be like to feel so part *of something?* she wondered.

"Mr. Friend . . . will you sing 'Baa, Baa, Black Sheep' to me?"

There was a cold silence. "I thought we agreed never to speak of that again."

Tommy laughed, and she gave a little skip. "Oh, if the ton could have heard you. You have a fine voice."

"That I'll agree with," he said easily. "I'll escort you back to the carriage, Tommy, but I'll have the driver take you back to London. I'd like to stop in to see my sister, perhaps ride back to London tomorrow."

She smiled. "You're fond of your sister."

"My sister is a trial. And she is currently immensely with child."

"In other words, you're fond of your sister."

He laughed.

Laughing with him was strangely a bit like drinking champagne. She wanted more of it, and the more she had of it, the giddier she felt.

Interesting to know definitively that Jonathan Redmond was a man who naturally *cared*. Who put himself in the way of fists out of some sort of moral reflex. Who put his reputation and family name at risk by going to Miss Endicott about Sally. He'd gone well out of his way for both Tommy and a little girl who'd picked her nose, wiped it on her dress, kicked him, smiled at him, and forced him to sing "Baa, Baa, Black Sheep" for nearly two hours.

She cleared her throat. "Thank you for what you did for Sally." She said it softly and rather stiffly, because her gratitude was immense and humbling, and she was unaccustomed to being humble.

He seemed to understand this. "Friends help each other when they can, isn't that true, Miss de Ballesteros? I'll stay up nights thinking of ways you might repay me."

He shot her a wicked sideling glance.

Her mouth quirked. "You'll make a splendid uncle. You're very good with children."

"Bite your tongue." Somehow his words lacked conviction.

A bird sent a spiraling song into the companionable silence.

"You're good with them, too, Tommy. Or at least it seems so to me."

It was Tommy's turn to shrug.

He reached up and slowly dragged his hand through the leaves of a low-branch. "Why are they so important to you? Do you want a family?" He said it idly.

As if it weren't a question of monumental import. As if the answer wouldn't reveal everything important about her. As if it wasn't the thing she wanted more than anything else in the world.

"I like children," she said noncommittally. Hesitating to commit herself to an answer that left her open to more questions, to more vulnerability.

He had a way of uncovering her secrets. Perhaps he'd know that one eventually, too.

He looked at her askance, recognizing a dodge, but content to leave it lie for now.

Because he liked walking with her, he realized, on this cool sunny day in this village he knew and loved, just as he loved his own family. He could have found his way back to the carriage in the dead of night by simply listening for the sound of the wind in familiar trees, the timbre of the river's rush over a particular patch of stones, the rise and fall and texture of the ground beneath his feet.

The world felt somehow larger with her in it, somehow a bit brighter and easier.

She was probably the only woman he knew, apart perhaps from Violet, with whom he felt utterly himself. Ironic, and what did it say about him, given that she seemed to be a conduit for chaos. Though at the moment she, too, appeared to be at peace and content just to be in his company.

They crossed the little bridge over the river, and paused while they leaned over to peer into the water.

"I used to fish from this bridge when I was a boy. I seldom caught anything larger than my hand. My father brought all of us here—me, Miles, Lyon."

"Are you close to your father?"

It ought to have been an easy question, or one he could have addressed with a pleasantry.

"My father is a difficult man," he said instead, hesitantly. Not wanting to lie to her.

She didn't press him. She heard a good deal in those simple words. "And your brother, Miles?"

"Lyon was the oldest, but we always used to turn to Miles for advice. He was always the steady one, whereas—"

"SHITE!"

He jumped and turned, to find Tommy was tearing the laces at the back of her dress. She whipped it over her head, standing in just a shift. She kicked out her legs like a Lippizaner stallion and—*one! two!*—her slippers flew past his head like satin missiles.

And before he could so much as fling out an arm or make a protesting sound, Tommy clambered over the bridge wall.

"*Son* of a—" He lunged at the rail.

In time to hear the splash.

All that remained were ripples of water fanning out from the place her body had sunk.

Everything stopped. His heart. Time. His breath.

And then she exploded to the surface, spluttering, bobbing, flailing, and she heaved her body awkwardly forward, her shift floating around her like foam, slim white arms churning the water, determinedly if gracelessly moving ahead.

Ahead of her, just out of reach of her hand, bobbed that bright scrap of ribbon and metal, carried inexorably away by the lazy current.

He was in the water now. He didn't remember how he got there, or hurling off his own boots. Just the cold, the surrounding green.

He shot to the surface and lunged after her. He was an excellent swimmer, and he quickly overtook her, propelled by foul language and blistering fury.

"You bleeding *madwoman*. You belong in bleeding *Bedlam,* you bloody—"

He slung his arm around beneath her arms, pulled her into his body hard, and kicked off toward the bank.

"What are you—let me go! Let *go* of me, you *wretched*—"

He wasn't to hear the end of that sentence, for she writhed and twisted in his arms, dragging them both beneath the surface. River water rushed up his nose, but he hauled them both upward again, spluttering.

She thrashed her arms and actually landed a blow on his ear.

He swore something scorchingly filthy.

She attempted to bite his hand.

That was when he clamped his arm like a punishing vise beneath her breasts, and pushed the two of them backward toward shore. He was stronger and she was small. It didn't matter what she did, she hadn't a prayer. She kicked and swore; like retrieved shipwreck cargo, he gracelessly dumped her on the narrow bank.

She pushed herself upright.

He ground out words through heaving breaths. "Move *one inch* back toward the water and I'll wring your neck I swear to *God*, Tommy, don't think I won't."

Her hands were balled into white knots. She tried to get to her knees and stumbled again, coughing and hacking. "*Damn* . . . you . . . to hell . . ."

The anguished fury in her voice froze his marrow. He nearly stammered.

"Tommy . . . what . . . tell me what's . . ."

"It's getting away! *Please* . . . Jonathan, oh *please* get it—"

And she pointed a shaking hand at that damned red scrap of ribbon.

And he threw himself back in the water. Fortunately, whatever it was had been enjoying a relatively languid drift up the river, despite their water battle. He was a strong swimmer and he kept it in his sight; it did a pas de deux with a passing floating twig, flirted with some leaves, and was just was about to shimmy between a pair of rocks when he seized it.

Treading water, he held it up high like a torch and waved it at her, amazed at how far away she seemed now. He saw her bring her hands together as if in prayer and drop her forehead down to them, then sink to her knees. From a distance, she looked entirely carved in marble—white arms, shift, toes—a martyred saint. Apart from her hair, that was, which she'd taken from its pins. It poured in a dark river down the front of her.

He pushed off the rock with his feet and began the journey back to her. And now he felt the distance in his arms and legs; the yards seemed to stretch longer and longer. It had been years since he'd had a swim in the Ouse, and he'd never done it in trousers and linen before. He waded to shore and stopped, his lungs heaving, water pouring from linen and nankeen and hair.

He stared at her.

With self-possession and pragmatism, while he'd been swimming back to her, she'd begun to set up camp of sorts. All the pins from her hair lay in a small gleaming pile. She'd peeled off her stockings and laid them out flat to dry, like freshly caught fish. She hadn't removed a single particle of her wet clothing. It was plastered to her body, and he could see the petite outline of her, every curve of her thighs and legs, her slim arms.

He might have been more than intrigued in other circumstances. Instead, he longed to peel off the clinging linen of his shirt and hurl it at her.

He sank to his knees instead.

She looked at him hopefully. And then very likely alarmed by what she saw in his face, swiftly dropped her eyes and searched his hands. He'd kept the scrap of metal and ribbon tight in his fist.

Her lips were blue and gooseflesh marched up those slender arms. She really ought to take off every scrap of her clothing but he wasn't about to suggest it, and there was nothing to wrap her in anyway. He could just imagine the reception that suggestion would receive.

"Rub your arms, like so, Tommy," he said curtly. He demonstrated by chafing his own.

To hell with propriety. It was warm enough to dry them both, and he unbuttoned his shirt with stiff weary hands and shook it off his shoulders. He turned from her and hooked it to some shrubbery, quite conscious she was both staring at him and trying not to. Let her stare. He knew how finely he was built.

And then he looked down at the scrap of ribbon and metal in his hand.

It was, of all things, a Peninsular Medal. It was unmistakable. Struck in gold, with four short arms forming a cross. They were rare, and given only to men who'd commanded battalions.

He turned it over in his hand and read:

Thomas Cantor Moretyon
6th Duke of Greyfolk.

It made no sense.

Had she *stolen* it from the duke?

The silence while she waited for his reaction—and while he took in the information—was profound. Like a blow to the head.

"I've never seen any woman undress so quickly," he said absently.

She didn't look at him. "If that was a ploy to get me to ask 'how many women have there *been?*' well, you know how I feel about predictability."

It was what she would have normally said, but her delivery was decidedly subdued. And wary. And well she should be.

His fury likely rose from him like steam. She could lay her stockings over *him* and they'd be dry in seconds.

"Fifty-six and a half," he said shortly. Still absently. Glibness was a reflex for both of them, it seemed.

"I must be the half."

At any other time he would have said, "Why don't we make that a full fifty-seven now," and they would have had a laugh at the utter unlikelihood of this.

But he was shocked by the purity of his anger. He pulled in fresh draughts of it with every breath. He couldn't think through it, or piece together why she should be clutching a campaign medal with the Duke's name on it, or why the loss of it should turn the formidable Tommy de Ballesteros into a trembling, beseeching child.

She cleared her throat.

"Thank you for retrieving my possession," she said humbly and stiffly. Clearly "humble" didn't come naturally to her. "May I have it now, please?"

"No," he said instantly.

She turned her head swiftly toward him. Then just as swiftly turned away. She began plucking nervously at the wet shift to cover her knees.

He turned to her and said very slowly, "If you want it back, I'm going to need an explanation,

Tommy. And please keep it truthful and simple or I'll hurl this right back into the river."

"You're angry." She hedged. "About . . . my sudden bridge dive?"

He fixed her with a scorching, incredulous glare.

"I *can* swim. I learned many years ago."

"Oh. Well, then," he said mildly. "That makes everything better. Did you have a lesson?"

"Well, yes, in a manner of speak—"

"Excellent. I suppose they simply forgot to tell you that you aren't meant to suddenly leap over a ten-foot high bridge into a river and swim in a god-*damned DRESS?*"

Well. The last word dress cracked like an axe blow.

Birds burst from the shrubbery in alarm.

Dress . . . dress . . . dress. . .

That fury-infused sardonic word echoed in a very satisfying way all about them.

She was wide-eyed as a fawn and frozen in genuine alarm. He didn't apologize. He inhaled deeply, released the breath slowly. He pressed his fingers to his temples. His voice was weary. "You could have *drowned* tangled up in your shift. Or . . . dashed your damned head on a rock. You had no idea of the depth of the water."

"I had some idea."

He turned and stared at her long enough for her to turn away and start picking at her shift again.

"It's just that . . . Jonathan, the object you're holding is very important to me."

"Clearly." He said it flatly.

"And what would *you* do if your dearest possession fell into the river?"

Her dearest possession? It had *sentimental* value, then. Not just monetary value.

"Well, let's see. If I was a woman—a *sane* woman, mind you—I would have turned to the man standing next to me and asked for some assistance in retrieving it. If, on the other hand, I were a mad, willful, reckless, difficult, capricious, pig-headed woman, I would likely have torn off my clothes and thrown myself off a bridge with no warning whatsoever to my companion."

She had gone increasingly pink and was now blotchy with infuriated color. But she was also clearly baffled by this recitation.

This did nothing for his temper.

"How *dare* you, Jonathan. That is . . . I . . . I . . . I wasn't trying to be willful or capricious or reckless. I swear to you. I'm never any of those things. *Ever.*"

This seemed so patently delusional he didn't address it.

"Then why the devil didn't you point and say 'Oh, no!' when this went in the water? At which point I would have gone in after it, since I grew up swimming in this very river, or I would have done something clever and male to retrieve it, like fashion a fishing pole from a stick and a watch fob."

She was watching his mouth move as if he was speaking a language she'd never before heard. Mother of *God.*

"I . . . I didn't think to do that." Her voice was frayed now. She was staring at him wonderingly. And then she straightened her spine and threw her shoulders back, realizing his temper was driving her like a nail into the ground. "I just . . . *it's* just . . . all my life, if something needed to be done, Jonathan . . . well, then I have always simply done it. The medal was floating away and there was no time to discuss it, so it didn't occur to me to chat about it. You see, I'm just not in the habit of . . . that is, there's never been anyone who . . ."

She stopped abruptly. Clamped her mouth shut.

And now he was staring at her. She was pink and stammering, defensive, indignant. Her composure and confidence was warping, curling at the edges, as if he'd somehow just exposed her deepest shame.

Oh, God.

And silently he finished her sentence for her: *There's never been anyone who cared.*

And here he was bellowing at Tommy as if *this* was a crime.

"I didn't mean to upset you, Jonathan, I swear it."

He closed his eyes against her flushed face. He felt like . . . such an ass.

"I truly didn't mean to upset you, Jonathan," she said softly. There was entreaty in it. She sensed an easing in him, and she was going to work her advantage. "And I'm sorry that I did. Do you believe me?" Her hand lifted slightly, as though she meant to soothe him; he stared at it. She dropped it again.

She wasn't his sister Violet, for whom he suspected he would die without question (and knowing Violet, he still wasn't certain it wouldn't one day come to that), but who had gone about threatening to throw herself down wells and the like before she married the earl, knowing someone on the periphery, a brother of some sort, would always save her from herself. She was now the Earl of Ardmay's concern. And he was possibly the only man on the planet who could handle her.

Yet how on earth could he have known this about Tommy? He was about to learn more about her, and he wasn't certain whether he wanted to, and yet everything in him rebelled at the idea of her hurling herself off a bridge because no one else had ever pulled her back by her metaphorical elbows. A conviction settled over him.

He inhaled deeply, and sighed out a breath.

"From now on, you will take three seconds to assess whether whatever it is you're about to do is dangerous. If the answer is 'yes,' I want you to tell me, and if it absolutely must be done, I will do it instead. You can trust me to do it. Do we have a bargain?"

He expected mutiny.

She studied him, her expression cool, assessing, now.

"Very well," she agreed softly, regally, as if giving him a gift.

Strangely, the relief he felt made it seem as though he'd received one.

If a dubious one.

He suspected she was humoring him, but he felt better. After a moment, he nodded curtly.

"Now, where did you get this campaign medal, Tommy?"

"My mother gave it to me just before she died. She *was* from Spain. Even if she wasn't a princess. She fled during the war."

"Where did *she* get it?"

"From my . . ." She cleared her throat, and then

the word emerged sounding threadbare, as though she hadn't the right to it. ". . . my father."

"And who is your father?" His questions came clipped and quickly. He wasn't interested in treading delicately.

She turned to him slowly. It was her turn for incredulity. And then she mimicked him, more wearily than with rancor. "Read the goddamned medal."

Chapter 15

She looked at him expectantly.

He stared back at her, genuinely amazed.

"No need to curse," he said mildly, finally.

Which made her laugh.

Oh, God. He nearly closed his eyes. It was as though he had been held underwater until this moment. It went to his head like the first draught of oxygen he'd had in hours, the sound of her laugh.

And now he knew: There had been an instant when her head had disappeared beneath the surface of the river, when all the color and light and sound had seemed to go out of the world at once.

It had been like his own death experienced.

He didn't like knowing that his righteous fury at her was really a sort of terror.

He sat with these two new bits of knowledge, assimilating them, while she waited for him to say something.

"I don't mean to be insulting, but . . . does your father know he's your father?"

"I absolve you of any need to be tactful, Jonathan, as I don't know if you can withstand the strain. My mother was his mistress. She says he loved her, but he cast her off when he married his young wife, who was very jealous when she somehow learned of my mother. And my mother said she told him about me. She claims she even brought me to him when I was a baby. He wanted naught to do with us. At least that's what . . . that's what . . . Why are you staring at me so oddly?"

"You do both have a sort of little dent in your chin." He gestured to his own. "You and the duke."

He saw her breath stop. She seemed transfixed. Absently, wonderingly, she pressed her finger into her chin.

She dropped it as though she'd burnt it, as if she'd just remembered he was watching.

"It's called a dimple, Jonathan. Not a dent, for heaven's sake. Some men have even called it my most appealing feature."

"Were they . . . blind men?" he asked mildly.

She laughed, delighted, and her eyes scrunched at the corners. It was odd, but he loved how they did that, for it made them seem like stars.

"And then there are your eyes . . ." he said absently.

In truth, the Duke of Greyfolk's face was as cold and distinct and unyielding as any dead notable carved in effigy in Westminster Abby. Very like his own father, or how other people viewed his father.

"Do I have his eyes?" Her voice was too casual. Her absently plucking fingers had frozen on her shift. Hunger burned through the words and in her eyes.

No one else in the world has eyes like yours.

This thought blew through his mind and destroyed every other thought in its path. For a moment he couldn't speak.

He must have been staring blankly at her, for she frowned faintly.

"His eyes are green," he confirmed softly, hedging. "What became of your mother?"

"She died when I was seven years old. She told me all of this and gave me the medal just before she died."

Seven years old. Seven years old was so very, very young. "At seven! At seven *I* was . . ."

"Terrorizing your siblings, I have no doubt."

"I was the youngest. They tormented *me*. But I quickly became master of the game."

But he was distracted. What a small imperious fireball of a girl she must have been. Full of laughter, quick on her feet, and nimble of wit. Had she been terrified when she lost her mother? Lonely?

"What became of you? Had you any other family?"

"I was sent to Bethnal Green."

She said it quite matter-of-factly.

He was utterly unprepared for the words. They landed on him like an anvil.

The workhouse. She'd been sent to the workhouse at Bethnal Green. Which is what often became of orphans . . . that is, if they were lucky. And that's how she knew about these children.

She flashed him a grin, enjoying his discomfiture. "A far cry from Eton and Oxford—is that what you're thinking, Mr. Redmond?"

"I suspect it was," he said politely.

"Don't you *dare* think I was pitiful, Jonathan," she warned swiftly, reading his silence. "I was *never* that. I made a great many friends there, and I have friends still."

"Minions, you mean."

A smile started at one corner of her mouth and spread to the other, and was fully delighted when it was done.

"I wager you were a horrible child," he said tenderly.

"I was. Thoroughly impossible, but quite sturdy and clever and willful."

"And superior."

"And superior," she confirmed. "And cheeky. Always that. Doubtless my education at the hands of life has been far more useful to me in terms of survival than the sort *most* young girls receive."

And he would have believed her, would have been convinced by all of this bravado and offhanded pragmatism, if he hadn't seen and heard her anguish as that scrap linking her to anyone at all floated away.

He had an entire family of people to anchor him to life, to both torture him and provide a net of safety. *She* had a tenuous grip on a campaign medal. And, if she was to be believed, she also had a terrifying father.

He knew a little something about terrifying fathers.

"And the medal . . ."

"I managed to keep it hidden with a friend of my mother until I was able to retrieve it. It's the only proof that I am who I say I am, for he gave it to my mama in better times, telling her it was his most cherished possession. I've kept it safe for him all this while. My mother told me to seek him out if I ever needed him, and to show him the medal."

"And you need him now."

And here she began to smooth her shift over her knees absently. "Perhaps."

There was a silence.

"Jonathan . . . may I ask . . . you are acquainted with him. What is he like?"

He hesitated. "What would you like to know about him?"

"Are you being careful with me?" She sounded indignant.

"Very well. Shall I be blunt instead? He's a thoroughly cold, ruthless, difficult, powerful, wealthy man. He lacks charm, at least in my point of view. He doesn't like me. He *does* like my father, who is, in fact, very like him. And you do look more than a little like him."

"And he's a very handsome man," she said suddenly. "At least the parts of him that I could see were."

"Oh, yes. Your looks, such as they are, are probably the only reason anyone tolerates you at all."

She laughed again. And then with a swift sudden motion she captured her hair, which had begun to flutter and curl and puff in the sun, in one fist. She twisted and twisted until it was a knot at her nape, which she then secured in some graceful and impatient and deft and mysterious female fashion. Women didn't know how often they betrayed their whole selves in these gestures, how moving and endearing and irritating all at once they could be. Such things could ensnare a man more than mere calculation.

"It won't stay," he muttered. He meant the hair.

He wondered how that rich mahogany color would feel against his palm. It looked as though it would always be warm to the touch, like a fire burned low.

"Nothing ever does," she said philosophically. Proving them right, a strand popped out of its little knot prison and circled her ear like a fishhook out to snare hearts.

And now that he was restored to his usual reasonable temper, his other senses were asserting their rights with vigor. And when her arms raised to attend to her hair, he could see—because naturally he looked—the dark peaks of her nipples through the damp shift. The sight went straight to his head like a shot of raw whisky. Her breasts were little and arced upward, and he could suddenly vividly imagine what it would be like to take one into his mouth, and this notion seemed to communicate immediately with his groin. Her shoulders were creamy and smooth and narrow, and the line of her body, from her shoulders to her little waist to her hips and thighs, down to her bare ankles and toes, seemed suddenly unutterably carnal.

Tommy seemed to sense a change in the air. She looked toward him with a querying brow arched. And then gave a slow crooked smile.

Wench knew *precisely* what she was about. It amused and impressed him, given that it was effective.

He self-consciously swept back his wet hair with one hand.

It stayed where he swept it.

She studied the result. "Fetching." She clearly meant the opposite.

He just smiled and casually stretched indolently and leaned back on his elbows. He knew her eyes followed the line of his body when he did, as surely as if her gaze was tethered to him, and he knew she was trying to pretend this wasn't the case. He knew very well how finely he was made. He possessed his own measure of vanity.

And he had wiles of his own.

She followed suit. They both leaned back on the shore, against sand and matted reeds and flattened wildflowers, and let the sun set to work on drying them. And it was warm and high now, mercifully aiming itself right at them.

Where was the harm in a little exercise of vanity? Jonathan thought. They were semi-bare and alone, and the sun lay over them like a soft layer of warm silk. They rested in easy complicity of their own charms, knowing they were safe from each other's wiles, because they were of course smarter than nearly everyone else, and they were not in the least what each other wanted.

She shifted her feet, and he glanced down at them in time to see a neat bracelet of shiny pink skin around one.

A scar. Perhaps a burn.

So many things he didn't know about her. So many things about her should have warned him away long before now. And yet here he still was.

He frowned up at the sky. She might be a petite temptress. He didn't doubt for a second she was strong.

But it was in ways that could either serve or defeat her. And she might have the bloods of the ton eating from her hand. But she hadn't met the likes of the Duke of Greyfolk.

He rolled over, propped himself on his elbow, and looked down at her.

She looked back up at him, a query in her eyes, which had gone a bit drowsy from the sun.

"About the Duke of Greyfolk, Tommy . . ."

"Yes?"

"He may not take kindly to having his orderly existence interrupted by the appearance of an unexpected daughter."

For Jonathan, that amounted to circumspection.

"Would *you* turn a daughter away?"

A startling thought—the having a daughter part. He thought about Sally. She'd been someone's daughter. What had become of her parents?

"I'm not a duke with a fortune," was how he avoided answering that question.

"I'll manage it the way I manage everything else," she said complacently.

"That's what I'm afraid of. I don't think you're managing things, Tommy, so much as you're dodging or lobbing events back as they come at you, a bit like lawn tennis."

She snorted softly.

"And where do you get money, if you're not yet a rich man's mistress?"

He wasn't certain yet whether this was true. Something told him it was, and yet his breath suspended.

She hesitated. "The occasional win at the hand of cards. The occasional shilling the countess can spare. And that's it, I swear to you. As a friend."

He exhaled. "What do you want, Tommy?" he said softly, vehemently.

"What do you mean?

"Five years from today . . . what does your day look like? Are you in those rooms in Covent Garden? Are you still dodging bullets and lascivious doctors and stealing children? Are you married to a dull man with a title? What do you *want?*"

She paused.

"Why does he have to be *dull?*"

"They invariably are."

"Said the man who doesn't have one."

"There's always time," he said shortly.

She smiled lazily. And then she exhaled a long breath. "Very well. I always wanted . . ."

"Yes?"

"You won't laugh?"

"No promises."

She sighed. "When I was very little, I was driven in a cart from the workhouse past a house . . . I don't remember where. A row house. And a little girl was running down the stairs right into the arms of her father, and her mother stood at the door smiling, and there were flowers in the box at the window and . . . that's it." She gave a little embarrassed laugh.

He didn't laugh. He was struck motionless by the fact that she may have just described the only necessary ingredients for happiness.

She wanted a family.

How very fortunate he was in so many ways.

And just then she pushed back a strand of hair over her ear, and his eye watched the movement of her breast arc against her wet stays.

And for a moment he couldn't breathe.

He wasn't made of stone, for God's sake. He ought to get the two of them covered up.

He didn't move.

"I haven't had much time to think of another dream," she said defensively.

He was still thinking about the shadow of a nipple against the damp white.

"It's a fine dream," he said absently. "But I didn't hear anything about marrying a title in that," he said finally.

She pressed her lips together. And hesitated. And then: "It's just . . . well, you won't betray my secret to the ton?"

"Which secret? You've a *legion* of them."

"This one: I just want to . . . choose my life. I don't necessarily *want* to marry anyone."

"The heresy! Ah, you see? We have a dream in common. I don't want to *have* to marry anyone, either."

She laughed.

"Why *did* your father issue that particular edict, Jonathan?"

He turned away from her then. "My father," he said dryly, "doesn't think very much of me. He thinks I'm on the road to perdition and a marriage ought to put me right."

"Surely that's not true!" she said with flattering shock.

"I didn't put it quite the right way. Nothing has been expected of me. *He* doesn't expect anything of me, apart from what I've always done. I'm to be dispensed with before I can do something to embarrass him."

She mulled this somberly. "It's hard to imagine he wouldn't be proud of you."

She meant it. He knew it.

He stared down at her and said nothing. And in the silence her unusual beauty lulled him, sunk into his bones, much the way the sun had, in a way he'd never before dared allow it to do. The slight cant of those sorceress eyes, that pale gold slope of her cheeks, the lines of her elegant slim limbs were why his breath was suddenly shallow. He suddenly felt her in his body as something primal, the way he felt the need for air or water, and he shifted restlessly. They were too long here, too little dressed, too alone.

"Tommy . . ." he began, his voice soft now. ". . . just because you survived being shot, and you've lived this long . . . doesn't mean you're . . ."

He was about to say "invincible." And he realized it probably wouldn't matter. And it was something he didn't want to take from her: her belief in herself.

Besides, how did he know she wasn't invincible, ultimately?

He would just have to hope he was there the next time she decided to put herself in harm's way. Whether it was a midnight foray to steal a child, or an encounter with a duke.

Suddenly her mouth started to waver and turn up at the corners. She was stifling a laugh.

"What?" he said irritably.

"It's just . . . Jonathan you look so . . . you should see your *expression*. You're staring down at me as though you fear I'm flammable. Or covered all over in quills."

His eyes were darker, unblinking as a rifleman's. It wasn't quite the look he wore when he threw those scissors at the wall. But it was close.

Still, he didn't say a word.

She realized then that the atmosphere between them had shifted subtly.

A faint warning knell sounded somewhere in her, a warning about their stillness and closeness. *His eyes are blue.* She was suddenly alarmed by knowing this so definitively. Jonathan's eyes are blue. Not like cornflowers, or the sea, or anything so safe and ordinary. They were more like . . . the sky just after sunset. That blue-purple of day finally surrendering to night.

A subtle color.

Funny, but subtle was definitely not a word she'd ever associated with Jonathan Redmond.

He still didn't speak.

"I'm neither as dangerous *or* as fragile as all that, Jonathan." For some reason she whispered the words, as if they were in a church. Such was the gravity of his gaze.

He hesitated. And then:

"No?" he said at last. With devastating softness and great, great skepticism.

And then tentatively, softly he laid his hand against her cheek.

Lightly as a moth it landed there. And softly, softly he dragged the backs of his fingers along her cheekbone, tracing that distinct line of her jaw, that might very well look like her father's. Gently, purposefully. As though testing the blade of an exquisite weapon.

And it was as if his fingers had found the loose

link in that chain mail wrapped round her soul and tugged, starting up a slow dangerous unraveling; she felt it in the filament of heat that seemed to start right at the crook of her legs, and travel up her spine.

"Because I fear," he murmured thoughtfully, more to himself than to her, as if arriving at a troubling conclusion. "That you're both, Tommy."

She curled her fingers into the ground, an attempt to anchor herself to earth.

He's going to kiss me, she realized, shocked. It was the fault of gravity, she supposed, and the fact that they were both more bare than usual, and if two pairs of lips hovered that near each other long enough, a kiss was bound to happen.

She hadn't been kissed in . . . so long.

And he did. His lips bumped hers gently, once.

It was downright chaste.

She was on the verge of finding this very funny when his mouth returned to brush over hers, slowly, light as a breath.

Testing.

Lulling.

Mmmmmmmmm.

Devil take it, but now she was curious.

She didn't stop to reflect that curiosity had been the downfall of many a woman.

She would have thought him a taker. But this kiss was subtle, subtle like his eyes. It coaxed. It lured. It revealed to her, with deliberate delicacy, a world of sensation in her lips alone. Somehow with just his lips Jonathan marshaled nerve endings in far-flung places in her body, setting them one by one aflame, and coaxing nearly everything that *could* stand erect on her body into an upright position. The fine hair on the nape of her neck and arms, her nipples—as if they all wanted to see what the fuss was about.

The world she'd once known was dissolving into a new world of heat and decadent texture. Honey. Satin. A rich male sweetness. It invaded her veins like a fine liquor and spangled her thoughts. And she knew all of this because her mouth had opened beneath his like a flower opening to the sun, because why wouldn't it? She was already drunk with it. Close to trembling.

When their tongues at last met, she moaned with relief.

She felt the sound of it arc through his body like a lightning bolt.

For his breath caught, and he tensed. And then he saw his advantage and took it immediately; the kiss became demanding, searching, and she met him hungrily. He raised up on his arms, bridging her body with his, then lowering down, down, gently down. And this was when some well-honed instinct for self-preservation made her flatten her hands against his chest, but this a mistake. It was like touching a warm satin-covered *wall*. She could feel pure lust humming beneath his skin, dangerous, unpredictable, as a riptide. His heart drummed beneath her palms. She almost felt betrayed, as though this hard, beautiful, unequivocally male body, this kiss like quicksand, were weapons Jonathan had hidden from her.

A different instinct said: *Give him whatever he wants. Take whatever he'll give.*

He moved his mouth to her throat and she

arched to abet him, to urge him lower. She knew he must have felt the thump of her pulse there. Lower, lower, now, to the valley between her breasts, and she prayed his mouth would skim her nipple. And instead of pushing him away, her fingers trailed down the gorgeous deep furrow made by the muscles ridging his spine, slipped into the gap of his trouser waist, slid over his hips. Another inch and her fingers would delicately skim his cock, which swelled against his trousers impressively.

"Tommy." Her name evolved into a gasp that sounded like surfacing deep from the river again. He went still, pulling away suddenly.

He stared down at her stunned for a moment. And then fell like timber away from her.

And all she could hear now was breathing. Hers and his.

A duet in breath-catching.

It was a bit like the aftermath of an explosion, she surmised. Everyone surprised and a bit abashed to have screamed and run about like ninnies, but relieved to have escaped with their lives.

God. She'd actually *moaned*.

She almost moaned again at the memory. It was with a great effort that she refrained from throwing an abashed arm over her eyes.

Jonathan *Redmond* of all people.

And he was the one who'd had the sense to *end* it.

"So . . . I take it you've been kissed before?" He was trying for irony. But his voice sounded odd. Thick and pensive. As though he'd sustained a blow to the head.

"As have you, I suspect." Hers sounded very like his in her own ears. She suspected they were both struggling to speak over the sensual tumult in their bodies. She felt like she'd been tossed rudely about on some kind of wave and thrown roughly to shore.

There was a pause.

"Apparently not," he finally said cryptically, half to himself. He still sounded dazed.

She didn't ask him what he meant. Speaking seemed superfluous in the wake of that, anyway.

When *he* said nothing more, she took him in a surreptitious sidelong glance.

He was lying flat, staring up at the sky as if he'd just plummeted to earth. One hand rested on his rib cage as if he'd been shot there. She watched that hand rise and fall, rise and fall with each breath, still deep but settling bit by bit. She wondered if he was trying to muffle the galloping sound of his heart. It was precisely what she was tempted to do, for she could still hear her own clanging away in her ears. The whoosh of blood heated to boiling in what felt like mere seconds.

She studied his profile as if she'd never seen it before. And so she hadn't, not really. His dark brush of lashes cast a little shadow on his cheek. A faint line was cut into the corner of his blue eyes from years of squinting from horseback into the sun. The hollow of his cheek was filled with shadow, and this seemed fascinating and new. It occurred to her that she wouldn't mind lying here all day watching how the shadows played over the curves and angles of his face. She suddenly wanted to see him in every kind of light.

And at that thought she felt exposed, and she was shivering. "My clothes," she said suddenly.

"I'll get them!" He shot to his feet like a sprung trap, scrambled up the riverbank, crashed through the underbrush, and vanished practically before she had time to blink.

Very like a man ecstatic to have an excuse to bolt.

Leaving Tommy alone with her thoughts, seldom a pleasant state of affairs.

And then he came into view on the bridge. Much smaller. Quite a distance they'd come, both literally and figuratively it seemed.

From a distance seemed a safer way to watch him, and she found herself avidly studying him as though he were a new species she'd never before seen: a lean, well-built, dark-haired man, bending to scoop up clothes. Not extraordinary from afar. Nor dangerous.

She watched him gently shake out and then neatly, carefully fold her dress, and for some reason this touched her unutterably. He retrieved her slippers, first one, then bending over to retrieve the other, yards away from the first, and she saw how small and absurd they looked in his big hands. She knew a sudden vertigo of understanding, of what hell he must have experienced when she had kicked them off and gone over the edge.

His hands. Skating her jaw, just so. She gave her head a rough shake and sucked in a long, hopefully cleansing breath and exhaled. Why should she feel *abashed*? She'd kissed men before and enjoyed it, though she certainly rationed her kisses, as she was practical above all else. She was hardly made of stone.

None of those *other* men had had the unmitigated gall to mine her very soul with a kiss.

She distracted herself from the tumble of her thoughts with tasks: she rolled on her stockings. She finger-combed her riotous hair, which was exhibiting dandelion puff tendencies, deftly braided it, then pinned it into a coil.

And then Jonathan came crashing through the brush like a great beast again, sliding down the bank, grabbing fistfuls of greenery for balance on his way down.

He froze when he saw her and stared. As if he, too, were seeing her for the first time. As if he couldn't decide whether she was predator or prey.

"Catch." He tossed her bundled dress to her.

She caught it effortlessly. He raised a pair of impressed eyebrows.

She shook it out gently, then gave it an extra shake, just in case any insects had taken a notion to explore it while it lay abandoned in a heap.

"Ought you to put it on over your . . . wet . . . things?"

The tone was all concern, but his face remained impassive, and *surely* that pause was deliberate and innuendo-drenched.

Wicked, wicked man. She could feel heat starting up in strategic places when he said it.

"I'm very nearly dry now," she said pointedly. "But thank you."

After a moment, he shrugged, and he gave a quarter turn, a superfluous bit of manners given that he'd seen her nipples through her shift, but hadn't touched them, more's the pity. But it was a bit of ceremonial reimposition of propriety.

She dropped the dress over her head and pushed her arms through.

She reached behind for the laces and drew them as tight as she could. He didn't offer to assist.

He was already dressed, shirt buttoned and safely hidden behind his coat, and his gorgeous polished boots covered up to his knees reflecting the sway of leaves above, and his hair was drying in waves that bordered on comical. Part meringue, part Beelzebub.

"Why are you smiling?" he said irritably.

"Do this." She smoothed her hair with both hands.

His hands flew up to his head. He began patting. "Thank you," he muttered. "Damned Byronic *nonsense* . . . I ought to have it shaved down to a nub."

"Don't!" The words were out of her before she could stop herself.

He lowered his hands slowly. He eyed her speculatively.

She stared back at him. Lips pressed together.

"Like the curls, do you, Tommy?" he asked after a pause. His tone was neutral. And yet there was a waiting, cautious quality to his stance.

He probably thinks I'm going to cling and swoon over him now. Like the rest of the women in the ton.

Little chance of *that*, since she wanted nothing more than to bolt at the moment.

And yet she hadn't a rejoinder. Her wits had been kissed into a stupor and clearly hadn't recovered all the way.

"You'll need these." *One! Two!* He whipped her slippers at her.

She shrieked and ducked and threw her arms over her head. The shoes thumped harmlessly to the ground just shy of where she stood.

The bastard was laughing softly.

"*That* was for nearly taking out my eye when you kicked them off on your way over the . . . side of the bridge." He repeated to himself, incredulously, as though just remembering how they'd gotten here. "Over the side of the bridge. When you tore off your clothes and leaped into the *water* over the side of the bridge. For the love of *God*," he muttered.

"We've been over this," she said easily. "And honestly, Jonathan, an eye for an eye is childish."

"If I wanted to take out your eyes with the slippers I *would* have," he said idly. "Believe me."

She did.

She shoved her feet into them, smoothed her dress, patted her hair, squared her shoulders. "Well?" She swept her arms down her person.

The stillness of his face as he studied her was deliberate. He was hiding his thoughts.

"You'll do," he said gruffly.

Another awkward little silence ensued.

We've forgotten how to talk to each other. The notion panicked her.

"Come on, then. You can't climb very well in those shoes. I'll need to tow you up the embankment like a barge." He thrust out his hand.

She looked at it.

Her hand moved toward his like a mouse trying to steal cheese from a trap.

She expected him to smile or tease. He didn't. He simply waited.

And once her hand was in his he closed his fingers over hers deliberately, so that she could feel every single one of them. He gripped her for a second with something that felt like irrevocability. That felt peculiarly like a vow.

Then he gave a short nod, and tugged.

She trailed him like a child, allowing herself to be led. A strange feeling. She could not have said what he was thinking as he climbed up the embankment, capturing and holding back shrubbery so it wouldn't lash her in the face, speaking only to point out the best foothold. *She* didn't think or speak at all. The world had narrowed to that place where their hands entwined. She wondered if he could feel her pulse kicking away in there. She wondered why she wanted to pull away at the same time she would have been willingly led anywhere by him at that moment.

But soon they were on the road again, and he freed her hand as though releasing a bird he'd nursed back to health. He didn't look at her while he did it.

"How did you get that scar on your wrist, Tommy?"

She stared at him, her mind blank with surprise.

His voice was even. But he wasn't blinking. And he wasn't looking at her.

"Childhood mishap." Her voice was faint.

"Ah," he said. "Onward then."

It was the last word either of them spoke for a while. The sun was lowering and tinting the edges of leaves gold, spreading big cognac-colored pools of light on the ground, and everything was too beautiful and strange for speaking, and Tommy was weary. Too weary to wonder what made Jonathan quiet.

The medal was safely in her possession once again, gripped tightly in her hand.

"About what happened today . . ." she said as they made ready to part.

"The bridge dive, the revelations about your parentage, how *blindingly* pale you truly are— "

"Don't be obtuse."

"Very well. 'About what happened today . . .'"

"Well, it won't happen again, of course." She said it lightly but firmly. Searching his face for their usual concord.

He didn't speak for a moment. He seemed to go rather still. She cursed the lowering light, for she couldn't quite read his expression.

"Oh, Tommy," he said at last. "You are stupider than you look."

She jerked backward. And then indignation sent her voice out at whistle-pitch. "*I—*"

He winced. "Don't squeak."

"Then don't be enigmatic! It doesn't suit you."

"Very well, then. I'm afraid it's like this. Picture, if you will, Tommy, the fuse of a cannon. Now, when one touches a flame to a fuse, what happens? It's consumed bit . . ." He stepped toward her, so close that his boot toes nearly touched the toes of her slippers.

She sucked in a breath. But she stood her ground when his knees brushed hers.

". . . by bit . . ."

His voice had gone perilously soft. ". . . by bit. Until . . ."

His breath fluttered her hair.

His mouth was next to her ear now. "Boom."

It was really more of an exhale than a word. Still, it made her jump a little.

He slowly stepped back and looked down at her. She could see herself in the big dark mirror of his pupils. She imagined her own pupils were just as huge, and that in that moment they reflected back to each other infinitely, without giving anything in particular away.

"But of course it won't happen again." He was suddenly jarringly crisp. He said it with faint mockery and a hint of something strangely like anger.

It made her want to kick him.

He didn't wait for a reply.

"Enjoy your trip back to London, Miss de Ballesteros."

He touched his hat to her and strode off, whistling something that may have been "The Ballad of Colin Eversea."

Chapter 16

KLAUS WAS TINKERING WITH his press when the bell of the shop jangled. He glanced up idly.

Then shot to an upright position immediately.

An angel was standing in the doorway.

He gawked momentarily, basking in the flawless, serene English Rose beauty: the golden hair, the round blue eyes, the complexion of cream.

His beleaguered first few months in England suddenly seemed worth it. Jonathan Redmond was surely a genius.

He bowed, low and elegant and deferential.

"Good afternoon, madam, and welcome to my humble establishment. I would be delighted to be of some service to you today, if I may."

"I am Lady Grace Worthington, Mr. Liebman. And . . . I received a message . . .

She had indeed received a message, on Klaus Liebman & Co. stationery:

Your name was submitted to us privately by more than one gentleman as an example of all that a Diamond of the First Water should be. We would

*be honored if you would accept our invitation to
pose for a very special edition deck of fine playing
cards paying homage to the loveliest young ladies
in London. An appointment will be set for you at
two o'clock Wednesday next, should you wish to
be immortalized thusly.*

She paused and blushed, fidgeting with her reticule.

But this first arrival was bold, despite her blush.
She was apparently unaccompanied, and she kept
glancing over her shoulder.

"Ah, Lady Grace. Say no more. It is obvious to
any man with eyes why you are here. You honor
Klaus Liebman & Co. by accepting our humble invitation. It will not take our skilled portraitist very
long to capture the purity of your beauty, if that is
what you wish. A sketch will be all that is necessary. If you will please have a seat in the window,
like so, where the light will make the most of your
complexion, and our Mr. Wyndham will join you
presently. May I bring you a cup of tea?"

"Tea would be lovely, thank you."

Lady Grace Worthington settled into the chair
by the window and folded her hands demurely,
while Klaus ducked into the back room, and via
a series of eyebrow wags and chin nudges communicated her arrival to Mr. Wyndham, who had
agreed to sketch for a percentage of the profits.

He peered out, looked back at Klaus and mimed
a whistle, and Klaus grinned.

At half past the hour, Miss Marianne Linley
strolled by in the company of her brother, Mr.
Harry Linley. The two of them had been invited by

Lord Argosy to meet in a tea house just next door to the printer at precisely that hour.

Marianne Linley's brother came to an abrupt halt at the vision that was Lady Grace Worthington rising from chair in the window to admire what appeared to be a sketch held by a man who had the eyes of a rogue, the hair of a fox, and the shirt of a painter—splashed profligately with color.

"Oh, this must be the printer Argosy mentioned! The Diamonds of the First Water decks."

Marianne, a petite brunette with snapping dark eyes, was immediately alert. She fancied *herself* precisely that. Certainly she had cause for it, since any number of men had lavishly complimented her this season.

"What you do mean by that?" she demanded. "Diamonds of the First Water decks?"

"Liebman will be printing decks of cards featuring all the most beautiful girls in the ton as the suits. You know, say . . . Lady Gra—er, you, as the Queen of Spades."

Her eyes narrowed.

The most beautiful girls!

"Why is *Lady Grace Worthington* sitting in that chair?"

"I don't know. Perhaps she was invited? Rumor has it Jonathan Redmond will be drawing a bride from the deck before the year is out." He gave a short laugh and shook his head. "Redmond."

Marianne gasped. "Does he really mean to do that?"

Marianne fancied herself in love with Jonathan Redmond, and had suffered greatly when it became clear he hadn't fallen in love with her. Pri-

marily she was in love with the *idea* of Jonathan
Redmond, since he'd been so unattainable and everyone else wanted him. Yearning and competition
made her suffer, and certainly suffering meant she
was in love.

Her brother, who hadn't any idea of this,
shrugged. "Who knows? But he has devilish luck
with Five-Card Loo, so why wouldn't he have luck
with *this* game, whatever it—where are you *going*?
We're supposed to meet Argosy in minutes."

Marianne had pushed open the door to Klaus
Liebman & Co. "Fetch me later, Harry. I intend to
have *my* portrait done."

And Lady Grace Worthington and Marianne
Linley assiduously avoided each other's eyes as
they passed, one going into the shop, the other
leaving.

HE WASN'T PRECISELY avoiding her, Jonathan told
himself.

It was just that invitations continued to ava-
lanche the Redmond town house; he accepted
them, relieved and reveling, for a time, anyway, in
familiar pastimes in which he was relatively certain he would not be shot at or arrested or required
to dive into a river, and conversations that were so
predictable he could have held them entirely on his
own rather than with lovely, interchangeable blond
women. There honestly was no time to go to the
salon that week.

And yet nights were a different story.

"Mein freund! You look as though you have
not slept," Klaus exclaimed as they pored over the
books.

That would be because he hadn't, not really.

Something about being alone in a bed at night—
for that's precisely what he'd been, alone—well, the
moment he closed his eyes all he saw was Tommy's
face after he'd kissed her: soft, stunned, vulnerable.
The feel of her arcing beneath him, lithe as a flame,
and her hands skimming his body, and her mouth.

Oh, her mouth. The wonder of it.

Kissing her had been rather like coming to know
her: layers upon layers of revelation. He'd never
dreamed a mere kiss could be like a punch to the
head. In the best possible way.

He'd seen stars.

And never had it been like that before. Like a
torch to straw, just that fast. A lust so consum-
ing and raw-edged it both shook him bodily and
rattled him into stopping, because, despite what
anyone else might think, Jonathan Redmond was
sensible. And he knew more than a little about control. But he would have taken her, right there on
the riverbank, swiftly and hard. He could imagine
it all too well.

He sucked in a breath.

No. He'd been sensible to stop. Not *afraid*—
sensible.

It was just . . . it was just that he hadn't touched
nearly enough of her.

Perhaps just a little more would take the edge
off the need.

He suspected this was the sort of mental conversation future opium addicts had with themselves
after that very first taste.

"I'm thinking deep thoughts about our business
at night, Liebman."

Which was, as he predicted, thriving. Their first hastily printed and distributed decks of court cards sold out rapidly, despite their cost (two pounds!), and several shops in the Burlington Arcade had ordered more of them, and Almack's had ordered one hundred decks of them, White's twenty-five, at least five different gaming establishment a good hundred more, and Klaus had begun daydreaming about building a second printer while Jonathan began daydreaming about doubling profits.

They'd earn back the entirety of Tommy's investment within just weeks at this rate.

"And I am reaping the benefits of it during the day," Klaus said dreamily.

As a steady stream of beautiful women had come to sit in his window to be sketched.

It was a veritable cascade of competition and vanity, a parade of cold looks and cold shoulders, as the cream of London young womanhood filed in and out of Klaus Liebman & Co. to sit for Wyndham in the window, which was rapidly becoming just a bit famous. Passersby slowed to admire them.

Unsurprisingly, Argosy had begun to show an interest in commerce. For surely that was the reason he stopped in at the Bond Street shop.

The orders for them were piling up. Hundreds of them so far. Two hundred alone, the day after Klaus Liebman & Co. had advertised in the broadsheets.

"How shall we choose the final faces for the suits?"

"Oh, I suppose we could draw names from a hat," he said absently.

He was trying to imagine what sort of deck

Tommy would fit into. The Most Problematic Women of London, perhaps. Men would arrive in droves to purchase the deck, grateful for the warning. They could print a fresh deck yearly, with new faces, just like a calendar.

Jonathan smiled to himself. Ideas *were* capital.

"Are you really going to choose a bride from this deck, Redmond?" Liebman was wistful. He would love a similar opportunity.

Jonathan thought of the ball he was due to attend this evening, and all the lovely women he would be obliged to dance with.

"But of course, my dear Klaus. Can you think of a better way to choose a bride?"

Klaus, a German, and generally optimistic, didn't quite catch the whiff of irony surrounding those words.

ONE, TWO, THREE . . . one, two, three. . .

He could do it in his sleep, the Sussex Waltz. He very nearly was at the moment, although the beautiful blond woman whose hand he was holding and whose waist he touched didn't seem to know it.

"Papa says the shooting is excellent. Grouse all but fly right into your hands."

"Oh, that's a shame. What makes it a sport is that animals you are trying to shoot are generally trying not to be shot."

Lady Grace Worthington missed the irony.

"Well, there's always riding, too. We live near some of the loveliest woodland left in England. You know how it was all cut for shipbuilding for the war. Papa made a *fortune*."

Jonathan was all too aware of her fortune. His father craved an association with her father.

"And do you enjoy riding, Lady Grace?"

"Oh, yes! And walking is very pleasant, too."

"Oh, I concur. When I'm trying to get from one place to another, walking or riding are usually my choices."

That whirring noise, he thought, was the sound of irony sailing right over her admittedly very handsome golden head.

Jonathan was enjoying himself, but not for the right reasons.

"There are ruins, too," she enthused. "Quite pretty ones."

"I'm sure there are." There are ruins bloody *everywhere* in England.

He wondered if babies felt this way when rocked. He'd never dreamed a waltz could actually put him to sleep. Not too long ago it was considered utterly scandalous, the waltz. Men and women touching each other for the duration of an entire dance. Like sex standing up. How very carnal.

How wrong they were.

Although, like everything else in life, it likely depended upon one's partner.

"And a folly, where we can picnic." She was still talking.

"Follies are jolly." By golly!

"Yes, aren't they!" She smiled. Teeth arrayed like pearls. Her short top lip sat atop a slightly plumper lower one. Her mouth *is* like a bud, he thought, somewhat bemused. Poets aren't *completely* mad when they write that sort of nonsense.

Tommy's mouth had the generosity of . . . a just-opened rose.

Somehow it didn't feel at all like nonsense when he thought it.

"I often take my embroidery out to it on fine days."

He frowned very faintly. She took her embroidery out to where . . . ?

Oh! the folly!

"What sorts of things do you embroider? Do say butterflies."

"I do!" she smiled. "And flowers and bees. Handkerchiefs and the like."

He really had nothing more to say to that. Unless it was: *Yes, but what in bloody hell do you* do *all day?*

He didn't say it. Because it wasn't just patently unfair, it was mad. If an English gentleman did his job correctly, the women in his life wouldn't really need to *do* anything. Embroider. Knit. Raise the children, with assistance from a battalion of servants. Manage the household. Beam adoringly at her husband from across a breakfast table.

A woman shouldn't need to steal abused orphan children to be considered interesting.

He should be very unhappy, indeed, if Tommy de Ballesteros had robbed him of his pleasure in meaningless conversations. They were practically evidence of gentility. They were as comfortable as featherbeds. They were as English as the Union Jack. Meaningless conversations were as much a part of his life as the Sussex Downs, and always had been.

Then again, veterans of war often returned to

England, bored and lost and purposeless after the noise and trauma and variety of the battlefield. Perhaps Tommy was his metaphorical battlefield.

But his thoughts seemed tethered to her, and the lead was short, and he was forever being yanked back to her side.

He imagined how his hand would feel against her waist now—it would be like dancing with a hummingbird, all quick lithe warmth—and how her hand would feel folded safely in his, and his mouth so close, so close to her mouth . . .

Tommy would likely want to lead.

He wouldn't let her.

He smiled to himself.

The bands of muscle in his stomach tightened. He inadvertently squeezed Lady Worthington's hand.

She squeezed him back. And smiled so sultrily he realized he must have been smiling sultrily at her.

"What do you think of child labor?" he said suddenly.

She blinked as if he'd flicked something into her eyes.

And then her eyes went wide and a faint pink washed her cheeks. She could not have looked more nonplussed if he'd suddenly noisily broken wind.

He could undo it if he wanted to. He could change the subject. He could steer the conversation as surely as he led this dance.

He waited.

She cleared her throat. "We've a number of young servants. There's a good deal of work to do in a house that size, and servants are so expensive to feed and house, and the children, why, you can just get them very cheaply from the workhouses. "

Very cheaply. As if they were cheese, or eggs.

"Can you?" he said softly.

"Well, of course. Surely your father employs children."

"No," Jonathan said. "He doesn't. At least not the youngest ones. I think our scullery maid may be all of twelve years old. Do you think children ought to be working when they're very little?"

He watched her valiantly consider this, likely in order to please him. It wasn't the sort of thing she'd ever needed to think about. Servants just *were*. They kept the house functioning, and maintained the lifestyle to which she was accustomed. She didn't think much more about them from moment to moment than she did about her own, for instance, liver, or pancreas.

"Well, it's not as though they're like us, are they? They're servant children."

"No, I suppose they aren't like us. Apart from the two eyes, four limbs, same species, that sort of thing."

She nodded, looking relieved at what she interpreted as their accord.

He stifled a sigh.

It was official. He'd been ruined for purposeless conversations.

He abandoned continued efforts to sustain it. And his thoughts snapped back to Tommy de Ballesteros once again.

Lady Grace looked worried about his silence. He did nothing to ease her worry.

"Mr. Wyndham said the light loves my skin," she blurted. Then she blushed fetchingly. "He painted me for the Diamonds of the First Water deck, you know."

Jonathan was instantly alert. Artists *would* say things like that.

"And who *wouldn't* love your skin?" he said, and offered up a genuinely sultry smile.

The ballroom grew restless when he did that, and fans fluttered agitatedly, and feminine brows fought the urge to frown, because frowning brought premature lines.

He realized too late it was just the sort of thing that resulted in his face ultimately being slapped by Lady Philippa Winslow.

It wasn't his *fault*.

Her skin *was* flawlessly lovely. The rest of her likely was, too. A tasteful portion of her bosom was presented by that fashionable dress of hers, and it looked ample and white and soft. And yet he couldn't seem to muster interest in peeking beneath her dress, when just a week or so ago he'd had one distinctive daydream about it. She was a perfectly pleasant person, apart from a great, and understandable, streak of vanity, which he had exploited for the purposes of his deck.

Truly. He should be kind to her. Surely that shouldn't take any great effort. Surely he was so well bred that he could be nothing *but* kind.

"Do you really intend to choose a bride from that deck, Mr. Redmond?"

A bold question, that. He liked it. He wasn't bored by it, anyway.

"Where on earth would you have heard a thing like that?" he said idly.

"From . . . everywhere."

He smiled. "It does seem rather arbitrary, doesn't it? And rather presumptuous? If I chose a bride from the deck, why should I presume that she'd have me?"

He was interested in what she'd have to say to that.

"Surely you're aware you're the catch of the season, Mr. Redmond."

Said the woman who was entirely confident that *she* was the catch of the season.

Was he? He supposed every season needed one. And weren't there more titles on offer? Then again, the Redmond fortune rather trumped a number of titles.

"I've heard I've a certain amount to recommend me," he said humbly.

He would need to tread carefully. The last thing he wanted was for Lady Grace Worthington to go making assumptions about how two catches were like two peas in a pod.

But he also wanted to sell a *lot* of decks of cards.

"Then again, can you imagine anything more romantic than allowing destiny to choose a mate, Lady Grace? And what is destiny if not a meta-phorical turn of the card?"

All she'd heard was the word "romantic." Her big cornflower-blue eyes went starry.

"Do you believe in destiny then?" she breathed.

Did he? The word instantly called to mind that

damned Gypsy girl, Martha Heron, and his whole being reared away from it.

He'd opened his mouth to respond with polite scorn when his eye was caught by a flash of movement on the periphery of the ballroom. It was more of an impression, really, of bright hair, of liquid, almost primal grace. Rather like a wild creature, perhaps a fox, escaping into its burrow.

"Yes," he answered instead.

And he abandoned an open-mouthed Lady Grace Worthington without a word just before the last note of the waltz was played, and bolted cross the ballroom, turning heads, fluttering the plumes on turbans.

But revelers soon filled in the path he created, the way displaced water will.

Chapter 17

Tᴏᴍᴍʏ ʜᴀᴅ ʙᴇᴇɴ ʟᴇᴀɴɪɴɢ against the wall next to a statue (of what appeared to be Diana, the Goddess of the Hunt), her eyes hooded, her fan languidly sweeping beneath her chin, and calmly, quietly hating Lady Grace Worthington.

There was a rich variety of things to hate about her: the coronet affixed to her golden head, as though she thought she were a bloody queen; or the smile that implied everyone in the ballroom was her loyal subject; or that gown—a violet blue, like a certain pair of eyes, silk, achingly stylish. It had likely cost a queen's ransom.

Primarily she hated her because of the hand resting on her waist.

She in fact couldn't take her eyes away from the hand resting on Lady Grace's waist.

And in the rational depths of her mind, which still hadn't recovered to their full pragmatic strength in the wake of an ill-advised kiss, she knew all of this was absurd, since Tommy would have happily affixed a coronet to her head if she possessed one, and she was generally quite in favor of smiling, and there was no question that one could call the girl "beautiful" and not be accused of hyperbole. If one liked blondes, that was.

The man dancing with her—for the *second* time this evening—reportedly decidedly did.

Certainly he spent his days and nights touching them, if only socially, if only during waltzes and reels and the like. It wasn't as if she didn't know this already.

It was quite another thing to witness it.

He was smiling, too. And why watching him smile down at a beautiful blond woman was peculiarly like taking a pickax to her own heart, she didn't know. Especially since she had been particularly relieved when he hadn't appeared at the salon this week, which left her to flit from one man to another as usual, collecting compliments, distributing charm, lightening moods. All apart from her own.

And so it was torture. But she couldn't *stop* watching him.

Surreptitiously.

From behind statuary.

And the Countess Mirabeau's wig.

Tonight the Countess Mirabeau looked like a member of the Sun King's court, with her towering powdered wig and patches, and long trailing sleeves. She overlapped two hands on her cane, found a bench next to the wall long enough to accommodate her enormous bead-encrusted dress, and watched the proceedings with a faint pleased smile on her face, nodding in time to the music. It was really all the countess required of balls these days, to sit on the bank of the river of gaiety and watch it go by.

She'd entreated Tommy to accompany her, just as an escort, and Tommy now wished she'd thought better of it. She was gripping her fan so tightly she'd nearly snapped the sticks. And she knew an unaccustomed urge to flee, as if she'd been cornered by a predator, except that for the moment she was all but invisible. Which was ironic, given that she was usually the one wearing the metaphorical tiara, the recipient of smiles, the bestower of attention. It was just that no one would ever expect to see Thomasina de Ballesteros here, among the glittering entitled, the women who would grace Jonathan Redmond's infamous Diamonds of the First Water deck, and the men who visited her salon and fell over themselves to earn her attention. She was quite simply out of context. And her dress, her very best, was altogether ordinary.

She watched him dancing with the sort of woman he was destined to marry, and breathing became difficult.

What do you want? Jonathan had asked her.

The shame of the realization scorched her cheeks. He'd known full well her world was *literally* a demimonde, an in-between world, no world at all, really. She *had* no context. She didn't fit in among the people in this ballroom, and she didn't fit neatly into any other strata of London society, unless you counted the Building of Dubious Occupations a strata.

But *he* fit in. He would fit anywhere. She'd earned her confidence through use, and it was a muscular thing. He'd been *born* with his; it was his birthright. And in the face of that, watching him now, effortlessly charming, dashing, very male and sure of himself, she suddenly felt abashed and unworthy and absurd for wanting him. He'd dived into the Ouse without a thought to rescue her. He'd found a place for a little girl, by dint of his family name. He was extraordinary, through and through.

And who was *she*? She'd been proud of survival. But . . . *animals* were content to survive. She'd done what she'd needed to do to survive, which is precisely what animals did. More acutely than ever before, Jonathan Redmond reminded her how this was simply not enough. Of how desperately she longed to *belong*.

What did she *want*? Unhelpfully, she now knew more about what she *didn't* want.

She didn't want to *need* anything, particularly something—or someone—she quite simply couldn't have. Too much had been taken from her already, and she'd had enough of accommodating pain, of straightening her spine, of soldiering on.

And *that* was the danger in kisses. Or at least the sort he'd given her. They stripped away layers of defenses and exposed her life for what it was, as rickety on its foundations as the building she lived in.

She stirred when a little cluster of young girls, charming in white muslin, shyly approached the countess and stopped to exclaim over the countess's dress.

"Madame, c'est une jolie robe!" one of them braved.

"Merci, mademoiselle. Vous êtes très jolie ce soir aussi," the countess replied regally.

"Je pense que vos cheveux gros est très charmant."

If Tommy wasn't mistaken—her French was rudimentary, as her mother had only taught her a little of it before she died—the young girl had just told the countess she found her big hair charming.

The countess chuckled.

And as more schoolgirl French and giggles erupted around her, Tommy, like a wound spring, finally burst away from the wall to look for the foreroom.

She wasn't fleeing. It was just that she felt more comfortable when she was moving.

IRONICALLY, FOR A girl who could find her way through the labyrinth that was London in the dark, she got lost on her way to the withdrawing room.

Which she supposed was simply more metaphor. Or more evidence that she didn't belong in a house like this.

Her footsteps echoed across marble floors and she knew she was getting farther and father away from the ballroom when the sounds became mere echoes.

She stopped when she encountered a long low table pushed up against a pair of French windows. Clearly she could go no further.

When she was still she heard the footsteps echoing behind.

She spun, reflexively prepared for attack.

She froze when she saw him.

Standing not more than ten feet away from her.

Her heart leaped like a spring lamb.

They stared at each other for a moment. And then a wondering smile started at one corner of his mouth and slowly spread to the other.

All the tension went out of her, and her confidence exploded into full bloom, and doubt withered in the face of the fact that she now knew there was a world of difference between the smiles he gave the likes of Lady Grace and the ones he gave to her.

The smile he gave Lady Grace was a mask.

The one he gave to her revealed him completely.

In three long steps he was in front of her, so close she could reach out and touch him.

"Well, well, well," he said softly. "If it isn't Miss Thomasina de Ballesteros. And me without my pistol."

They couldn't seem to stop smiling at each other.

"Do you know, Tommy, my last dancing partner asked me if I believed in destiny. What do you suppose I told her?"

"You told her to pose for your deck of cards, and that she'd find out whether she truly believed in destiny in about a month or so."

"Mmm." He acknowledged this little barb with a little smile.

"How did you manage to find me here?" She gestured to the empty half-dark hallway.

"Me? I saw a crimson-haired woman moving unaccountably quickly, and I followed, much like a dog who has no choice but to chase a squirrel. Blind instinct."

She was suddenly too breathless to speak.

"It's not crimson," was all she said. Softly.

He just smiled at that. "Why *are* you here, Tommy? I thought surely I'd had too much of the god-awful ratafia and was hallucinating."

"The Countess Mirabeau received one of her rare invitations, and she wanted to come, so I was enlisted as a companion. She doesn't seem to need me hovering, however. She's doing well all on her own."

"Oh? Where is she?"

"Over in the corner, against the wall. If you go back the way you came and crane your head, you can just see the towering wig. She looks like Marie Antoinette tonight. I left her alone for a moment to go to the withdrawing room. She looks happy enough, doesn't she? Several of the young ladies are practicing their French with her."

"She looks happy," he said, though he didn't turn at all. It was if he thought Tommy would disappear if he blinked.

Another silence.

Boom, Tommy thought.

She fancied the air between them had heated. She could almost feel it, like a palpable thing, like warm velvet.

Though the heat might just have been her cheeks.

You can't stop a lit fuse, she thought.

She waved her fan. "Jonathan Redmond in his natural habitat," she mused. "Isn't this something your brother Miles would write about? The way he wrote about the natives?"

"I'll suggest it to him."

"And so, is this is how you usually spend your evenings? Heiress shopping?"

"Or being hunted by heiresses. However you prefer to view it. At least it makes my mother happy."

Oddly, he sounded somewhat sincere.

She clucked sympathetically. "What a sacrifice it must be to dance with the homely young Lady Grace Worthington . . . twice."

He paused. She saw him realize what she'd just inadvertently revealed: she'd been watching him.

For quite some time.

"It's true, you know," he said, stepping closer. She took one step back. "I don't know what I've done to deserve such punishment. Her limpid blue eyes are *so* disfiguring."

"And golden ringlets are such a liability in the marriage market. Her mama must *despair* of ever finding a match for her."

He took another step closer. She took another step back.

"Your sympathy is balm, truly, Tommy. For dancing so close to a bosom so snowy and well, there's really no other way to put it—*generous*—is well-nigh unendurable. It's an act of pure charity, I tell you."

They were really enjoying themselves now.

"How you must suffer!" she said passionately. "And yet, I'm certain your place in heaven is assured. For her rosebud lips are *such* an eyesore."

"Yes. I prefer to kiss lips made of lava and silk."

Their silence could not have been more instant, mutual, and shocked if he had slapped her.

She stepped backward until she bumped against the table. Her fingers flew to her mouth; she rested them on her bottom lip.

Jonathan's eyes followed them there. He frowned faintly; he swiftly sought her eyes.

She dropped her fingers and her eyes quickly.

In the history of the world there *may* have been other moments more awkward. But Tommy wouldn't have wagered on it.

She lifted her eyes, as she was no coward. He was still watching her. She was fairly certain he hadn't blinked.

"Lava ... and ... *silk* ... Jonathan?" She repeated on an incredulous hush, all trembling, tamped hilarity, and wonder. "That is ... did you really just say, 'lava and—'"

"Hush!" he said, stifling an amazed, mortified laugh, which was shot through with a peculiar torment. "I'm appalled, too. It just ... came out that way. *Shhh.*"

Their usual complicity and pleasure in familiar contempt was now charged with something prickly and dangerous.

And thrilling.

If only she didn't so *enjoy* that sensation.

She aimed her eyes at his cravat so she wouldn't have to look at his eyes. Which were watching her again with that fixed gaze that panicked and excited her.

Like a wall, she thought. He feels like a satin-covered wall, and I remember how it felt when his heart beat against mine, and how shockingly smooth his skin is, and behind those nacre buttons is a chest carved into sheets of muscle that one wants to trace with a single finger like a road leading to bliss.

She fidgeted with her fan, signaling nothing but her own discomfiture and the jagged run of her thoughts. Neither of them said anything.

Whap, whap, whap went her fan against her palm. She stopped when he frowned at it.

Now would be an *excellent* time to return to the ballroom.

"Sounds like it might be uncomfortable to kiss lips made of . . . lava and silk, was it?" she ventured into the silence instead.

"Oh, it wasn't comfortable at all. It was, in fact, very, very disturbing. I fear I may never be the same."

His usual quickness. But they were shoved over to her like a chess piece, those words.

Your move.

There was something new in his posture, a sort of wound tension, a watchful, waiting quality. And that new expression of his . . . guarded, she would have called it. Jonathan had never before been guarded. It was cousin to the face of a gambler who had just wagered high on a hand he wasn't sure of.

"I, on the other hand," she said, "was entirely unaffected."

His features went dark. As though she'd stabbed a finger into his solar plexus.

But if she'd hurt him—which seemed improbable—he certainly recovered with remarkable speed.

"Oh, Tommy. You missed your calling. You ought to have been a toreador."

"Too dull," she maintained, and felt it again, that swell of fierce joy in this dance they both did so brilliantly, that made colors brighter and champagne more effervescent. It drowned the useless little voice in her head warning: *Don't bait him, don't bait him, don't bait him.* "Bulls charge at the slightest inducement. Just like men. Simple, predictable creatures, the lot of you."

"Too right," he murmured sympathetically. "Nearly as predictable and simple as you are."

Hmm. Not what she thought he'd say next.

"I'm sure I don't know—"

"That you're lying when you said you were un-affected? Of course you know. That you're trying to goad me into kissing you? We *both* know that. But color me . . . 'induced' . . . anyway."

He was laughing at her softly. And first one, then the other of his arms bracketed her where she stood. *Slap, slap,* his palms landed emphatically on the table behind her.

She was quite expertly imprisoned.

They held perfectly still, in just that way, so close but not touching, long enough for the sway of their breathing to synchronize. And yet she was afraid to move because to move would be to touch him, and in the last few seconds she'd de-cided she wanted to do that more than she wanted to breathe. Her heart clattered away in her chest like a pair of castanets. His breath landed softly on her chin. She could count his eyelashes if she so chose. *His eyes are blue.*

From a thousand miles away came faint sounds of a ballroom. From somewhere in her conscience the underused voice of her good sense wheezed a warning.

"I can make you feel . . . a thing or two," Jona-than suggested on a whisper at last. Casually. As though it were a summer day and they were two bored people looking for something to fill the time.

"I doubt it."

He smiled faintly, almost pityingly. And slowly freed her from her prison by bringing his hands up to cradle the back of her head. Big hands, sure hands. Her head tipped into them too easily.

He gazed down at her for a second, one brow arched: *See how easy you are?*

And then his lips crushed hers.

No finesse this time. It was really more of an eager, mutual competition for pleasure, a devouring. She wanted to know, needed to know, if it was as good as she recalled. She threaded her gloved fingers through his hair to hold him fast, to open up to him, to take from him. His mouth was hot satin and tasted of cognac; their tongues clashed, twined, teased. And just like that, so shockingly swiftly, desire built upon desire upon desire in her, until she shook from it. It was a spiky need.

She made a little hybrid sound, part laugh, part moan, part despair. *No, no, no, no, no. Please, no. It can't be this good.*

"Feel anything yet?" He stopped long enough to murmur against her lips.

"Oh," she murmured "Have you begun affecting me, then?"

She felt his short laugh against her throat, for his mouth had traveled there, to that tender place sheltered beneath her jaw, and his hands, astoundingly bold and confident and far too quick for her to muster any kind of objection, slid down over her breasts. When he discovered her nipples were as erect as pen nibs through the silk, he paused and drew hard filigrees over them with his thumbs. Hot bolts of pleasure shot through her veins, nearly buckling her knees. He felt her sag; his knee came up between her legs, his hands cupped her arse to hold her upright, and they were suddenly fused groin to groin.

"I can make you feel. I can make you scream. I can make you come."

His voice was next to her ear. Hoarse, urgent. Half dare. Half plea. So delicious and filthy and wrong and dangerous, her vision nearly blacked.

And what an impressively enormous erection he was sporting.

"You can't." Her voice was a staccato raw husk. It was both a dare and a warning.

Neither of them laughed this time.

"You're almost there now." To emphasize his point he pressed her harder against his erect cock, and her breath snagged as pleasure drove a spike through her.

A heartbeat's worth of hesitation. And then:

"Hurry," she urged on a hiss.

He gave a short laugh then. They were conspirators now. His hands furled up her dress swiftly. "Don't take your eyes from my face."

She did as ordered. Their eyes locked and his fingers dragged between her thighs, and she saw again a flicker, there and gone, of something like pain, something like wonder. This expression nearly undid her. He'd slowed to savor the feel of her. He simply hadn't been able to help it.

And she expected his hands to be demanding, but the way he touched her she knew he was savoring the silky skin hidden between her thighs. He slid his fingers between her legs, where she was slick and hot.

"You. Are. So. Wet."

The husked words, his harsh breath, rushed over skin like cinders, a fresh wave of sensation, and she nearly buckled.

She couldn't speak. She could scarcely hear him over the low roar of her own breath. Her head thrashed back and caught a glimpse of her face reflected in a silver sconce, flushed, slit-eyed, distorted. And his fingers were almost too skilled; he was a man who knew what he was about and didn't digress from his mission. Within seconds she was grinding her hips against the swift hard circling of his fingers, and then the pleasure built and built and built until it roared through her, an uncontainable conflagration, and seconds after that his arm flew up to cover her mouth.

Because she did scream, right into the pristine sleeve of his gorgeous black coat. And she did come, white stars exploding behind her eyes.

And her body quaked in the aftermath.

He left his fingers against her, feeling every pulse and shudder of it, as though it was his reward, too.

Over in only a minute or two.

She looked up at him, dazed. His eyes were hot and dark.

And they were both breathing as if . . . as if . . . they'd just swum a mile in the Ouse.

"Is this our new hobby?" he whispered.

She gave a pained laugh, and then tipped her face into her hands and rocked it, with a groan, while he smoothed the skirt of her dress and discreetly availed himself of a pocket handkerchief.

She peeled her hands away from her eyes and looked at him almost accusingly.

So now she knew. It wasn't as good as she remembered. It was as good as it would ever be in a lifetime. It was better than anything she'd ever before dared imagine, but she *could* imagine it getting better. For instance, if they were to divest themselves of clothing, and he were to climb on top and give that a try. It was tremendously inconvenient and unexpected and quite frightening, in truth, though she wasn't one to ever admit to being frightened.

He correctly read her expression. "I don't like it any more than you do."

He meant this new explosiveness. They'd opened some sort of erotic Pandora's box.

"You started it," she said, like a child.

He was indignant. "I wasn't the one who tore off my clothes to go sailing over a bridge!"

"I inflamed your manly passions, is that it? You could scarce contain yourself?"

He sucked in a breath. "Tommy . . . do you really think you couldn't inflame the passions of any man?"

She smiled slowly and crookedly at this, utterly mollified.

They were quiet and fidgety together, because conversation in the wake of a ballroom orgasm, and in the quiet, her sense of unease took over.

"Jonathan . . . I feel one of us ought to say it. We are friends, are we not?"

He went strangely still. Almost as though he was bracing himself.

"We *are* friends?" she insisted, more urgently, worried now.

"Yes. Of course. We are friends." His voice was surprisingly gentle.

She exhaled in relief. "Because . . . because I need a friend more than I need . . . anything else now."

He understood immediately. "And you're implying that friends don't scream into the coats of other friends whilst in the throes of a bone-rattling orgasm."

"I'm given to understand that no. No, they don't."

And now they were both *smiling* at each other, and yet she read in his face that new restraint, that fear of too *much* delight. How very much she *liked* him. How buoyant life seemed with him about, and how giddy the mundane could become, how safe the world seemed. And she didn't know why she should feel her heart was both breaking and almost violently blooming all at once. All she knew was that she was very aware of it in her chest at the moment, the way one was aware of a noon sun burning down. It seemed inconvenient to possess a heart in that moment.

Jonathan cleared his throat. "Very well. Then it's agreed. We are friends, and we shall behave as friends behave. I'll braid your hair. You'll accompany me to gaming hells, horse races, whorehouses—"

"Jonathan."

He stopped.

Which is the first time Tommy considered that Jonathan was witty because wit kept all that was bleak at bay, kept it from sinking in. It must not be easy to be a Redmond.

And suddenly she felt a surge of protectiveness toward him. Toward this man who had volunteered to protect her, when no one in her life ever had. If only he knew how remarkable he was. How could his father think otherwise?

"I am honored to have your friendship, Tommy."

He said it simply, and with a lovely gravity that made her aware of the centuries of breeding that had gone into producing Redmonds. She knew he meant it.

"Likewise, Jonathan."

Sealing it with a handshake would have been absurd, and besides, she didn't trust herself to touch him again at that moment.

And as there seemed to be nothing else to say at the moment, and there was a ballroom filled with young women whose nights would be ruined if Jonathan Redmond did not return to claim a dance, he said, "Well . . . it's been a pleasure, Tommy." With only a hint of irony.

"Hasn't it? Thank you." She didn't add, "for the bone-rattling orgasm," because it was rather implied, and didn't seem to fit the moment's mood.

He just nodded, lofted an amused eyebrow, and turned away.

A peculiar panic set in as she watched him go. His back—the white of his collar meeting the dark of his hair, those broad shoulders that could so easily overcome her if he chose, suddenly seemed poignant and significant. She knew she was afraid. Of all she felt about him, about the tumult he roused in her body, and yet she knew the only real safety was distance from him. Still.

She opened her mouth. She suspected she meant to say, "Enjoy your evening." Instead:

"Cognac and satin!"

. . . was what emerged.

She clapped her mouth closed, astonished.

Jonathan slowed. Froze in place. Rotated slowly back to face her.

"What did you just—?" And then the comprehension gradually lit his face. His fingers went up slowly to touch his mouth.

And a fierce light surged into his eyes.

And oh, God help her. He knew what she meant. Cognac and satin . . . was how it felt to kiss him.

"It . . . just came out that way." Her voice was nearly a whisper. She was mortified.

He remained silent. Utterly still. His features seemed drawn tight with some suppressed emotion. Apart from that beam from those blue-purple eyes, so intense it made her breathless, he might have been statuary. He seemed to be searching her face for something, or compelling her to speak. God only knew what he saw in her face, apart from the color red.

And clearly he didn't find what he was looking for, because he at last he quirked the corner of his mouth ruefully. As if laughing at himself.

And gave a shallow bow.

And he turned and really did go dance with women who weren't his friends.

Chapter 18

THE MORNING DAWNED GRAY, which suited Jonathan down to his toes.

He arrived at the breakfast table earlier than he wanted to, and not even three cups of the blackest coffee made inroads into the lead that seemed to have replaced his blood. It didn't help that his father was already there, looking more alert than any man his age had a right to.

And then he realized why the coffee wasn't helping. It wasn't a *hangover*. It was a great bleak clog of thwarted desire.

Friend. That sexless word. A bloody pity, that. A bloody relief, too, in its way. But he'd meant it: He was honored to be her friend. For in truth, he not only admired her. He half suspected he wasn't entirely worthy of her.

And he'd never before thought of a woman in those terms, as though he needed to deserve her.

His father cleared his throat. "What's this I hear, Jonathan, about a Diamonds of the First Water deck of cards?"

Jonathan's fork froze halfway to his mouth.

He recovered swiftly, inserting his eggs and chewing them, then lay down the fork.

On the one hand, if his father had heard about it, they'd done their work skillfully indeed.

"What is it *you* hear about a Diamonds of the First Water deck, Father?"

"That you intend to choose a bride from it."

He was now staring at Jonathan. Examining him for more black eyes, perhaps.

Jonathan hesitated. "Oh yes. That rumor. I've heard that, too." A pause. "Where did *you* hear it?" he asked carefully.

"From your mother."

"From *Mother*?" He nearly choked.

"Who heard it from the Viscount Worthington."

"How the devil . . ."

"Who heard it from his wife."

Jonathan silently completed, *who heard it from his daughter.*

"Viscount Worthington said he saw you bolt through the ballroom last night. You left his daughter alone on the dance floor."

Oh, he *had* done that. He pictured it now. Jonathan was tempted to close his eyes. It was bad form, indeed, to abandon a girl whose only flaw, really, was that she wasn't Tommy.

But Lady Grace enjoys *walking*. Why, it's one of her favorite pastimes. She told me! She could have walked back all on her own. He was tempted to say it.

"I do regret that. It was admittedly bad of me. But I had an urgent matter to attend to."

"Too much ratafia?" his father said dryly.

"*One* cup of ratafia is too much ratafia, but no."

His father did half smile here. He didn't like to waste good gullet space on fussy drinks, either.

"No, but . . . along those lines."

His father chose not to pursue that line of questioning, perhaps because they were eating breakfast.

"Who is this Klaus Liebman?"

So his father had done a little research.

"A skilled printer who has developed the capability to print excellent color images in great volume."

"And what is your relationship to the business?"

"I'm the '& Co.' in 'Klaus Liebman & Co.'"

He had the gratifying sensation of watching his father go still.

"Are you . . . *working?*"

He said it the way someone else might say, "Are you . . . fornicating?"

"God, no. Liebman does the work. I simply provide ideas and support." In the form of cash and gossip and connections.

Which is all a gentleman should do.

His father took this in. A moment went by, filled with the scraping sounds of fried bread being buttered and marmaladed.

Jonathan knew his father was dying to ask about profits.

And then Isaiah could bear it no longer.

"How are earnings?" A brief avidity flared in his father's eyes.

Despite it all, something in Jonathan surged toward his father's genuine interest. Still:

"Modest."

Modest times seven, that was.

His father nodded, smiling wryly, as if this was only what he'd expected.

"Back to this Diamonds of the First Water deck nonsense . . . is it a publicity ploy for your business, Jonathan?"

"I suspect it may prove to be effective publicity." A tour de force of circumspection, that little statement. "As you said, I do have a 'certain amount' to recommend me, and the ton, as always, is interested in any potential nuptials. When you said: 'Dozens of lovely girls come eligible every day,' I thought, 'He's right! All one really needs in a wife is looks and breeding and preferably a title.' Surely one lovely girl will do as well as the next! And then you suggested I could always rely on the turn of the card for my future. I must thank you. Ideas truly *are* capital."

He didn't precisely bat his eyes at his father.

But he did fix him with his best ingenuous stare.

And then he sipped at his coffee. Somewhat noisily, because the absolute silence abraded his nerves a little.

Isaiah had frozen in the process of buttering his toast. Jonathan could see himself in the knife. Innocent as a babe.

"I never dreamed you were listening," is what Isaiah Redmond said finally, somewhat sourly.

"Oh—and you needn't worry, Father, about my caprices of character affecting my choices. Only women of impeccable pedigree are represented in the deck. We'll print our Famous English Courtesans of the Nineteenth Century deck in time for Michaelmas. Long after I'm supposed to choose a bride."

This won him, as he'd suspected, a censorious stare. "Certainly you have enough respect for the family name, Jonathan, not to print such a deck."

Always, always, always the family name.

"A jest," Jonathan said shortly.

Did his father *used* to laugh? It was hard to remember. He and his siblings all possessed senses of humor. Perhaps as a form of defense against Isaiah.

"Any progress with the Lancaster Mill?" Jonathan asked to change to a subject that was torturing his father, rather than him.

His father sighed. "I've invited the Duke of Greyfolk to dine with our family in Sussex in about a fortnight. We'll discuss his potential involvement in the Mercury Club then "Is the owner still proving capricious about selling the mill?"

"Well, the *owner* died without heirs and without a will, and dispensation of the mill is at the solicitor's—that would be Mr. Romulus Bean— sole discretion. And yes, he remains either deucedly inefficient or willfully capricious. I've requested a comprehensive list of the information he requires in order to begin purchasing proceedings, but he insists on feeding the requirements to us one by one. But we expect he'll be unable to decline an offer levied from the Mercury Club itself. "

We expect.

What would happen to Isaiah Redmond if suddenly the world didn't behave as he expected it to behave?

With any luck, he'd soon have an opportunity to find out.

THE COUNTESS MIRABEAU was dressed as an Egyptian today, or rather, her interpretation of an Egyptian. A gold armband wound round her arm, and kohl was drawn round her eyes.

Tommy wished she could paint *her* eyes with kohl, because the blue shadows beneath them were just a little too apparent, and some of the poets were incorporating them into the metaphors they were using to flatter her.

Her lids began to lower as she stood listening to Argosy describe the sort of jewels he thought would match her eyes. She staggered a bit, then righted herself with a start, just as he was saying, "Peridot, with perhaps a setting of silver—"

"Lord Argosy?"

"Yes?"

"I *am* a person. You may speak to me as if I'm a person."

She said it with an urgency that clearly baffled Argosy.

Argosy blinked. "Of . . . of course you are," he said soothingly.

She held her breath. Hope surged.

"That is . . . you're a *beautiful* person."

She whirled on him and stalked away. Leaving him as startled as if his favorite cat had turned into a snarling tiger.

She changed her mind and whirled on her heel and returned to him.

"Would you throw yourself off a bridge for me?"

"Would I . . ." He blinked. "Couldn't I buy you a bridge instead?"

She sighed. And then she took pity on him. "It

was hypothetical, Lord Argosy. I shouldn't want you to ever endanger yourself on my behalf."

She abandoned him then before she could see any sort of expression of relief cross his face, with a weak smile, and moved through the crowd. All those men pretending they weren't eager for her attention. And whereas before the exchange of pleasantries had been like imbibing champagne, she'd now lost her appetite for it.

None of them were Jonathan, and that was their chief flaw.

But the truth buffeted her at night as she lay in her quiet bed; she wanted him. More than she wanted to breathe. She lay rigid in the dark, eyes squeezed closed, imagining again his hands on her body, and she put her own hands on her body, an attempt to relive it, to soothe herself, to arouse herself, and burn away the need.

Nothing worked.

She'd done the right thing, of course. It wasn't as if there was anything to be gained but pleasure from it. And there certainly was a good deal to lose.

She just needed some air that wasn't being breathed by spoiled aristocrats and poets.

She wove out of the room, past the countess, her destination the windows flung wide at the end of the south parlor.

And then suddenly Lord Prescott stepped around the corner.

She gave a start, and clapped a hand over her heart. "Good heavens, Lord Prescott, you gave me a start."

"Miss de Ballesteros, you refuse to speak to me. You won't meet my eyes. And yet you accepted my gift, which has given me cause to hope. I haven't seen you wear it. Might I assume that you are overwhelmed, or perhaps still mulling my offer? I must know . . ." He extended a hand awkwardly, and then drew it lightly down her arm. It was all she could do not to flinch it away. "I must know your mind. Or dare I hope . . . your heart."

She'd known she'd be able to dodge Prescott for only so long. Panic knotted her stomach.

"I'm flattered indeed by your offer, Lord Prescott, and by your too generous gift," she began gently. "Was there a condition attached to the pearls?"

"Only that when you wear them, you will be mine and mine alone."

Oh. Only *that*.

"You are indeed insightful, and I must thank you for your patience. I am a bit overwhelmed, and I feel somewhat shy, you see, since the pearls arrived. My apologies if I have been less than gracious."

"Believe me when I say that I would be all that was kind and generous, Miss de Ballesteros. The finest modistes at your disposal. Your own carriage. Servants to command."

The offer had indeed been generous. It had in fact stolen her breath to think that a man had calculated her worth in pounds.

Her worth when she was naked and compliant, that was.

How did he know she wasn't covered all over with fur, or boils, or iridescent scales beneath her clothing? He wanted her primarily because everybody else wanted her. She knew a bit about manufacturing demand.

But he was a man of enormous wealth, and he of course assumed she had a price. For didn't everybody?

"I fear I would make a terrible mistress, Lord Prescott," she said bluntly, desperately.

He smiled slightly at that. "I doubt it, with your Spanish blood. I'm told your mother had quite a gift. And I am an excellent teacher."

She went still. And then a furious flush washed the back of her arms and up to her collarbone. Her eyes stung with humiliation.

And Prescott would likely interpret all that color as appealing bashfulness.

No one would ever imply that, for instance, Lady Grace Worthington's mother had quite a "gift" for pleasuring men. Or assume that *she* naturally would have inherited said gift. What the devil did that *mean*, anyway? No, Lady Worthington was a coddled, precious jewel, a commodity, of a certainty, but one who would go, in all likelihood, to the highest bidder, who would then perpetuate the coddling. She would know safety and respect for the rest of her days.

All of the men here viewed everything and everyone through a lens of class and context. Not one of them could imagine Tommy as anything other than what she was—an object to be adored and wooed and competed over, but certainly not a lady.

If Jonathan were here . . . she pictured The Doctor dangling from Jonathan's fist, and suspected something similar would be happening to Prescott right now, for the implication. For the offer.

Except that Jonathan hadn't the right.

He had no *right*.

She was suddenly as furious with him as if he
was the one who'd made insinuations about her
skills, even though presumably he knew better
than anyone. She was furious with him for the way
he kissed her, for the way he'd made her want him,
and for stripping her down to her true self, and for
making her nights sleepless ones, and for reminding her of what she wasn't and what she couldn't
have. And for making her days decidedly colorless
by his absence. For making her limbs feel like lead
today, because gravity was more punishing when
he wasn't about. Damn him.

She closed her eyes briefly against the image of
him walking away from her.

She'd *sent* him away.

And she wondered if he had no use for her now
that they were friends only.

But she also remembered the look in his eye
when she had. That watchfulness, that held breath,
that fixed guarded intensity in his eyes. He'd been
waiting . . . for something. *Cognac and satin.*

None of this could be helped. One of them had
needed to be sensible.

She couldn't leave her eyes closed for long, for
there Prescott stood, dark and gangly and maybe
resembling a marionette, but wealthy enough so
that his clothes were beautifully made and hung
on him properly.

And then she heard herself speak the words,
gently, as if in a dream.

"I'm afraid my price is higher, Lord Prescott."

"Than pearls? Than a town house? Than the allowance I described? Name your price."

She paused, and she felt oddly as though she were delivering her own sentence.

"I cannot be bought for anything less than your name."

It took Prescott a moment to realize what she was saying. And then his expression shifted subtly, and his head tipped. He studied her, assessing, re-assessing.

"I never realized that was your game, Tommy."

It wasn't an accusation. He'd said it thoughtfully. As if he was suddenly evaluating her in a new light.

"It's not a game," she said simply. "Now, if you'll allow me to pass?"

He stepped aside, and she made for the windows.

There wasn't enough air in the world today to clear her head or make her feel better.

BY EARLY EVENING it was drizzling, which suited her mood.

Tommy shoved her key into the lock of the Building of Dubious Occupations and turned it with an excess of feeling, pushed open the door, and let it slam shut behind her.

The entire building shivered as if Rutherford was in and stomping about, which he was not.

So intent on a cup of tea and a warm fire was she that she nearly missed the scrap of torn foolscap that cartwheeled away from her in the downdraft of the closed door.

She chased it, and bent to pluck it up and carried it with her into the rooms. She couldn't light the lamp quickly enough, and yet her hands were trembling, so it was slow going. And then when light flared into the room, she immediately inspected the foolscap for a message.

There was nothing at all one side of it, apart from half of an advertisement for Klaus Liebman & Co.

The irony.

She flipped it over, and there it was, the tiny message scrawled in charcoal.

She lowered it again.

A flush of a different kind started up along her arms, and she closed her eyes, and indulged in a tiny hosanna.

And then she picked it up, and closed her eyes, and kissed it.

For this particular message had given her an excuse to compose a message of her own.

AMID THE STACKS of invitations for Jonathan was one simple folded and sealed sheet of foolscap. He seized it. He stared dumbly at his name scrawled across it. Then he broke open the seal and devoured the words. There were only a few.

Jonathan lowered the message, struck dumb.

For a moment he stopped breathing.

And then he slowly lifted his head from it, blinking, surprised.

Could it be . . . could it be that the sun was shining for the first time in weeks? What other reason would there be for the fact that the dining room seemed saturated in dazzling color? And was that . . . did he hear . . . singing? Of course, it might be the residual strains of "Bah, Bah, Black Sheep" trapped in his brain, stirred to life again, like a fever.

Then again, it was entirely possible it was his heart singing. Poets had an unfortunate tendency to ascribe vocal chords to hearts. He was skeptical, but less of a skeptic than he might have been once.

And breathing . . . breathing was suddenly a fresh new pleasure. As if he was doing it for the very first time. The air was wine. He read the message again:

> *I'm contemplating something dangerous. I did promise to tell you. Care to be involved? Come today?*
>
>
> *—Your friend, T*

"What are you smiling at, Jonathan?"

His father sounded amused.

Jonathan gave a start.

He'd completely forgotten his father was sitting at the table with him. And not even the fact that he sat at the table breathing the same air could affect his mood. His father looked more colorful, too, somehow.

"It's a beautiful day," he said simply, at last.

His father swiveled toward the window, saw clouds outside and frowned faintly.

But when he swiveled back to Jonathan again, Jonathan's chair was empty, and still rocking a little from the speed with which he'd abandoned it.

Chapter 19

THEY DIDN'T SPEAK WHEN she opened the door to his knock.

They didn't speak on the stairs, or in the passageway.

And for an absurdly long, ever-so-awkward moment after she'd let him into her rooms, where a fire crackled and a pot of tea sat in the center of the little table, neither of them spoke a word.

At last he said softly. "Miss me, Tommy?"

A little silence.

"Didn't we *just* see each other?" She took pains to sound bored.

He gave her a slow smile.

Then Jonathan mouthed, "Liar."

She smiled and turned away abruptly, and she seemed, of all things, to be fidgeting. Two little spots of color sat high on her cheeks.

"You're looking well," she said politely. Which was funny, since she wasn't looking at him at all.

"Of course I am. Why don't you tell me what dangerous thing you're contemplating now?"

And so while Rutherford thumped overhead, Jonathan listened to Tommy explain what they were about to do.

It was sheer lunacy, of course. He'd expected nothing less of her.

Mad, dangerous, foolish. Quixotic.

After a long silence to absorb, through which he surreptitiously examined her for new bullet wounds or any other marks and was relieved beyond all proportion not to find any, the first question out of his mouth was, "Should I wear an eyepatch?"

Clearly he'd already decided to do it.

"An *eyepatch?*"

"Or a wig?"

"Do you mean . . . like a barrister?"

He sighed exasperatedly. "For God's sake. I resemble my father. At least somewhat. He's hardly an anonymous man. A mill overlooker with a particle of intelligence might be able to piece together who I am."

"Firstly, overlookers aren't known for their particles of intelligence, particularly this one. And no one on the face of the earth would believe him even if he did piece that together. For what is the nature of your reputation, Mr. Redmond? In what context are you usually found? You see, everything has its uses, including a reputation you've found somewhat burdensome of late. Is it that you want to wear a disguise?" she asked indulgently. "Will you sulk if you aren't allowed to wear one?"

He regarded her in cold silence for a moment.

"I don't have to do this at all," he proffered casually. It was very much a threat.

She arranged her features in an unconvincing expression of contrition. "I think it will all happen so quickly—it needs to happen so quickly— a disguise will not be necessary. In fact, I think it will be most effective if you look exactly the way you do now."

"Which is how . . . ? Desire incarnate?"

She just smiled and slowly shook her head, but her cheeks did look a trifle rosier. "Like a *Gentleman*, with a capital '*G*.'"

"And what will you be do doing while I'm inspecting the mill at the behest of the owner?"

The mill, ironically, his father wanted more than anything else in the world, and wanted more by the day, simply because he couldn't have it. The mill the Duke of Greyfolk wanted.

"Distracting the overlooker."

"And how will you distract the overlooker?"

"Oh, *please*," she laughed merrily.

She *was* distracting. He'd allow her that.

IT CAME INTO view about two hours into the ride in a hired carriage driven by someone Tommy trusted to take their money and keep his mouth shut: a behemoth of orderly red brick glowing in the sun, five stories spread out over a pretty acreage of trees and meadow, narrow rectangular windows punched in at even intervals. A benign enough looking building. Chimneys endlessly fed wisps of black smoke into the blue sky. The river shimmered alongside. A building that must have been the dormitory for the children sat a good hundred feet or more behind it. Always locked, Tommy told him. Always locked and guarded. And surrounded by a wall nearly twice the height of Jonathan.

The sort of wall no child could ever hope to scale.

It represented everything his father lived for: progress, potential, and profit.

Immense profit. And Jonathan felt his own blood quicken with the potential of it, and a tingling begin in his fingertips.

He saw it as clearly as they did.

But surely profits fueled by the sweat and blood of children were tainted.

Surely they didn't *have* to be fueled by the blood of children?

And did his father know that? Did the duke? Did they care?

The boy was named Charlemagne Wilkerson. Charlie for short. He was eight or nine years old, perhaps younger—no one knew for certain, Tommy told him. A scrappy little fellow who'd been beaten by the overlooker more than once. According to her contact at the Bethnal Green workhouse, Charlie been sold to the mill owner less than a year ago, and worked as a scavenger or a piecer, which meant he scrambled under the gigantic, incessantly moving frames and wheels with a brush sweep, beneath the wheels of the machines, lest little bits of cotton clog them and bring commerce to an untimely halt, or he ran between frames to tie the snapped bits of cotton.

Scavengers, Tommy explained, often must throw their bodies flat on the floor to avoid being scalped or run over by the wheels. That's why the littlest ones were used.

Many a child had been scalped that way.

"So be careful how you get his attention. You could kill him."

He was humbled by the things she knew.

"I might say the same of you," Jonathan said. Except the "him" he was referring to was the overlooker.

She knew it, and gave a smile that bordered on the sultry. *Her* job was to keep the overlooker, a nasty piece of work named Mr. Tabthwaite, occupied, if not enthralled, while Jonathan found Charlie somewhere on the factory floor and slipped out of the building, child in tow.

What could *possibly* go awry?

Fortunately, he had a plan. Or rather, two plans.

The first was a mad plan, but could nevertheless work well, indeed. He had little Sally to thank for the inspiration.

The second plan involved his pistol and a lot of running and dodging.

And he wasn't certain whether he was doing this mad thing for Tommy, or doing this for himself, or whether there was any distinction anymore.

All he knew was that he wanted her to admire him the way he admired her. He wanted to be brave for her.

"Good day, Mr. Tabthwaite. I'm Lord Ludlow of the Edinburgh College of Physicians, and this is my assistant, Miss Edwina Burns. You'll be expecting us, I believe."

He concluded this with a faint, politely imperious smile.

The man stared up at him. One of his eyes was strikingly smaller than the other, and both had that peculiar, flat lightlessness of the truly cruel. His eyebrows were half an inch wide, and curled in an unruly fashion upward, like the antenna on an insect. Tabthwaite's hair was oddly glorious, a mane of carefully tended brown.

Jonathan was reminded of the children who were scalped beneath the machinery.

He saw Tommy's eyes looking in the same direction.

"I dinna ken a Lord Ludlow." Tabthwaite said it with an abruptness that bordered on insolence, but his eyes kept wandering toward Tommy, as surely as if they were magnetized. Tommy rewarded him with a smile that was as demure as her neckline was dangerous. The man smiled faintly in response. A reflex. It was what men did when they saw Tommy.

He jerked his attention forcefully back to Jonathan when Jonathan spoke again.

"Mr. Romulus Bean, Esquire, your current employer and payer of your wages, will have informed you of our visit today. He is the very model of efficiency, so I'm certain he has done his duty. Perhaps it has slipped your mind?" It had the faintest whiff of censure, delivered in cutting aristocratic tones. "Miss Burns, if you would please make a note of this."

The name "Romulus Bean" straightened the man's spine. He cleared his throat.

"What be the nature of your visit, Lord Ludlow? Are you wishin' to buy the mill, then?"

"Miss Burns," Jonathan said crisply. "If you would show Mr. Tabthwaite our papers."

Tommy produced a sheaf of frightfully crisp and official looking documents, decorated with gleaming seals, enormous important looking signatures scrawled at the bottoms, and thrust them into the hands of Tabthwaite, who accepted them, puzzled.

"By order of his majesty, we are here on a matter of public safety. Our visit regards a redheaded boy named Charlemagne Wilkerson, who is employed here. Our research has revealed that he is the last surviving member of a Scottish village, which perished in a strain of plague known as Chrysanthia Pestis, or the Violet Plague. You may know it more commonly as the collywobbles. Young Mr. Wilkerson is most certainly a carrier of the disease."

Both of the man's eyes widened in alarm.

"Collywobbles . . . but . . . but . . . I thought collywobbles was just nervous stomach!"

So *that's* what it was.

"Perhaps the word has evolved to mean such in your part of England," Jonathan said smoothly. "I can assure you the condition is quite serious, name aside. Will you tell me, please, on what floor of the factory I can find young Charlemagne? I've been instructed to remove him from the premises for quarantine and study."

Tabthwaite frowned.

"Are you . . . reluctant, Mr. Tabthwaite, to cooperate with an order issued by Mr. Romulus Bean?" Jonathan said it softly. It was a threat.

"I'll . . . I'll go and fetch Charlie for you."

"With all due respect, Mr. Tabthwaite, it's wisest

you stay here. If you haven't yet had the collywobbles, it is best not to put yourself at any further risk, despite the fact that you've experienced some exposure. Miss Burns will stay behind to query you about the child whilst I fetch him. I am quite immune, having been exposed some years ago, and I am familiar with the care needed to transport the diseased."

"W-w-w-hat about the *rest* of the children?" Mr. Tabthwaite was genuinely alarmed now. "What about *me*?"

"If it's all the same to you, sir, if you would be so kind as to watch them for symptoms. A tendency to rebellion is one of the early signs. This tendency is caused by a fever of the brain."

"That be Charlie! Many's the day I've broken a stick over the boy's hide. Was forced to knock him senseless once."

Jonathan went silent. *How very, very much I would like to break a stick over your hide and knock you senseless now.*

Mr. Tabthwaite must have sensed his thoughts, for he took an unconscious, infinitesimal step back. The hands holding his sheaf of entirely invented official documents rattled a little in his hands.

"The trouble with beating the infected child," Jonathan mused, "is that the disease tends to rise from the child's skin and attach to whoever's nearest. We therefore don't recommend beating an infected child as a form of discipline, unless one is eager for an early death. And undue exertion, such as laying a stick upon a recalcitrant child, can cause a latent disease to manifest. In other words,

if you beat a child, you are more likely to fall prey
to the disease, and it kills adults more quickly than
it does children. Now, on which floor will I find
Charlemagne?"

It was a moment before the man could speak.

"Third," Tabthwaite choked after a hesitation.
His face was gray now. "The stairs be that way.
He's a ginger. Freckles, too."

Jonathan nodded shortly, then turned to Tommy.
"Miss Burns, will you kindly stay here and complete our query while I fetch the subject?"

"Yes, of course, my lord," she said very quietly,
eyes downcast.

Which was the most abiding Tommy had ever
sounded.

Fifteen minutes, they'd agreed. She'd distract
him for fifteen minutes, then return to the carriage.

Blood singing with the first triumph, Jonathan
made for the stairs.

THE DIN WAS extraordinary; the movement dizzied, then mesmerized, then stunned. The air was
choked with dust and the smell of oiled machinery.
Dozens if not hundreds of children, and men and
women, too, moved like buzzing bees among long
row upon row of huge spinning frames. The spin-
dles were a rotating blur as the wheeled frames ad-
vanced toward each other on great iron tracks and
drew back again, as if in the throes of a perpetual
reel. And in this way cotton became yarn, and yarn
became weaving material, and thusly everyone in
England would have their tablecloths and sheets
and underclothes.

How had he come to this? How had he become a man who sang "Baa, Baa, Black Sheep" at the command of a little girl and was now about to steal a child from the din of a cotton mill? The answer was "Tommy."

Jonathan held his breath as one of the children darted forward and quickly knotted the pieces of thread broken under the strain of the stretching and twisting. Stunningly deft work. One moment of miscalculation and he'd be crushed beneath the wheels or between the moving frames.

The child had bright red hair.

Jonathan was unnoticed as of yet by the workers, many of whom looked away from their work at their peril.

But the boy glanced up, saw him, and bolted for him, darting like a hummingbird in flight among the machinery and other laborers.

He planted his hands on his hips. "You be Mr. Friend? Sent by Tommy?"

"Charlie!" a man bellowed from the opposite end of the row.

"Aye, Charlie. We must go now. Quickly." Jonathan seized him by the hand and hauled him back the way he'd come.

They were halfway down the first flight of stairs when they heard another faint: "*Charlie!*"

"Here, guv." Charlie led him toward a long passage, at the end of which was a narrow wooden door. The one that allegedly led out to the river.

Jonathan lunged for the knob. Bloody *hell*. The bloody thing was locked.

"Stand back, Charlie."

Jonathan inhaled, and then drew back his foot and threw his entire weight into a kick.

It splintered in the frame with a crash, and they both jumped away with a wince. Jonathan pushed it. It gave.

Charlie gave a delighted hoot.

Jonathan surveyed the destruction with grim satisfaction." And now we run."

THE EXPANSE OF grassland and shrubbery between them and the mill seemed to stretch and grow and unfurl like the Atlantic Ocean itself. The boy was quick but his legs were short, and he took four or five steps to Jonathan's every one. And then Charlie halted and yanked his hand away.

Which is when Jonathan saw raw abrasions on both of the little boy's wrists.

In very nearly the same place as those scars of Tommy's.

His stomach flipped unpleasantly with a dark suspicion.

"I needs to take a piss. Now." Charlie planted his hands on his hips and squinted up at Jonathan. He was about four feet tall and feisty and rude as a fighting cock.

Oh . . . Christ. Jonathan swiveled his head around. "Well, all right then. Do you see a likely bush? We need to hurry, Charlie."

Charlie pointed to a ragged hawthorn near the river. Jonathan turned his back.

The boy unfastened his trousers and turned, aiming for the shrub.

"Charlie . . . how did you get those wounds on your wrists?"

"They chained me up, di'nt they? Bracelets round me ankles and wrists."

Jonathan's stomach clenched. He tried to keep his voice casual. "Do they chain everyone?"

"Just the ones what run," Charlie said offhandedly. "I got out the gate quick like, when it was open to a farmer's cart, got as far as the road before they caught me. Legs too short." He looked down with grim resignation. "They'll be longer than yours when I'm grown. I'll be taller than you by far. Drained!" he announced at last, whirled, buttoning his trousers.

"Excellent. Can you run, Charlie? Would you like me to carry you?"

"Carry! I've legs, don't I?" Nick said scornfully. "I'm no' a baby, ye daft cove. I'll walk on me own. And you smell!"

"*You* smell," Jonathan said.

Well, he wasn't proud of it. It was a reflex.

Charlie snorted at that. "You smell *worse*."

Jonathan knew from experience this sort of disagreement could go on forever.

"It's a shame you want to walk, Charlie. I might have given you a ride on my back . . . like a horse."

Charlie turned to him, his eyes huge and disbelieving. Then he turned away again, and shook his head to and fro.

"Bedlam," he muttered, throwing his arms outward as if to an invisible audience, shooting Jonathan a sidelong look. "Ye belong in with the loobies. Like a horse! A grown man run like an *'orse*," He snorted. "I've 'eard it all, now, I 'ave."

Jonathan shrugged.

They walked on. Charlie took about four steps to Jonathan's one. He counted now. He couldn't tell what was louder—his heartbeat or his footsteps.

"Ye'd . . . gallop, like?" Charlie said with studied casualness.

"I'd gallop."

"And I can kick you? And shout 'Hi-*ya! Ya! Ya!*'"

"No. You may not shout or whoop at all. And if you kick me, I'll buck you off immediately."

But his palms had begun to sweat when Charlie conceded grandly, "Very well. Mayhap I'll give it a go."

Jonathan dropped to a crouch. "Loop your arms *loosely* around my neck. I'll hold beneath your knees. NOW!"

Amazingly, the child did as told, too surprised to do anything else, probably.

And Jonathan took off at a run.

Charlie predictably whooped.

"I SAID NO WHOOPING."

Good God, he sounded like his father.

He ran like a racehorse spooked by a hornet with a smelly, delighted, and terrified little boy clinging to his back, and soon the carriage and—oh, sweet merciful Mary—Tommy, too, came into view. Tommy, who was hopping up and down anxiously, as if to encourage them to go faster.

But when she saw them she burst into laughter.

He nearly snarled at her, but he spun about and tipped Charlie into the carriage, seized Tommy by the waist and lifted her up before she could squeak a protest, then he flung himself back against the seat.

One fist pound to the ceiling and the driver emerged from the stand of trees, and they were rolling onto the road again.

And it was Jonathan who whooped.

Chapter 20

"*Tommy!*" Charlie fell into her arms, and she buried her face in his dirty hair.

And the moment Jonathan saw the expression on their faces he realized he would likely have happily stolen the crown jewels for her.

That was a terrifying thought.

And when Tommy at last released him, Charlie had flung himself backward on the plump seat and immediately began swinging his legs extravagantly. He kicked Jonathan in the boot.

He eyed Charlie balefully.

Which only made Charlie grin, and of course, do it again.

"If you kick me again, Charlie, I shall not hesitate to kick you back."

Charlie paused in the leg-swinging for a moment, his eyes wide and fascinated and fixed on Jonathan's face. "I shall not 'esitate to kick you back," he imitated cheekily.

Jonathan closed his eyes and slowly, slowly banged the back of his head against the seat. Thrice.

"I wouldn't leave your eyes closed for very long,

if I were you. They get up to things," Tommy said.

He opened them. Fixed her with a stare so controlled and expressionless she fought a smile.

"It's a short ride back to London," she reassured him. "I know a song to pass the time. 'Baa, Baa, Black Sheep . . .'"

"Would you like me to kick you?" he asked mildly.

She beamed at him.

He turned his attention to the boy again. Charlie was still regarding him unblinkingly, with some fascination, and a trifle shyly now.

"Will ye say that again, wot ye just said?"

"I shall not hesitate to kick you back? Because I won't."

Charlie mouthed the words to himself. It was funny watching someone shape his elegant crisp consonants and round vowels, that distinctively upper-crust British he spoke that must sound practically like Norwegian or Chinese to this little boy.

Charlie tried it again.

"Very good!" Jonathan approved firmly.

The boy tried not to squirm with pleasure. "Will ye teach me to speak fancy like?"

"Like a gentleman, you mean?"

"Sure," Charlie said indifferently. As if to say, "If *that's* what you want to call it." But the little boy was no longer trying to suppress his avidity. His sharp elfin eyes were taking in Jonathan's clothes, not tallying their cost the way a thief would, but with the dawning of hero worship, and comparing them, no doubt. To his own.

"There's quite a bit to being a gentleman, Master Charlemagne." He shot a warning look at Tommy, in case she wanted to chime in with her droll opinion of just what that "quite a bit" constituted.

Instead of kicking Jonathan, Charlie began drumming his heels rhythmically against the seat. Each kick vibrated like a blow struck directly to Jonathan's temples.

Jonathan leveled his head up and fixed him with his very best quelling stare.

The heel drumming stopped immediately. Charlie's eyes were wide and uncertain, and he was frozen as a hare before a fox.

"Thank you, Master Charlemagne," Jonathan said sternly. "As our first lesson, I should tell you that gentlemen do not drum their heels against seats. And gentlemen always say thank you, even when the thank you in question regards the cessation of torture. And the drumming of a certainty was bothering the other passengers in this carriage."

Charlie probably had no idea what any of that meant, but he caught the gist, because he grinned infectiously. "All right, guv."

Jonathan sighed. "It's Mr. Friend, to you, Charlie."

But Charlie didn't do any more thumping. Luckily, what he did was doze off seconds later, feet shoved up against the wall of the coach, head pushed against Tommy's thigh.

She gently tucked her shawl around him and left one arm resting across his shoulder.

"That's quite a frightening look you've got in your arsenal, Mr. Redmond," Tommy congratulated in a lowered voice. "I think it grayed a few of my hairs."

Jonathan shook his head to and fro. "They're bloody exhausting. It's always 'don't!' and 'stop that!' and 'be quiet!' or 'speak up!' . . . they're *completely* anarchic creatures. *Animals* make infinitely more sense."

"Children?"

"What else!"

Oh, how Violet would laugh and laugh at him.

But then he looked at one of Charlie's skinny raw legs poking out from beneath the shawl, and his gut clutched. Yes, he would steal him again.

There was a quiet, during which their nerves relaxed into the shapes they normally took when they weren't stretched beyond recognition. Tommy gazed out the window, probably mostly sightlessly. Dozing Jonathan admired the warm pearl glow the sun gave to her complexion, and that kitten point of her chin, and the achingly soft slope of her cheek.

He'd been trying to decide whether to ask the question that haunted him. But he had no choice. It was an anguish in him. He needed to know.

"He has scars on his ankles and wrists like yours."

Her spine stiffened almost imperceptibly. "Does he?" She said it absently. She continued gazing with apparent disinterest out the window.

He was afraid to ask the question. But it had momentum now.

"Were you shackled at a mill, Tommy? Were you sold by the workhouse at Bethnal Green to a mill?"

She slowly turned to him. Held his gaze for a moment, as if to steady him. And said very carefully and expressionlessly, "Yes."

He was silent. Suddenly he couldn't hear over

a high-pitched whine in his ears. He supposed it was the sound of every cell in his body screaming in protest at the image of a little redheaded girl chained round the ankles.

Had she been beaten?

His stomach heaved.

Her wrists and ankles even today were so narrow and fragile looking. With their shining rings of scars, faint now. But they would always, always be there. He tried not to look at them now. He tried not to swallow.

He breathed in, for it was all he could do.

"Why is it so important for you to know?" she asked into his silence. Her voice was calm.

"Because you didn't want me to know."

He said it before he could think about what it meant. *Because I want to know you.*

It was too late. Deeper and deeper in. He was beset by a peculiar sort of gravity when it came to her. The more he tried to resist, the more entangled he found himself, and the less he minded the entanglement.

"And that wasn't because I walk about crippled by the trauma of it, or because I'm ashamed, or because it's so indescribably difficult to talk about. It's because of the look on your face now. They don't shackle boys who go to Eton now, do they?

It was faintly acerbic.

"Not as a matter of course, no," he told her after a moment.

"So it's a bit much for you to take in, I imagine."

He said nothing for a time. Just long enough for her to hear the faint whiff of self-righteousness in her own tone. Just long enough for the silence to become a whispered rebuke.

"I don't like picturing you in shackles. No," he said evenly. Quietly.

His hands were cold; his face felt stiff. He suspected all the blood had left it.

They stared at each other a moment as the benign country rolled by. They still weren't being followed by hounds or villagers with torches and pitchforks or anything at all, really. How easy it had been to steal a child.

A child that nobody wanted. Disposable as kindling.

Just like Tommy had been.

"Jonathan . . ." she said softly, suddenly. She leaned forward impulsively. And she laid her hand softly on his knee. She was offering comfort for what he had to picture now. And she knew how to give comfort and solace, in large part because of what she'd endured.

He drew in a breath, and sighed it out. And then he gave a short nod.

She gently took her hand away.

By rights they ought to be in each other's arms, and his hands ought to be sliding beneath her skirts.

She sat back again. That wouldn't be happening. They were *friends*.

"How did you go from that—" He gestured with an appreciative sweeping hand at her person. "—to this?"

"The exceptional representative of womankind I am today? Well, I was shackled after the first time

I ran, for they caught me. I was eight years old. But they didn't catch me the second time. I got away."

"How?"

"I'd diligently sharpened a twig that I found in the yard and hid it in the seam of my skirt. Little by little, against the rail of my cot. So they chained me up and the whole while I was chained I was sweet as candied ginger and docile and even pious whilst shackled—I really had learned the error of my ways! It really had been what was best for me! That sort of thing. They were *enchanted.* And after that pig of a foreman unshackled me with a great deal of blather about seeing the error of my ways, I waited for just the right moment. When no one was looking. And I stabbed him."

Jonathan was both horrified and enthralled by the story.

"Dead?"

"Probably not," she said indifferently. "I stabbed him in the thigh, which was as high as I could reach. Unless somehow a splinter found its way into him and he died a slow painful death from infection." She seemed to brighten a little at the possibility. "He screamed like a little girl and *I* ran like a spider out of that place. I remember hands grabbing at me; they missed. I knew the area now, and even though they sent out dogs, it was much too late. I kept to the river. They never saw me again. It took some doing but I returned to London—it's about a day's walking, and the roads are marked. I did have friends to look after me, after a fashion, and I knew where to find them—in the very building where I live today. I ran a bit wild, living from hand to mouth, on scraps I could steal, and on what charity was extended to me."

"And yet you don't sound as though you were raised in the gutter."

"Well, I wasn't. Not entirely. My mother once did the Countess of Mirabeau a good turn, and she'd wanted to return the favor. When she learned of were I was living, she got hold of me, made certain I acquired some polish, the sort of polish my mother had tried to impart, and a little education. I loved to read, and she found a few books for me. She'd like to see me settled, I know. But I think she has in mind for me a life like my mother's."

The unspoken words being, "But it's not what I want." He recalled her vision of a little girl running into the arms of a man at a town house.

"So the celebrated Tommy de Ballesteros is in truth a fugitive from justice."

"They called me Thomasina Bell, back then. And yes, I suppose I am. Are you going to turn me over to the authorities?"

"I might, if you force me to accompany you on any more jaunts like this one."

She laughed at that, knowing he was lying.

But he didn't say anything else.

"It's all the same, isn't it?' she mused. "If you're a mill owner and you've enough money, you can buy children by the handful from the workhouses. Society has to do *something* with them, so why not put them to practical use?" It was all said very sardonically. "I was promised I would learn to be a fine lady there, and I was bid to sign a paper and given a shilling to seal the bargain. And the so-called bargain gave them the right to me until I reached the age of twenty-one. And I was eight years old when I made that decision."

The thought of it was unbearable.

"It's wrong." His voice sounded gruff, abstracted in his own ears. Such pallid words. He wanted to unsay them the moment he'd said them. "There are laws . . ."

"But they aren't sufficient, and they aren't enforced well enough. What are you going to do about it, Jonathan? Destroy every mill?"

"Perhaps."

She quirked the corner of her mouth humorlessly.

"It's the sort of thing a man like the Duke of Greyfolk can influence," she said. "He could *help* make laws. He has that sort of power and wealth and position. Someone needs to make it *stop*." Her voice was quiet but fierce.

He noticed then she was gripping the bloody medal again. A good luck charm?

He thought he'd better tell her.

"Tommy . . . that mill is for sale, and The Duke of Greyfolk wants to buy it. As does my father. But the solicitor has the final say over who purchases it, and he seems to have decision-making criteria known only to him. So now my father is trying to woo the duke into the Mercury Club Investment Group, I suppose because their combined wealth and influence couldn't help but sway a lowly solicitor," Jonathan concluded dryly.

Tommy took this in thoughtfully. "Jonathan . . . you and I can only help one child at a time. But someone like the duke . . . with his power and name and money . . . oh, Jonathan. Just imagine. What if . . . what if I told him about what became of my mother, and what became of me . . . *surely* he'd listen. It would be unconscionable not to see him. It's time to stop being a coward." She glanced down at her medal.

God, how he hated the words, "you and I can only help one child at a time." How he chafed at his limitations, and youth, and how his ambitions were so hobbled by his resources. He could protect her from sinister doctors or from drowning in the Ouse. But he hadn't the power to change the whole world for her, and people like the duke and his father . . . almost certainly did.

And likely wouldn't.

"You're the bravest person I've ever met," he said with low ferocity.

Her eyes went wide at that, and then she smiled, a beautiful flush of pink entering her cheeks. And she turned away, abashed a moment, considering herself in this new light.

"And if you do go speak to the duke . . . I hope the meeting is everything you want it to be."

"I'll go tomorrow," she said quietly. He saw her knuckles tighten to whiteness over the medal.

Next to Tommy, Charlie muttered in his sleep, rolled over, and farted.

Jonathan sighed. "Did you have to rescue such a determinedly fetid one?"

"I'm sure *you* always smell like starch and soap and bay rum."

It startled both of them into a moment of awkward silence, the sudden inventory of how he smelled.

"You left out, 'and a certain ineffable manly goodness native only to you.'"

She rolled her eyes. But he saw the blush at her collarbone.

He was on her mind. Right there at the surface. Of course he was. For she was on his. More specifically, he lingered in her senses. And in all likelihood, at night, when it was dark and they were alone in their respective beds, she thought about how he smelled, and how his hair felt against her hands, and the cognac and satin—*cognac and satin!*—taste of his mouth. Because he knew he relived again the feel of her skin, the silken slide and give of it beneath his palms, and the way her body fit against his, how lithe she was, how wild and alive and hungry she was when he touched her. He hadn't touched enough of her, not anywhere outside his imagination, anyway.

And he didn't know about her, but he knew what *he* did while he was thinking of her at night.

When really, he ought to be counting blond heiresses instead of sheep in preparation for choosing one.

The silence between them was different now. Both more peaceful and less. He realized this secret of her scars, that unspoken part of her history, had created a subtle tension between them.

The remaining tension had to do with how he smelled, and how she *knew* how he smelled, and all the associated unspoken things. But they weren't going to discuss that.

Because they were *friends*.

"Jonathan . . . I know it's new to you, and difficult to hear. But everything that happened to me was such a very long time ago now that it's almost like a dream to me. And it's a blessing, really, in many ways. Because of it I'm no longer really afraid of anything, that there's very little I can't do, and that I'll do whatever I need to do in order to get what I want."

Her smile was serene. Her spine straight.

Jonathan stared back at her and realized: She believes it. She actually believes it.

Oh, Tommy. You're afraid of so many things, and you don't even know it.

And it was an odd moment, knowing this so definitively about her. Tommy was so very clever, so worldly-wise, so cynical. He was sometimes uncomfortably in awe of her. But there was innocence left in her: her expression when he'd dragged his fingers along her jaw, that fire and yearning and amazement and fear that she was human after all, and could get lost in someone, and could get hurt. Her expression when she'd asked him about her father—that uncertainty, that hunger to *belong* to someone. She was the bravest person he knew, but there was a world of people—people like the Duke of Greyfolk, or his own father—of whom she had no knowledge. Whom she ought to fear. Who had the impersonal powers of destruction possessed by an iceberg. She truly had no idea, for nothing in her existence had yet prepared her for them.

"Then I suppose it's best for all of us that what you want to do is rescue children, rather than conquer the British Isles and set yourself up as a despot."

But he couldn't help but say it gently, which won him a faintly suspicious frown.

"What makes you think I *don't* want to do that?"

He snorted.

But he had a terrible suspicion that if she should choose to do that, he'd help her.

Chapter 21

JONATHAN PEERED IN THE window of Klaus Liebman & Co. to make sure no Diamonds of the First Water were sitting in the posing chair.

And then he pushed the door open, and the bell jangled merrily.

"Klaus! I've brought you an assistant."

Klaus turned around, saw Charlie, beamed, then rattled off something enthusiastic in German. Charlie stared up at him with enormous fascinated eyes. The only word Jonathan understood from all of it was "kinder."

"He doesn't speak German, Klaus," Jonathan said wryly. "He's an *English* child. And his name is Charlie."

"My apologies. I am pleased to meet you, Charlie." He bowed.

"You can bow to Mr. Liebman."

The boy did, albeit a trifle cheekily. The way, Jonathan had discovered, he did nearly everything.

"Can you handle a broom, Charlie?" Jonathan asked.

"Can I handle a broom?" he snorted to his invisible audience. "I brushed beneath *wheels,* guv."

"Charlie," he said firmly. "A gentleman answers questions when one is addressed to him. Shall we try again? *Can* you handle a broom?"

"Aye. I can handle a broom." Still cheekily, but at least he'd looked the two of them in the eye.

"Thank you. Excellent. Do you think you can handle tea, crumpets, and guinea fowl for dinner?"

The boy flinched, as though he'd been jabbed by a hot poker. His eyes flew open wide, and his gaze swung between Klaus and Jonathan.

And then to their astonishment, his face crumpled and he began to weep bitterly.

Jonathan exchanged a bewildered look with Klaus, who shrugged uncomfortably.

Argh. He wished Tommy was here.

Jonathan dropped to his knees. "Charlie, Charlie, look at me. What is it? What is the trouble? You can tell me."

Charlie peered up at him with watery woeful eyes. "Dinna tease me, guv," he begged. "I'll be good. Oatcake is just fine. Ye needn't say the rest. I'll stay and work and be good."

"Tease you?" Jonathan was bewildered. "Charlie, tell me what you mean."

"There willna be crumpets or tea."

"There will," Jonathan said firmly. "But what makes you say that?"

"They told us there would be before they took us to the mill. Just oatcake, guv, and a bit of milk. Nivver tea. Nivver butter. Never anything else. Dinna tease me guv. I'll eat the oatcake."

Oh, God. Lies on top of lies on top of lies had been used to exploit these children.

Jonathan looked up at Klaus and gestured with his chin. Klaus turned on his heel and disappeared into the back room, where they kept the food.

And Jonathan contemplated Charlie. And he felt it again: that swooping sense of vertigo, the consciousness of what a perilous condition childhood truly is. And that willingness to trust . . . it was a gift. In a way, a child's trust blessed anyone to whom it was given.

What a heinous crime it was to exploit it.

You and I can only help one child at a time. He'd hated hearing those words from Tommy.

But she was right. One at a time just wasn't enough.

"Charlie . . . listen to me. You will work and sleep here, but you will have a comfortable bed of your own. You will have three meals a day and more. You will have bread and cheese and tea, and you will have cakes now and again. You will listen to Klaus and do as he bids and learn to be a gentleman and you will never be hungry. And you will learn to play cricket." Jonathan had added that impulsively. Because Charlie was fast, and wouldn't it be fun to teach a cocky, quick little boy how to play cricket? "Do you believe me? I will never lie to you."

Jonathan hoped *that* was true. He'd never tell a big lie, anyway. An important lie.

And he realized everything he'd just said was tantamount to a sacred vow. There was no way he could say these thing to this child's face and not somehow remain a part of his life.

The idea, he realized, wasn't repellant.

Klaus emerged with tea and what appeared to be cheese and bread on a tray.

"We shall eat, all right, Charlie, and come to know one another? And then I will show you how to help me here."

Jonathan raised questioning brows at Charlie.

Charlie nodded. He opened his mouth to say something, and belched. And giggled.

Jonathan sighed. "He's all yours, Klaus."

ODD TO REALIZE that it required considerably more of her nerve to go in the front door of this enormous building than it had to slip through a wrought iron gate at midnight, creep around the back, and spy through French windows.

Tommy's palms were icy inside her gloves. She gave herself a little shake, to rouse her bravado. She inhaled deeply and exhaled, and then she did again.

She squared her shoulders.

One would think meeting one's father for the first time was an athletic event.

If he would see her.

She suspected her name, if anything else, when she presented it to the butler, would at least rouse the man's curiosity.

She watched, as if in a dream, her hand reach up and grip the knocker.

And she watched, as if in a dream, as she stood waiting for the door to be answered rather than turning around and *fleeing* down the stairs again after she'd rapped the knocker.

She jumped a little when the door swung wide. "May I help you, miss?"

The butler was a tall, gray, impassive man with a spine rigid as a ship's mast. It was clear from the swift professional sweep of his eyes over Tommy that he hadn't the faintest idea how to place her. She was well dressed, but not ostentatiously so. She was young, but she wasn't the bred-within-an-inch-of-her-life aristocrat with whom he'd be familiar.

She cleared her throat. "I wondered if I might speak to his Grace, the Duke of Greyfolk?"

He didn't blink.

"And who may I say is calling upon him?"

She hadn't a card, of course, and this would reveal more about her station to the butler than her clothing.

"Tell him, if you would, that it's Miss Thomasina de Ballesteros. And that my mother's name was Carolina de Ballesteros."

"If you would please wait here."

She stood on the steps, and couldn't decide what she wanted more: to be let into the house, or to be told to leave.

The choice was taken from her.

"If you would come with me, please, Miss de Ballesteros."

And she was inside, and the door was closing behind her.

Her head felt a bit as if it was floating above her body as the butler led her through the house. It smelled of wealth, of wax candles and linseed oil and profligately burned wood. Light ricocheted from the aggressively polished furniture, which looked as though no one sat upon it. The house was probably filled with dozens of parlors similar to that one.

She craned her head as they passed a room of heart-stopping grandeur, carpeted in swirling gray and blue. Over a white marble fireplace that climbed nearly to the soaring ceiling was a painting of the duke. In it he was slim and dark haired, as he must have been when her mother had been his mistress. He wore an expression of proud satisfaction, while a beautiful blond woman rested her hand on his shoulder, and two little blond children, a boy and a girl, leaned against his knees.

She tripped over her feet. Then righted herself as the butler glanced behind him, one brow upraised.

Her heart in her throat, she craned her head toward the portrait as she was led up a marble staircase to a room.

"Miss Thomasina de Ballesteros, Your Grace." The butler bowed low, and ushered her inside.

He was seated behind a desk vast as a ship. She could see herself in it, and what she saw made her straighten her spine.

It was a moment before she remembered to curtsy.

He rose at what appeared to be his leisure and bowed only slightly. A begrudging bow, as if he'd only a limited supply of them to spare.

"Have a seat, Miss . . . de Ballesteros."

It was the first time she'd heard his voice. His Spanish—the liquid rolling treatment of that "r"— was impeccable. He'd served in Spain. She wondered if he spoke Spanish to her mother, and her heart gave a little leap at the thought.

"My father's voice is very commanding, with a gruff edge. Exposure to gunpowder in the war, you know. He

won a medal for distinguished service." She imagined saying this to friends and acquaintances.

Her thoughts were jerked back to the portrait in the other room.

He'd had a family the entire time. Another whole family. She had *siblings*.

She stared at him. It seemed impossible he was real, that she would no longer need to—or be able to—simply imagine him. He *did* have green eyes. Pale, not quite like hers, but nevertheless. He was a hard handsome man. The lines of him—chin, cheekbones, nose, lips—were all clean-drawn and unforgiving. As if life had worn away any softness he might have once possessed.

And there was no denying the voice was as impersonal as the cold wind she'd bundled against.

She sat, slowly, gracefully. She'd dressed carefully, in a gown with a subdued neckline, covered in a pelisse of brown, all of which nevertheless flattered her coloring.

"My daughter is lovely," she imagined he might say to someone else. *"She looks well in brown. She has my eyes, but her nose is her mother's."*

He studied her across the mirrored surface of his enormous desk. He was positively motionless. *Not a man who fidgets,* decided Tommy. He's very controlled, my father. He assesses a situation and then—

And then she saw that his knuckles were white against his desk.

She slowly looked up into his face, schooled to stillness.

He was afraid of her.

"I'm told I have your eyes," she said.

And at those words, he seemed to stop breathing.

And slowly, before her eyes, high, angry color flooded into his face.

"What do you want?" His voice was even and cold.

Her hands folded together even more tightly. "She named me for you. My name is Thomasina." The faintest bit of desperation in her voice now.

"What do you *want?*"

"I wanted to meet you."

The ensuing silence did nothing but turn her stomach into a cauldron. He did have a dent—a dimple—in his chin. It suddenly struck her as astonishing that anything could have dented the granite of this man's features.

The pendulum on the clock behind him swung with maddening steadiness. Emphasizing a silent few minutes.

" 'I've heard your name, Miss de Ballesteros. I'm given to understand that you're a courtesan of some type."

The shock blanked her mind for a moment. For a moment she couldn't feel her limbs. She felt heat rush over the back of her neck, over her collarbone.

"I fear you've been misinformed."

"Have I? How is it that you make your way in the world, then?"

"I'm an investor." Thank you, Jonathan, for the ability to say that.

He smiled, slowly and unpleasantly. "And what do you invest? The funds from wealthy, gullible men whom you've blackmailed or otherwise coerced into giving you money?"

She flinched. This was his strategy: attack.

And her strategy was to charm. It was nearly impossible to smile in the face of his smile. It had frozen her face, as surely as if she'd walked into a snowstorm.

"I know this must come as a surprise to you, but I swear to you that I'm here only because I wanted to meet you. I grew up without a father, and *surely* you can understand my curiosity . . . the desire to meet my . . ."

To know whether I have your eyes, or your chin, or your way of moving, or whether you have a facility with words, or if you can bend your thumb all the way back because I can, or if anything that is good about me is because of you. To feel as though I'm anchored to this world by a family.

And she'd never stammered in her life. He'd reduced her to a child. She failed to remember who she was before she walked into his office. Such was his power.

"I'm sure I don't know what you're talking about."

And that's when her temper slipped its tether. And she spoke with a clenched jaw.

"You left *her*. You left us. She was loving and lively and she taught me not to think badly of you. I *loved* her. She fell ill and died in penury and left me alone when I was seven years old."

She might as well have been shouting into a storm. Her words seemed carried away by the cold wind of his entitled indifference.

"Taught you not to think *badly* of me? Miss Carolina de Ballesteros and I had a business arrangement, which I concluded when I no longer had need of her services. What she allegedly taught you about me is none of my concern."

Services. Her mother had *serviced* this man, in his point of view. I'm a result of a *service*, Tommy thought furiously.

There was no give in him. She could feel herself almost physically weakening, winded as though she'd spent the last ten minutes pushing and pushing and pushing against something immovable. A continent, a glacier. He was a man used to shaping circumstances to suit him. Circumstances probably generally *vied* for the honor of pleasing him.

I saw you pull your trousers from your crack, you nasty old sod.

Two could play at staring.

"Do I look like her?"

And she saw it then: a flicker of memory heating the back of his eyes, a twitch, a darkening, a memory.

But he said nothing.

"Do I *look* like her?" This time she said it through clenched teeth. The arms of the medal dug into her palm.

Another of those supercilious smiles appeared. "Miss de Ballesteros, if that is indeed your name or who you are—"

She abruptly thrust out her hand, palm up. He flinched infinitesimally.

She kept her hand outstretched. She was proud of its steadiness.

He cautiously leaned forward and peered. Then adjusted his spectacles and stared.

She saw the recognition, surprise, flicker over his features. But what a very controlled man he was. Or perhaps it was just that his emotions were no longer elastic; he'd no choice but to snap back into coldness.

He leaned slowly back again. "Where did you get that?"

Just those words, delivered slowly and heavily, sounded like a threat.

"From you, essentially. For you gave it to my mother, didn't you? Because you loved her once. Didn't you? And when she died, she gave it me. She told me to come to you if I ever—"

She halted immediately. Her pride prevented her from saying anything more, because she suddenly knew exactly how the duke would hear it.

A cynical gleam was already dawning in the duke's eyes.

"Miss . . . whatever your name might be. I am hardly in the business of acceding to the wishes of opportunistic whores. It's very clear you want money. I will never give you any, because in my experience your sort would never be satisfied with asking just once. If you attempt anything remotely resembling blackmail, I assure you that things will go very badly for you, indeed. I sincerely hope for your sake you do not intend to trouble me *or* my family again. Now, if you will return my possession to me."

She took every one of those words as if they were slaps. *Opportunistic. Whore.*

My family. The pride and possession he'd imbued those two words with.

Her skin felt stung. As though the mill overlooker had taken a stick to her.

A heavy silence ensued. He was quite satisfied

he had, in fact, vanquished her. He was clearly equally confident she'd give the medal to him.

"It isn't your possession any longer. You gave it away. You could always, of course, try taking it from me."

She got up abruptly enough for him to flinch just a little. She stood looking down at him, the desk between them, and she calculated how quickly he could lunge.

And she knew he wouldn't.

"I thought not. I find it ironic that the hero who faced down his enemies in war and won this"— and she dangled it before him—"is so very afraid of me."

And she curtsied before she turned her back on him and departed, because God help her, she didn't want her father to think she was a peasant.

Chapter 22

"Jonathan, are you unwell, dear?"

"I'm fine. Thank you for asking, Mother."

"It's just that you've stared at your food without tasting it for the last several minutes."

Jonathan gave a start. He had been staring down at his plate.

His father glanced up, ascertained his health, glanced down again.

Suddenly Jonathan remembered when his father had taken his boys—Jonathan, Lyon, Miles—fishing. And his father had been so patient, so exacting, so filled with pride when Jonathan had caught his first trout. Learning to ride. Learning to shoot. Manners and comportment.

Regardless of who Isaiah had become, Jonathan knew he owed many of the best parts of himself to his father. Both directly, and indirectly, he was who he was because of his father. He took for granted not only his father, for better or worse, but his entire family.

And Tommy had no one.

He knew now why he hadn't been able to touch

his food. He was actually nervous on her behalf. For she'd intended to speak with the duke yesterday, and Jonathan couldn't bear not knowing whether this had actually transpired.

She could, of course, even now, be immersed in warm reminiscence with the duke, and seated at the table with his family, gathered into their bosom.

He doubted this.

He was actually *worried*. Not that she would take a sharpened stick to the duke. But that the duke had somehow taken a metaphorical sharpened stick to *her*. Which struck Jonathan as infinitely likely, because he knew how men like the duke could turn a single word into a weapon. *Droll*, for instance.

She'd borne enough alone.

He shoveled a few more bites of breakfast into his mouth, chewed with a rapidity that made his mother wince, and excused himself with graceless haste before either of his parents could say another word.

HE WAS BREATHING hard by the time he'd reached the Building of Dubious Occupations. He knocked. Twice. Hard. And waited.

Nothing happened. He pressed his ear against the door. He could hear no one stirring..

He did it again. This time, insistently, rhythmically, a fancy elaborate knock, with his fist.

The door was flung open.

She stood.

"Didn't you hear me knock?" he said mildly.

"My apologies," she said tonelessly, after a strange hesitation. She stared at him, but he wasn't convinced she truly saw him. When he arched his eyebrows, she stirred into life, and finally turned around and headed back to her rooms, leaving the door open.

He followed her inside. But her silence continued. It was an empty, heavy silence, as if she were a chair or a rock, something that had never possessed the powers of speech.

So he spoke. "Did you . . . meet with the duke?"

She stirred again. "Yes. I met the duke."

It was that same flat, abstracted tone. She was holding herself very still, as though if she moved too quickly in a particular direction she'd risk disturbing an injury.

And then she smiled. But it was as though her face was a frozen snowbank, and her mouth couldn't force its way into a curve. Quite the travesty of a smile.

It was really very alarming.

He didn't know which question to ask next, or how to ask it. Nothing about her stance encouraged questions.

"What happened?" he asked quietly. Suspecting he probably already knew the answer.

"What happened . . ." She twisted her mouth, and crossed both arms around her, and looked up at the ceiling. She inhaled deeply, then exhaled. "Well, he quite elegantly, mind you, told me how he felt about opportunistic whores. He assumed I wanted money, told me he would give me none because my sort would never be satisfied with asking just once. He sincerely hoped I wouldn't trouble him or his . . . f-family again. His manners are really very elegant, and he's a very handsome man."

He couldn't make a sound.

She seemed to stir to life; she smiled, and she'd tried for rueful this time and mostly succeeded.

"I showed him the medal." She uncurled her hand and it lay there like something crushed to death. Her voice was faintly wondering, almost amused. Full of self-mockery.

She looked up at him. That bitter, resigned, half smile knotted his lungs. There was defeat in it, and that terrified him.

He still couldn't breathe to speak. Fifty emotions pinned him like a martyr to a Catherine Wheel.

"I actually showed him the medal," she repeated, faintly, incredulously. And she gave a short laugh. The talisman, the lifeline of her childhood. Its power stripped by a man who could take away meaning from things or people simply by virtue of his title. Who could *take* things or people to use or throw away at will. "But I wouldn't let him have it back." Her chin shot up then. "You should have seen his face *then*."

He'd never hated himself more for being silent.

And then before his eyes her face slowly crumpled in on itself. Like a rose blooming in reverse.

And her fist went up to her mouth.

Oh God. Oh God, oh God, oh God.

He would much rather be flayed raw and dipped in vinegar than watch a woman weep.

Panic was the reflex; fleeing was the impulse. They so often wept for baffling reasons and at baffling times. God help them if they would *tell* you why.

She turned swiftly away from him. Clearly she

was going to try to be quiet about it. Or subtle about it.

And all at once it was like that dive from the bridge into the river. He didn't remember crossing the room. He only remembered his hands on her shoulders, turning her to face him. She wouldn't look up at him, wouldn't take her hands from her eyes; she didn't want him to see her. So he wrapped his arms around her like armor, making a shelter for her to fall apart.

She clutched his shirt and wept hopeless, shamed, wracking near-soundless sobs. Every one of them was a hammer swung at his heart.

She would survive this, too. Of this he was certain. He didn't like to think of how this particular wound would heal. What part of her she would decide to scar over in order to create an even more effective shield from the world.

He surreptitiously rested his cheek against the top of her head. That rich hair was too silky and fine and warm, and her narrow pale part seemed ridiculously pale and vulnerable as a fontanelle. Here, it seemed to say, was proof that Thomasina de Ballesteros could be broken. Cracked like an egg. That she was human.

The rage he felt then toward the duke was almost euphoric. Almost holy.

This is how crusades are born, he thought. With this kind of a certainty about right and wrong, good and evil, and the need to avenge.

And that's when Jonathan knew, with surprise and a certain distant fatal amusement, that he was sunk.

So this is what it feels like, he wondered. It's horrible and magnificent all at once.

And it's even a little funny, given that she doesn't love you.

This, he realized, didn't matter.

He'd never been conscious of fragility in himself. Before today he'd been well-nigh indestructible. Now he felt as breakable as she was, and more powerful than he'd ever dreamed he'd feel. He was in love.

She was breathing evenly now.

And for a moment he simply held her and she held onto him.

It might have been the most perfect moment of his life so far.

Then she sniffed noisily and looked up into his eyes. Her eyes were particularly brilliant green in their scarlet rims.

"I never cry," she said finally, bemused.

"Remind me to bring you a dictionary so you can look up the word 'never.'"

She laughed, and gave another mighty sniff and another sigh that sounded conclusive.

"Here. You need a bit of mopping up."

He both reluctantly and with relief put her away from him and fished a handkerchief out of his pocket. His initials had been exquisitely embroidered into it by his sister, Violet, who was meticulous about such things: *JHR*. He thrust it at her.

"Thank you." She examined it, running it through her fingers, admiring its fineness. Then she looked back up at him. "And oh, look at your shirt. You've a soggy patch. The second time in as many weeks I've gotten you wet."

"I suppose that makes us even."

She frowned slightly, puzzled. And then a gratifying array of expressions stormed her face as his meaning set in. Outrage and shock and then, bless her, always that wicked delight. She concluded by turning a glorious shade of vermilion.

"Jonathan! H.! Redmond!" she scolded on a scandalized hush. And with that, he'd effectively vanquished every last bit of her tears.

She looked away toward the window, flustered. He enjoyed that. "What does the 'H' stand for?"

"Horatio. Are you going to mock me for it?"

"Of course," she said, surprised he would even ask. She dabbed at her eyes and gave her nose a honk, then held it out to him.

"Keep it. I've enough wet linen for now."

They were silent for a moment, and it was a more comfortable silence than one might have supposed.

"Sorry I acted like such a girl," she said hesitantly, twisting the handkerchief in her hands.

"It was bound to happen one of these days."

She smiled again, the slow crooked one that was like a fishhook that yanked hearts from chests. "I haven't offered you any tea."

"And I've been holding a grudge about that since I've arrived. I'll make it."

"*Can* you?"

He rolled his eyes. "You really *do* think I'm helpless, don't you?"

He found a tin of tea and filled a kettle full of water, settled it on the fire.

"You frightened him, you know. The duke." He said it carefully. "His world is very orderly. He's used to things the way he wants them to be and . . .

he lashed out at you. He wasn't prepared for you."

"He's cruel. Really a ghastly man. He said such hateful things."

"That may be. But keep in mind . . . we all have different ways of showing our fear. Of adjusting to change."

And he thought of his father.

Jonathan, in truth, agreed that the duke was "cruel" and "ghastly." But he found he didn't want to take her hope away completely.

And in some ways it was his hope for her, too, that one day she really would have a father in her life. That the duke would perhaps magically transform.

He could all but hear her considering it. And he was aware of her eyes watching his every move.

She was steeling herself to say something. He could feel it.

"Jonathan?"

"Mmm?"

"Why did you come today? Was there a particular reason?"

He turned. Her breath seemed to be held.

Because I couldn't stay away from you. Because I couldn't bear the idea of you hurting alone. Because I love you. What would happen if he said it? The thought gripped his throat like a fist. He would likely frighten her away completely. Could he withstand her pity, and then the loss of her as a friend?

But if he never said it, he could remain in her life, and make sure she was happy and safe.

Jonathan Redmond, martyr. Who would have thought? No one, that was who.

What if she loved him, too?

Now who was afraid?

"I came because I thought you might like to know how well Charlie is doing with Klaus."

A celestial light illuminated her face. It was bloody breathtaking.

And it hurt in the sweetest way to look at her now. Will I only get to touch her when her heart is breaking? Will I ever know what it feels like to kiss her now that I know I love her? Because *surely* that would be a transcendent experience? Not to mention how it feels to be *naked* with someone he loved.

He could make her *want* him any time he chose, of that he was confident.

And perhaps . . . it wouldn't hurt to remind her of that, just a little.

How about that? He was the shortest reigning martyr in history. Because surely martyrs didn't have those kinds of intentions.

"Thank you, Jonathan."

"You're welcome, Burden."

She laughed, and handed him his hat and great-coat, and their fingers brushed. And the moment stretched.

And he thought, *go ahead and breathe me in. Starch and soap and bay rum. Want me. Want me.*

"I'm off to Sussex. Try not to pine."

And though at the moment it felt a bit like tearing off a limb, he crammed on his hat, and left.

Chapter 23

I‌T WAS A FAMILIAR scene: the long table set with a snowy tablecloth, the lit candles arrayed down the center, exchanging dazzle with the chandelier overhead, maids and footman padding unobtrusively in and out, in and out, for the endless reel of the Dinner of the Enormously Wealthy.

Isaiah sat at the head, as usual, his family grouped around him.

His family grouped around him except for *Lyon*, of course.

The Earl of Ardmay at his right.

The Duke of Greyfolk sat upon his left.

Jonathan had been in Sussex for an entire fortnight, spending his days riding, visiting his family, aiming dart after dart flawlessly into the board at the Pig & Thistle at night And in a moment of weakness, visiting the very bridge Tommy had leaped from, finding his way back down to the bank, staring at the water that had nearly carried away the Duke of Greyfolk's medal. She'd risked her life for that medal, and that man had eviscerated her with just a few words. And now Jonathan tried, but failed, not to stare at the duke. The man's heavy handsome head turned this way and that, bestowing his attention on various diners as if it were a benediction, and in short supply.

"I understand you've become a partner in your own concern, Mr. Redmond."

"Yes. Klaus Liebman & Co. You ought to see our decks of cards. They're . . . droll."

There was a surprised little hush at the table. The duke regarded him thoughtfully.

"Are they? I suppose it's is a fine thing for a young man to have a hobby. I see your bruise has healed."

"Bruises do that," Jonathan said cheerily. "Your Grace . . . I wondered if I could ask your opinion regarding a business concern. Given your decades of superior experience."

Greyfolk nodded, granting an audience.

"We've employed a young boy to do the sweeping and errand-running for us. Tell me, Your Grace . . . I understand you're interested in the Lancaster Mill. Do you have an opinion about the uses of children for labor? From what I understand the mill's employees are almost primarily children. Small ones."

"Well, it's an efficient system, clearly. Quite sensible, from my point of view."

"Efficient, Your Grace?"

Jonathan had an inordinately tight grip on his knife. *"I was holding it too tight,"* he imagined telling Tommy. *"It slipped from my grasp and flew right into his throat. There was really nothing I could do about it."*

The duke tipped his head. "Tell me, young Mr. Redmond . . . are you aware of the inner workings of a cotton mill?"

"Just vaguely," he lied.

"The machinery is such that only small children can help to maintain it."

"Is that so? Oddly, I've heard some mills employ adults solely. Were you aware, Your Grace, that children obtained from the workhouse are lied to about the conditions to expect at the mills? At ages as young as six, they're promised the moon, apparently, and then are made to sign a paper committing them to servitude until they're twenty-one years of age."

"They receive wages, Mr. Redmond."

"Oh, well. As long as they're paid. Although . . ." Jonathan furrowed his brow. ". . . It isn't wage enough to buy penny sweets, from what I understand."

"Jonathan. This is hardly lighthearted conversation, dear," his mother reproved gently.

"Jonathan dear, do go on," Violet encouraged. She'd been following this with increasing fascination. She sensed a windup to something.

His father was listening, too. He seemed poised and alert. But Jonathan scarcely paid him any attention. The duke was his dartboard this evening.

Jonathan's tone was deferential. "Well, Your Grace, you have children, do you not? Now, I understand that children who work for the mill are often beaten if they so much as sit down for a moment. That they're on their feet more than twelve hours a day. That they're given scarcely anything to eat. That they're caned and shackled if they're perceived to be misbehaving. They often lose their hair in the machinery. Or their lives.

"Jonathan . . ." his mother warned again.

Violet shushed her mother with an irritated wave of her hand. She was watching Jonathan in dropped-mouth avid glee.

And Jonathan was struggling now to keep his voice even and dispassionate.

The duke's eyelids were lowered. One of the beloved defenses of the Important, Jonathan had learned, was to effect boredom. Nothing more rapidly deflates a plebian.

"If you intend to be a businessman, you will one day come to learn the necessity for maximizing profit and minimizing expenses, Mr. Redmond. As I have. And quite simply, unwanted orphan children are an efficient source of labor. And as many of them are from a decidedly unruly underclass, it's often necessary to beat them to instill the necessary discipline. If they were not put to some good use, they would be running amuck in the streets and will soon fill our prisons and cost us money, rather than contribute to the country's economy. And if they should lose their lives through carelessness, well, it is a fact of life that others will take their place."

Jonathan pretended to mull this. "You're right, of course. And it's not just orphans who work for the mills. I understand that occasionally the unwanted illegitimate children of wealthy influential men end up in workhouses."

And suddenly the silence was charged with something threatening and dark. The duke had walked into a trap, and was only just realizing it.

He slowly straightened in his chair and fixed Jonathan with an inscrutable, searching stare. As if he was seeing him for the first time.

And the silence went on. No one knew what quite what to say or what precisely had happened, only that something significant had been said. He thought he saw a flare of swift savage emotion in the duke's eyes, but that could just have been the flickering in his pupils.

Jonathan gave the duke a small tight smile. He searched the duke's face for a twitch, a tensing of muscle.

And at last the duke simply gave him a slow unpleasant smile. The smile that said, *"No matter what you say, you can never touch me. You'll never be a duke."*

"If this is in fact true, what a fortunate thing that the workhouses and mills exist to shelter these children. Or they might meet a more dire fate on the street or at the hands of the law."

Jonathan stared at him. Neither blinked.

"Evil bastard," Jonathan said thoughtfully.

A gasp went up. Every head at the stable shot up and pivoted toward Jonathan.

Then whipped toward the duke.

Violet looked more cheerful than she had in weeks. Clearly she should have been requesting a little controversy when she'd been asking for marzipan.

". . . is what I suspect one might say to you if one *objected* to the practice of employing children in mills. Given that some minor reforms are in place, I expect some people do object. I've heard rumors of such a thing."

No one was fooled.

Jonathan didn't *want* anyone to be fooled.

"Jonathan." His father's voice was frigid. The voice of a man who would probably love to take a cane to his youngest son at the moment. "Child labor is a common practice."

The duke was staring at Jonathan now. Candle flames danced in his pupils. The effect was entirely appropriate. Jonathan wished him in hell.

"Is it?" the duke asked icily. And almost indulgently.

But Jonathan knew that tactic, too, thanks to his father.

"But surely Mr. Bean will sell the mill to you," Jonathan pacified. "Once, of course, you meet whatever his inscrutable requirements might be."

I will defeat him, Tommy, Jonathan swore to himself. *If it kills me.*

"Of course. Why wouldn't he?" the duke asked idly. "I can't imagine he's had a better offer than the one extended by the Mercury Club, especially given that my name is now attached. I expect he's merely somewhat inefficient, and hasn't yet considered our bid thoroughly enough to respond. Your father and I—"

"Mama?" Violet's voice was a small strange thing. Choked and faint.

And yet somehow they all heard it, as people will hear a foreign sound, a warning sound, in the midst of a crowd.

They all turned to her.

Her face was colorless. Her eyes were wide and shocked. "Something . . . something's amiss . . . I think we should . . ."

And then her head tipped backward, and she crumpled, sliding from her chair.

The earl lunged for her before she struck the floor. He lifted her torso, and her white throat arced back over his great forearm.

And he turned a taut face up to them. "Send for the doctor."

THEY SENT FOR the doctor.

Five hours later they sent for the vicar.

And they sent a somber and silenced Duke of Greyfolk back to London.

The Earl of Ardmay had taken up a position in the parlor, facing the wall, one hand against it, as if he could push back the encroachment of death.

Jonathan sat slumped on the settee, feet propped on a stool, staring into the space Violet had occupied just the other day, knitting something blue. He smoked.

A few hours ago he'd heard his sister scream, an unearthly, ungodly sound that made him want to drop to his knees and pray, or weep like a boy.

And then they closed the door and no one downstairs heard anything else at all.

The baby was early, and breech, they'd been told. But the women were privy to more of the truth, and the truth was clearly rather more severe.

Particularly since the towering blond vicar had been sent for, and had bolted up the stairs when he arrived.

Funny. He'd never thought of Violet as religious, despite the fact that they all attended church regularly. Would she care if the vicar held her hand while she died?

Miles sat next to Jonathan, similarly slumped. He was staring at Isaiah, who was uncharacteristically slouched in a chair across from the two of them. Jonathan longed to ask his older brother what he was thinking. Miles, who had been the one to whom the siblings all turned for strength. Miles, who had married for love, and whose wife Cynthia was Violet's best friend, but wasn't welcome in this house because she wasn't everything his father had schemed for in a wife for his son.

He'd warrant Miles was thinking the same thoughts about love.

And if Violet died, would Lyon ever forgive himself for not being here?

Would *Jonathan* ever forgive him?

Isaiah's skin had a grayish cast in the low light of the fire that no one was tending. Some life force had drained from him. This was one thing he couldn't control: whether the earl's heir would kill his daughter.

He loves us, Jonathan thought. He must. Why it should feel like a revelation, he didn't know. *Surely* his father knew about love. Had been in love once. Whether he loved their mother now was a mystery known only to his parents. Or perhaps only to Isaiah.

Would it take the death of one of his children for Isaiah to realize that love was the only important thing?

And then Jonathan remembered what that horrible Gypsy girl had said.

She will break hearts.

And he shifted in his chair, and closed his eyes.

A slow chill filled his gut. Oh, God. How many hearts would be broken if *Violet* died?

Not Violet, Jonathan thought fiercely. Better me than Violet. *Please not Violet.*

What the bloody hell use were predictions like that? He was suddenly impotently furious with that Gypsy girl. They caused nothing but havoc, her predictions. What use was it to *know?*

Jonathan had already smoked himself sick, but he still lit another cheroot.

Wordlessly he handed one to Miles, who took it wordlessly. And then he extended the humidor to his father, and his father took one, too.

And in silence they smoked.

The earl still had his face to the wall. Perhaps he's praying, Jonathan thought. Perhaps he's savoring every memory he has of Violet, going over and over them, like rosary beads.

And in his weariness, only one word came to Jonathan, like a prayer. *Tommy,* he thought, invoking what was good and real. *Tommy.* The word for love in his world right now. *Tommy.* And he supposed the word that occurred to you in your darkest moments . . . well, that word meant love. That was how you knew. And perhaps that was the purpose of dark moments.

HIS HEART CLOGGED into his throat when the vicar came downstairs to them.

They shot to their feet, all of them. The earl turned around. And Jonathan would never forget the expression on his face for the rest of his days.

There was something about Adam Sylvaine. The vicar brought a peace into the room with him, and Jonathan felt the edges of his fear and anger and weariness soften, blunt, as if the very presence of the man filled in the jagged places. A product of prayer, or of being worn smooth by the cares of others?

"Mother and baby are fine," Reverend Sylvaine said immediately. "You have a daughter, Lord Ardmay. It was hard and a near thing, and she will need to rest in bed for a while. Go and see—"

But the earl had already vanished up the stairs.

Adam Sylvaine watched him go, a slight smile on his face.

The three Redmond men exhaled. His father slumped, and dropped his head into his hands.

The vicar was weary, too, Jonathan saw. And it occurred to him then that the vicar's work—seeing to deaths and births and weddings and secrets and cares—was the kind that Tommy would have approved of. Doing good, some small good, one parishioner at a time.

He wanted to be a man she admired. The way he admired her. He wanted her to think of him as brave. He wanted to be *better* because of her, and for her.

He *was* better because of her. She'd changed him irrevocably.

And it occurred to him that the moments in which he had felt most worthy were because of her. Of comforting a little boy. Or holding her while she wept.

You need to care about something, Violet had said to him, to his outrage.

And now he understood with humble stark clarity what she meant. There were degrees to caring. And depths to his heart that might have very well been left unexcavated for an entire lifetime, if not for Tommy.

"Thank you for coming," he said to Reverend Sylvaine. Because somebody needed to say it.

"If I helped, I'm glad," Reverend Sylvaine replied simply.

"Drink?" Jonathan asked.

His father slowly looked at him then, a habitual warning. One doesn't feed and water one's alleged enemies was what the expression was meant to convey.

Jonathan didn't care. Adam Sylvaine might be an Eversea cousin but he'd shot out of bed in the dead of night to pray over his sister, and whether he'd helped at all, Jonathan would be *damned* if he couldn't give the man a drink.

And furthermore he'd just wed the most improbable woman imaginable, crushing the dreams of a legion of women in Pennyroyal Green and Greater Sussex. And Jonathan understood now something of the courage this must have taken.

He saw Adam hesitate. "Thank you. Brandy, if you have it."

"We have everything."

Adam Sylvaine grinned. "I suspect everyone will need a little of everything after tonight. And congratulations to you all."

Chapter 24

TOMMY WAS AN ISLAND in the midst of a sea of ambient noise at the salon. Baritone voices swelled and fell in social rhythms, laughing, lilting, arguing. She drifted among the people there not with intent but with instinct, riding the ebb and flow of conversation like a leaf on a breeze. Her smiles and comments were reflexes. She wasn't trying at all to charm. She didn't think anyone particularly noticed.

Image fragments returned to her again and again: Jonathan's face when he'd departed for Sussex—he'd stared down at her as if he was memorizing her, willing him to memorize him. As if it was the very last time he'd ever see her. His hands on her back when she'd wept into his shirt, the tenderness and strength. The surreptitious touch of his chin against the top of her head, when he'd rested it there. The moment where he'd taken his handkerchief and knocked a crumb from the corner of little Sally's mouth. His instinct was to protect the vulnerable. She sifted through these moments as if they were jewels in a treasure chest, each moment faceted, dazzling.

Because it was all she had of him; she hadn't seen him in weeks. He'd devoured her with his eyes, and then he apparently abandoned her completely.

"Miss de Ballesteros."

Argosy's voice was suddenly sharper. Which made her realize he'd likely said her name more than once.

She turned to him with some surprise, eyebrows raised. She'd listened to him wax enthusiastically about his new high flyer, and then received a compliment about . . . something. She couldn't recall.

"He isn't here," Argosy said gently.

And all at once the bottom dropped out of her stomach. She stared at him, too stunned to speak, and this in itself was quite damning.

"Forgive me, Lord Argosy, but I'm not sure what you . . ." Her voice was too weak. She heard it, and nearly winced.

"Redmond is in Sussex. Or at least, if he has returned to London, I haven't yet seen him."

She gave a nervous little laugh. "Forgive me, Lord Argosy, but I still don't—"

"You keep looking at the place next to me, as if you expect to find someone standing in it, and when you don't see him, your face quite loses its light. "

She was speechless. Imagine, Argosy seeing her as a human for the first time. Her feelings must be transparent indeed if this was possible, and that would never do.

The silence between them became awkward. And yet she could find nothing to say.

He saved her with a little half smile. "You could do worse than Redmond."

She found she was able to produce a reasonably convincing smile. "I think you're mistaken, Lord Argosy."

"I'm not," he said easily.

She was still too stunned to respond properly. A silence more honest than any of the conversations they'd held so far descended between the two of them. And while Argosy looked at her, she looked down at her slippers. And then she stared at his dazzling buttons, saw her tiny face reflected in them. She gazed unseeingly out over the salon, as if it were the sea.

"Do you know that I lost my first love to Jonathan's brother Miles?" he said finally. Conversationally. Without a shred of melodrama.

She studied Argosy, whose dark eyes were watching her, not without sympathy. With something akin to wryness.

"Surely I'm not your love, too, Mr. Argosy," she said gently.

He paused. He seemed to be contemplating what to reply. Such a gloriously handsome man by anyone's standards, and he likely would become more so as he grew older, and yet he moved her not at all.

"No," he admitted after a moment. "But one occasionally desires the feeling of romance, without the potential pain of it, and you, Miss de Ballesteros, are intoxicating after the fashion of champagne."

Ah, that word. *Pain.* It was what leaped out at her from that sentence. It frightened her. It seemed so inextricable from "romance," as he called it. He'd just delivered a strange compliment, and a truth. She was a pleasant diversion, anesthesia, a way for him to forget. She was that for many of the man here, but they likely had mistaken this for desire. Very like the way Prescott had.

Somehow she wasn't insulted by Argosy's statement. She liked truth better than she liked illusion.

She wondered if Argosy understood that romance and love were two different things. Love, she suspected, was warm arms wrapped around you while you wept your loss and humiliation into a man's shirt. Love was a man throwing himself into the Ouse to retrieve a scrap of metal and fabric that anchored you to whatever family you might have.

At this realization, a light seemed to fill her chest. She wanted to close her eyes to be alone with this newly discovered truth.

She wondered if Jonathan knew that he loved her.

Or even if he did know, what difference it could ever make.

She wondered if that's why he'd disappeared.

She collected herself. "I am delighted I can help keep your flirtation prowess honed, Lord Argosy, until the day comes when *love* finds you."

She wasn't sure if he noticed the distinction she gave the word. He quirked the corner of his fine mouth, as if he doubted the day would come. "Regardless, I expect we shall go on enjoying each other as we were, Miss de Ballesteros."

"Naturally. Thank you, Mr. Argosy. And you are quite mistaken, you know, regarding . . . Mr. Redmond."

It needed to be said, even if they both knew she was lying, and Argosy knew she knew that she was lying. It quite simply wasn't something she could or would ever admit aloud.

"Yes. Just as I'm certain you don't interest him at all."

She tried and failed not to smile slowly at that.

And another little silence ensued.

"Would it please you to know that your compliments *are* the finest?" she soothed.

He smiled at that, somewhat mollified. "I have you to thank for the inspiration."

She twirled her empty glass in her fingertips, and looked away from him.

"Does Mr. Redmond know what a good friend he has in you?" Her voice was low.

"He does. Even if it's all I can do to tolerate his inexplicable need to make money. I do understand it."

"From what I understand, he possesses a . . ."

A tall gangly figure had just moved into the room. Every muscle in her body went taut. Prescott didn't look at her directly, not immediately. Perhaps he hadn't yet seen her. She watched him speak to others present, watched him as he was deferential and charming to the countess.

She would need to make her escape now.

"Lord Argosy, if you will excuse me?"

And for fifteen minutes she was like her father's campaign medal bobbing in the Ouse, drifting from conversation to conversation just out of reach of Prescott, again and again. But she felt him on the periphery of awareness like an approaching storm. Not that he intended any destruction. It was just very clear that Lord Prescott was quite full of something, some sort of news, some *intent*, that would very much change her emotional weather.

She hoped it wasn't more suggestions about her potential sexual prowess.

A woman could only drink so much champagne without needing to visit the loo. And if she did, she would need to leave the room, and Prescott would corner her. But there came a time when she could postpone neither for another minute.

And predictably, as she returned from the water closet, Lord Prescott emerged from the shadows of the small parlor that separated the water closet from where the countess's guests mingled.

"Miss de Ballesteros. May I have a word?"

She halted, a good five feet from him. Just out of reach of his arms. "Lord Prescott. At least you didn't leap out at me this time."

"I never mean to startle. I hope you'll forgive me. It's difficult to find a moment to speak with you alone."

How about that. Then my plan is working.

"I shall be brief," he said. "I have given some careful consideration to what you said the other day, Miss de Ballesteros. And since my fortune is substantial, and I am not constrained by my family's requirements, I may marry as I please."

Constrained by my family's requirements. A statement that described Jonathan Redmond rather well. And very unusual for an aristocrat not to be constrained by his family's requirements.

Then the word "marry" knelled in her mind. She was suddenly paralyzed by what she sensed was about to happen.

"And if my name is what is required for me to partake of the pleasures of your body, Miss de Ballesteros, I should be pleased indeed if you would consent to marry me."

There was a buzzing noise in her ears. *Marry me, marry me, marry me.*

The words seemed to echo, double, reverberate in her mind. I'm going to faint, she thought. Surely this was impossible. Of all the things she'd experienced in her life so far, a proposal from a viscount who was a virtual stranger shouldn't be the one thing that caused it.

He stepped closer to her.

She couldn't disguise a reflexive flinch.

The ramifications swarmed her mind like bees. She would be Lady Prescott. *Lady.* She would have endless funds at her disposal, a carriage, servants, fine clothing, an allowance. She would forever be a part of the family tree of this ancient title; likely her portrait would be made and would hang over the mantel of his town house, or one of their country homes, Prescott wearing a self-satisfied expression, his hand resting on her shoulder, their gangly children leaning against his knees. She might even be able to persuade him to use his influence politically, to forever abolish child labor.

No more living in a rickety, thumping building. No more living hand to mouth, from day to day.

No more freedom, and no more excitement, and no passion, and no love.

And the only price for immediate comfort and safety was to lie in bed next to this man, and to submit to being touched by him, and to touching him, for the rest of her days.

To bear his heirs.

To marry this stranger with whom she'd primarily shared flattery and witticisms about the king's many indiscretions. She scarcely knew him. He of a certainty knew her not at all.

She could hear her own swift panicky breathing now.

One man might have offered her comfort and the shelter of his arms in which to weep.

This man offered her forever.

And if Prescott had asked a month ago . . . If he'd asked the day before she'd encountered Jonathan Redmond at midnight outside the Duke of Greyfolk's house . . .

Ah, but she was a different woman now. One kiss had changed that.

And a ballroom orgasm.

What made Prescott think she was worth it? She longed to ask. What was it about *her*, in particular? She was aware of her beauty, but then, the ton was filled with beautiful women, all of whom seemed to have danced with Jonathan Redmond at that ball. Was it the fantasy of her, that Argosy had described? The desire to win over all the others that every wealthy men seemed to share?

If only her investment in Jonathan and Klaus's business had paid off by now.

"Lord Prescott." Her voice trembled. She cleared her throat. "Your offer honors and humbles me. I am quite bowled over and flattered and quite astonished, truly. I beg of you a little time to consider your proposal."

He exhaled, and his head went back in some

surprise. And he was silent, mulling her. Apparently she'd done the unexpected yet again.

"Very well. But bear in mind that I won't ask again, Miss de Ballesteros. I know I don't need to explain to you that offering you my name and title truly *is* an honor and not without some risk to my reputation. I shall expect your reply within a month. Surely that is time enough to . . . weigh your other offers."

She stared at him. Well. She'd underestimated Lord Prescott. Or perhaps, more accurately, she hadn't fully estimated him. Simmering beneath that surface was yet another man certain of getting what he wanted. Because he likely always had.

He wasn't pleased at being made to wait for a decision as momentous as this.

The men who hold the power are all alike, Tommy thought. Astonished when someone cannot be bought.

She jerked her chin up high.

"Thank you, Lord Prescott. It's helpful to know that your desire for me will expire by a particular date."

"Much like the desirability of any woman. You of all people should be fully aware that a woman's bloom doesn't last forever. Nor does her ability to bear children."

Threats! How very romantic.

"Thank you for reminding me. It slipped my mind, temporarily."

He nodded, smiling a little, acknowledging her little barb. "Good day, Miss de Ballesteros. I am not a man without feeling, and I think I shall depart now, to recover from the decidedly ambivalent receipt of my proposal."

She smiled a little at that.

"Good day, Lord Prescott. Perhaps I should retire, too, to preserve my bloom."

He bowed and left her, presumably to collect his hat and coat from the footman.

She backed into a corner to wait for him to leave. She couldn't return to the salon, not in the wake of this. And she closed her eyes, and counted to one hundred very deliberately to prevent herself from thinking of anything or anyone else at the moment.

And she, too, fled, without saying good-bye, and darted on her labyrinthine path home, lest anyone attempt to follow her, find her, know the real her.

Chapter 25

"THANK YOU FOR THE marzipan raspberries," was the first thing Violet said when Jonathan was finally allowed to see her alone.

He paused. "Are you delirious?" he whispered.

She gave a weak laugh. His beautiful sister looked as though she'd been dragged along the bottom of the Ouse. Damp and white and exhausted and hollow-cheeked. But her eyes glowed, and there was an inner light to her. A sort of private joy. Imagine, a peaceful Violet. It had only taken nearly killing her to do it.

"Are you truly all right, Vi?"

"Yes, I'm fine, or I will be if I lie still for a few days and allow people to wait upon me, but that's enough about me for now."

Enough about me. Words he'd never heard her say in his entire life.

He was about to ask if she felt different now that she was a mother, but she'd just rather answered the question.

The culprit, the baby, was cocooned in white, and making little clucking sounds, waving fists the size of tea cakes. She was almost as formless as a blancmange, with a tiny little nose and mouth. Tremendously solemn blue eyes looked back at him. A thick fluff of dark hair topped her.

He peered down. "I'm your Uncle Jonathan."

She waved a fist like a maraca and gazed somberly as a clergyman at him.

He tentatively gave one of those little waving fists a finger and she held onto it, like an anemone.

"What is her name?" he asked softly.

"Ruby. Ruby Alexandra."

"I like it," Jonathan replied, as Ruby tried out her new hands and squeezed his finger.

"Ow," he teased her gently.

"Don't feel too special," Violet said. "She squeezes everyone."

He laughed lightly. He allowed Ruby to hold onto his finger. How silky her skin was. What a dangerous, amazing thing it was to be a baby. He suspected Violet and the earl would be the equivalent of having a lion and lioness for parents. This child would be safe and fiercely loved. *She will break hearts.*

"What was all that bit about children and mills, Jonathan, last night? I wondered if *you* were delirious. You sounded rather . . . impassioned. Almost as if you . . . *cared* about something."

As if this was a condition he'd never before suffered. She sounded insufferably amused.

He didn't answer. He couldn't answer. And he wanted to admire Ruby. Or rather he studied her curiously, since, if he was being very truthful, she looked more like something that oughtn't to have left the cocoon yet.

"I'll be your favorite uncle," he vowed.

Violet just watched him and smiled know-ingly. "It's a woman," she announced. And then a thought occurred to her. "Dear God, it's not Olivia Eversea, is it? But she's been seen out walking with Landsdowne."

He snorted at that. And ignored the question. But he rather understood Olivia Eversea. Almost . . . almost rather wished her well. He sent a silent message to his brother: *Lyon, wherever you are. Your woman is out walking with Landsdowne.*

He wasn't his brother, and thank God for that.

"Vi?"

"Mmm."

"I'm glad you didn't die."

"I love you, too, Jonathan," she said.

"Will you promise to stay alive while I return to London? There's something I need to do there straightaway."

"Of course," she yawned.

He believed her.

He lightly touched Ruby's little nose, because it was like a button, and how could he not?

And then he kissed Violet's cheek and departed.

THUD, THUD, THUD.

Tommy winced as Rutherford walked from one end of the room to the other. London on the whole seemed noisier than usual lately. But perhaps that was because her nerves were abraded since Prescott had issued his proposal, and her thoughts were an almost ceaseless cacophony. She tried to read a horrid novel loaned to her by the Countess Mirabeau, and failed, and stared at the swinging pendulum on her little ormolu clock instead. Perhaps she could be mesmerized into some measure of calm.

It was no use. She almost regretted knowing how it felt to be held by Jonathan, because now it was all she wanted. It was the only thing that would soothe her.

A knock sounded on her door. An urgent one.

She nearly leaped out of her skin.

A fancy one. A long complicated one.

She sprung off the settee and smoothed her skirts, scrambled through the passage and down the stairs, and peered through the peephole.

There really was no mistaking the tall figure that stood out there, despite the fact that she could see only from about his second button to his cravat. She threw all the various locks on the door, and swung it open for him.

They stood in dumb silence, absorbing the intoxicating impact of each other on their senses.

His expression when he saw her was at first startled, then rapt, and then relieved. As if there had been a moment when he thought she might have entirely been a figment of his imagination.

He was strangely pale and a little nervy. He plucked his hat from his head.

"May I come in?" he asked politely. When it seemed neither of them would speak.

She stepped back. "I . . . yes. Of course. You look as though you could use some strong tea. Or maybe a whisky."

"Tea would be grand." His voice was threadbare. As though he hadn't slept in days.

She led him into her rooms, and he followed silently.

Where *were* you, she wanted to demand, when a viscount was proposing to me and warning me about my perishable bloom?

She said nothing. She allowed the silence and the tension to speak for her.

He'd done a somewhat perfunctory job of shaving, she could see, and his eyes were shadowed beneath. But he was staring at her with an undisguised fierceness. She would have called it intent.

As though she was the heart of the target.

Eventually, it stole her breath.

She found her voice. "I'll . . . I'll make tea."

"Tommy . . . wait."

She stopped.

But he said nothing more. He remained motionless, looking about her rooms as if he'd never seen them before. He didn't sit.

"Jonathan . . . is aught amiss?"

"Amiss . . . Well, first you must congratulate me. I've a new niece. Well, my first niece, really. Her name is Ruby."

Joy surged in her. He knew how much he loved his sister, and a new baby was quite simply a gift.

"Congratulations! My goodness, she's early, isn't she? Is she beautiful?"

"She looks a bit like a worm topped with a quantity of dark hair. A little yelling worm with fists the size of tea cakes. Or rather, they look a bit like crumpets. Nose like a button." He pointed to his own nose.

She knew him well by now. "Ah, so she's beautiful, in other words."

The corner of his mouth quirked. "She has pretty eyes. Blue ones. I expect she'll arrange to be beautiful. Neither of her parents are homely."

"Blue is an excellent shade for eyes," she said softly.

He blinked. And the slow smile he gave her then about buckled her knees.

"I know," he said.

She laughed, suddenly weightless, and the happiness of being near him swelled her close to pain.

Another little silence passed. During which he continued to stare at her with intent.

"And how is her mother?" she prompted.

And here he was quiet for so long she began to worry.

"They called for the vicar."

Oh, no. Oh, God, no. Not his sister. Not Violet.

She felt the floor begin to move beneath her feet, felt a real terror that something may have happened to someone he loved.

And now she understood he hadn't wanted to say it aloud. It made it all too real.

She impulsively took a step toward him.

"And he's an *Eversea*, the vicar is—well, their cousin, really. That's how certain they were that she was going to die. It was bad, Tommy. Very bad, indeed."

His voice was a raw scrape.

Her heart lurched. "Oh, Jonathan. And she . . ."

"She lives on," he said hurriedly, emphatically, as if the more strongly he said it the more true it became. "She is, in fact, beginning to thrive. I expect her to begin plaguing me again shortly."

She exhaled. "Thank God."

"Yes, he may have had something to do with it."

The relief swept through her. She knew as surely as she knew the beat of her own heart how it would have devastated him if anything had become of his sister. And she wasn't sure how she could not have borne his pain.

How, in a matter of weeks, had his happiness become somehow inextricable from her own?

There was a silence.

"You ought to sit, Jonathan," she tried gently. "You look a bit . . ."

"Ill-used?" He smiled faintly. "Oh, yes. It's hard work, sitting amongst white-faced men doing absolutely nothing but bargaining with God, whilst your sister nearly dies in childbirth. I've never felt so useless in my entire life." A faint whiff of bitterness there.

"*Never* think that," she said with low ferocity. "If only you knew . . . how important you are. How *good* you are. How necessary you are. To the people who love you."

To me. To me. To me.

She didn't say those last words aloud.

But he heard it.

They were silent for God only knew how long. Assessing, thoughtful, watching each other.

"I couldn't imagine a world without her. It was simply impossible." His voice was abstracted.

The way he said it she knew, somehow, that what he spoke had everything to do with her, too.

Her heart skipped.

"And all I could think, Tommy, was . . . there are

all these children, just cast away as if they don't matter, used up as if they were kindling to fuel a factory. As if they were just that dispensable. And when you consider what it takes just to *get* them into the world . . . and how Sally has this dimple, and how Charlie is so *quick*, and . . . how . . . how can *anyone* just . . ."

He stopped. He took a swift breath and sighed it out. Steadying his emotions.

"Yes," she said softly. "They *all* matter."

"Life is short, Tommy. Short and dangerous. A bit like you."

She gave a startled laugh.

"Tommy . . ." He drew in a long breath. "Enough. There is something I came here to say."

Slam. Slam. Slam. Her heart could compete with Rutherford for thudding.

He seemed to be either deciding which words to use, or gathering courage.

She waited. On the precipice of something.

And the silence stretched.

He breathed in, and exhaled to steady himself.

"I've dreamed about the feel of your skin every night since I first touched you."

"Jonathan . . ." she said softly, startled.

"And what it might be like to feel your cerise hair trailing over my naked body." He took two steps closer to her.

"It's not cerise . . ."

"Sorrel then," he said impatiently. "And I think . . . I hope . . ." He paused. "I hope you feel the same way."

There was much that was unspoken, and she

couldn't blame him. "Love" was a big and terrify-ing word.

"No."

He went utterly still. "No," she continued softly. "I haven't thought at all what it might be like to lie completely naked beneath you, my legs wrapped round you. Nor have I lost a minute of sleep won-dering what your skin would feel like next to mine."

He closed his eyes, and his head fell back, and a great sigh of relief moved his shoulders up and down. He opened them again, and the expression she saw there nearly buckled her knees.

"Tommy . . ." His voice was a hush. "Tell me then . . . why the hell else are we alive if not for this?" Something—fatigue, emotion—cracked his voice.

It was like the moment she'd walked the railing outside of this building. Don't look at the ground, Tommy. Don't look at your feet. Don't wonder how it is that you're balancing so precariously. Just do it.

He'd offered her nothing but himself. Not a future, not forever.

She had never chosen the easy way. Safety wasn't her nature. And if love was so dangerous neither of them dared say the word, that was fine, too.

She moved closer to him, and let her head fall back to look up at the giddy height, the beautiful view that was his face.

His hands glided up over her throat, and cradled her head. "For this. This is what we're meant for," he whispered.

Before his mouth touched hers.

Their lips melted together. And little by little,

his kiss unraveled her. At first slow, then deep, so deep, then nearly desperate. She felt it in every layer of her being, until she was sure she'd been created by it.

She pulled away, ducked her head into his chest, shook it to and fro. "Jonathan . . ." Her voice trembled. Still a murmur. Still a warning.

But his hands were on the laces of her dress, and she didn't stop him.

His voice was low in her ear, like a spell, so close it might as well have been the voice of her own heart, and she was helpless not to follow its dictates. "Tell me you haven't thought about me every single night. The taste of me. The feel of me. The smell of me. Tell me you haven't been haunted the way I have."

"Haunted? Not for a single moment," she murmured, as she unbuttoned the first of his buttons. "Not by your smile. Not by your laugh. Not by how your thighs look in those trousers."

This won her a little smile. "I always knew you were a liar," he murmured back. He'd finished with her laces and had nudged her bodice down over her shoulders, and his mouth trailed to the slope of them, leaving gooseflesh in their wake.

She unbuttoned the second button. And then slipped her hands into his shirt, and oh, the wondrous relief to be touching him. Her hands slid over the smooth hard muscle of him and the crisp curling hair and the glorious heat. She lay her cheek against his chest and listened to his heart beat. She dragged her fingers down the seam between muscles that led to the buttons of his trousers. She had the intense pleasure of feeling his belly leap when his breath snagged, of feeling his hands tighten around her, drag softly up her spine, over the nape of her neck, leaving a trail of heat. She licked his nipple.

She suspected she *did* have a gift for pleasuring. But only for a man she wanted to pleasure.

"I am going to take you every imaginable way," he promised on a whisper, tugging her bodice lower.

"Excellent," she murmured. She tugged his shirt from his trousers.

"Right side up, upside down, sideways, sitting, standing. You on top. Then me on top."

"A brilliant plan." His shirt fell from his shoulders. Oh, his shoulders. The vast glorious curve of them. She couldn't wait to lick one.

"Backward, forward. On the bed, on the table, on the settee."

He paused, and lifted her dress off over her head with all the ceremony of an unveiling. It fell to the floor.

"And then?" she whispered.

"And then we'll do it all over again."

It was the never-ending story!

And yet when they were at last completely nude, he seemed a bit wonderstruck. A bit like a man who hardly knew where to begin, since the options were endless and he'd been presented with a feast.

So she wrapped her arms around him and pressed her body against him, and felt the jump of his belly from his sharp intake of breath, at the blissful shock of at last being skin to skin. She placed a soft hot kiss into the center of his chest, and then another, a little lower, and she followed the kisses with the slide of her hands down over his belly, then over his thighs, teasing, and then she cupped his swelling cock, and stroked it, gently at first, then enclosed it in her fist.

His breath snagged again; his head tipped back on a soft groan, and his hands played over her spine.

"Don't stop," he whispered.

So she did it again,. His hands cupped her arse and pressed her closer to him as he took her mouth again, and oh, the pleasure of it.

"I left out one way," he murmured against her lips.

"What's that?"

"Quickly."

His best idea yet.

He lifted her up, and she wrapped her legs around his waist, then looped her arms around his neck, and he carried her to the bed and lowered her down. She landed with a soft thump.

He gazed down for a second or so longer, baldly admiring her, his eyes dark and wondering. Long enough to make her blush. As if he didn't want to forget this moment.

She reached up for his hand and pulled him down.

Oh, the unthinkable magic of touching him and being touched by him. The astonishing privilege of feeling his body against the length of her body. She finally understood the true purpose of skin, of fingertips, of lips. She wanted to taste every inch of him, every hollow, every slope, but there was time for that later. For now they lay folded together, limbs entangled, his lovely enormous erect cock pressed against her belly, and kissed, and allowed their hands to greedily wander, to discover, purposeless, yet every stroke, every touch, every kiss, every breath, inflamed and aroused. His hands filled with her breasts, and he stroked her nipples until she was gasping, arching, *begging* for it. He slipped down the length of her and took one into his mouth and bit gently.

She threw a leg over his hip, and he teased her, sliding his cock where she was wet, and hot, and swollen with need for him.

"Oh, God, Jonathan. *Now, now, now.*"

He hovered over her, and she wrapped her legs around him. She didn't want to savor the moment of joining. She didn't want finesse. She wanted what he wanted, and that was to be inexorably, thoroughly claimed. She arched beneath him as he plunged into her, pulling him closer with her legs, urging him deeper and deeper. She reveled in how black his gaze went, how fierce, and how he closed his eyes against the nearly intolerable pleasure.

"*Jonathan . . . please . . . fast . . .*"

She didn't have to beg. His white hips drummed swiftly, driving them toward a shattering release. And it was Jonathan who shook in her arms, and her name that was a hoarse cry against her throat as he shuddered.

LATER THEY LAY silent and limp and spent. He'd pulled all the pins from her hair and combed it out until it fanned over the pillow.

"Russet," he murmured to himself.

"No," she murmured again.

He drowsily tangled his fingers in the length of her hair.

"No one has ever kissed me the way you do," she said.

"Have there been many?" His voice was languid. As far as he was concerned, it wouldn't matter. She understood this.

"No," she admitted.

"It's the only way I know how to kiss you. It was like I had no choice."

"What do you mean?"

He tipped back his head in thought. "What did Shakespeare say . . . something about a woman and infinite variety, or some such?"

She laughed. "Oh, fine grasp of Shakespeare, Oxford boy. You're asking the wrong girl."

"But that's you. Kissing you is . . . kissing you is its own world."

She knew what he meant. The fact that he could speak it moved her immeasurably and she could say nothing at all. "Have *you* kissed many . . ."

"Not one of them counted until you."

She was thunderstruck. She stared at him. Then she drew a strand of her hair over her face, moved and overwhelmed.

He peeled it away gently. He looked down at her thoughtfully for a long moment.

She gazed back at him. His brow furrowed, as though he meant to say something profound. She held her breath.

"Backward now?" he suggested.

"Are you going to call out our lovemaking like a billiards game?"

He laughed. God, how she loved his laugh.

Thud, thud, thud. Upstairs Rutherford walked across the room.

Tommy thought, how about that? I've added my own thumping to the building at last.

Chapter 26

AFTER TWO HOURS OF luxuriously lying with each other, Tommy had discovered more things. For instance, how his thighs were so marvelously, shockingly hard. A delicious benefit of all that riding horseback.

As her hand wandered down and between them, he optimistically opened them a bit wider, encouraging her to attend to the swelling between them.

"You've marvelous muscles in your thighs," she murmured, as she slipped a hand between them.

"It's true. Best be careful. If I close them too quickly, I might accidentally snap your wrist like a twig."

She laughed. She bent to place a kiss on that pale smooth place deep inside them where horseback riding had worn away his hair. She saw his cock twitch and leap a little.

"The thighs are all well and good, but I think you intend to go higher." He sounded distracted. It was an erotic sound. It was the beginning of him losing his mind with pleasure. "Perhaps you need a map."

"Patience," she ordered, but she bent and indulged him and drew the head of his cock slowly into her mouth. Then traced it with her tongue, and slid her lips down over it harder, and followed it with her fists.

He groaned. "Oh, God. Christ, I'm a lucky man."

His hands twined through her hair as she slid her lips over him, slowly then quickly, and he arched, his breathing hoarse now.

"You wouldn't consider riding me, would you?" he asked politely.

"You've lovely manners," she purred. "But of course."

She climbed aboard, and eased down over his cock, and . . . Oh God . . . she half sighed, half moaned with the pleasure of it. She felt him everywhere, her fingertips to the soles of her feet. Her head went back, eyes shut. So. Good.

His big hands spanned her back, and they moved together slowly at first, eyes locked. Each daring the other, teasing with a pause, a slow slide. He allowed her to dictate the rhythm. Slow, and then stop. A rise, a pause, then a fall. Sensual torment. The cords of his neck grew taut, and his head thrashed back as his chest heaved against hers. He moaned as she rose again. The sweat sheened his throat, and his eyes were black now. She licked him where the sweat traveled to his collarbone.

"Please, Tommy. Have mercy. I need . . . *please* . . . GOD . . ."

He bucked upward, and she had mercy. She met him hard, and they rocked together, a frenzy of joining now, her nipples chafing his chest a lightning burst of sensation, her fingers clawing his shoulders, as she swore and urged him on harder, and harder, and deeper, and deeper, until he made a roar of her name.

"*Tommy!*" His head dropped back and he shuddered.

And she buried her long soundless cry in his throat as she shattered.

FOUR HOURS LATER he discovered things about *her*.

For instance:

"You've an arse like a peach," he said as he gently nipped one cheek. He'd kissed his way down her spine while she lay on her stomach, sated, her head resting on her arm. He licked the sweet little indentation at the base of her spine, and she stirred and sighed. He slipped his fingers between her thighs, delicately, lightly, tracing the downy hair there, until she sighed again, and her thighs shifted open wider.

He obliged her, sliding his fingers between her legs, to where she was slick and satiny smooth, and he slid them in and out again.

She groaned softly and bridged her hips up.

"Do you like it?" His voice was tense.

"Please don't stop." A prayer if she'd ever prayed one.

"On your hands and knees," he ordered softly.

She arched her body up to obey him. And he shifted to his back, and slipped his head between her legs, and reached his hands up to cup her arse, and then brought her down to his mouth.

And he thrust his tongue hard along her wetness.

Mother of God. The *shock*. The exquisite *shock*. She hissed the pleasure of it as it lightninged through her bud. The hiss evolved into a helpless carnal groan. "Oh, God. Oh, please . . . Jonathan."

"Again?" he murmured.

She nearly whimpered.

He did it again, circling this time, then sucking lightly. It rushed to her head, the bliss of it; she nearly fell. He held her fast.

He feasted, his tongue silken, deft, insistent, a revelation, driving her to the brink of madness with a pleasure she'd never dreamed attainable. She heard her own breath like the ocean in her ears, and the animal sounds of pleasure and encouragement she'd never imagined she was capable of making. And then he sucked hard, and sensation rushed over her, like flames.

And as she screamed her release, he slipped from beneath her, and turned, and seized her hips and guided his cock into her, and sank into her deeply. He withdrew, then drove hard again, pulling her hips back into him, taking her deeper and deeper still, their bodies colliding hard, her fingers clawing into the counterpane, until she felt it, amazingly, once more, the pleasure swelling against the very seams of her being. She heard the roar of his breath, and his groan of helpless bliss as he plunged ever more swiftly. And then he went still. He came on a hoarse cry. And seconds later she did, too, nearly weeping from the unthinkable, nearly unbearable pleasure.

So good. So endlessly, endlessly good. She would never, never have enough of him.

He collapsed next to her, and scooped her, sated and boneless and thoroughly pleasured, into his arms. They were both sweat-shiny and limp.

"That's upside down taken care of," he murmured. "For you, that is."

She couldn't wait to find out what upside down for him meant.

ROUND ABOUT THE seventh hour they both fell asleep, Tommy splayed half on top of him, his arm wrapped around her.

He snored.

She woke before he did, and pressed her head against his chest, and listened. To his soft snoring. To the faint gurgle in his stomach. To the steady beat of his heart.

I am so blessed. So very, very lucky.

So privileged to love him. Because she did.

She knew he loved her, too.

There would be time to worry about what it meant, or think about the future.

For now there was only this man and his heartbeat, and the rise and fall of his breath as he slept.

Chapter 27

J ONATHAN DIDN'T RETURN TO his parents' town house on St. James Square for a fortnight.

He didn't go to White's. He didn't go to the opera, to balls, or to the theater, and he missed a few dinner invitations.

He most certainly didn't go to the salon.

He told no one where he was sleeping at night. Not because of any great need for secrecy. In a haze of sex and happiness, he simply forgot that someone might wish to know.

He ventured out only to buy food. And then he returned to the snug little nest in the rickety building in Covent Garden, where he exchanged life stories with Tommy, and made love and slept and made love some more.

And to think he'd thought he'd been *happy* before. This was something altogether different. Something anarchic he couldn't command, something unreasonable and likely untenable in the long run. A dream, surely, for he could see no way of transferring it to the life he lived in the ton. But for as long as he possibly could, he wanted only to feel, not to think.

AT THE END of a fortnight, Jonathan stopped in at Klaus Liebman & Co. on Bond Street.

Klaus and Argosy, who was leaning against the counter and watching Wyndham sketch a certain handsome Miss Elizabeth Francis, whom Jonathan had danced with perhaps once, all turned and gaped at him.

"Who had 'Jonathan Redmond is alive?' in White's Betting Books?" Argosy said dryly at last.

"I'm in the Betting Books?" Jonathan still felt pleasantly cushioned from real life by happiness.

"For the past week you've *dominated* the Betting Books. Someone else wagered that you had disappeared along with your brother Lyon Redmond. There's been much debate over whether an Eversea was responsible."

Oh, God. He could only imagine what his father would think when he saw that. Not only was the name "Lyon" invoked, but someone had thought to poke the embers of the Eversea enmity while they did it.

He *knew* he shouldn't have ventured from the Building of Dubious Occupations.

"And there's another wager, too, Jonathan," Argosy said carefully. It was Argosy's tone. "If you'll just come with me for a moment?"

Argosy beckoned him into the back room.

Argosy's expression was portentous.

"What?" Jonathan said, irritated.

"I know, Redmond."

"What do you know? Apart from the best horseflesh and where to buy gloves that cost one hundred pounds?'

"I know you've been with Tommy de Ballesteros this entire time."

Jonathan could feel the blood drain from his face.

"What makes you say that?

Argosy was amused. "You should see your face, Redmond! Don't worry. I'm not going to call you out. I could see the writing on the wall. *You* are hardly inscrutable, at least to me. And no woman is quite that interested in *investing*."

"You'd be amazed at what women are interested in, Argosy." He was carefully, surreptitiously assessing his friend for evidence he felt betrayed. But Argosy was remarkably sanguine for someone whose heart was broken, since he'd made just such a production over Cynthia Brightly breaking his heart.

"Who else knows?"

"I don't think anyone *knows*. Well, apart from me, now, because you as much as admitted it. But . . . this is what I wanted to tell you. There's a wager in the books about the two of you. You and Tommy."

"Christ! Who wagered it? And why?"

"The trouble is that you *both* rather vanished from the London scene right about the same time. This coincidence was remarked upon at White's, and Harry Linley, well he'd had about a couple pints too many, and he decided it answered a question about where the two of you had got to, so he wagered Edmund Rickburn. How Linley intends to win that bet is beyond me."

Jonathan thought quickly. "Have you seen my father in White's?"

A hesitation. "Yes. Or rather, he's been seen at White's. Deep in discussion with the Duke of Grey-folk."

Jonathan sighed, and yanked off his hat, and slumped back against the wall. "Damn," he muttered. "Damn, damn, damn."

That didn't mean Isaiah had read the Betting Books. Or had heard or taken to heart prurient gossip. But his father had his ways of discovering what he wanted to know.

Damn.

"So what is it like?" Argosy ventured casually.

Jonathan looked up at him dangerously.

"What is *what* like?" he said with clipped politeness. Knowing full well what he meant.

Argosy simply stared at him incredulously, an eyebrow arched.

"Horrible." And Jonathan smiled slowly.

"Oh, yes. I'm certain it's horrible. You're positively gaunt from all the vigorous shagging you've been doing. Would you like a piece of cheese?"

Jonathan laughed. Then sighed. "I best take a look at the books here to see how the orders are doing."

"What are you going to do, Redmond?"

"I don't know. I've never been in love before."

"*Love?*" Argosy was shocked into choking the word. "You mean, what I had for Cynthia?"

Jonathan hadn't the patience. "With all due respect, Argosy, that wasn't love. Trust me, you'll know it when it happens."

IT WASN'T THE day of the salon—which Tommy had in fact utterly forgotten to attend for the past two weeks—but since Jonathan had gone down to Bond Street to Klaus Liebman & Co., and the Countess Mirabeau had sent a note asking her if she would call upon her that morning, Tommy went off cheerfully.

The house seemed very quiet without the usual hubbub of the guests. Later Tommy would come to think of that quiet as portentous. It was a bit like the way birds fell silent right before a nasty storm.

She smiled and accepted kisses on the cheek from the countess, who was dressed, startlingly, in the height of fashion, a turban wound round her head, a plume arcing over it, her dress plum-colored silk.

The countess whispered in her ear, "He asked for an introduction to you, my dear, and since he's clearly a very wealthy and important man, I thought it in your best interests to effect it."

Countess Mirabeau was pleased with herself. She wagged her brows up high, and took herself out of the room.

Tommy was still.

And she swiveled.

Rising to his feet from a chair was an older man, an extraordinarily handsome man, a man with the sort of presence that made one's breath catch a moment.

And intangibles . . . the height of him, the way he held himself, that set of his shoulders, the way his body straightened as he rose from the chair to

greet her—it was eerie. It was like glimpsing Jonathan thirty years from now. Like him, and yet not
like him.

He bowed. "Miss de Ballesteros, I presume?"

"Mr. Isaiah Redmond, I presume?"

If this surprised him, he showed no signs of it.
He has green eyes, too.

"I wondered if I could perhaps have a word with
you. Will you sit down with me? It shan't take long."

She moved warily into the room, her eyes mark-
ing him as if he was a wolf. She knew a bit more
about his kind now. The immovable powerful men
of the world. The builders and destroyers.

She sat gingerly in the chair across from him,
and folded her hands in her lap. She turned to him
expectantly. *Breathe, Tommy.*

"It's my understanding that you've taken my son
as a lover."

The words harpooned her.

It was a moment before she could breathe again,
and she was certain he'd noticed. For he was the
sort who noticed everything. And it was too late to
protect Jonathan or deny it.

"I fear you misunderstand the nature of our association, Mr. Redmond." She was proud of her
steady voice.

"Oh, I doubt that."

He was too experienced at this sort of thing.
He'd read her quite easily.

"I do wonder what business it is of yours?" she
asked politely, almost disinterestedly. She was
proud of her cool tone, given that her hands were
already clammy.

He paused. Either for effect, or he truly was gathering his thoughts.

"Do you have a family, Miss de Ballesteros? A mother, a father, siblings? People you love, and who love you in return?"

And thusly he twisted the spear. He must know, somehow, that she had no one. Had he spoken to the duke? Did he know?

She was breathing shortly now. She could feel the heat starting up in her cheeks.

He was satisfied that her silence was a response.

"Because unless you do, I don't know if you can understand what his family means to Jonathan, or what he means to the family. And if he marries inappropriately, everything he cares about will be denied to him—his home, his family, his past, his inheritance. Not only that, but the usual opportunities for advancement and connection afforded a young man of wealth and stature will be denied him if he marries into a class other than his own. He will, quite simply, ultimately be miserable. Perhaps at first he will not be, but in the end, he will. I can assure you. Someone like Jonathan doesn't simply abandon everything he knows."

Tommy's nails dug more and more deeply into her palm, a reminder to steady her temper. She stared at him, amazed.

"You don't know your son at all," she said slowly, allowing her amazement to show. "You underestimate him greatly. And you may one day soon regret it."

She was beginning to wonder if all men who possessed green eyes were bastards.

Something about her tone—her icy bearing, her utter confidence—made him pause. He studied her curiously for a moment. Jonathan was right. Here was another man like her father, she thought. She was scarcely worth his notice. Scarcely worth any minute amplification of emotion.

"Oh, I doubt that, too," he said finally, easily enough. "This is what I came here to say to you. If you care for my son, you'll refuse to see him, and allow him to go on to the future that was meant for him. It's bright, and he has a chance to be happy, and if you want his happiness, surely you'll let him go. Because if he continues his, shall we say, association with you, he'll be cut off from his sister, his brother, his mother, his rightful inheritance, and his birthright. It is absolutely nonnegotiable, Miss de Ballesteros. I will ensure it happens. And believe me, I have the power to ensure that it remains that way."

Breathing was more of a struggle now. Oh, how she hated men like him. Who had earned money in order to bully people with it, in order to shape the world the way they wanted it.

She was the proverbial wayward nail, pointing up out of the plank, and he thought he could hammer her into place again.

"Didn't you threaten another son, Mr. Redmond, with something very similar? Tell me, will he be dining at your table this evening? Will you see him tomorrow, or the next day, or the next day? Or did he, in fact, disappear entirely?"

She watched fury slowly infuse Isaiah Redmond. It was subtle, but apparent, and fascinating. And his brand of fury was a cold bitter thing, she could see. He would never lose his temper in an ugly way. It stiffened his muscles, and tensed his jaw, and his eyes went cinder gray.

And in that moment, she loved the power to make someone like him furious. For the only way to make him furious was to know his weaknesses.

"You won't see a penny of Jonathan's family money, Miss de Ballesteros. I shan't worry, however. Women like you always land on their feet. It was just that I felt, as a father, I should appeal to whatever affection you may hold for my son. He has no future with you, and you should release him now, before he is hurt. For above all, I shouldn't like to see him hurt."

Yes. I'm sure your motives are just that altruistic, Tommy thought.

She jerked her chin high. I will not cry, not even furious tears, in front of this man.

"You are correct not to worry about me, Mr. Redmond. And isn't it fortunate for you that Jonathan will shortly be choosing a bride from a deck of cards? For aren't women of fine families all interchangeable? One is very like another, and surely his happiness is guaranteed as long as your expectations are met. Surely he'll never be hurt as long as *you* are satisfied. And you may rest easy. *I* never posed for any deck of cards."

He smiled faintly. "I'm glad we understand each other, Miss de Ballesteros."

He stood again, and looked down at her for a curious moment. As if memorizing her.

And then he bowed, and departed without another word.

AND THAT AFTERNOON, Jonathan bolted up the stairs, rushed in, and flung off his hat, and loosened his cravat.

"You on top!" he announced gleefully and lunged for her.

She laughed, she couldn't help it, as he swept her up in his arms, his hands cupping her bottom. She wrapped her legs round his waist and her arms round his neck and he dropped backward on the settee with her straddling him.

"Kiss me," he ordered on a whisper, while she worked open his trouser buttons, and she did, while he furled up her dress, stroking the tender insides of her thighs above her stockings. His mouth was hot and sweet, it was opium. There was a ferocity, a new urgency to him.

And she shifted to slide her wetness against him, teasing, and he closed his eyes, the chords of his neck taut with the pleasure of it.

"Tease me," he whispered.

And so she did. She slid down on him, and moved over him slowly, so slowly. Until a long moan of pleasure was dragged from him. Until his brow beaded in sweat. Until she could scarcely bear it herself. She played toreador with hot spiky pleasure building, building in her; and then she played toreador with his pleasure.

She dipped her tongue into his ear, traced the whorls of it, and his groan evolved into a short laugh of near despair.

"Had enough torture?" she whispered.

He seized her hips and urged her on. They rocked together, hard and furious, graceless and

greedy for the extraordinary pleasure they knew
would be theirs in seconds.

And their cries mingled together

"Boom," he whispered. His head tucked beneath
her chin.

She felt every precious rise and fall of his chest
as his breath mingled with hers.

She threaded her fingers through his hair. So
soft, like a boy's. Glossy dark.

His hair, of all things, was going to make her cry.

She slipped from his arms, and straightened
her dress, and sat next to him on the settee, hands
folded tightly on her lap.

And didn't look at him.

He stared at her, eyes still dreamy from lovemaking, surprised she was able to even move.

She inhaled for courage. And then turned to him.

"Jonathan . . . there's something I need to say to
you."

She met his eyes.

His eyes went from dreamy to wary. He studied
her closely.

She bravely withstood his scrutiny.

And then his eyes narrowed. "My *father*," he
spat. "My father spoke to you."

She was shocked.

"How did you—? No."

"Don't *lie* to me, Tommy. I know it's true. It's
something he would do. And I know the look of
someone who's been *got to* by Isaiah Redmond.
What the bloody hell did he say? Did he try to
warn you away from me?"

He was fastening his trousers now. Movements
quick and jerky, furious.

"Jonathan," she tried softly. "No matter what you think of him . . . he's right. You'll come to hate me. Because he'll cut you off from everything you love if you stay with me, and you'll be cut off from the society you know, and from opportunities you might have."

"I love *you*."

Oh, the words. The precious words. *She loved him, she loved him*.

She closed her eyes.

"You love me, Tommy. I know you do. Say it."

"What difference does it make, Jonathan?"

"Say it!"

"Jonathan . . ."

"Don't *do* this, Tommy. Not yet. Not yet."

"Then when? The day before you wed Lady Penelope Moneystacks? No, it's better we end it now."

"Because you're afraid."

She stared at him incredulously. And now she was furious.

"You're bloody well right I'm afraid! Of never having anything permanent to call my own, of reliving my mother's life, of watching you marry someone else, of knowing someone else sleeps next to you at night! I'm afraid! I'm afraid of you growing to hate me because if you choose me while everything else you love is forbidden to you. . . . The way I see it, I get to choose the way in which I'm hurt, and I choose this way. Now, rather than later. Now, with my pride intact and other options before me."

He went still.

"What other options?" His voice was low and taut.

She inhaled, knowing the words would be like a dagger driven into him. "Lord Prescott has asked me to marry him."

He took the words like a blow. She could see the blank shock, the flinch. He shook his head. *"Prescott?* But . . ."

"Because he *wants* me, Jonathan. Just the way you do. And apparently that's the price he's willing— and able—to pay."

She could tell the news was reverberating through him.

"Prescott. Prescott gave you the pearls."

She didn't deny it.

"What did you give him in return?"

"Unworthy, Jonathan," she said. "I gave him nothing, and you know it. But it's what he wants that matters here."

"What *he* wants?"

"Think about it. If you love me, would you rather I live day to day like I am now, in this building, or in a measure of safety and comfort and security— all the things that someone like your sister, or Lady Grace Worthington, will always have? Why shouldn't I have it, too?"

"You don't want to marry him."

"Of course not, you ass!"

And that shocked both of them.

But now she was near to weeping with fury and futility and fear. "And there you have it. My other option. Unless you count the possibility of our fortune arriving tomorrow. But we haven't a fortune yet, have we, Jonathan?

"No," he said. "But we will. Don't do it, Tommy. Not now. You don't have to do it now."

"He gave me until the end of the month to give him a decision."

He closed his eyes. "Mother of God."

And then he swore violently beneath his breath. She flinched.

"Jonathan . . . think about it. Do you want to live like that, cut off from everything else you love? Do you want me to live like this forever? *Do* you?"

She couldn't bear it. He was moving as though he'd been scalded, dressing furiously, jamming his arms through his shirtsleeves, knotting his cravat as though he wished it were a noose for his father.

He stood staring down at her. Gulping her down with his eyes.

"My father won't win, Tommy. *I* will." He said it quietly, evenly. It thrummed with the conviction of a blood vow. "I'll have everything I want. And so will you. You just have to decide whether you trust me. And whether you love me more than you fear the future."

They stared at each other in furious weighted silence.

Fear. How she hated to be accused of it. But she wasn't prepared to make that decision now, when fear of the pain of losing him outweighed every other consideration. For it was that she couldn't bear.

"You best go now," she said gently. "I need you to go now."

He closed his eyes. And when he opened them again, his expression almost made her say, "I take all of it back. Don't go. Don't go. Never leave me."

He didn't move. He was tensed as a closed fist.

Instead, she said, "Are you looking for something to throw?"

He didn't find something to throw. He found something to kick, however.

The door. Hard. On his way out.

Chapter 28

In the days that followed, Jonathan returned to the Redmond town house on St. James Square as if he'd never left. He was all that was polite and glib at the breakfast table.

His father didn't ask any questions. If he cast one or two lingering, querying looks in Jonathan's direction, assessing him for signs of rebellion or heartbreak, Jonathan simply smiled benignly.

You won't win, Father. I will.

It was his only thought as he passed the marmalade to his father, as he shaved in the morning, when his head hit the pillow in the evening. It was in the air he breathed.

His behavior was so faultless that Isaiah departed for Sussex again to oversee business there.

Jonathan frequented the print shop to see to the progress of orders, to review the plates, to pore over the books. Men and women had begun to commission decks of cards featuring *their* visages only on all the suits. Because they were single orders, requiring the preparation of unique plates, Klaus gleefully charged an exorbitant fee. Ah, the money to be had from the rich vein of vanity that ran through London.

And Jonathan himself commissioned a special deck.

"I'll need it quickly, Wyndham. By the time the Diamonds of the First Water decks are prepared."

And then a scientist wished to publish a book featuring colorful anatomical illustrations, and Klaus was beside himself with possibility. Soon after that, a publisher commissioned Klaus to print colorfully illustrated limited editions of Miles Redmond's famous South Sea Journals. Klaus had built two more printers and hired another helper at fair wages, a young man from the Bethnal Green workhouse named William, to help with all the extra work. But Charlie was quick and clever and thriving, and would soon be capable of more than sweeping and errand-running.

And in every waking moment, in every step he took, Jonathan quietly seethed with purpose.

And when his investment in the recent silks cargo *finally* paid off—nearly triple the original investment—Jonathan Redmond realized he was, officially and quite apart from his family's money, wealthy. Modestly, yes.

Certainly not *Isaiah Redmond* wealthy.

Yet.

But it was all his.

He used the money to repay Tommy's investment. She wasn't wealthy, but she now had choices, which really was what she'd wanted all along.

And he knew a fierce satisfaction that he was the one who had ensured she would be comfortable and safe. If she didn't want to live in a building made of kindling anymore, then she certainly didn't need to. If she didn't want to marry a man with a title, she didn't need to.

If she didn't want to marry anyone at *all*, she didn't need to.

He deposited her share in her account and sent round a message to tell her simply that.

And he added:

You wanted choices. Now you have many.

P.S. Don't do anything rash. —J

Hardly a love note. But he wasn't going to beg. If she trusted him, she quite simply wouldn't do anything stupid, like leave London, or marry a viscount.

And then he went to visit a solicitor.

Romulus Bean, Esquire.

The sign swung in a light breeze. His offices were in a rather unassuming location for a man who had caused Isaiah Redmond and the Duke of Greyfolk sleepless nights of tormented covetousness.

Jonathan blew out a breath. And climbed the stairs, and opened the door.

It was a tiny office, sparsely and elegantly furnished, impeccably neat. Mr. Romulus Bean was behind his desk, and like his office, he was a compact neat man, whose spectacles had slipped to the tip of his nose, and whose few remaining hairs clung to his head like shipwreck victims to a raft.

Jonathan bowed. "Please forgive my intrusion, Mr. Bean, but I'd hoped you'd have a moment to speak with me."

Mr. Bean adjusted his spectacles and peered up at Jonathan. Evidently approving of the clothing, the accent, the bearing.

"My name is Jonathan Redmond."

And that's when a hint of irony darkened his features.

"Are you related to . . . Mr. Isaiah Redmond?"

He said it gingerly. And it was curiously uninflected. The way he said it rather called to mind how Jonathan felt about his father.

"Yes, but he doesn't know I'm here. I'm here entirely on my own behalf."

"Ah. Please do have a seat, Mr. Redmond. What then is the nature of your inquiry?"

Jonathan settled into the chair across from the man's desk. "I understand you're the solicitor charged with the sale of the Lancaster Cotton Mill."

"I am indeed."

"I would like to purchase it."

Mr. Bean fell as silent as if someone had dropped a dome over him.

And then slowly, absently, he began rotating a glass of water on his desk round and round, slowly, with his fingers. Twisting it to and fro. To and fro.

"I've a number of buyers interested in the property, Mr. Redmond. Can you tell me the nature of your offer? Perhaps your plans for the property?"

During his long silence, Mr. Bean had clearly decided to be kind and to humor him, that much was clear. He didn't believe for a moment that Jonathan had the capital.

"I propose to pay for a portion of it in cash, a portion of it in a percentage share of my printing business, and to make payments on the rest. I can provide statements of my earnings and an accurate forecast of my future earnings."

A little silence ensued.

"Payments." Mr. Bean said the word delicately. As if he'd never dealt with anyone who would need to do anything so plebeian as to make payments. But it wasn't unsympathetic. He had the look of a man who would love to glance at the clock in order to usher Jonathan along, but who was too innately polite.

"And my plans are to either cease altogether the use of child labor, or institute dramatic changes. My first attempt will be find ways to train the children working there in a legitimate lifetime trade, find homes or apprenticeships for them, and hire adults."

Mr. Bean leaned slowly back in his chair then.

He went still. Thoughtful.

"Even the girls?" His voice was clipped now.

"Of course."

Mr. Bean leaned forward again. He folded his lips in on themselves. He recommenced idly turning the tumbler of water. It was winding Jonathan's nerves tauter and tauter. He was tempted to reach out and flatten a hand on top of Bean's to make him stop.

Too late. It finally wobbled and tipped, and water cascaded everywhere.

Jonathan leaped backward.

Mr. Bean shot to his feet. "Good heavens, I do apologize, Mr. Redmond! It's just . . ."

"Please don't worry about it. It's just water."

Jonathan fished out a handkerchief and handed it to Mr. Bean, who, flushed and abashed, diligently mopped and dabbed in silence for a time.

He folded Jonathan's handkerchief into neat little fours. "My apologies for drenching your . . ." He pushed up his spectacles higher on his nose again. He ran his thumb over the corner of the handkerchief.

He looked up slowly. His expression was odd.

"Will you do something for me, Mr. Redmond?"

I'll kiss you on the mouth if you sell me the mill. "What might that be?"

"Will you say"—he cleared his throat and intoned—" 'Get off him, you fetid bastard!' In a quite furious tone?"

Jonathan blinked. "I beg your . . . well, if you insist. 'Get off him . . .' "

He halted.

Because then he *knew.*

"It's *you!*" they shouted simultaneously. Gleefully.

"*You* saved me from those ruffians!" Mr. Bean was beside himself.

"You were the fellow outside the Plum & Pear who was beset by those . . . fetid bastards!"

"They did stink!" Mr. Bean said happily.

"Powerfully!"

"You gave me your handkerchief! I bled all over it!"

Jonathan silently, with great ceremony, rolled up

his sleeve. "And I have a nice little knife wound. It impresses the ladies."

Mr. Bean admired the gash, then sat back, beaming, shaking his head wonderingly.

"It's the oddest thing, Mr. Redmond, but I've been inscrutable about my reluctance to sell the mill to certain parties, and it's . . . for the very reasons you cited. That mill is a moral burden to me. I loathe the use of child labor. And the only way children will be treated more humanely, that things will change, is if passionate, influential individuals fight for stronger laws. I wonder"—he leaned forward—"have you considered running for parliament, Mr. Redmond? I strongly suspect you'd have a good deal of support. You seem to have the boldness of a politician. Saving my life makes an excellent story—quite revelatory of character, wouldn't you say? Certainly the Redmond name holds a good deal of sway, and you've an undeniable presence."

He had an "undeniable presence," did he?

It was Jonathan's turn to lean back in his chair and study Mr. Bean. "I *have* been told I've a certain amount to recommend me."

He closed his eyes. The idea spiraled, glittering, like a guinea into the well of his mind.

And he knew, just knew, in the way he always did, that the idea was brilliant and right. And a peculiar sense of peace came over him.

"I think, Mr. Bean . . . you've just said something very important."

"Splendid. I look forward to supporting you in the next election, Mr. Redmond."

Jonathan grinned.

And they sat for a moment in bemused, delighted silence.

"Well," Mr. Bean said finally, with a drum of his fingers. "This is serendipitous. You don't know how I've longed for an opportunity to thank my rescuer."

Jonathan leaned back and folded his arms behind his head.

"Tell me, Mr. Bean . . . just how grateful are you feeling?"

Chapter 29

THE NIGHT BEFORE THE Diamonds of the First Water decks were due to appear in stores was a sleepless one for hundreds of members of the ton.

All the young ladies who'd posed for Wyndham stared up at their ceilings, rigid with tension, praying that Lady Grace Worthington hadn't been chosen, and that they had.

Lady Grace Worthington lay awake all night trying to decide just how many decks she would purchase, for she was confident she would be featured. She hugged herself with pleasure, imagining her face in Almack's and at every fine house in all of England.

And dozens of young men worried over the wagers they'd placed via White's Betting Books on the young women who would appear in the deck. And who Redmond would choose, if indeed he did choose, as he'd said he would do.

And just before dawn, Charlie and Klaus and Klaus's new assistant, William, began loading up the cart under cover of predawn darkness. The deliveries to shops all over London, in particular to the Burlington Arcade, would need to be finished by the time they opened.

And each and every one of them wondered: Would Jonathan Redmond really choose a bride from a deck of cards?

AND OVER IN the Building of Dubious Occupations, Tommy de Ballesteros hadn't slept a wink, either, and not just because Rutherford was home all evening apparently entertaining a lady guest who must have been the same size as he was, such was the crashing and thumping. *Rhythmic* thumping. She tried hard not to imagine it, and then felt envious, and lonely, and achingly sad, and frightened.

Because she knew today was the day the Diamonds of the First Water decks were meant to be delivered to shops.

And the day Jonathan Redmond was rumored to be choosing a bride from the deck.

If she rolled over and breathed in, she could still smell him faintly on her pillow. Or so she imagined. This made her spring upright and sit at the very edge of her bed and admire the stripes sent through her blinds by the moon. She pushed her feet into them, as though they were a soothing stream.

She needed soothing. Today was an important day for her, too.

For she'd come to a decision about Jonathan and Prescott.

HE HADN'T SENT word ahead to his family that he would be leaving London for Pennyroyal Green.

He simply rode all the way home, relishing the brisk weather, the opportunity to gallop, the time to plan and savor his mission.

At Redmond House, he leaped from his horse, gave the reins to the groomsman, and dashed up the stairs to the house, handing off his coat and hat to the waiting footman.

He paused only to smooth his hair in the mirror, knock the dust from his boots, and then he took the marble stairs two at a time up to his father's library.

His father was ensconced at his huge shining desk in his brown and cream refuge of a library, bent over documents spread out the length of it. Jonathan could see a thinning spot on the top of his gray head. For a moment it was poignant. Isaiah Redmond is not indestructible. He will fray at the edges, crumple, return to dust, like everyone eventually does.

Knowing this only solidified Jonathan's resolve.

He remained still for a moment, watching his father, lit by the light of the great window, unguarded, absorbed, frowning faintly. Probably still wondering why Romulus Bean still refused to sell the mill to him, but unworried; he would find a way to get what he wanted, for he always did.

Jonathan rapped at the open door and his father's head shot up.

Surprise flickered in his eyes. Followed by a fleeting moment of what may just have been a bit of unease.

"Well! What can I do for you Jonathan? Have you come to make me the proudest man alive by telling me you've drawn a bride from a deck of cards?"

"It is indeed the designated day," Jonathan said calmly, unsurprised his father knew. "But I thought you might like to do the honors. Since you inspired the idea."

He slipped his hand into his coat and retrieved the deck of cards. Gestured with it.

This his father clearly wasn't expecting. He stared at him, surprised..

"Jonathan . . . I honestly . . ."

Without invitation Jonathan strode over to his father's desk and pulled up a chair. His father swiftly collected his documents, as if he feared Jonathan's cards might taint them, but not before Jonathan saw the words written across the top of one: "Mercury Club Proposal for Acquisition of Lancaster Mill."

Jonathan pushed the deck of cards over to his father.

"Go ahead, Father. Turn over the first card. Because that's who my bride will be."

His father shifted his gaze, making a great show of looking at the clock behind him, then heaved a long suffering sigh, hiked a brow, delicately plucked up the top card, and turned it over.

The Queen of Hearts lay on the table.

They were silent.

"Beautiful color printing, wouldn't you say?" Jonathan coaxed. When it seemed his father would say nothing.

"It's quite fine," Isaiah said absently. He seemed riveted by the image.

Jonathan watched thunder slowly gather in his

father's face. His hands trembled. His jaw turned to granite.

His father looked slowly up at him.

"What the devil do you mean by this?" Every word was etched in cold fury.

"Her name is Thomasina de Ballesteros. But you already know that, as you had a little conversation with her. And there it is, right there"—Jonathan tapped the card—"printed right across the bottom in tiny letters. I am going to marry her. And you will love her. Because I love her."

His father's mouth was trembling in fury. It was a moment before he could finally make words emerge, and they were scraped raw. "How *dare*—"

Jonathan held up a hand. "I repeat: You will love her. You will receive her in this house. *And* you will allow Cynthia Brightly into this house. And you will love her, too, because I love her, and Miles loves her, and Violet loves her. Because it is *you*, Father, who has caused the upheaval and division in your family. You who are causing your own unhappiness with your attempts to make yourself happy. Not your children. You. And the only thing that matters in life is that you have people to love. Surely, somewhere inside you, you know this."

His father's jaw was dropped now.

And then he clapped it shut again swiftly. And his words emerged an arid hiss.

"How *dare* you speak to me this way." It was a tone of voice that would have terrified Jonathan when he was a child. "If you marry this girl you won't receive another pen—"

"And with regards to my allowance," Jonathan

continued smoothly, as if his father hadn't said a word, "you'll find the entirety of what I have been paid for the past two years in your account. I've doubled my wealth inside a year. Next year I intend to triple it. And if you care to know the reason why, it's because *I* now own the Lancaster Mill. I sat with the solicitor, Mr. Romulus Bean, yesterday, and we made if official. I'm also in discussions with Mr. Bean to purchase a part ownership in the cotton mill in Northampton. I won't *require* another penny from you. But I will be happy to discuss investment opportunities with you, for I'll be forming my own investment group. One of the group's first priorities is helping Miles find the funding for his next expedition."

His father took all of this in, as if to say, "You're . . . jesting."

Jonathan sighed. "Feel free to write to Mr. Bean to inquire, but I do have the deed—" He slipped it from his coat, a coat of horrors as far as his father was concerned, and slid it over to him. "—right here."

His father gingerly dragged the document toward him and stared down at it.

He looked back up at Jonathan, his face entirely unreadable now.

Jonathan put his palm over it and slid it back into his possession. "I'll just take that back now, shall I? And do you know why he sold it to me? As luck would have it, I saved him from some thugs in a street brawl. Right outside a gaming hell. Of course, I had funds, too, thanks to my prior investments, or Mr. Bean wouldn't even have bothered to speak with me. I've been investing in silks and similar cargos for the past two years. As I told you."

His father levered himself gingerly back in his chair, as if he'd suddenly become brittle and feared he would shatter. He stared at Jonathan as if he'd never seen him before.

And in many ways, of course, he hadn't.

Jonathan would warrant his father wouldn't make *that* mistake again.

"One thing that *might* cheer you: Thomasina's father is, in fact, a duke."

And there was a flicker of something on Isaiah's face then. Hope or surprise. More likely a reflexive response to the word "duke," perhaps, knowing his father and his hunger for a title that the king forever dangled before the Redmonds and Everseas, and which still remained out of reach.

"You can't tell anyone, however. She's *quite* illegitimate."

Jonathan was enjoying himself a bit too much.

"And I suppose I ought to tell you we already have children. A good hundred or so of them. Well, in a manner of speaking."

His father slowly closed his eyes. His lips moved in what might have been a prayer.

"One final thing, Father. You may want to stay on my good side, because I'm running for parliament to dismantle the practice of child labor. And I have every intention of winning. I expect when you've time to recover and have had a good think, you'll be proud of me. Apple doesn't fall far from the tree, that sort of thing. And of course you'll be able to turn it all to your benefit."

Isaiah's green eyes snapped open again. His hands remained flat on his desk, as if the earth was moving and he was attempting to hold it still.

Jonathan stood. "And oh . . . you may have realized this, but that isn't the Diamonds of the First Water Deck. It's a special edition. The only deck I'd ever consider drawing from."

Jonathan winked at his father, slipped the Queen of Hearts back into his pocket. And then he slid back his chair and left the room.

Short, shocking, and to the point. Jonathan had honed that skill playing darts.

But, of course, he'd first learned it from his father.

ISAIAH SAT STUNNED for another moment, staring at the doorway.

And then he drew in a long breath and idly pulled the deck toward him. He was appalled to find his hands shaking.

He turned over the top card.

The Queen of Diamonds.

He peered: This particular monarch had green eyes, and tiny slanting black brows, and red hair, and a regal tilt to her head. She wore a proud secret smile.

An unmistakable face.

He cautiously, slowly, turned over another.

It was the Knave of Spades.

He held it in his now-shaking hands and inspected it. The knave was wearing pantaloons, but scandalously; it was clearly a woman. Red hair knotted at the nape, and an elegant profile, a large slanting green eye with extraordinarily long lashes.

He turned over another card.
And another.
And another.
Every single court card, every last one of them,
featured an image of Thomasina de Ballesteros.

Chapter 30

LATER, THE BROADSHEETS WOULD report it as "The Burlington Arcade Stampede." The aftermath was still being dealt with the following day, when bits of ribbon and scraps of net—perhaps torn from bonnets or the sleeves of dresses—a glove, and even a slipper were swept up by the merchants' assistants. One young lady turned her ankle and needed to be carried out. Another fainted, though that may have just been dramatics.

All anyone knew for certain was that a milling, restless, generally well-bred, brilliantly well-dressed crowd poured into the shops to snap up their Diamonds of the First Water decks, and claim the ones they ordered in advance, only to find that, much to everyone's surprise, two different decks had been delivered.

The Diamonds of the First Water decks were torn open and rifled through, and shouts of glee and howls of protest went up. Fierce arguments and fits of weeping broke out, money changed hands as wagers were won or lost.

And in one appalling instance, a certain Lady

Grace Worthington was rumored to have shouted something unrepeatable when she at first couldn't find herself in the deck. It was whispered that the first word began with an "F" and the second was "Hell."

And then she found herself in the deck and stared, appeased and captivated.

"But what about Redmond? Where's Redmond?" the cry soon went up. For more wagers needed to be settled.

The merchant called for silence.

"From what I understand, Mr. Redmond is formally making his choice in a private ceremony at his home in Sussex. But you can find his choice in this *very* limited edition deck."

The merchants gestured at the other deck held behind their counters, and soon those decks vanished, too.

Silence descended as they all rifled in confusion through the deck.

Then muttering ensued.

Then a hush, as realization sank into each of them.

"But she's not even blond!" Lady Grace Worthington howled.

Or so it was rumored.

And then she succumbed to overstimulation, fainted prettily, and needed to be carried away by two bloods who had lost money in the wager and considered a look at Lady Grace's ankles a consolation.

SHE MUST HAVE dozed off, because Tommy awoke with a start when she heard the knock.

A long knock, as it turned out. A fancy complicated one.

Her heart leaped like a bird sprung from a cage.

She scrambled out of bed, shoved her arms
into her pelisse, and ran barefoot down the stairs,
through the corridor, and then came to an abrupt
halt.

A message—this one written on foolscap, folded
neatly, and formally sealed with red wax—had
been slipped under her door.

She stood on tiptoe and peeked out the peephole. Not a soul stood there. She opened it a few
inches and peered out.

Nothing but a dim, none-too-sweet-smelling
London alley. Not even a cat or a rat strolled by.

She closed and locked the door and turned
around abruptly, pressing her back to it. Then
she plucked up the message gingerly. She ran her
thumb over the seal—something had been pressed
into it, a signet of some sort—but she couldn't read
it in the dark.

Her heart pounding loud enough to drown out
her footsteps, she slowly carried it up the creak-
ing stairs, back down the corridor, into her rooms
again. She crouched down next to the fire, and
peered.

Into the red wax were pressed the letters:

JHR.

She traced it with trembling fingers. Might as
well have been his heart.

Pity she needed to break it to read what was
inside.

She slipped her finger beneath it tenderly, and
snapped open a sheet of foolscap.

There was no letter. No preamble. It was simply what appeared to be a numbered list, written in a hand as tall, dark, and bold as JHR was.

1. Walk twenty paces and turn left at the building with the red door.
2. Go straight for forty paces and turn right.
3. Walk up the stairs to the second story, turn around three times, touch your nose, then go twenty paces forward.

And on and on it went.

And then she burst into laughter and bounced on her toes, her heart singing. The beast! What on earth was he *about?*

She skipped to the bottom:

22. When you reach the carriage, board it and stay aboard until it stops. You'll find a picnic repast inside to help you pass the time.

Unwrapping the gift inside will also pass the time.

Just as he'd said he'd never seen a woman undress so quickly when she'd flung herself off a bridge into the Ouse, he likely would have said he'd never seen a woman dress so quickly as she did this morning. But she dressed *carefully*. She hadn't seen him in three weeks, a veritable eternity. She wanted to look spectacular.

She locked the door behind her, and gamely embarked on a labyrinthine journey very like the one she'd led him on the second midnight she'd met him.

Down narrow streets, up staircases, once doubling back to do it again.

She smiled like a looby the entire way.

"Greetings, Tommy!" Jasper called when she passed him the alley. He was leaning against the wall.

"Greetings, Jasper!"

She mulled how very Jonathan of him to effortlessly find his way to her when she needed him, labyrinth or no. Just as he'd effortlessly uncovered her secrets. But that was simply because he'd been born knowing the secret to her. He was hers and she was his. Just as there was one key for every lock.

At last, on Drury Lane, she found what appeared to be a brand new, quite spotless carriage pulled by four beautiful matched grays.

The driver was leaning against the side of it, arms crossed over his chest, beaming.

He helped her aboard.

"We'll be traveling for just a few hours, madam. Please make yourself comfortable."

It wasn't difficult to do as the seats were well-sprung clouds; she nestled into them, sighing. Across from her was the basket mentioned in her message. She fished about, and inside were tea cakes, bread and cheese, a flask of tea. Ah! And there it was.

A little bundle wrapped in ribbon.

With trembling hands, she unwrapped it.

It was a key.

She stared at it for a moment, puzzled. Then she closed it tightly in her palm, holding onto it the way she'd once held onto her father's medal.

AN HOUR INTO her journey, the roads began to look familiar, and she knew, just knew, where she was bound. And so though she wasn't surprised when the low red brick of the Lancaster Mill came into view, her heart began to slam.

The mill was quiet now, closed for the evening, twilight hanging swaths of mauve and blue clouds behind it, as if the mill itself were festooned for a party.

The driver assisted her down.

And he nodded at her to go the rest of the distance alone.

It was so quiet she could hear the river moving behind the mill. Hear the wind stirring in the trees. Hear her own footsteps echoing on the path.

A sheet of foolscap was affixed to the door. On it was written:

USE THE KEY

Laughing, breathless, her hands trembling and a trifle awkward, she inserted the key into the lock and turned.

She gave the door a gentle push, and it swung open noiselessly. She approved of the well-oiled hinges.

The silence inside was resounding. She peered into the twilit cavern; not a living creature stirred. The immense machines were like a pride of slumbering beasts. All the children were in the dormitory for the evening. Bits of twilight pushed through the narrow rectangle windows.

And a row of lit lamps were arranged on the floor, forming a path of sorts toward the overlooker's office.

Something rustled; she took a step backward. Below her feet another sheet of foolscap affixed to the floor. She crouched down and read:

Go left for twenty paces and open the door. Follow the lamps.

She measured off those paces as though she were walking a high wire. Dizzied, and shaking, and giddy, and hopeful, and exhilaratingly frightened. *Don't look at your feet, Tommy,* she warned herself. The way to achieve the impossible is to simply do it as if it were the most possible thing in the world.

Twenty paces later she found herself staring at the door of the overlooker's office.

She sucked in a shaking breath, closed her fingers around the knob, and pulled it slowly open. The room was dimly, warmly lit by a pair of lamps.

Jonathan was seated at the desk, his long legs crossed up on it. Arms folded behind his head. Very like he owned the place. Very relaxed indeed.

There ensued a moment during which they merely stared at each other. They never could speak to each other until that first wave of fierce joy and desire had washed each of them, and they had both caught their breath and gathered their wits again.

He caught his first.

"You made good time. In a hurry to see me, Tommy?"

A drawl, soft as a silk shawl drawn round her shoulders.

But she detected the slight tremble in it. And the tension in the arms that seemed oh-so-casually folded behind his head.

She knew then he hadn't been certain she would come.

"Didn't I just see you?" she said softly. Feigning boredom.

He didn't smile. He stood, drawing his legs gracefully down from the desk, and slowly came to her. As if he, too, were walking a high wire.

He stood staring down at her.

"Here is what I have to say, then, Tommy." His voice was still soft. What an untold pleasure it was to hear his voice again. The very sound of love. "You wanted choices, Tommy. I have two choices for you."

He reached into the pocket of his coat, and came out with a folded sheet of foolscap. It rattled a bit in his hands. He drew in a breath, and exhaled. And then he held it out to her.

"This is a deed to this mill. It's in your name. In short, this mill now belongs to you, if you want it."

She blanked in shock.

Suddenly she couldn't feel her limbs at all.

She took it from him gingerly. The foolscap rattled between her trembling fingers. A haze of emotion moved over her eyes, and it was a moment before she could read.

But she did read. In the dim silence, while Jonathan held utterly still, she read.

And she saw that what he said was true.

She looked up at him.

"But . . . how . . . ?"

"I bought it. And the reason I was able to buy it is indirectly all because of you. I've another deed—I had the solicitor draw up two of them—that says something entirely different. It says the mill belongs to me. I'll tell you about that next. For that's where your choice comes in. First, I wanted you to know, Tommy . . . that I chose a bride from a deck of cards yesterday."

She reared back. And now shock slowly iced her palms and the pit of her stomach. She longed to look over her shoulder. Longed to flee. But she was trapped here now.

Surely . . . surely the mill wasn't an apology, or a thank you for services rendered? Was this a cruel trick?

And now panic shortened her breath.

"Would you like to see who I drew from the deck?" he asked. His expression gave away nothing.

She stared at him. Iciness had given way to a feverish heat in her cheeks. Fine. There was nothing she couldn't endure. She straightened her spine and jerked up her chin, and thrust out her palm.

And he pulled a card from his right pocket as she took a bracing breath.

He settled it into her palm.

"Look at it, Tommy." he ordered. When it appeared she never would.

So she looked.

And then she looked harder.

It was the Queen of Hearts. She was wearing a green dress, and her eyes were a vivid green rimmed round in gray, and she had a little pointed chin and delicate slashes of eyebrows.

Most striking of all was the hair.

"Copper-colored hair and all," he whispered.

She couldn't see it through her tears. "Copper!" she choked wonderingly. "*Yes.*"

"*Burnished* copper," he embellished triumphantly, still on a whisper.

She laughed shakily. "Yes!" she approved on a whisper, too. "But . . . how . . ."

These seemed to be the only words she was capable of speaking today.

"I commissioned a deck, Tommy. Wyndham had already done your portrait, so he painted it from that. I made him work around the clock for a few days. And I made sure you were the only person in that deck. Not only that, but you can buy the Thomasina de Ballesteros deck in the Burlington Arcade."

She recovered then, and choked a laugh. "I hope we make an immense profit."

He heard the word "we."

She understood how he heard it when he went suddenly very still and alert.

A man *alive* with a hope he hardly dare harbor.

She couldn't postpone it any longer. She'd best tell him what she came to tell him.

"Jonathan . . ." she said hesitantly. "It's . . . I'm afraid I have something to tell you, too."

He'd survive a few moments of torture, the beast. It was only what he deserved.

She almost took pity when she saw how instantly gray and taut his face went. *He loves me. He loves me. He loves me.* The thought was a hosanna, and exultation. And she took no pleasure in hurting him.

Still, a little theater wouldn't kill either of them. She'd get the torture over with quickly.

"Very well. Tell me what you need to tell me," he ordered curtly. Still tense and slit-eyed and gray-faced. Like a man braced to have a bullet extracted from his flesh.

"Close your eyes and hold out your hand."

He hesitated, much the way she had. And then he inhaled for courage and thrust out his hand.

And slowly, with great ceremony, she poured the strand of pearls into his palm.

He blinked. He looked down at them and frowned faintly. "I don't . . . that is . . . what are . . ."

"When you deposited the money in my account, I used all of it to buy them back from Exley & Morrow. I'll have them returned to Prescott tomorrow."

And the dawning of realization on his face was glorious. "You believed in me," he said slowly. "You trusted me."

"Of course I did. That, and I love you more than life itself."

She saw her words enter him like cupid's arrow. He closed his eyes swiftly, as if bracing against an onslaught of emotion. He mouthed something that might have been "Hallelujah."

Then he opened them again, as if he couldn't bear not to see her in the aftermath of those words.

"Say it again."

"I love you." Those magical powerful words that she never dreamed she'd be able to say to anyone.

And look, look what it did to Jonathan Redmond's face when she said them. What a humbling power she held.

He recovered, and smiled a slow satisfied smile. "Of course you love me. How could you help it?"

He gathered her abruptly into his arms then, and he bent to kiss her senseless.

And then her senses congregated again and clamored for his touch everywhere she could possibly be touched.

"And you'll marry me?" he wanted to know. He murmured this in her ear, before he applied a tongue to it. Her breath caught, and she turned her head to press her lips to his throat. How swiftly his heartbeat was beating. For her. *He loved her.*

"I'll marry you," she gasped.

Because he'd dragged his hands softly down over her breasts and cupped them, and she felt the surge of wildness overtake her.

He kissed her again, and his hands went to work on the laces of her dress.

"Excellent. Because, as I may have mentioned, I love you, Tommy, and I really think I may perish without you."

"Will it kill your father if we marry?"

He gave a laugh. "You sound just a bit hopeful. But never fear. My father will love you, too."

"How is that possible?" She'd gone to work on the buttons of his shirt.

"Because I told him he will. Oh, and he will. For you and I, my love, my dearest Tommy, and our children, and our children's children, are not only going to own much of England one day . . . we're going to rule it, too. Starting with this mill. This mill is *ours*. Starting with laws about child labor. Let me tell you how."

He lifted her up onto the desk, and furled up her skirts, his mouth never leaving hers. She reached for his trouser buttons, and had them open with scandalous rapidity.

"Our children's children?" she whispered.

"Our beautiful, brilliant, fearless, scrappy, courageous, copper-headed children. We ought to have at least ten of them. I have it on good authority."

Though in a way, they already did have hundreds of them, just as he'd told his father. In mills all over England, waiting for their help.

Imagine that. That Gypsy girl had been *right*.

"Ten? We'd best get started, then." Tommy was practical.

And so—for the sake of England's future, of course—they got started.

And didn't finish for *hours*.

Epilogue

❧

THERE WAS AN EPIDEMIC of stiff necks in Penny-royal Green.

Generally Pennyroyal Green parishioners had no difficulty deciding where to point their eyes during Sunday services—after all, one simply *wanted* to look at the Reverend Sylvaine regardless of what he was saying—and not even his recent marriage to the most unlikely woman imaginable had dimmed his ability to fill the pews.

But for six Sundays in a row Reverend Sylvaine had competition for his parishioners' attention.

Breathlessly, silently, frozen with fascination, everyone listened and watched. Isaiah Redmond had neither blinked, nor flinched, nor smiled while banns were read for his youngest son and a certain Thomasina de Ballesteros, a heathen name if ever there was one, some sniffed. (Mercifully, no rumors about Tommy had yet wafted from London to Sussex on the winds of gossip.) Others surmised she *must* be of Spanish royalty, what with her fine looks and bearing, or otherwise Isaiah Redmond never would have countenanced the match. For

Isaiah Redmond's back remained straight, his gaze remained focused, his expression remained mildly interested, and he never so much as twitched a muscle or raised a brow, let alone a protest.

He also never once looked at Jonathan or Tommy. Let alone spoke to them. Nor did matriarch Fanchette Redmond, though one had the sense that her neck was quivering with the effort not to turn. But then she was a mother, and looking at her children was a difficult-to-combat instinct.

The parishioners hardly knew *where* to look.

Jonathan weathered his silent father and the curious stares with a shifting blend of wary aplomb—inscrutability was an art form with Isaiah Redmond, and one never quite knew what the man had up his sleeve—and serene certainty, for love had encased him in a bubble of invincibility that concerns about the future couldn't penetrate. Tommy bore the curious stares of the townspeople like a queen, and if while the banns were read she surreptitiously gripped his hand the way she used to grip her father's medal, Jonathan would look down to where their fingers twined, awestruck and honored and grateful that the bravest person he knew would turn to *him* when she needed courage. It was what he was born to do: ensure her safety. He would endeavor to deserve her trust every day of his life.

For three of those weeks Jonathan and Tommy stayed with Miles Redmond and his wife Cynthia in a Sussex estate Miles had rented nearby, but Jonathan divided much of his time between London and Lancaster and Sussex.

During the fourth week, a parishioner who

happened to be awake exceptionally early one Saturday—namely, Mrs. Sneath—witnessed Jonathan and Tommy leaving the church in the pale gold morning light, followed by Mr. Miles Redmond and his wife Cynthia, the Earl of Ardmay and his wife the former Miss Violet Redmond, and the celestially handsome Lord Argosy.

But not, it was noted and much discussed, by Mr. Isaiah Redmond.

Or by Fanchette Redmond.

And *this* supplied conversation kindling throughout the town for yet another week. When word of Jonathan's marriage spread through the village, the disappointment at being deprived of a spectacle of a wedding was grave—for not a word had been spoken about the event in advance—yet was rather offset by the revelation that the popular young Mr. Redmond had never looked more gloriously handsome and so *happy*, and that his bride, heathen name or no, looked like the sun itself, as beautiful as an angel, and Mrs. Sneath relayed this story so well at the weekly meeting of the Society for the Protection of the Sussex Poor that there wasn't a dry handkerchief after the telling of it, and much of the embroidery was inconveniently dampened.

Today the excitement at church continued.

The parishioner's necks quivered with the effort not to whip to and fro like weathervanes, from Redmond to Redmond to Redmond. For Violet Redmond's new baby was to be baptized after Reverend Sylvaine read the first lesson, and instead of the traditional two Godmothers and one Godfather, it seemed the little one was to instead have *one*

Godmother—Mrs. Cynthia Redmond—and two Godfathers, Mr. Miles Redmond and an almost unbearably dashing, blond, more-than-ever-so-slightly dangerous looking gentleman by the name of Lavay, the first mate of the earl's ship. For Violet Redmond of course wouldn't be able to resist exciting a bit of controversy even after she was safely married.

Jonathan was not immune to the temptation to whip his head around the congregation, too, but he managed to do it surreptitiously, with glances. His eyes snagged on Olivia Eversea, who was wedged between two of her brothers. She must have sensed it, because her eyes flicked toward him; for a second, they held gazes. Olivia, who like Tommy, was driven by a passion for causes. Olivia, who had allegedly broken Lyon's heart and driven Lyon away. And Jonathan had a swift traitorous thought: Did Lyon deserve her? What drove Olivia? Did she miss his brother as much as Jonathan did?

He jerked his stare away when the tiny lace-bedecked Ruby opened her mouth in a howl that elicited sympathetic clucks and chuckles from the congregation. Suddenly the memory of roars of Gypsy laughter echoed in his head: *ten children, ten children, ten children* . . .

He must have tensed just a bit, because Tommy squeezed his hand and the corner of her mouth twitched, suppressing a smile. Over the past several weeks Jonathan had spent his time between Pennyroyal Green, Lancaster, and London. With the assistance of Tommy and Mr. Romulus Bean and even Argosy, who had been conscripted into the process but had proved startlingly useful once given something to *do*, they'd made headway into finding loving homes and excellent apprenticeships for nearly all of the youngest children, and hired adult replacements for them; at a higher cost, to be sure, but Jonathan was certain he would be able to offset the cost with increased profits. And he'd also introduced Tommy to Violet. Violet had first regarded Tommy with gratifying astonishment, then stunned glee—for Jonathan's sudden engagement was highly unexpected and delightfully controversial. And then she'd collected herself and had become a cool haughty silence and a stare that nevertheless spoke loudly: *Prove to me that you're good enough for my brother.*

And so for a time, Tommy and Violet had eyed each other with the wariness of cats while Jonathan looked on. Until:

"I've always wanted a sister," Tommy had finally said truthfully yet cautiously—for one would need to be a bit mad to *wish* for a sister like Violet. And Violet, made magnanimous and soft by motherhood and still inclined to weep a little at sentimental things (which infuriated her, as she was fiercely loyal but not at *all* sentimental), swept Tommy into her arms. Jonathan doubted the friendship between two such . . . distinctive . . . personalities would always be quite so effortless and giddy, but this would do for a beginning.

His father and mother, however, had not spoken to him in weeks. Not since his father had turned over the Thomasina de Ballesteros card.

Jonathan hadn't precisely avoided them. And it didn't appear, at least, that they'd been avoiding Jonathan. But the silence was just rather tacit. And he knew that Violet and the earl had been invited to join his father and mother for breakfast after the baptism. Quite pointedly, a similar invitation had not been extended to Jonathan and Tommy, or to his brother Miles and his wife Cynthia. For Cynthia wasn't welcome in the Redmond home, either.

Little Ruby Alexandra predictably and understandably roared in astonished outrage when she was dipped in the font. Jonathan looked forward to telling his niece about the time her mother had threatened to throw herself down a well after an argument with a suitor.

And that's when he glanced toward his father and mother now, a reflex, and saw his mother reach for his father's hand, much the way Tommy had reached for his. Jonathan was beginning to understand how much could be conveyed in utter silence between two married people.

He just wasn't certain precisely what was being conveyed between his parents in that moment.

And then the service was over, and everyone stood to file out of the church.

Just as the sky opened up and the rain plummeted.

With disconcerting rapidity the pathway into town turned into a bit of a muddy soup, driving all the parishioners who'd walked to church into the warm welcoming arms of the Pig & Thistle across the road to wait out the downpour.

Leaving a cluster of silent Redmonds standing bemusedly in front of the church. For Jonathan and Tommy and Miles and Cynthia had walked to church in the clear cold morning, while his father, mother, Violet and the earl had arrived in the Redmond carriage.

For a moment, the silence was taut enough to be thumped like a drum.

And then his father turned and addressed Jonathan as if they'd spoken only yesterday.

"Why don't we put the ladies in the carriage and have them taken back to the house? The four of will surely survive a walk in the rain if it continues."

The ladies. Meaning Cynthia, Violet, Tommy, and their mother.

And Jonathan, for a moment, was speechless. As was Miles, apart from a brow that shot up.

The ladies in question seemed to be holding their collective breaths.

"Why don't we?" the Earl of Ardmay said smoothly.

And thusly a quartet of silent, astonished, wide-eyed ladies and one baby were duly assisted into the carriage, which rolled away.

Leaving a quartet of silent men behind.

"We could walk back now," Jonathan mused. "Or . . . we could have a game of darts at the Pig & Thistle and wait it out."

His father turned to him. His face was unreadable. And then the corner of his mouth twitched. "Darts it is," his father said.

"I'll win," Jonathan said, after a moment, unable to resist.

A hesitation.

"Perhaps," his father said easily, after a moment. "Perhaps not."

With a smile that was faint but real.

It was the perfect answer, as far as Jonathan was concerned.

And they all made their way into the Pig & Thistle.

"PACKAGE FOR YOU, sir."

The Duke of Greyfolk looked up at the footman hovering in the doorway, and beckoned him forward with a sweep of his hand, as he settled his haunches into the indentation in his favorite chair in the library where Thomasina and Jonathan had peered in at him one midnight.

He accepted the small paper-wrapped bundle and sliced the string with a letter opener.

The first thing revealed was a folded sheet of foolscap. He thumbed it open and read:

> *This gave me courage when I needed it. I hope it will remind you of how brave you can be.*

He parted the layers of tissue and stopped when he caught a glimpse of red.

And carefully, from its generous nest, he lifted his medal.